'An assured and complex début, its themes of racism, misogyny, fracturing machismo and male emotional impotence are served up in a demonic patois'
Sunday Times

'Much more than a heart-warming tale about how music can conquer hatred and intolerance . . . Sutherland's acute, slangy representation of the Glasgow underworld is unquestionably one of the best novels about jazz since Rafi Zabor's masterful performance, *The Bear Comes Home*'
Daily Telegraph

'The authenticity of *Jelly Roll* gives the book much of its power'
Scotland on Sunday

'A remarkably assured and accomplished first foray into literature. On its most obvious level, the book is a pacey and thoroughly nineties odyssey through Glasgow's hip, flip, and unutterably bohemian West End . . . In fact, Sutherland's book is a much more subtle and complex work, addressing a wider set of agendas and drawing upon an eclectice range of influences'
The Herald

'To say Luke Sutherland is talented is like saying the Empire State Building is quite high – an understatement of some magnitude'
i-D

'A refreshingly rich novel, a cliché-lite tour of the Highlands with a jazz band'
New Musical Express

Also by Luke Sutherland
JELLY ROLL

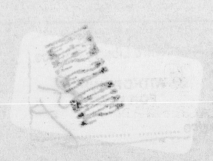

sweetmeat

LUKE SUTHERLAND

BLACK SWAN

SWEETMEAT
A BLACK SWAN BOOK : 0 552 99920 2

Originally published in Great Britain by Doubleday,
a division of Transworld Publishers

PRINTING HISTORY
Doubleday edition published 2002
Black Swan edition published 2003

1 3 5 7 9 10 8 6 4 2

Set in 11/13pt Melior by
Kestrel Data, Exeter, Devon.

Black Swan Books are published by Transworld Publishers,
61–63 Uxbridge Road, London W5 5SA,
a division of The Random House Group Ltd,
in Australia by Random House Australia (Pty) Ltd,
20 Alfred Street, Milsons Point, Sydney, NSW 2061, Australia,
in New Zealand by Random House New Zealand Ltd,
18 Poland Road, Glenfield, Auckland 10, New Zealand
and in South Africa by Random House (Pty) Ltd,
Endulini, 5a Jubilee Road, Parktown 2193, South Africa.

Printed and bound in Great Britain by
Clays Ltd, St Ives plc.

For Brian Duncan

and remembering Cathy Haswell (1947–2001)

Thanks Bex, Mum and Dad, Paisley, Fritha,
Kyle, Merric Davidson, Bill Scott-Kerr,
Tam Dean Burn, Tommy Udo, David Sweeney,
Iain Baird, Susanna Grant, Ruth Emond,
Karen Lumsden, Fraser MacDonald, Kelly Mendonça,
Paul Cox, Margaret Fiedler, Alan Benzie, Jon Roberts
at Butler's Wharf Chef School, the London Arts
Board. Thanks also to Dominic Aitchison,
Stuart Braithwaite and Barry Burns for the
top deck ghost stories.

The fact that kings are habitually seen in the company of guards, drums, officers and all the things which prompt automatic responses of respect and fear has the result that, when they are sometimes alone and unaccompanied, their features are enough to strike respect and fear into their subjects, because we make no mental distinction between their person and the retinue with which they are normally seen to be associated. And the world, which does not know that this is the effect of habit, believes it to derive from some natural force, hence such sayings as: The character of divinity is stamped on his features.

Blaise Pascal, *Pensées*

head

head

In which the head chef of a Thames-side restaurant, while reflecting upon the disparity between body and soul, is swayed from catastrophic action by a strange omen.

I love you I love you I love you I love you I LOVE YOU. If only writing it over and over was enough to make you love me. Enough to conjure you here and now, to relieve the beating of this unhappy heart. If only.

You're way beyond me. You always were. The more I wanted you, the faster you seemed to recede. And then, the wedding announcement of one month ago . . . I can't tell you how that made me despair.

I resolved, there and then, to 'seduce' you with the few God-given gifts I have. I'd throw myself wholly into the making of your wedding meal. Would, as it were, offer myself to you on a plate. Delicious dishes to express what circumstance has never allowed me to say. And you'd respond, because by dining on my handmade delights, you'd absorb every ounce of love I have in my heart. A love that, burning brightly as it does, <u>WOULD BE ENOUGH TO MAKE YOU LOVE ME</u>. But alas, I no longer have the energy, or will.

You are all that kept me here. All I ever wanted. A look
or kind word from you was enough to transport me out of
this world. Sweet but fleeting relief, as I always feel I would
be better off somewhere I am not.
    Even the Elephant Man found acceptance in his lifetime.
Not so me. Most people look at me and see only a freak, a
man-woman, a monster,

He glanced at his candlelit reflection. Looked away
and looked back. Couldn't stop a curse slipping
between his lips. A heartfelt, —Fat cunt, because his
face was more like two faces: the first's boyish beauty
seduced by the second's chocolatey wads, his features
fouled by flab.
    A tap on the mirror's edge gave him full view of the
super-smooth cumulus of his chins. It was like looking
down across a bank of cloud; as close to flying as he
would ever get because there was no plane that could
hold him.
    The high nobility of his brow was almost wholly
incidental, for here was a natural point of tension – the
skin simply strained under the weight of his face.
Sometimes he worried about the effect of all that
pressure on his brain, because quick wit and creativity
were his only gifts. On darker days he felt as though
his fat foiled all forms of thought, every cerebral
impulse. But with the help of a cup of curaçao and a
dash of passion fruit, he usually managed to soothe
himself with the knowledge that men were mostly
made of water, that water was a fine conductor and
that he was an Aquarius: a water carrier.
    He parted his lips, baring too-white teeth. Stuck out
his tongue, lifted it, twisted it, curled it back against
the roof of his mouth, exposing the underside's
gruesome roots. So long as he was awake, his tongue

14

always obeyed orders. It was the only part of his body that did and he rarely wasted a word. When he was asleep, however, it lapsed and folded and rolled down his throat, choking him awake every half hour, compounding the mounting strain on his heart.

His eyes were calm pools in the tumult – sky blue windows to a golden soul – indisputable proof of how human he really was. He tried not to scowl at the permanent shadow around them. Held himself back from the urge to hack and scratch at the liner on his lids, the mascara on his lashes, the stick on his lips.

The make-up had started as a youthful salute to the hermaphroditic cool possessed of great art and artists. But coupled with his size and shade it'd made him look cartoonishly camp. After a sex life characterized by whispered propositions from circus freaks, the future chef threw himself into what he knew best: food. Food, its consumption, and in time, its preparation became his *raison d'être*. He bought sackfuls of slap, applied extravagant splashes in tight-lipped protest over former failures, and then soiled himself on soups and sweetmeats, charcoal grills and honey roasts, goulash and stir-fries, puddings and pasta. The make-up swung from a come-on to a fuck off; warpaint more or less: the warning flash of Admiral wings, lava-blotched backs of poisonous toads and rouge like deadly nightshade.

But cooking and cosmetics weren't cathartic enough and all that anger turned to apathy. One afternoon he swallowed nine hundred milligrams of temazepam, went to bed and slept until woken six weeks later by a clubber who fell through his window. The girl, in the process of making an escape of her own, recognized the plight of a twin spirit and hauled him out of bed. An hour-long shower shifted all the shit and mould growing in the folds of his somehow expanded fat, and doused the lacerations on her arms and legs. As they dried themselves and measured up in the mirror, her scars seemed smaller but certainly permanent, while he was left with a faint imprint of make-up around his eyes and mouth. Fourteen years on, it was still glimmering.

but I am a man; capable of greatness. If only I could bridge the vast chasm between who I am and what I seem to be.

Perhaps if I had expressed these things to you in person, we'd be living happily ever after right now. Maybe there's still time. An eleventh-hour intervention. A stay of execution. Just one sign that my wishes might come true and I'd

He held his breath at the sound of a distant door opening. Put down the pen and glanced away from the page. The last of the staff had left the restaurant hours ago. The whole block was stoppered and locked. Swaying to his feet, he spilled the stash of sleeping pills across his desk and rumbled to the window where he peered between the curtains. Falling snow made halos of the Tower Bridge lights. It hid every whiff of the city beyond Blackfriars. On tiptoe, he squinted down at the courtyard, saw the iron gate was ajar.

—Queer, he said, and staggered back as something clattered against a drainpipe. Scratching, scrabbling, whispers and laughter. He edged towards the door, frozen stiff by a rapping on the window. —My God? he murmured. —What horror is this? Thieves? Devils? The fates come to fetch me at last?

The knocking grew more insistent with every blow. A voice above the buffeting: —Bohemond! Bo!

He shrugged on his quilted dressing gown, drew the

curtains and opened the window, as always, almost offended by the man looking up at him. Paris, the maître d', had climbed thirty feet up the face of the tenement in a blizzard. He oozed into the room, the weight of his body wringing water from his suit as he wound around the window ledge and rolled onto the floor. —Top notch, he gasped, and reeled to his feet spluttering snowflakes.

Bohemond blinked as a naked arm flopped up over the window ledge, its long-fingered hand groping for a grip. Paris grinned and grabbed hold. One foot set against the wall, he leaned back to drag whoever was on the outside, in. A body clad in a blue-glitter ballgown slithered giggling through the window, the momentum forcing Paris over on his ankle, and he crashed into a cabinet, shattering a lamp and scattering titbits: cashews and raisins, petits fours and panettone. The stranger sprawled, legs spread, hems riding up over caramel-coloured thighs.

Paris gathered himself again and stooped to help his friend stand up. They stood head to head, gasping as they gazed into one another's eyes, the woman's hands gripping Paris's lapels, Paris's hands on her waist. Bohemond clutched the butt of a bedpost, marvelling at the newcomer's obvious androgyny. Her face and neck were a little bit boyish, so too the crew cut that dovetailed at the nape. There were no breasts or bottom to speak of, just the easy air of someone less than a man, a delicate elegance around what little there was of the hips, and slight ladylike hands.

Paris turned to Bohemond, holding his companion by the wrist. Too much booze on his breath, he said: —I lost my keys; and motioned towards the bed. —May we?

—No wait, I . . .

The guests kicked back onto the vast mattress. It sank in the middle like a trampoline. Gold folds almost swallowed them whole, only a wink of blue glitter and Paris's hand visible before the springs sprang them back and they bobbed up lopsided, both laughing.

Bohemond closed the window and drew the curtains. He scooped up some of the spilled sleeping pills and put them in his pocket along with the letter.

—How do you sleep in this? Paris patted the duvet.

—Practice.

Paris nudged the stranger with his shoulder. —See what I mean? Isn't he just the biggest fattest *weirdest* thing you've ever seen?

She hooted. Literally. Like an owl.

—He's an athlete though, said Paris. —Eats for England . . . *no, France!* And look, you can see the make-up and mascara and shit on him. Look. *Look!*

Eyes gleaming with awe, the stranger leaned into the light and gave out something like a gasp.

—Actually . . . Bohemond managed a half-hearted shrug —. . . I was just about to retire.

—By the way, said Paris, —This is Jo. Jo, meet Bohemond, our very own French gourmet.

Jo nodded almost cautiously. There was glitter in her lipstick, pricks of stubble and mismatched eyeshadow. One of her sandals hung half off, its instep straps shorn clean through and that foot's big toe, bruised blue.

—Ask us what we was doing, said Paris.

—Please, Bohemond sighed. —Would you just go.

—Ain't really the weather for it, but we was on a boat in Little Venice, right. Lili and Faulkner and them were playing at a dinner party. I went along for a laugh. Come back with Jo here.

Bohemond bowed his head, bit his tongue, looked

up and let go: —And does Jo know that you're in a long-standing relationship? That six months from now you'll be a married man?

Paris sneered at him. —Jo knows the score. Hermione knows Jo. No big deal. Don't you or anyone else be trying to start anything with me.

—I wasn't trying to start anything with you.

—I already had one fight tonight.

—Paris, please.

—Gig on the boat got ugly. We had to swim for it.

—You *swam*? Bohemond backed against his desk. —And Faulkner. Did he swim too?

—Faulkner's hard as nails. He'll be in here tomorrow, onstage, telling stories, doing his thing, as usual.

—That band is bad news.

—They're all right.

—And yet you want them to play at your wedding.

—Hermione's idea. Her granddad and Faulkner go back a-ways.

—After what they did to Vic, I can't believe she'd want them. They should be in jail.

—The band on the boat tonight, Paris directed his words at Jo but kept his eyes on Bohemond, —mad fuckers, but good guys y'know. They come into the kitchen last weekend looking for liqueurs and the drummer, this guy Jugs, starts giving it all these ju-jitsu moves with Vic, the Chinky chef we got working here. It was just a laugh, y'know, but Vic got a bit out his depth and accidentally smacked a cigar out of Jugs's mouth. So Lili, the bass player, what does he do? He splits Vic's lip with a rolling pin, and once he's hit the deck, rides him like a rodeo. It was so funny. Ends up the band drag Vic into the dry store, lock the door and fuck knows what they was doing to him in there, but when they come out, twenty minutes later, casual as

19

you like, Lili's got all these scratches down the side of his face. We found Vic in there, shirt ripped to shreds, chunks of his hair on the floor, all bleeding bald patches on his head, and fucking *teeth marks* on his neck. He asked for it though. Arrogant twat.

—Those wounds were serious, said Bohemond. —I had to put him back together again. He's been having problems since.

Paris laughed. —Did he say what they done to him?

—He won't talk about it.

—Shame.

—And I doubt whether he'll come to the wedding if Lili and Co. are there.

—I doubt you'll be there either after what they done to you.

Jo grunted and stuck out her tongue. Paris glanced at her. —I don't know how they managed it, he said, —but apparently, last Christmas, Lili, and Mr Lewis, and Petra and all them got our Bohemond here to do a striptease. Can you imagine it? Giggles fizzed to his lips. —They said he's got a cock like a toothpick.

—That's not true! Bohemond blushed, too weak for rage. —I don't even know how that rumour began. But it certainly won't stop me from coming to the wedding.

—I doubt Hermione would give a fuck either way.

—And where is Hermione now?

—Don't you worry about Hermione. Paris pinched a pack of Lucky Strike from his inside pocket, flicked the flap, bit out two cigarettes, lit both with a silver Zippo and handed one to Jo. —You've got to love it though, eh? he said. —She practically built this joint up from scratch. Delphi is her baby. She can have the pick of the crop – fucking royalty in helicopters on Hampstead Heath. But what does she do? She gets it on with Paris, her head waiter.

—It amazes me too, said Bohemond.

Paris frowned, cocked his head a little. Bohemond lowered his eyes, shifted against the desk, the damp towel under his dressing gown rubbing up a rash. —Are you getting out of your depth, fatty?

—You're drunk . . . would you please just leave . . .

—Are we going to have to see what you're made of?

—Please, Paris. I just want to go to bed. Get today over with.

Paris stubbed the barely started cigarette on the sole of his boot, flicked the butt across the room and lit up another. Jo put a hand on his knee, braced against the eddy of the mattress, the two of them swaying gently. —Give us a look, then. They bounced off the bed. Bohemond waddled away, spitting sugar and shit as he stepped on splintered lamp. Without warning Paris grabbed the bow of his dressing gown belt. Bohemond's hand shot out, gripped him by the wrist.

Paris's lips thinned a little. —Come on.

—*Leave me alone*. He wobbled back, too late to see Jo on all fours at his heels. Delphi thundered as he tumbled, the dressing gown belt whipping away like a kite tail, Paris rapidly receding as if he were miles down on the ground flying Bohemond over England. His legs swung over his head and he knew he'd been exposed, not just by the cold air on his crotch, but by a glimpse of Jo's face, mouth open, eyes wide, darting no doubt from his cock, to his hole, to his tiny black balls, the rollicking sponge of his stomach. He landed flat, pills skittering from his pocket.

Paris looked down at him. —Have you ever seen anything like it?

Jo didn't reply, winking disbelief, her face enflamed by the sheen of Bohemond's baby-oiled skin.

—The rumour's true, muttered Paris, and held out a

hand as he made for the door. Jo skipped after him, linking a single finger with one of his.

Bohemond rolled over, the envelope meant for his farewell note squashed under his nose, script smudged with snot: HERMIONE. He bashed his head against the floor. Clamped the carpet between his teeth.

antipasto

In which Bohemond expounds upon the role of the gourmet, the extent of his Frenchness, and the symbolic suitability of olive oil as a wedding feast ingredient.

Beyond the kitchen, through the little Victorian laundry, lay the mess-room. The cooks went there to relax between shifts or for drinks last thing. Occasionally they'd celebrate a good night, sometimes they'd drown their sorrows.

The mess had the same glass-domed ceiling as the dry store. Its walls and skirting were painted gold, an imitation of sunlight meant to encourage the plant life because the room was more like a grove. Partly flagstone, the floor dissolved to soil towards the back, and it was here that Bohemond grew his garden. Cajeput, caper-bush, wintergreen, sweatleaf. There were China-berries and little citrus trees, common box and dogwood, gingko and juniper, sweet fern and even sea-grape amongst real curiosities like persimmon and papaya, wax-myrtle and hardhack that Bohemond couldn't even remember planting. An apple tree drooped over the table at the edge of the plot and behind it, to the right, a baby sequoia soared towards the skylight.

The garden was so overgrown that Hanswurst the kitchen porter claimed he lost his way in it one night. It'd seemed a singular spot for a Christmas kiss with Loretta the waitress, but they couldn't find their way out again. After three hours of fighting through thicket she ran off screaming hysterically. At first Hanswurst thought she'd lost it over the prospect of perpetual trekking, but in fact she'd spotted a python wrapped around the trunk of a blue gum eucalyptus.

Bohemond found the porter face-down on the mess-room floor the following morning. He hauled him into a chair and revived him with salts. Calmed his nerves with the vapour of crushed camphor leaves. Hanswurst was adamant he'd been in the woods for three days.

The previous Easter a fox had bolted from the under-brush, skidded through the laundry, the kitchen, jumped over a table in the crowded restaurant, dashed into the foyer and up the stairs.

Everyone was waiting for another miracle.

The morning after Paris and the stranger had fallen into Bohemond's bedroom, the senior cooks sat in the mess-room waiting to begin the day. Seeta the sweet chef was there. Innocent the sous-chef and Vic the still-wounded sous-sous sat on either side of her. They lounged around the table drinking beet borscht that Innocent had prepared the night before, hardly glancing as the floor rumbled, the cutlery rattled and the leaves shivered on the trees. —Game on, said Seeta, and Bohemond bowled in. Fat French chef like a lifesize Brueghel, basin bellied in brass-buttoned clogs – eyeshadow, liner, lipstick and long hair. *Homer's Bohemond*, blundering like a young god, both hands beautifully smooth to the tips of nails starry-dark with varnish.

Seeta rose to the stove and poured Bohemond a mug of borscht as he eased himself into his cast-iron throne. —Morning, he said, his greeting met with sleepy eyelids and lazily cocked heads. Innocent looked whacked and Vic, who never said very much anyway, had become even more withdrawn since the night Lili dragged him into the dry store.

Bohemond's drink set before him, Seeta squeezed what she could of his oversized shoulder and shuffled back into her seat.

Vic glanced at Innocent. The old Pole scratched his nose. Bohemond sipped his stew and gazed out the window. It was still snowing.

—Hermione was looking for you, Chef, said Seeta.

—Oh?

—The wedding.

He sighed. —I'm still getting used to the idea.

—Me too. Paris is just a fucking *animal*.

—*Seeta*.

—You're telling me it's not a mystery to you why Hermione's getting hitched to him?

Vic nodded but Bohemond blew out. —I suppose she's in love, he said.

—In *denial*, more like.

—Denial?

—Come on. You spend your life looking for someone to love, don't you? When you're young you can be fussy. But when you get older and you want to settle down, you start making do with wankers you wouldn't have given a second glance before.

Innocent laughed. —You are so young to be such a cynic, Seeta. Hermione and Paris *are* in love.

—The only person Paris is in love with is himself.

25

—Nonsense.

—A guy like that: you think he's going to stop sowing his wild oats just cos he's married?

Bohemond swallowed rising winds. —What are you talking about?

But Seeta was quick to duck and mumble, —Nothing.

—So maybe Paris looks at other women, said Innocent, —but we must wish him well. He's marrying a beautiful girl in Hermione. At the end of the day, eyeing up some beauty queen in a bikini is small beer compared with committing to a marriage. Besides, show me a man who doesn't get hot under the collar when Miss World walks around the corner.

—Bohemond, said Seeta.

—*Me?* Bohemond's gut rumbled. His bowels budged.

—Bohemond is not interested in girls, said Innocent. —For him, it's an interest in personalities.

Seeta rolled her eyes. —A *what*?

—I'm an artist, Bohemond puffed weakly. —Not for me the carnal appetites of mere mortals.

—You're *a chef*.

—Yes, said Innocent, —but *what* a chef.

Bohemond bowed a little. Innocent responded with a curt nod of acknowledgement.

—A chef that's not interested in women, said Seeta.

—As a chef, said Innocent, —you are interested in *everyone*: men, women, young, old, big, small, pretty, not so pretty. You bring all people together. People you would never expect. Make them feel like they belong. Soothe them with delicious dishes . . . The meal becomes like a symphony of many move-ments. The chef enchants his diners with food just as the composer enchants his audience with beautiful music . . .

—Very nice, said Seeta. —But all I'm saying is not

every guy you meet wants to climb into your knickers.

They all looked up as the door swung open and Morrissey the potwasher came in; as Seeta had it: Bohemond's little mulatto masseur. He rustled into the mess, wearing bootcut pinstripes with a shirt to match, ruffled Vic's hair and swerved around the table, belching loudly as he slumped into the chair beside Seeta.

Vic hissed at how his uncovered cuts nipped. —*Prick!*

Morrissey raised an eyebrow.

—Seriously though, Seeta, said Bohemond. —Have you any proof that Paris has done anything wrong?

—Ask Paris.

—You have proof, then?

She twisted the ring off her index finger and put it in her pocket. Wouldn't look up. Morrissey ducked towards her, skin rippling from his furrowed brow to a close-shaven crown. —Sour grapes?

Seeta turned towards Bohemond. —Can you tell clothes-horse to piss off already? He doesn't even know what we're on about and he's off.

—Let me guess, said Morrissey. —Seeta's in a strop because someone's having a good time.

—What would you know, you slimy little *shit*?

—I know you.

—All right, she gestured round the table, —you've got everyone's attention, *as usual*. Say something.

—Time of the month? Problems at home?

Face flushed with fury, Seeta shot Bohemond a red-hot look. He backed up, flapping his hands beneath the table, shaking his head, all wide-eyed innocence and worry.

—Children, children, said Innocent, glancing from Seeta to Morrissey. —Thank God it's not you who is

27

getting married. Marriage is a very special thing. You give yourself to the other person for ever. Trust them with feelings that could kill you. They are always there, to catch you at any time. They become a part of you – sometimes all of you. You look into their eyes and you see yourself. You see the whole world differently. *All that joy*. Some people never get that. I look around at London, and this is a big city. So many people. So many men, yet so many unmarried women. You see them on the Tube all the time, these beautiful women without wedding rings, and their hands look naked and small and the women look so lonely. Sometimes you want to say something, but you never do. You just watch and grow a little sad . . .

Morrissey frowned, obviously offended. —Where the fuck did that come from?

—I'm sure plenty of those women are quite happily unmarried, said Seeta, her rage, to Bohemond's relief, speedily receding.

—But Hermione and Paris are so lucky, replied Innocent. —Everything from now on is double. Double love.

—Double disappointment.

—You haven't heard then? Morrissey puckered his lips, waiting for a response. —About how Hermione attacked Paris. Had him by the throat in the dry store, knife to his crotch, ready to chop off his bollocks.

Bohemond, Seeta, Innocent, Vic – an awed chorus: —*NO!*

—Loretta saw them, a month ago or so. Right round the time they announced the wedding. Surprised you didn't know.

Seeta sneered, gasped, scratched the table with her fingernails. —Bullshit!

—And we all know how that girl Loretta loves to talk, said Innocent. —If this thing happened in the dry store and she was aware of it, I think at least one of us would have been too.

—OK, Morrissey smiled, —maybe it wasn't the dry store . . . maybe it was the kitchen, or the *restaurant*, shit . . . maybe it was up in the office. Or was it the bar?

—Make up your mind. Seeta glanced towards the garden. —That's the whole building, apart from Bohemond's flat at the top.

—Maybe it was there . . .

—I knew this was more of your bullshit.

—Well, Morrissey? Sweat wet Bohemond's inner thighs. It logged his clogs. —Is it true?

—I'm just telling you what I heard.

Everyone sighed. Bohemond clutched his left breast, drove a thumb towards his heart. Too much to hope that the wedding was already on the rocks. —To get back to the point, he puffed, —much as some of us might hate to admit it, Innocent was right. Hermione and Paris will be two people living as one and that's where we come in.

Seeta slurred, —Really.

—Come on, Seeta, please.

—I'm trying.

If anything could deliver Bohemond from the depths of his despair, it was Seeta and her sweets. He needed her, but could see she was in retreat: the way she slouched over the table; her hair no longer pulled back in a black ponytail, but pressed down under a net; the sickly sheen of her skin; the lack of sparkle in her remarks; no flicker of fun. This woman who could once have been his muse, certainly the best sweet chef in the city, brimming with bile and blues as though

29

she couldn't give a fig about food. And if she couldn't give a fig about food, how could she help him hex Hermione? Especially now he'd been given a sign that his love might not go unrequited. —I propose, said Bohemond, interrupting the flow of conversation, —a meal that complements both bride and groom; one that compounds their love; that fortifies their bodies while it enriches their minds. Marriage is a meeting on many different levels and the feast we prepare should reflect and consummate that union.

—Calm down, muttered Morrissey, —it's just a bit of grub.

—Just a bit of grub? said Innocent, his neck reddening. —It is to be their first meal as man and wife. It is going to be a grand affair.

—Hermione's folks are loaded aren't they? said Morrissey. —They bought her this place, right?

—Old money, said Bohemond. —The wedding's at their mansion on the banks of Loch Torridon in Scotland.

Morrissey smiled. —I was in Scotland a couple of years ago. Wound up at some Roman toga orgy on the Isle of Skye would you believe?

—Oh now there's a coincidence, Seeta came on all camp. —Hermione's dad's Italian.

—*Fuck me*. What does he make of our Paris?

—Why would he make anything of Paris?

—Italians aren't too keen on the black Negro race, are they?

Seeta scowled. —Morrissey, what kind of animal are you?

—*It's true*.

—My brother used to go out with an Italian girl.

—Yeah but your brother isn't black, is he. He's Indian, or Bangladeshi or whatever it is.

30

—He's black enough. You watch too much TV.

—I get on well enough with Hermione, said Bohemond.

—She can't be Italian then, said Seeta. —Or you can't be black.

—Apparently I'm not.

—What?

—Lili and his bandmates, and Paris too for that matter, seem at pains to impress on me that I'm more like a fat white woman.

Morrissey grinned. —Lili's a cunt.

—What, Seeta muttered, —and Paris *isn't*?

—Paris is Paris, said Morrissey. —Lili's got real problems. That *whole band's* got problems.

—Well, brace yourselves, said Bohemond, —they're going to be playing at the wedding.

Everyone huffed and heaved.

—Faulkner as well? Seeta took the ring out of her pocket and wedged it on the end of her thumb.

Bohemond nodded. —The whole band. Hermione asked them to perform. But don't worry, from what I hear, her mother rules the roost with an iron fist.

—Is Hermione's mum Italian too? asked Morrissey.

—Turkish, said Seeta.

—So her dad likes dark meat after all.

—Are they all as stupid as you in Liverpool? Look at Hermione.

—Yeah, but she's not full-blooded though, is she?

—And not all Turkish people are the colour of fucking *coffee*.

Bohemond raised his hands. —That's pretty much what I was getting round to, he said. —. . . What if the wedding feast was to comprise elements of Paris and Hermione's ancestry? For instance since Hermione's father is Italian and her mother's Turkish, we begin with an Italian antipasto and move on to a Turkish-influenced second course, and so on.

—What about Paris? asked Morrissey.

—Certainly African, said Bohemond.

Seeta puffed. —Paris is *English*.

—But his bloodline isn't English.

—Like yours isn't French?

—Seeta, I was born in France. I am French. I *feel* French. I have the immediate cultural responses and tastes of a Frenchman. But that has no bearing on the fact that a part of me *is* African and that my physical and even spiritual lineage stems from Africa. I don't doubt for one second that African things and Africanness carry resonances I can't help but be consciously or subconsciously affected by. If I were making this meal for Hermione and myself, I would include an African element.

—Yeah, said Morrissey. —An African beef injection.

—But Bohemond, said Seeta, —you were brought up in a convent. – *By nuns*.

Innocent nodded. Morrissey glanced at a bewildered Vic. Seeta shaded her face with a hand, glanced at Bohemond and mouthed a silent apology.

He smiled sadly, avoiding every gaze.

—Fucker never told me that, muttered Morrissey. —When?

—A couple of days after I was born, said Bohemond, —my mother abandoned me. She left me on the steps of a convent deep in the heart of the Dordogne with a note fastened to my crib. It said: God forgive me. I brought this child into the world with no means of supporting him, please take care of him.

—Jesus, you're Jesus!

—Not quite, Morrissey. I still have the note. It wasn't

signed so I don't know her name. Don't know anything about her. The Missionary Sisters of the Sacred Heart of Jesus brought me up. And because I'd survived what they thought a great ordeal, they named me after one of the hardiest and most famous of all Christians: the Crusader, Bohemond, sometime Prince of Antioch.

Innocent patted Bohemond's arm. Let his hand rest for just a second.

—It's not a big deal, said Seeta. —This ancestry stuff's bollocks. I mean like you say, Chef, you were brought up by French nuns, but you've lived in London for ages. You don't even have a French accent any more. Yeah you're black, but you're blue-eyed too, and you've got straight hair. So when I hear you go on about the spirits of Africa, I'm just like: *what*?

Bohemond shrugged. —So what am I?

—*Fuck knows* and who cares. You're a hundred things. Which is why all this national dishes nonsense is bollocks. *I'd* feel queer if there was prawn korma and nan bread at my wedding.

—How would you feel if there were lamb and beef croquettes on the menu?

—Why?

—That, Seeta, is part of the point I am trying to make. Some foreign dishes are so common one might quite excusably think them English.

—Lamb and beef croquettes?

—Traditional Indian, said Bohemond. —Kofta ring any bells?

—Nope.

—All culinary development is dependent upon the importation of foreign foods and condiments, which are themselves transformed even as they're absorbed into the recipient culture.

—So?

33

—So, said Bohemond, —remind me at some point to give you a potted history of the potato. Let me warn you now, though, it's a bloody tale of fallen nations and fledgling empires, of savage Spanish Conquistadors and slaughtered Incas, of miracle cures and dreadful disease, of paranoid peasantry force-fed at gunpoint. A caseload of carnage just to convince you that mash, chips and crisps et cetera are international variations on a South American theme.

Morrissey shook his head, looking even more appalled than he had done at Innocent's sympathy for unmarried women. —Fucker never told me he was a monk. And now *this*.

—It's still patronizing, said Seeta.

Bohemond licked his lips. —Perhaps, he said, —it would be a little inappropriate if we were to serve spaghetti bolognese followed by chicken chop suey. But we can be subtle enough to make the transitions from dish to dish seem seamless. Simplicity is the key. It's entirely possible we can affect the bond between bride and groom through the food we prepare for them.

—You believe all this stuff, don't you?

Of course he believed it. Eating had shaped the human view of the world. Since the dawn of time, men and women had been able to make the distinction between foods that would kill or sustain them. That age-old discrimination was now considered a virtue: *taste* – the tendency to avoid all things foreign; to stick to the tried and tested. No wonder modern man found himself immediately wary of worldly diversity. Acquisition of taste was at the root of his prosperity, but it was also at the root of his xenophobia and ignorance. Bohemond needed Seeta's help to expand the narrowing palate with dishes that celebrated

34

difference. Because he was sure that the way to Hermione's heart lay in the mingling of their ancestries, the combination of their cultural DNA. Temperance at an end, he might've stormed in with: REMEMBER, SEETA, FOOD IS FUNDAMENTAL TO OUR EXISTENCE! IT'S NO EXAGGERATION TO SAY, HE WHO CONTROLS WHAT GOES IN HAS <u>NO SMALL INFLUENCE</u> OVER WHAT COMES OUT! But instead all he said was: —Yes.

Innocent, slouched in his chair, eyes closed, nodded along.

—What about asparagus? beamed Morrissey. —Cock food. We can get them all jiggy with it.

Bohemond groaned. —The food/sex connection is for TV chefs. We should aim for something much higher by looking deeper. Hermione is half-Italian, so I suggest that our antipasto incorporate some olive derivative since olive trees, olives and olive oil have been at the centre of the ritual, cultural and creative life of the Mediterranean for thousands of years.

—*Whoopee.*

—Mock all you like, Morrissey, but olive oil is a kind of holy water. The stuff you buy bottled from the local deli was once used to consecrate priests, temples and churches. It was used to anoint every king of France from Clovis right up to Louis XVI.

Morrissey folded his arms, shrugged and said, —Shite.

—What do you mean, shite? The kingship bestowed by the oil is irrevocable, inviolable. Do you understand? We'll use it to consecrate the marriage of Hermione and Paris.

—All marriages end in divorce.

Innocent spluttered on his borsch and Seeta said,

—If Hermione and Paris don't know all this stuff about olive oil, what's the point?

—Remember, said Bohemond, —even though I'm French, it's entirely possible that what African blood there is in me could be stirred by African things whose real meaning I have no knowledge of.

And if that was too new-age for them, they could surely appreciate the associated symbolism: Noah's dove returned to the ark with an olive twig in its beak; in later days, heralds and envoys brought olive branches into enemy camps as a sign of peace and conducted their business without fear of ambush; Olympic champions were presented with olive wreaths, which they wore as a sign that all the virtues of the civilized world were combined within them; when Odysseus built his marriage bed he made one of its four posts an olive tree that was still rooted in the ground . . .

—. . . every one of them's fucked. Morrissey finished saying something, but since Bohemond had soared from the foot of Odysseus' marriage bed to winging it over the Aegean with Icarus and Hermione – all three of them soaring northwards, heavens above, oceans below – he'd missed the point. —So, olives! he said, suddenly saddened. —Immovability. Constancy. Inviolability. Peace. Civility. Tolerance. Regeneration. Aren't these characteristics you would wish of any marriage?

Seeta shyed away from a smile.

—This place you mention, said Innocent, —the home of Hermione's mother and father. It's near water?

—Loch Torridon on the West Highland coast, said Bohemond.

Innocent rubbed his wrists together. —Perhaps then, it might be an idea to begin with fish.

. . . fish . . . *Bravo!* Just as the sea was a symbol of the human psyche, so fish signified its hidden riches. It was here, in her unconscious, like fish darting through a sunken wonderland, that Hermione's deepest desires for Bohemond lay. If she was to become conscious of these passions, she must first attain a state of pure emotional enlightenment; a level of ecstasy Bohemond could induce with the right fusion of foods . . . —Polpettone di tonno?

Morrissey, half laughing: —Fuck off.

—Polpettone of tunny fish, said Innocent.

Bohemond nodded. —For this we'll need olive oil, tunny fish, eggs, capers and fresh black pepper . . . Pulp the fish in a food mill with generous amounts of olive oil. Beat the eggs into this purée and season the results with the pepper. I like to add a little fresh sage at this point, since, when it is absorbed into the settling tuna it endows the finished dish with an elusive flavour I can only describe as teasingly reminiscent of a lesser smoked prosciutto. Stir in the capers making sure they are spread evenly and then tip the mixture onto a floured board and mould it into the shape of a fat sausage. Sprinkle more flour over a doubled butter muslin, wrap the fish pulp in it and tie up the ends salami-style. Lower the bundle lengthways into a pan of boiling water, reduce to a gentle simmer and leave it bathing for an hour and five minutes, before hanging it up to drain and cool. Don't unwrap it until it's cold and then serve it cut into slices, preferably with an insalata di patate. A rather cool cut for summertime don't you think?

Innocent leaned forward and slapped the tabletop with the palm of his hand; applause of a sort.

Seeta rested her cheek on a fist and said: —I quite

37

like the sound of this polpettone. I'd definitely be tempted to go for that as a fish starter.

—But it . . . sounds like a big fat *cock*, said Morrissey. —I thought you weren't going for the food sex thing.

Seeta ignored him. —What about veggies though, Chef . . . You think they're crap, eh?

Intoxicated by the scent of her surrender, Bohemond hammed up. —*Crap?* he wailed, quite the outraged gourmet. —*Crap!* How could I despise a way of life endorsed by the likes of Pythagoras and Plato. How could I deny the biological *rationale* of Plutarch who tells us that meat-eating is unnatural as the human condition is not suited to it. According to him, man's teeth are too *tiny*, his tongue is not *rough* enough, his digestion too *dainty*. He has no hooked *beak* or talons. No real *carnivorous instinct* . . . We could have insalata di carciofi, uova sode agli spinaci, insalata di peperoni gialli, peperoni sott'olio, insalata di pomodoro, antipasto misto, insalata di finocchi e cetrioli, all with room for plenty of olive oil.

—You're just taking the piss now, she said.

—As if . . .

—It is quite romantic though. I mean even if all this symbolism and stuff is baloney, it's a nice way of thinking. It's just a shame Paris is the biggest prick on the planet.

—What a *bitch*, said Morrissey, and pushed away from the table.

Seeta pouted. —Touchy.

—Back to work, said Innocent. He watched Morrissey flounce out and looked at Vic; —Shall we? Vic nodded. They rinsed their mugs in the sink and trudged into the kitchen.

—What's up with those two? Bohemond frowned.

—Hungover, said Seeta. —They were in here drinking late last night.

He stretched and began to get up. —I was on a roll, he said. —Just getting started.

Seeta skipped around the table and helped him to his feet.

the sacred weight of sweetmeats

In which Bohemond soothes Seeta's blues with a fairy tale.

After lunch Bohemond retired to the mess-room to water the plants. He found Seeta there, sitting at the table, cradling another mug of borscht. She didn't look up as he came in.

—Is everything all right?

—What did you say to Morrissey, Chef?

—I'm sorry?

—About *me*. You heard him this morning: problems at home, he said. How does he know?

Bohemond's heartbeat slumped. —Seeta, you've got to believe me, I didn't say anything to him.

—You're the only person I told.

—You were winding each other up, as you always do. He got lucky and hit a nerve.

At last she looked at him. —Are you sure?

—Oh, God, Seeta . . . *no* . . . I'm not sure.

—Chef!

—All I said was that you'd had a row with your father and spent a night here, in Delphi.

—Did you tell him about this? She yanked on her lapels, exposing the skin below her collarbone, the blue-black rim of a bruise.

—No. Eyes down, Bohemond glanced across the floor. —Course not.

—Cos if you did . . .

—I didn't.

—. . . I'll never speak to you again.

—Seeta, *I promise*.

She let go of her overalls. —I don't get why you let Morrissey work here anyway. He's such a creep.

—He keeps my feet on the ground, said Bohemond. —Stops me overreaching myself.

—Is *that it*? I can do that.

He tried to laugh, but gasped and grabbed his cast-iron throne. —May I? Seeta didn't reply and so he sat down beside her. —Please don't get angry with me, he said, —I only ask because I care about you . . .

—Jesus . . .

—. . . but . . . are you still having problems with your father?

—Not any more.

—Seeta, that's good news.

—I moved out.

—*You what?*

—Got a place in Kilburn.

—But that's the other side of the city.

—I wish it was the other side of the world, she said. —But hey, let's not dwell on it, Hermione and Paris are getting married. Hurrah.

—Bad timing? said Bohemond.

—Just a reminder of everything that's shit about my own life.

41

—Such as?

—How about my dad laying into me for starters?

—Seeta, you said it was an accident.

—What's he doing laying his hands on me in the first place? *Idiot fucking man.*

—You said he's never done anything like it before.

—He hasn't.

—So what did you do to make him so angry?

—Oh, so it's my fault now, is it?

—No . . . no . . . Has your mother said anything yet?

—Not one word . . . *I hope your womb dries like a desert!* he's shouting at me, and my mum was there in the hall, nodding away . . . same fucking woman who told me, two days before, when my dad makes love to her it's as though she doesn't need to *be there.*

—Your *womb*? Seeta, what have you done?

—My little sister saw him push me, and she went hysterical, *Why is daddy killing Seeta?* And my dad's like, *Because she has brought the greatest shame down on all our heads.* And he's off on one: *Twenty years,* he says, *Twenty years we have been living in this god-forsaken country, and still they tell me, Paki go home! And I say, This is my home, the best place for my family, the education of my son and daughters. You go home! Twenty years of struggle, Seeta, and now this is how you repay me!*

—*Good God* . . .

—Textbook curse, eh . . .

—You're not . . . ?

—What?

—Pregnant.

Tutting.

—Well then what? I can't believe you've done anything that awful.

42

—Maybe you don't know me as well as you think you do.

—What happened?

—. . . I fell in love. OK?

—But that's great.

—My dad didn't think so.

—He went berserk because of a *boyfriend*?

—It's nothing, Chef. Just leave it.

Bohemond scratched his head. Gnawed the inside of his cheek.

—Just leave it.

—It seems to me, he said, —the only people who're happy right now are Hermione and Paris.

—*There you go again*. Seeta wrung her hands. —How do you know they're happy?

—Why else would they commit to spending the rest of their lives together?

—*I told you*: security. Paris is at it behind her back, but he's a known quantity.

—Gossip is a dangerous pastime, Seeta. I've seen strange things too, but like you, I have no real proof.

Her eyes gleamed. —*What!* What did you see?

—Paris, in what I thought was a compromising position.

—*See?*

—I can't be sure . . .

—Wasn't it obvious?

—Not obvious . . . .

—Did you tell Hermione?

—I intend to, but Seeta, Hermione is my oldest friend, and I've come to realize that my priority is to make her as happy as possible. Believe me, I don't think Paris deserves her either, but she does, which can only mean we don't know the whole Paris. Perhaps

43

we'd do better to accept that love doesn't always crop up where we expect it.

Seeta sighed, a slight tremor rippling the long exhalation. —What's Hermione like, really? I mean *really*. You've known her for ages, yeah?

—Fourteen years.

—She's a good laugh . . .

—The funniest.

—And she's no wimp, right?

—Fearless.

—And she loves life and everything . . . you've had good times . . . ?

—Too many to mention . . .

. . . like the time they ate hash cake on the top floor of the dry store; the time they hunted for poinsettias at the Columbia Road Flower Market; the time she kissed his fingers when he burned them on the hotplate; the time she cured his cold with a cupful of flowers, slept by his side until the fever died; kisses under mistletoe, walks along the riverside, supper on the back lot, dancing in the moonlight, sharing spare ribs on a boat ride to Greenwich . . . and suddenly there was Seeta, sitting beside him, something buckling deep down inside her. —I just feel so . . . *young*, or something . . . like I don't matter . . . or I'm invisible . . .

—But Seeta—

—Chef . . . I'm twenty-one years old, I live in a shitty bedsit in Kilburn cos my dad's thrown me out the house, and I'm a *sweet cook* in a tiny restaurant.

Sweat sprang up on the nape of Bohemond's neck. It trickled down the backs of his ears. —You shouldn't underestimate the worth of what you do here. The times we've both heard people exclaim about the desserts you've prepared for them. The men who line up like dizzy suitors outside this very kitchen to compliment you on the splendour of your sweets. That gift is not to be sniffed at.

She bit her lip, gaze gone misty. —You make it sound *so* romantic, as always . . . but it's not really like that. Yeah, I can bake a cake, but so what?

—Seeta, don't go. Please. I need you here.

—You don't need me.

—Sometimes . . . I think I wouldn't manage without you . . .

She glanced at him sidelong, unsure.

—Believe me, I need you. And believe me, the grass is always greener until you get there.

—I'd still like to see the other side of the hill, though.

—But that's why Hermione and Paris are getting married. They understand that you don't have to go to the ends of the earth to find excitement. You only have to look into the eyes of your loved one.

—Please don't.

—No, seriously, Seeta. You talk about going off on great adventures, discovering the world and its secrets, but all anyone is really looking for is love. You could travel to the ends of the universe and come back feeling like a goddess, but it would be for nothing if you had no-one to share your treasures with. If you truly love this man your father is forcing you to give up, you should use all your energies to stay here and be with him. Your love *will* find a way.

—No. All that's *bollocks*. Paris is a tosser, but everyone's making out like there's this big happy romance going on. Five years down the line Hermione's going to wake up and find she's with the wrong guy. Everyone knows it, but they're standing round going, Yeah! Great! Wedding! Like it's some kind of fairy tale ending.

—Fairy tales aren't too bad a blueprint, Seeta. Think about it: love conquers all, even death; it drives men and women on to great deeds that are rewarded with eternal rapture and glory; hatred and evil are always confounded. Living happily ever after isn't impossible and there's nothing foolish in wishing for that end. It's all anyone wants. You say the world isn't like that, it's an unrealistic view. But if it's so unrealistic, why do so many people subscribe to it? There's no reason why dreams can't come true. Why fairy tales can't be made flesh . . . There's even hope for me that way.

—Do you . . . really think you'll end up with someone?

—I believe that by doing good, good things will come to me, regardless of how I look or feel about myself.

—Honestly?

—Why else bother?

—With what?

—With *anything*.

She smiled, tears beginning to glisten.

Bohemond covered her little fist with his own gargantuan hands and glanced out the window at the sun-gilt snow. —Hundreds of years ago, he said, —before those Spanish Conquistadors slew the Incas in Peru, but not so long after Clovis was crowned king of France – there lived, in Naples, a rich merchant by the name of Giovanni. He had three daughters, the youngest and most beautiful of whom was called Rosa.

One summer Giovanni lost a ship's cargo to pirates. After he'd paid off his debts, all he had left was a run-down cottage on a little bit of land. So, with no other choice, he moved out there to work as a farmer. The two older sisters, Maria and Clarice, didn't like that, especially as, they said, they'd had offers of marriage from some of Naples' most beautiful sons. The problem was that now, however, Naples' most beautiful didn't want to have anything to do with a pair of penniless scolds.

Life in the cottage was hard, especially for Rosa, whose sisters bullied her into doing all the chores. But then one day news reached Giovanni that his ship had docked in Naples with part of its cargo intact. Tremendously excited, he made ready to leave, and before he set out he asked his daughters what gifts they'd like him to bring back.

I want a cloak spun from pure gold, said Maria.

I want a silver bracelet, said Clarice.

But Rosa said, Just bring me a rose.

Maria and Clarice fell about laughing at that, but their father was only too happy to grant his youngest daughter's wish.

When he got to the port, Giovanni was accosted by angry merchants who insisted that since he was still in debt to them, the cargo was rightfully theirs. And so it was with a heavy heart that he made his way back home. He spent the last of his money on Maria's cloak and Clarice's bracelet. Since Rosa's rose was a simple present, he resolved to pick one from a garden on the road back.

At sundown, he lost his way in a forest. A sudden storm forced him to take shelter under a tree. Wolves howled, drawing nearer as the gale heightened.

In his panic the old merchant spotted something glowing in the trees. He ran in that direction and saw that the light was shining from the windows of an ivory palace. Sprinting up the steps, he flung open the door and hurried inside, amazed to find himself in a great glittering hall. A fire burned in a golden hearth, and by it stood a table laden with glorious dishes.

Walking all day had given him quite an appetite, so he sat down and ate.

After the meal he climbed the stairs and found a bedroom already prepared. It all seemed quite strange – a deserted palace in the middle of nowhere, food on the table – but in truth, so relieved was Giovanni to be out of the forest, he felt no fear.

In the morning, he woke to find new clothes and shoes at the end of the bed. He put them on and walked out into the gardens where he spotted a rose-bush with the biggest reddest rose he had ever seen growing at its centre. Goodness, he thought, that would make Rosa a lovely present. But no sooner had he picked it than, to his great horror, a dreadful monster jumped over the wall. The beast roared, I bring you into my house, feed you, give you a bed to sleep in and you return my hospitality with theft! How dare you! That rose will cost you your life!

Giovanni fell to his knees. Please sir, he cried, spare me, I only picked the rose as a gift for my youngest daughter, Rosa.

At these words the monster's rage abated and he said, You will live, on one condition; that you bring your daughter here to be my queen. Fail me in this and I will hunt you down, kill *all* your daughters before your eyes, and then slow-roast you over a fire before I split your skull and eat your brains.

Giovanni said that he'd do as the monster requested even though it might break his heart.

The beast then told him to go into the palace vaults and pick out as much treasure as he liked, he would send the booty on in a few days.

When Giovanni got back to the cottage Maria and Clarice tore their presents away from him. But Rosa was just happy to have him back. He handed over the rose and promptly burst into tears as he told them all that had happened.

Maria and Clarice were hysterical. See what you've done by asking for that rose, you silly little bitch! Now we're all going to die.

Rosa, however, kept calm. The giant won't hurt any of us if I go and live with him, she said, so that's what I'll do.

Maria and Clarice thought it a great idea, but Giovanni cried his eyes out begging her not to go. It was no good. Her mind was made up and the others knew it was the only way they could hope to stay alive.

When the old man woke at dawn, he found a chest full of treasure at the bottom of his bed. The monster had kept his word. He hid the hoard in a cupboard, got dressed and found Rosa ready waiting in the kitchen. Without further ado they set out for the ivory palace in the woods.

When they got there they found the table in the great hall set for two people. But given the circumstances, neither of them felt that hungry.

They were disturbed eventually by an ear-splitting roar, and the monster crashed into the room. Rosa's heart sank, for the beast that stood before them was far darker and more twisted than she could ever have imagined. But she did well to hide her disgust.

The monster sent Giovanni on his way saying, If you ever come here again without my invitation, my wrath will be terrible. Now, take this bag of gold and know that I will provide for you and your family for the rest of your lives.

Full of sorrow, the old merchant kissed his daughter goodbye and left. Rosa went off to bed where she cried herself to sleep.

Next morning she found beautiful clothes waiting for her as her father had done during his stay. The room, as well as the rest of the palace, she discovered, was full of everything she'd ever need.

As she ate dinner that evening the monster clattered into the hall and asked if he might sit with her.

Of course, she replied, it's your house.

On the contrary, said the monster, all that you see is yours.

Rosa smiled, starlight shining in her eyes.

The monster gaped at her, absolutely stunned, and said: Do you really think I'm *that* disgusting?

Beauty is only skin deep, she said. And you have a kind soul.

Then marry me? he said.

Well, Rosa's poor heart almost stopped. She didn't know what to say. How hurt would he be if she refused? In the end she could do no more than be honest. Truthfully, sir, she said, I have no desire to marry you.

The monster sighed and left the table.

Every dinner after that the beast proposed to Rosa, and every time she turned him down.

One day while they were strolling in the gardens, the monster pointed to a vast tree with huge green leaves. This, he said, is the tree of sadness and joy. When the leaves turn upwards, your house is full of happiness, but when they droop, it is full of sorrow.

A few weeks later Rosa found the leaves turned up and asked, Why is it so?

Your sister Maria is getting married, replied the monster.

Please, please, she said, can I go to the wedding?

Of course you can. But don't go for too long or I will die.

He handed her a ring set with an onyx stone. Take this, he said, and if the stone gets light you will know that I am in danger. Promise me that you'll come back to me at such time.

I promise, said Rosa.

Take whatever things you like from the treasury as wedding presents for Maria, and be sure to put them in the chest at the end of your bed before you go to sleep.

This she did and next morning she woke up in her father's cottage. Everyone was pleased to see her, even her sisters. But as soon as those two heard how kind the monster was and saw how happy and rich Rosa seemed to be, their generosity turned to spite, especially as Maria was marrying a shepherd. They took the monster's ring away from her, saying they'd love to try it on, but as soon as they were out of sight they hid it. By the end of the week Rosa was almost in tears pleading with them to hand it over, but they only did so after Giovanni ordered them to.

Poor Rosa. How quickly her delight turned to horror when she found the onyx stone looking a little cloudy.

In a panic she fled back to the palace. The monster was nowhere to be seen. She spent hours calling him but it was no use. At last he showed up to dinner looking very sick indeed.

I was ailing horribly, he said. If you had left it any longer it would have been the end of me. Don't you love me any more?

Of course I love you, Rosa blurted, surprising even herself.

Then marry me, said the beast.

Oh no, said Rosa. I'm sorry, but that I cannot do.

Two months later the leaves on the tree of sadness and joy were turned up again.

What's going on? asked Rosa.

Your sister Clarice is getting married, replied the monster.

Can I go?

Of course, but don't be gone too long or it will be the death of me.

Rosa gathered presents as she had before, went to bed and woke up in her father's cottage.

Her sisters did nothing to hide their jealousy this time. Not only was Clarice marrying a butcher, Maria's husband beat her.

They managed to steal Rosa's ring again and refused to return it. When she did finally get it back she was horrified to see that the stone had completely clouded over.

She hurried back to the palace but this time the monster didn't even *show* for dinner. He came to her next day, looking much weaker, and said, I was ready to die. Next time it will be the end of me.

A few months later Rosa found the leaves on the tree drooping so low that they brushed against the ground.

What is happening that is so bad? she asked.

Your father is dying, said the monster.

Rosa almost fainted. Oh let me go to him, she said, I promise I will come back in time.

Make sure you do.

She sped to her father's bedside where she tended him day and night. Her presence alone seemed to aid him on the road to recovery and soon it was clear he would live.

One day she left the ring on a sideboard while she washed her hands. When she went back to fetch it, it was gone. She knew her sisters had taken it again and she pleaded with them to return it. In the end her father rose from his sick-bed and ordered them to give it back.

This time, save for the tiniest notch at one side, the onyx stone had turned white.

Rosa raced back to the palace but it was dark and windswept, the sky overcast and thunderous. She ran through the jewelled halls screaming and crying for her monster but there was no answer.

At last, finding him in the garden, lying under the rosebush, looking as if he was done for, she flung herself upon him, kissed him and cried, I love you! I love you! Please don't die. Live so we can be married and I'll never leave you again.

At these words the sky opened up, silver light shone from the palace windows, the trees re-blossomed and music filled the air. The monster disappeared and in his place stood a handsome prince.

Rosa remained on her knees. Who are you? she wept. I want my monster back.

I was the monster, said the prince. A wicked sorcerer imprisoned me in that body and I was forced to remain a beast until a beautiful woman proposed to me just as I was. Your love broke the spell.

He took Rosa by the hand and she fell into his arms. As they turned towards the palace they saw Giovanni on the steps smiling and waving. Maria and Clarice were also there, but their jealousy had eaten away at them so much that they had become weightless, and they floated up into the sky, out of sight. As far as I know they're still drifting.

The young prince became a king, made Rosa his queen, and they lived happily ever after.

perfumed plates

An unexpected asthma attack.

Once he'd finished the story, Bohemond sat in silence with Seeta, ten minutes before she rose without a word and wandered through to the kitchen to make a start on the evening sweets. As he struggled to his feet he let go a gasp – small wonder, as always, at how he seemed even heavier than he had only moments ago. Bow-tying his housecoat, vindicated and saddened by how little belt there was left to secure the knot, he squeezed through the mess-room doorway on to the back lot.

Wind blew snowflakes in his face, forcing him to huddle up and keep his mouth shut. Hands in his pockets, he loitered under the lintel, stamping his feet. The blizzard had obliterated most things of note, only the toolshed stood out. Weak winter sunlight smattered the yard with gold, snow-infused shadows no darker than indigo.

Eventually he tottered towards the courtyard door. Icy fluff streamed under his collar, tickled his tongue whenever he clenched his teeth. His shoulderblades ached and his brow throbbed with frowning. From the middle of the plot he peered up the tenement wall, tracing the drainpipe from the ground to the guttering. It passed fully three metres to the left of his bedroom window. If Paris and the stranger had shinned it, they must've jumped to reach his window ledge, but he couldn't see how, especially given the figure-hugging fit of the blue-glitter dress. They might've dropped from higher up the pipe, made the most of momentum and trajectory, but that seemed a pointlessly life-threatening exercise. The most likely explanation was that they'd taken a ladder from the scaffolding on Curlew Street, but there'd been none of that kind of clatter last night. This mystery was another omen. A sign that Bohemond was on the side of righteousness.

It was possible his very *intention* to win Hermione for himself would force fate before the wedding. If not, the meal would be his salvation . . . Hermione in her full bridal gown at the head of the banquet table . . . one mouthful, no, a single *whiff* of his polpettone, and she'd be overcome. Spun into a whirlwind of mad love, she'd scream his name, renounce her vows, uproar that'd send the spread flying into the air. And as the knives and forks and skewers rained down, they'd pin Paris's cuffs to the table, hold him prisoner long enough for Hermione to run and jump onto the back of Bohemond's waiting horse and off they'd ride, into the sunset . . . nothing but a cloud of dust on the horizon . . .

He twitched and turned around at the sound of the courtyard door opening. It was Hanswurst, stiff-limbed in a donkey jacket, his greying perm crushed beneath a green wool cap. —All right, Fats.

Bohemond grunted. —You're very early.

—Gotta catch up on some reading.

—What have you got?

The porter pulled a copy of *Vogue* from the inside breast of his coat. He slid around beside Bohemond, tilted the magazine towards him and flicked through a thousand perfumed plates of serpentine torsos, knock-knees and turned-in feet.

Bohemond stumbled away, bile frothing up in his gullet.

The women in the magazine were too beautiful.

december menu

In which Bohemond bewitches his beloved.

Bohemond bombed back into the mess-room, lungs bubbling whenever he breathed in, windpipe dwindled to a pinhole. He fumbled for the inhaler in his pocket, plucked it out and sucked two shots of Ventolin, the hit spinning him into a slump against the sideboard where he lowered his head into his hands and waited for the pressure to lessen. Grinning, gurning, *growling*, Hanswurst peered in the window. He blew against the glass, licked it free of mist and lumbered around to the dry store door; hadn't set foot in the mess-room since the night he lost his way in its garden.

Dizziness deadened down, Bohemond sidled through the restaurant into the foyer and climbed the stairs to Hermione's office on the first-floor landing. The door was open. Voices murmuring. He knocked. Paris peeked around the post, slouched on the edge of the desk, one foot swinging lazily, the other planted on the floor. His hand hung over a thigh, two gold rings on the thumb, an unlit cigarette between his fingers. Delphi's man of action. Decked in a black vest and matching slacks, with silver-buckled shoes and steel-covered toecaps, all he lacked was a cape and mask. Hermione sat below him, almost obscured, but quickly wheeled herself away as Bohemond came in. —I've been looking for you, Bo, she said. —Sit down.

He puffed back the humid reek of wood glue. Dragged the cushioned copper throne from the corner of the room.

Paris rocked to his feet, no hint in his tilt or tone of what had happened the night before. —He's cool the cook, isn't he?

—Not half as cool as you, muttered Bohemond, and he sat down.

It looked darker outside. Much more like winter. A single table lamp buffed up the duskiness in the room.

—I'm out of here, said Paris. Hermione sprang up to kiss him, but he opened his mouth, waggled his tongue. She sucked the tip, brought a hand up to his throat, pushed him back, laughing as he fumbled with the fly of her palazzo pants. One long genuinely loving look and he dashed down the stairs.

The door closed and locked, Hermione swung her chair around beside Bohemond's. Cherry scent wafted up as she sat down, slowly simmering back to the sweetnesses of sweat, black coffee and spearmint breath.

—I was looking for you too, he said.

She licked a finger and reached out to scrape some crust away from the corner of his mouth. —Oh yeah?

Eyelids fluttering as she touched him, he stuttered, —Next month's menu.

—Ditto. Her finger became a thumb, smoothing over any rawness the scratching might have left. —Bit of biscuit, she said, and leaned back, squinting at the problem spot.

Bohemond swallowed, mumbling modesties.

—No-one would've noticed unless they were kissing you.

—Thanks.

—Don't mention it.

—You must be very excited, Hermione.

—Getting married? Yeah. All the twittering has made me and Paris a bit like strangers. In a good way. It's kind of like hallucinating or something. He looks larger than life . . . She laid a hand on his knee. —It means a lot to me, Bohemond . . . you cooking for me on my wedding day.

—Wouldn't have missed it. He glanced at the scar on her wrist, the one he knew flared in a curve all the way to her elbow. —Besides, it's the least I can do. You saved my life.

She withdrew, wisps of long black hair sliding down over her shoulder. —Hardly.

—I'd do anything for you, Hermione.

—Ditto. Again.

Falling snow flared gold as it passed the window. Bohemond sniffed. Bowed his head.

—Anyway, she said. —What are you making for the wedding?

—It's a surprise. What you can tell me though is, am I right thinking your mother's Turkish?

—Yeah, why?

—And your father's Italian.

—You know that already. He loves you. Never stops going on about the figpeckers you cooked him last summer.

—Just checking. What about Paris?

—His mum's from Guatemala and his dad's American.

—*African* American though, right?

—*Bohemond?*

He scratched his nose, sweat beginning to seep onto his top lip. Now or never. —One other thing . . . I have to ask because the rumour didn't go down too well in the kitchen. But will Faulkner and Lili and Petra and Francis and the rest of them definitely be playing at the wedding reception?

—Come on, Bo, Faulkner's almost family. And my dad thinks he's going to pop his clogs soon. It's the rest of the band I'm not so thrilled about: Lili and them. They're going to run riot.

—They were playing a boat party last night, weren't they?

—Were they?

—I thought you might have been there with Paris. I hope he didn't wake you when he came in last night?

—You mean, you hope I didn't wake *him*.

—*You?*

—I was out with my mates. He was dead to the world when I got back.

Steady but breathless he said, —You must have come home very late. He climbed in through my window around three thirty this morning.

—He *what*?

—He didn't tell you?

—No.

—He said he'd lost his keys, so he climbed up here with . . . what's her name . . . ? Is it Jo?

Hermione's eyes darkened. —*Jo*.

—I think that's what he said.

—Really slim? Little bit boyish-looking?

—That's right. Goodness knows how they managed to scale the wall.

—He had *her*, in here?

—Just last night.

Her jaw hardened, a flush budding in her cheeks. —Have you got the December menu?

Sweat drizzling from his fingers, Bohemond fumbled for the notebook in his pocket and opened it at a marked page.

—Wait a minute. Hermione slipped off her seat. Ducked down to a tiny glass-fronted fridge built into the wall beside the desk. Bohemond watched her work, tried to gauge the weight of his revelation, how far he was out of his depth. She rose holding a bottle of passion fruit Looza and a crystal tumbler. —Don't say I'm not good to you.

He smiled thanks as she set the glass on the table and poured him a drink. —Are you all right, Hermione?

—Fine, she said and stretched, arms spread, back arched, the hem of her skin-tight long-sleeved top riding up to unveil a pierced navel. —Why wouldn't I be?

Bohemond huffed, averted his eyes, took a sip of syrup that calmed his panic and the side-effects of the Ventolin. Short-lived luxury, for as Hermione sat down, kicked off her trainers and swung her bare feet up onto Bohemond's lap, his mouth filled with spit, his gut bubbled, his nipples twitched.

She closed her eyes. —Whenever you're ready.

Bent double, trembling, Bohemond began reading in a whisper.

HEAD FIRST

Caciotta-encrusted potato and spinach cream
torte

•

Sterlet roe with shredded eddoe crepe
and roast earthnut

•

Roman bruschetta: an assortment of market-fresh
tomatoes and basil on brie crostini

•

Charcoal-roast cloves of garlic mingled with
braised feta nuggets, marinated olives and
winter-christened artichoke hearts on rosemary
and thyme-baked crostini

•

Inkfish and tiger shrimp tossed with lemon
pepper linguini

•

Blue-dewed butterhead lettuce with
a belle-alliance cider vinaigrette

•

East Pacific mussels steamed with toasted chillies,
rubbed sage, fresh ginger in a white wine and
coconut milk broth

•

Garbanzo bean dahl with a medley of root
vegetables atop Swiss chard with a mint yoghurt
raita

•

Flame-grilled, honey-glazed calamari on
a bed of crispy roots with a tangy black bean
and corn salsa

LOVEHEARTS

Pan-seared chicken with steam-baked leeks,
stewed yellow peppers and penne in a cashew
nut besciamella

•

Spit-roasted ortolan wrapped in vine leaves and
Parma prosciutto, with a seasonal herb crust and
tarragon risotto

•

Spinach and ricotta ravioli in a walnut and
pumpkin sauce

•

Flash-poached Queens scallop, shiitake, portabello
and porcini mushrooms in a roast garlic relish

•

Fusilli with veal bolognese sauce, fava and
parmesan

VELVETY BELLIES

Oven-baked Atlantic mackerel accompanied by
flame-roasted ribbons of parsnip, pepper and
courgette, herb-crusted black rice and a citrus
beurre blanc

•

Grilled aubergine steaks in a red pepper–mushroom ragu,
served over a bed of black bean and plantain-studded
rice with market vegetables and a warm spinach–fennel
vinaigrette

•

Arctic char baked on rum-soaked cedar planks
with beet bauletti, grilled winter veg and
blackened citrus

•

Medallions of peanut-crusted pork tenderloin,
cumin-roast parsnip, pepper, courgette, broccoli
and shallots drizzled in olive oil, with spicy root
vegetable chips and a tangy rocambole marmalade

•

Potato pasta with an assortment of grilled
vegetables smothered in a savoury vegetable jus
over sautéed spinach

•

Marinated breast of chicken with grilled yams,
seasonal vegetables in a coriander cream sauce

•

Honey-roast rump of lamb with baked
Mediterranean vegetables and garlic polenta in a
green pepper and chilli salsa

•

Flame-grilled tournedos steak with roast potatoes
and chorizo cake in a sauce béarnaise

SWEET TEETH

Candied mandarin jujube with sugar-scorched
kiwi fruit in a vanilla cinnamon sauce

•

Deep-fried banana cutlets dunked in blood-red
Xeres with an almond chocolate sauce

•

Panocha with raspberries and grappa

•

Honey-blazed cheesecake in a pool of apricot
dew

•

Par-frosted orbs of watermelon, peach, mango
and nectarine on a rum-infused raft of coconut
and katemfe

•

White chocolate and strawberry parfait

•

Blackberry compote

•

Grilled pannequets

•

Baked peaches stuffed with molten macaroon

•

Fig pudding

•

Chef's own chocolate cake

Hermione opened her eyes and sighed: —Fuck me, I should be marrying you.

Bohemond's heart skipped. He saw a bit of bliss in the lazy gaze she gave him, the look he wanted to wake up to every morning for the rest of his life.

He eased to his feet and excused himself. Left Hermione chewing her lip.

The cooler climate of Bohemond's bedroom stiffened his sweat-sodden clothes. No time for a bath (each one requiring so much water that he washed just once a week), he stripped off and scrubbed his face, pits and pouches with a hot wax-smeared sponge. A fresh set of whites brought the life back into his limbs. He threw the soiled suit in the bathroom washbasket, whistling Ganger's 'Capo' when the phone rang.

—Hello.

—It's me.

—Hermione.

—Oh Bohemond.

—What? What is it? He heard the office door open. Paris singing.

—Got to go; her voice suddenly bubbly: —*Speak soon. Bye.*

—Hermione?

The line fell silent; Bohemond, inflamed *and* utterly deflated that it was possible to feel so brittle-boned. He closed his eyes and cried, —*So lonely!* But once the words were spoken, his lips wouldn't let go of them. —*So lonely . . . so lonely . . . so lonely . . .* Over and over, held down, but still high-pitched and hysterical: —*So lonely . . . so lonely . . . so lonely . . .*

He replaced the handset and, whispering as he went, slowly sank towards the floor. On all fours, he sifted through drifts of shattered biscuit, picking out sleeping pills until a dazzling apparition of Paris, all forked tongue and silvery glitter, rocked him back onto his heels.

His ankles and knees cracked and popped as he struggled to his feet. The floorboards seesawed. Pills in his pocket, he didn't check his reflection in the mirror on the way out – daylight didn't do too much for him.

As he locked the door he heard a voice, maybe Faulkner's, further along the landing. But when he started walking and the windows rattled in their frames, the talker bolted along with whoever he'd been talking to. Bohemond listened to the two sets of feet scramble down the stairs, slowing to a walk once they slid into the foyer.

The air at the top of the staircase was heavy with a scent of lavender that thickened as he descended. He glimpsed Hermione sitting behind the desk in her office. Paris, crouching down beside her, could have been begging forgiveness.

Thom was on reception, madly thumbing the keys of his mobile phone.

—Did you see anyone come this way, Thom?

No acknowledgement, just: —Text frenzy.

—Faulkner perhaps?

—Someone went in there, he raised an eyebrow towards the bar. —Don't know who though. I've been busy.

Bohemond padded across the foyer and leaned around the bar door. Lili, Petra, Jugs, Francis and Mr Lewis were cruising through a soundcheck. Faulkner waltzed between the tables making his way to the stage, proof enough for Bohemond that it *was* his voice he'd heard upstairs. But who had he been with? The footsteps had been far too light for any of the heavy-weights onstage. He looked left. Just missed someone slipping behind the bar. A flicker of fur all he saw as the gate swung shut. One step in that direction was as much as he managed before Lili boomed, —BAND ONLY! and lobbed a beer bottle at him. Bohemond jerked back, gasping as glass shattered against the closed door. Thom didn't blink, glaring at his phone.

Three more mouthfuls of Ventolin, Bohemond glanced up at Hermione's office and made his way through the building. None of the waiting staff eyed him as he sidled through the restaurant. Hanswurst, his head sandwiched between double-D headphone cups, was busy mopping the dry store floor. Vic and Innocent were pottering around their chopping boards in the kitchen.

He found Seeta in the mess-room, flicking through the copy of *Vogue*. —Hanswurst gave me it, she muttered. —Said I could do with a few tips.

—Charming, said Bohemond. —You weren't just up-stairs were you?

—Nope.

—OK . . . The trail gone cold. —Feeling better?

—I hate to say it, Chef, but your fairy tale put me in a good mood.

—If you need anything, Seeta. Anything at all.

She didn't look up, but her face brightened with a smile.

heavenly cuisine

On Bohemond's gift in the kitchen, and how he and his
staff are humbled by a Russian.

Saturday night was a sell-out as always. The cooks
sweated behind the scenes, half the kitchen obscured
by steam, thundering to the dishwasher's rinse runs.
Hot spotlights and fully gunned ovens heightened the
spiny scents of onion and garlic; plumped up the
blunter puff of marjoram, thyme, basil and rosemary.
Knives chimed and plates clattered. Oil sputtered and
sprayed.

It was here that Bohemond came into his own. Too
fat for an athlete maybe, but his rhythm in the kitchen
was heavenly. Co-ordinates fixed at the centre of this
culinary cosmos, whole worlds revolved around him: a
few short steps and pans passed under his hands,
cleavers swung into his grip, and skillets somersaulted
from the bottom shelves onto the worktops at a flick
from either of his feet. Ingredients gravitated towards
his fingers. He segued easily from preparation of
purées, to forging agrodolces, from dressing knuckles
of mutton, to whipping up fricassees. Fine-tuned

timing and simple increments of discrimination balanced the requirements of intricate dishes like sultan's delight and cèpe-stuffed quail, with the more elementary pig liver and deer spleen, calf hearts and starling brains.

Seeta opened a box of chocolates and keeled over as a cloud of tortoiseshell butterflies fluttered out. They formed a V and flew through a flambé, the sudden flash of kindled wings sucked up in a plume of smoke that unfurled along the ceiling and fanned flaming ash around the room. Morrissey, mid-dive for the fire extinguisher, upset a bucket of live shellfish, assorted crustaceans scurrying for cover as a round red-faced man with a waxed-stiff moustache clopped into the kitchen. Dressed in a sky blue suit, bowing a violin cradled in the crook of his arm, he serenaded the cooks with the tale of how he'd fallen under their spell the moment the fried fig starter had passed his lips. Never had he tasted such exceptional food, even in his native Saratov, and he pledged eternal devotion to whoever made the honey-crusted cheesecake. Glowing embers of butterfly sifted down around him. A yellow budgerigar flew through from the corridor. But the man sang on, even as a colossal pink-shelled crab scuttled between his feet and the budgerigar alighted on his shoulder.

blood

In which Faulkner tells the first part of his story.

If everything Faulkner said was true, then he was around one hundred and thirty years old. He'd fought in the Sioux–Cheyenne Wars from the age of fifteen, first on the side of the government troops and had switched to ride with the Amerindians. He'd seen Red Tomahawk kill Sitting Bull, barely escaped with his life from the massacre at Wounded Knee and was always quick to show off old Hotchkiss wounds. He'd been a pearl diver, a train driver, a pilot, a foreign correspondent, a machine gunner, a horse trainer and lion tamer. He'd worked as a film extra. Claimed you could see him in *Spartacus*, *Ben-Hur*, *Guys and Dolls* and *Gone With the Wind*. He'd hung out with Jelly Roll Morton and his Red Hot Chilli Peppers, with Louis Armstrong, Cab Calloway and Duke Ellington. Spent six months playing trumpet for Chick Webb. He'd even done a stint with the Warner Brothers cartoon orchestra: the brass that passed for Jerry's laugh and the marimba tinkle of Tom's broken teeth were his best-known works, although his favourite was the sound of stretching telegraph wires, the ones that Wile E. Coyote used to catapult himself after the Road-runner. Faulkner had played that jewel with a bottleneck on a Gibson semi-acoustic.

He'd headed the band at Delphi as long as Hermione had been in charge, a loyalty left over from the days he and her great-grandfather had been friends. Rumour was that he'd sired Lili, Petra, Francis, Jugs and Mr Lewis with different mistresses and that even now his libido still rippled.

The group played in the restaurant bar Thursday, Friday and Saturday nights, sometimes on Sunday afternoons. Faulkner joined them every so often, singing like he'd seen it all, or telling tall stories. Stick-thin, intricately wrinkled, slightly stooped in a two-piece suit, he delivered his tales in a transatlantic patois that ricocheted between Middlesex and Massa-chusetts.

A few hours after the blue-suited Russian had crooned for the cooks in the kitchen, Faulkner, or The Kid, as Lili occasionally called him, stepped up to the mike.

First I fell in with Roosevelt was the summer of 1921. I was working in a small town, Cherryville, South Carolina, driving deliveries for one Theodore Coulthart, a grocer who sold nickel trinkets on the side. He did OK at that though – only guy I knew had a truck with his name on it. Roosevelt worked down at the railroad along with just about every other Negro in town and I'd seen him around, knew him well enough to exchange a word or two.

One morning, middle of summer, as I was coming out a tobacco store well off the main, I saw him crossing the street headed for a lane intended to shortcut the trek to the railroad. A beautiful blonde was walking in the opposite direction. She smiled at him, he nodded, turning to eye her as she bounced past. I saw him grin, shake his head and carry on. Two white men, one fat, one thin, stepped off a veranda. Came trotting up behind him. Fat one had a gun. He whipped Roosevelt on the back of the head with the butt; shattered the handle. Roosevelt squawked and sprawled in front of the alley, these two goons laying in, forcing him back into the blackness. All he'd done was say hi to some strumpet and these guys were gonna kill him for it.

Downstate, in Spartanburg, a black boy going by the name Will Fair had found himself acquitted by an all-white jury a few years before. He'd been charged with assaulting a white woman and got himself thrown in jail. Mob that came looking for him tried to blow up the jailhouse with dynamite they were so damned eager, but all they got was an assful of bullets courtesy of Sheriff W. J. White and his deputy. God only knows how, but Will Fair survived until his trial and, to add insult to injury, got himself excused by a jury of white men. He became a legend. Case was breakthrough. A landmark for the anti-lynching lobby. But it pissed a lot of people off. Lot of people still out looking to even the score.

I ran down as Roosevelt struggled up grappling for the gun. Thin guy turned at the sound of my steps, pulled a knife but I swung in low, impact bowling us all to the ground, and the shooter went off. Blast burst my fucking eardrum. Fatman's brains sprayed across the lane. I think about that moment every day. How if I'd gone in sooner or higher or harder the guy might not've been killed. How if I'd stayed in bed one minute longer that morning I probably wouldn't have seen a thing. But I didn't. I did what I did and I had to live with it. Guy who died, died by accident but he must've expected some powerful karma comeback trying to snuff an innocent man. We reap what we sow. Just so happened I was the instrument of retribution. Truth is I'd've done the same for anyone I saw outnumbered, black, white or electric blue. I wouldn't have had any other choice. There's a split-second of helplessness, the instant when your soul strikes out and all you can do is go with the flow. But it's the shit that comes after – the things you do to cover your ass that you can't write off as heat of the moment – that's the stuff keeps you awake at night, turns you inside-out, blackens your heart. That shit never stops.

We fucked the other guy's face with our feet. Cut his throat when his nose caved in. Left nothing to chance. Besides, this was a skirmish in some kinda civil war.

Roosevelt leaned back against the wall, out of breath. Blood on his boots. Gun in his hand. Shadow cut his face in half – no eyes and all mouth. He bit his lip, fingers twitching, and right then I knew it was for ever.

You are one crazy white sonofabitch, he said. You know they'll kill you too now.

Sure, I said, but they'll come for you first.

It wouldn't be long before a mob was out looking to rip him apart and if they couldn't get a hold of him they'd lynch his folks.

I had nothing to lose but my life.

We jumped into the truck, Roosevelt lying on the floor, out of sight, me driving as he described the route to his folks' house. His mother and father were there with his brothers, Jacob and Walter. Jacob's wife, Onlie, was with him along with her brother Sol and his good friend Clarence B. Jones. Roosevelt whipped up a small storm of panic. Told them how I'd saved his life.

How there was a mob coming. His mother and father wouldn't budge, pleaded with us not to run, that justice would out, but the rest gathered what little they could and leaped into the trailer. Roosevelt kissed his mom and hugged his dad. Promised he'd be back before they knew it. Looked like they believed him too.

We ran out of gas not long after midnight. Nothing for it but to tip the truck over a ravine and go on walking. Onlie was exhausted. Looked like she was coming down with something bad. Jacob got spooked. Started whining about turning back. Tried to talk Roosevelt into giving himself up. Wound-up Sol threatened him with a throttling if he didn't shut his mouth. Roosevelt turned on them all. Told them going back meant death for sure. That the first to make a move would do better by shooting themselves in the head right there and then.

An hour or so later we found a log cabin at the edge of a forest. Light shone from a window. Coils of smoke rising from the chimney. I told the others to stay hidden and went with Roosevelt to check the house out. He had the revolver he'd lifted from the fatman and I carried the shotgun I always kept in the truck.

I snuck around the back of the shack, Roosevelt round the front. There were a couple of chicken coops and a pigpen, nothing much else.

We met around the other side and peered through the window. A white woman was asleep in a chair by the fire. She had a twelve-bore laid across her lap. On her left was a long wood table, more chairs and behind her, a couple of bunks. I gave Roosevelt my gun and knocked on the front door. He pressed against the wall, out of sight.

Who is it? An accent I'd never heard before.

A hungry someone looking for a bite to eat, I said.

The latch snapped and the door creaked open. She smiled up at me, hunched over the barrel of the shotgun; younger looking than she'd seemed in sleep. Prettier too.

Roosevelt swung around the doorpost. Levelled the revolver at her head. Her smile faded, she stepped back, eyes darting between us. Couldn't have looked good at that time of night: two men, one black, one white, black one with a gun.

I raised my hands. Ma'am, I said, we got some friends out here, men and women who've been travelling all day and night. Now, if it's all right with you, we'd just like to take a rest, maybe impose upon you long enough to get a little to eat.

She lowered the gun and made to take a peek out the door.

Just let me call my friends over, I said. You take a look at them and if you aren't satisfied, we'll leave you in peace.

Roosevelt cocked the hammer of the revolver and she nodded. I summoned the others with a wave. They limped across the clearing, heads down. Soon as Onlie appeared the stand-off was over. The white girl leaned her shotgun against the wall and virtually carried Jacob's swooning wife over the threshold.

Her name was Petrova. She was Hungarian. A twenty-eight-year-old widow as she told it. Husband had been killed years ago in some dispute over gold and she'd taken care of the house ever since. She laid Onlie down on the bed, brought blankets and sheets for everyone else, then set about making us supper. We had a beef stew laced with sweet paprika that she called porkolt, followed by crepes and apricot jelly.

77

After supper we sat up drinking wine, each of the men taking turns to keep a lookout, except Jacob, who fell asleep on the bed with Onlie. Roosevelt told Petrova what'd happened that day. He missed out the killing. Just said we'd kicked the shit out a couple of racist motherfuckers. Told her about Will Fair too. Sol, Clarence and Walter had stories of their own.

Walter told us about a white guy, Luther Wilson, out of Dade City, Florida, blacked himself up with grease-paint and attacked his sixteen-year-old cousin. Idea was that he'd have his wicked way and the girl'd lay the blame on some vicious sex-starved Negro. But some of the paint rubbed off in the struggle and she recognized him. Mob found him later, kneeling by a creek, trying to wash the black shit off his hands and face.

Clarence had a tale all the way from Doddsville, Mississippi, about a plantation hand, Luther Holbert, and his wife. Company of two hundred men chased the couple through four counties over as many days, because rumour was they'd shot one James Eastland, master of Holbert's plantation. Posse found the worn-out runaways asleep in a forest near Sheppardstown and dragged them the one hundred miles back to Doddsville. They were tied to trees in the shadow of a Negro church, believe it or not. No trial. No chance. Mob gathered, over a thousand strong: ricket-struck hicks, hayseeds, Klan and other assorted white trash trampling the shit out of each other fetching wood for the funeral pyres. Meantime the man and his wife had all their fingers hacked off and given out to the crowd as souvenirs. Luther got his cock sliced off, was made to eat most of it and say he liked it. He was bludgeoned with pipes till his skull split and one eye hung out. Both had their ears cut off.

Before the fires were lit, some goon rednecks jumped up with a huge corkscrew and they skewered those poor niggers like they were bottles of Beaujolais. Bore so deep into the arms and legs, most times it took two of them pulling with all their weight to withdraw, and course, every time they ripped out great chunks of meat and gristle.

Petrova didn't even want to hear Sol's story. She turned to me, almost whispering. What about you, Faulkner? There's some would say this isn't even your fight.

Guy was going to get killed for no reason at all, I said. What was I gonna do? *Nothing?*

Roosevelt smiled at me. Said, I've never met anyone like you.

I shrugged and crawled under the blankets that made up my bed. Clarence and Walter did likewise. Onlie was talking in her sleep.

Wasn't long before I dozed off, but I couldn't settle. One time I looked up I saw Roosevelt and Petrova whispering to each other. They were sitting on the floor, hardly moving, lazy-looking when they did. She had a hand on his arm.

Next time I woke up they weren't even in the room – just firelight glinting on the empty glasses.

We left before dawn. Onlie couldn't move. Jacob wouldn't leave her. Roosevelt gave them his gun. Kissed them both goodbye.

Plan was to make it to Norfolk, Virginia, where Roosevelt said he knew people could ship us to New York. Clarence thought he'd go for Nova Scotia. Mad motherfucker had heard some fairy tale about niggers out there living like kings. We laughed as he mouthed off about building his own castle – knights

79

and servants and shit. Big black Lionheart riding to the rescue of his beautiful Nubian princess.

Early afternoon we were trudging down a pass. Sol was singing. Walter reached the bottom first and turned with a finger over his lips, head cocked against the breeze. Sol, still singing, marched right into him. Walter pushed him off, hissing for quiet. The rest of us froze, listening, trying to separate ripples of wind from the sounds in the background. Took a few seconds before I recognized the hoarse holler of bloodhounds.

I hear that, said Clarence.

Roosevelt's shoulders sagged. He muttered something like, Sweet Jesus, and kicked off, long loping strides on down the meadow. We charged after him, Sol first, head down, gasping, Go! Go! Go!

Shotgun held me back so I tossed it into the scrub. A few hundred yards and we scrambled down into a dell. The barking died out, just the puffing and panting and the rumble of our footsteps. Trees grew thicker. Deer bolting from the dash. Fawn-coloured flashes of backside as they scattered. Walter tripped over a stump. Sol skidded back to help him, the two of them lumbering like cripples. Wood petered out up ahead. Spores and flies spiralling up sundry rays of sunlight. Roosevelt glanced over his shoulder. River, he said, but we didn't stop sprinting, clearing the bank mid-stride, somersaulting into the water. Clarence bust his head on a rock. Left us, floating belly up. So much for Scotia. I grabbed Roosevelt's shirt. He cradled my waist. Sol took hold of my hand. But the current dragged us under, came between us, pulled us apart. I lost my shoes in the shallows, flailing for an out-crop. Walter crashed in at my back. I rolled over choking, soaked to the bone, lungs like sponges with the water I'd taken on board. Sol was dangling from an

80

overhang, Roosevelt draped over a log, drifting downstream.

Walt and me lunged along the grassbank. Fished Sol out the water. Roosevelt we found a half-mile upriver. The log was jammed between two boulders that squeezed the water white and I almost fainted when I spied that big beautiful Negro crawling up the rock face. All hands helped him up, collapsing in a heap as he reached the summit and we lay there until the baying drove us on.

All day running for our lives. Sure, respect to Pheidippides, ancient Greek hero who bust his heart making that legendary long-distance dash from the plains of Marathon to the streets of Athens. But truth be told, that motherfucker had it easy. Nothing more exhausted, more *put-upon*, than niggers fleeing a mob.

We hit a cornfield around dusk. It stretched out like the Atlantic. The mother of all trees hovered at its far horizon – a huge blue-green bush that looked like a low flying cloud. I knew once we got there we'd be OK. Sky turned Idaho pink through matt blue. Stars came out, moon too. Night not quite falling. The blueness of the sky hemmed everything in. Sounds changed, colours, everything; it was like being in some big motherfucker's living room, running through the carpet. Bloodhounds and the mob sounded like they were right down the hallway.

The corn came up to my chin. I knew where the others were by the furrows they ploughed as they ran. Roosevelt was way ahead. Must've been him that startled the flock of golden birds. A low murmur at first, rising to the heights of a hurricane, the entire sky glittering for a moment as if the cornfield itself had taken flight. I watched still running, the birds flickering at first, then, as they arced higher, shimmering like stars.

Guns firing, voices, horses snorting, the chopping of too many hooves. I lost Roosevelt in the panic.

Sol screamed, threw up his hands. Blood sprayed my face. Something much bigger than a bloodhound savaged Walter. I didn't see it, just heard the single snarl, like a fucking mill-saw, ground up with a dreadful retching that could only have been that poor old bastard chucking up his own guts.

I ran into the shadow of the low cloud tree. Ground broke up into shallow waterlogged barrows, deeper the nearer I got to the trunk. Fish rose to the surface, flashing silver-white as they turned over and torpedoed back into the depths. I ended up wire-walking across an exposed root, almost knocked off-balance by a pair of white-palmed hands swung down from the boughs. *Up*, I jumped, grabbing hold and Roosevelt hauled me into the tree.

We lay spread out on our bellies, watching the posse approach. They charged into the pool, dismayed at how deep it was. Horses and dogs and men swimming in the water way below us. Some hung back, fired shots into the branches but the bullets didn't even reach us. They all looked so far away.

Roosevelt stood up, ragged, panting, balancing on a branch. He leaned against the trunk and closed his eyes. His brother and Sol hadn't made it. If they were still alive they wouldn't be for long. Strung up for sure.

I rolled onto my back. Took in the tree. The branches fanned out into the gloom of a night sky. Moon was up there, but closer and paler than I'd ever seen it, and far off, almost obscured, the gold birds still glittering. Left and right, nothing but branches. I glanced at the ground again. Mob was pulling its horses out the water.

We gotta go, said Roosevelt.

Go where?

He didn't reply, just cocked his head that way I'd learn meant he didn't want a discussion.

What about Walter and Sol?

Good as dead now.

No mention of Onlie and Jacob, he led off, further into the tree. I followed on, careful of my bare-footing, but stepping between the boughs was like skating over a polished oak floor. God only knows what kind of a place that was we were in. Any other day and I woulda got the Hell out of there, but I wasn't about to let some nigger-hating white trash rabble corkscrew me. No sir.

We walked over an hour. Tree was more like a forest. Full of life. More flocks of birds, butterflies, deer, skunks and shit. Ended up we killed two wild turkeys and roasted them over a fire. Roosevelt found a fresh-water stream and we drank long and deep. Some of the gold birds came back to roost. Lit up the wood like a Christmas tree. Warmed us somehow too.

As we sat up after supper, Roosevelt said: You remember that girl yesterday? The one who smiled at me and got us in this mess? Well, I know her.

Really.

No. I mean I know her. Like really know her. Her name's Beatrice. We're lovers.

Oh man, I said. This just goes from bad to worse.

Don't it? He pulled an envelope out his pocket. Glanced at it before he tossed it over to me.

We had plans, he said. We was tryin to save up enough money to get outta Cherryville, head north to New York, maybe sail to England. I had dreams about goin to Hollywood and bein a film actor, but America

83

ain't any kinda place for any kinda nigger. Things is happenin in England. Niggers got more opportunity over there. Maybe I ain't got so much chance gettin into films, but the theatre over there's got everyone else's beat, hands-down.

You're serious?

Damn right.

You and Beatrice were going to travel *together*?

These folks I know in Norfolk who's gonna send us on to New York, they was supposed to help Bea and me when we ran away together. Things is a little different now.

You could send for her in time.

He glanced up at the golden birds like maybe he was thinking he'd just up and fly away.

Would you read out that letter to me? It's from Bea.

I felt a little embarrassed. Can't you read?

Course I can read but if you do it, her voice ain't just be in my head.

But this is a private letter. It's between you and her.

Please.

Given the rest of the day, what he was asking was pretty simple. I opened the envelope. There was a single page inside that smelled real strongly of lavender. Roosevelt lay on his back, one arm crooked over his eyes.

I can't get you out of my mind. All during the show last night I wanted you with me but I had to sit with Clifford. I cannot understand why my parents want me to marry him. He is unbearably dull, unlike you. You are my reason for being. I have always loved you and I always will.

I am so sickened by the folk in Cherryville and can't wait to run away with you. I hate seeing you in the crowd or walking by you downtown and not being able to talk or laugh with you. I have never told you this before but sometimes I go home and weep. I cannot wait for the day that we are able to walk the streets without fear. But I know that we will have to go far far away before that is possible.

I love you more than life itself and if anything were to happen to you, even though I know it's a sin to say so, I'd kill myself. I'd go to Hell but maybe God would pardon me because he'd recognize that I'd died for love and he'd pull me up into Heaven where you and I would spend all eternity together.

My love, if I could cut myself open and hide you inside, I would. I'd carry you around in my belly (so intimate!), feeding you with all the love that is in my heart, and give birth to you when the world was ready for us to be together. Love is greater than color, my darling, and I want to believe that deep down most people feel the same way, but sadly, besides the deeds of a few good souls here and there, I don't see much proof that they do. I know that the way things are is not the way things are supposed to be, but I think God won't let this injustice last much longer. Until then we will have to be strong.

I can't wait for tomorrow night. Don't keep me waiting.

Yours,

'DEVOTED'

I folded the letter into the envelope. Tossed it back to him. Damn, I said, she really loves you.

He didn't reply. Didn't even make a sound until five minutes later when he said: Love at first sight. Once in a lifetime kinda thing.

Oh yeah?

Hell yeah. I'd just made a bust from a chain-gang over in Kentucky. Nuthin but hunger got me into that shit in the first place. All I done was steal a string of

85

sausages from a butcher in Bluefield, and the judge gave me *three years*' hard labour for it. My first Christmas on the gang, each of us cons got a shot of whiskey and back to barracks early so the governor and the guards could go on up to the house on the hill and eat roast turkey with their families.

Festive spirit, goodwill to all men and so on, they only left one guard on watch. Poor fucker couldn't have been much over sixteen years old. Way too trustin. A big old German tricked him into the ring and choked him with his chain. We took his keys. Ran free under cover of a blizzard.

Seems all I done in my life is run. It's got so it's about all I'm good for. I guess that's how I made it, on my own, over the Appalachians, *and* the Blue Ridge Mountains, all the way down into my home state of South Carolina. First thing I met with when I hit the plains was the sound of bells and the smell of lavender. It was gettin dark so I hid. Watched someone in a sleigh drawn by six deer slide right on by. Bells was on the deer's reins – *ting ting ting* – like Santa Claus. Hundred yards off it all broke down on one side. I ran through the trees. Drew level. And that's when I realized it was a woman drivin. She was all done up in real fine furs. Talkin to the deer. One of the skis on the sledge was snapped clean in half. I didn't see no gun or nuthin, so I stepped out the trees, in my jailbird rags, said: May I be of assistance, ma'am? And did she flinch? No sir. None of that, *Oh my god here's a nigger's gonna rape me and blow my brains out!* Not a twitch. All she said to me, as cool and beautiful as you like, was: My name is Beatrice, if you help me fix this here sledge I'll give you a lift into town. It hurt. Golly it hurt. She was so damned beautiful. Venus de Milo kinda beautiful. And there was I, stepped down offof the mountain right into her arms. Call it fate, call it what you like, but it turned out we was both headed for Cherryville.

I can't tell you how I knew, Faulkner. But all the time I was helping that woman, the words 'She is the one' kept comin in my head, especially when it got too dark to see anythin except the pale of her face; and the burnin blue of her eyes.

Once we got the ski fixed, she pulled me right up into that sledge and we set off. She opened her coat, wrapped me up inside of it with her. Covered us both with fur blankets. I will never forget how she felt that first time. Me after six months on the chain-gang, hard and dry as a strip of leather, and her soft as snow but warm inside, and that lavender scent like the breath of an angel.

Journey was like a spell she put on me. Stars above seemed closer than ever, like we was almost up there, flyin through em. That's how me and Beatrice is fixin on dyin now. No joke. We'll be ninety-nine years old, just about ready to fade away and we'll climb up into our sleigh and get all cosy in furs and blankets, then we'll let those deer damn well pull us through a million miles of snow right off the end of the earth and up, up into the sky all the way to the gates of Heaven.

It was almost daylight by the time we reached Cherryville. She dropped me at a bar on the outskirts of town. Owner was an old Negro called Ike. He asked no questions, gave me bed, board and work. I stayed there a while before I went back to my folks' house. I'd been away so long I guess they thought I was dead, and I needed time to work up to seeing them anyway.

Ike had a club he ran above the bar after hours. Called it Coffee and Cream. It was a place that black and white folks could mix, drink and love like they wanted. That's where I met Beatrice mostly. Where we made the most of our outlawed love. One night in there I got caught up with her and some others in a game of strip poker. Middle of a hand, some fucker comes bustin in, all hollerin that the sheriff's on his way down and everyone had better make a break for it. I was so drunk I could hardly walk. Butt-naked too. But Bea, who's a better drinker and a better poker player than damn well anyone I know, threw me over her shoulder, climbed out the window and got us clean away. What can I tell you? She's the reason I breathe.

When me and Roosevelt woke next morning we found the forest floor covered with feathers that the birds must've shook off when they took off. Each one of them weighed a couple of ounces and was made of solid gold. We grabbed as many as we could cram into our pockets and made off through the branches.

We came out of the woods about a mile away from Norfolk. Had to climb down a trunk to get out, just as we'd had to climb up one to get in. I don't know how many days we spent travelling through that tree, if indeed it was a tree, but we saw nobody, we never went hungry and we always slept soundly.

As I stepped out into the sunlight weighed down by gold, I felt a little sorry to be leaving the peace and quiet. But at the same time I was glad to be rid of all the blood and guts. Glad to hear an end to Roosevelt's horror stories.

Niggers being made to eat their own severed dicks, hands cut off, eyes scooped out, burned at the stake, fingers, ears and teeth dished out like relics. The only other motherfuckers to get that kind of treatment are those with religions named after them, those with their own stained-glass windows, or those with statues built in their honour. Martyrs like Joan of Arc. Niggers going to the wall for nothing other than living their lives – in my book that makes them saints.

Faulkner stepped back, warming to the applause. He unclipped the mike, swung his arm in a ragged arc and drove the band into a super-slow-burning version of Cab Calloway's 'Minnie The Moocher'.

wagging tongues

How a short meditation on the nature of decadent societies
leads to a portentous violation of privacy.

Bohemond's bath was more an indoor swimming pool.
Carved out of a marble dais at one end of his bathroom, it was bordered by a forest of pot-plants.
Hundreds of fallen summer-coloured petioles carpeted
the bottom. Sunlight had bleached the once-tan banks
white. Red and blue chequered tiles scrolled out from
the rim to ivy-smothered walls, giving way on one side
to a brass staircase that ascended from the wood-plank
floor by the toilet.

He climbed the steps and walked around the tub,
grinding homemade bath salts in a porcelain mortar.
The smell made him smile: a mixture of oils and
essences meant to invigorate his skin and soothe his
rheumatism. He slung the powder into the bath, trod
on the knob that applied the plug, turned on the taps
and ambled back into his bedroom.

Vogue lay glowing on his desktop. He'd found the
magazine in the mess-room after Faulkner's performance and had brought it back to his bedroom only to

find he couldn't bring himself to read it.

. . . Hermione was beautiful enough to find her way onto those pages. And when finally her passion transformed Bohemond from harpy to heart-throb, he'd be invited to pose as a centrefold in a full-colour pull-out supplement: OLD-FASHIONED VALUES – *How Hermione And Bohemond's Traditional Tastes Made A Love To Last A Lifetime.* Interviews, frank confessions, top-ten likes and dislikes, tips on preparation of the perfect Christmas dinner, framed around improbably glossy photographs of Bohemond dressed as a chauffeur in a blue rubber greatcoat with matching gloves and cap, and Hermione as a governor's daughter in tight white riding-breeches, with maybe a whip and red-hot lipstick. A 1920s American pastoral pastiche – complete with fake trees and hand-painted backdrops of ex-slaves bringing in the sheaves – devised by stylists who'd skulk off to sulk in a corner, vacant and amazed that *this* celebrity couple were so toned and photogenic any attempt to apply make-up to their faces proved pointless. Out of the blue, perched on a haystack, the interviewer would ask them to share the secret of their sex lives with the nation, suggesting they start by revealing how often they had sex. At which point Hermione would turn, wink at Bohemond and say something like 'Every day'. Or 'Lots but not often enough'. And the readers would know that by 'lots' she meant 'most of the time'. 'Lots' as in she might, in jest, suggest that Bohemond's sex drive be criminalized, as it was matched only by how much she lusted after him, a hunger so violent, so maddening, it had to be illegal. And Bohemond would nod and say, Outlawed love, beaming at how his patience had paid off. How fourteen years of waiting had made him all the man Hermione would ever need. Then suddenly a moment of doubt. A vibration in the base of his skull. Syllables hissing in his ears. A lament, like the wind, almost choral: the voices of the overweight come to lull him back to obesity? *No.* Eventually, and with no little relish, he'd realize the sound was actually that of women the world over sighing in awe of his delicious lasciviousness. Women so *hopeful* that just one of his kisses would bring them to their knees, ready to beg. Although all their eagerness would be as nothing next to an hour of Hermione's sexual healing. She'd use the photoshoot to tease him – whispering pure filth in his ear, brushing against his crotch with her bottom, revealing just enough of her cleavage to get him in a sweat, so that back in the changing room – he butt-naked, she in just jodhpurs – both a little tipsy on free Buck's Fizz, she'd spread his legs, grip his prick, tug and suck and laugh as Klansmen from the Carolinas to California turned in their graves. And as Bohemond surrendered, Hermione'd look at him as though she'd never wanted anything more; the expression of pure *desire* in her eyes when his cock went POP! like a champagne bottle, spouting a fountain of jism that turned the room into a jacuzzi. No! A lagoon! A storm-tossed sea! Waves and breakers, oceans of the stuff, gushing . . .

A moment more and the tub would overflow. Bohemond grimaced, blinked, wiped his eyes, scooped the magazine off the desk and stomped back into the bathroom.

The brass stairs were warm and wet, the terrace tiles sparkled. He turned off the taps, switched out the lights and stepped out of his dressing gown, dropping the magazine as his arms came free.

Capped with a panoramic view of the sky, Bohemond's bathroom shared the dry store's glass-domed roof. Moonlight glazed the plantlife and burnished the bathwater. It stretched the shadow of the window frames, magnifying drifts of snow that arced around the ledges. Phantom passages of piano filtered through from some other attic. Bohemond recognized Satie's *Trois Gnossiennes*, murmuring an accompaniment as he slumped down onto the side and slowly slipped into the bath.

Eyes closed, he groaned as the warm water rose up to his chest. When it lapped against his head and neck he smiled and said, —Eureka. Candy-scented steam curled towards the ceiling dome. Silt sifted between his toes. He swung both legs to the surface, and there he floated, belly-up, almost laughing – the big fat French head chef lounging in a moonlit lake of petals.

The swell nudged him to the other side and carried him back again. He plucked *Vogue* from the bankside, flicked through a couple of pages and tossed it away, weighed down by heartache. As he sank to the bottom he tried to stay under, but the water wouldn't let him. It sucked him back to the surface through rays of moonlight. And yet despite his depression, Bohemond felt all the physical grit and friction ebbing away; a reasonably easy yield thanks to the careful combination of oils and essences he'd mingled in the mortar.

The only good he ever wrought outside the kitchen was in imitation of his skills as a chef. He used the same method to blend bath salts and balms as he did to fix dishes. It was simply a question of balance.

Hitting any kind of effective equilibrium required skilful orchestration of measure, moderation, proportion, perspective, presentation and context. Cooking, *his cooking*, was undoubtedly an art and, therefore, cause for celebration. OK, so the portraits in *Vogue* were artistic, but there was nothing celebratory about them. The photostrips ripped off Raphael, Rosso, Botticelli, Donatello, Cellini and Michelangelo whose depiction of gorgeous souls was intended as a triumphant fuck-you to the body-bashing depravity of recently departed plague. Their art embraced its spectators, but the faultless flesh in the fashion mags was exclusive rather than inclusive. It dictated rather than celebrated, even aggravated Bohemond's asthma. As a gourmet, concordant with the creative outlook of these early Italian artists, he aimed to please. But it was quite clear that *Vogue*'s take on Renaissance painting was aimed to displease and dismay.

There was so much subterfuge in capitalist-assisted art, whereas his own endeavour was doggedly honest. He cooked to create happiness. Lived for the rapturous glances he garnered from satisfied diners. What *killed* him, though, was that these looks amounted to little more than coquetry. They were aroused by his mastery with food rather than by *him*. The very people who looked like they'd lay siege to Seeta, bombard her with gifts and passionate appeal until she succumbed and let them fuck her, looked upon Bohemond with pity and guilt. It broke his heart that his immeasurable appetite for what people most admired about him, was what made him so repulsive to them: he was God's own gourmet and a big fat black bastard.

He kicked back down to the bottom of the bath and rose to find Morrissey standing over him, chomping on gum as he leafed through the magazine. Hip cocked and topless, in tight white shorts and leather sandals, he wore a towel over his shoulder, a bottle of oil jammed between his waistband and abdomen. —Hello monkey.

Bohemond hooked his forearms onto the tiled side. His breathing uneven.

—*Monkey?*

—Monkey, as in monk. As in you never told me you were brought up by nuns.

—I'd no reason to. Believe me, Morrissey, there's nothing exciting about life in a convent. Nothing exciting about my life at all. I did the chores, got an education, ended up tending the gardens, left at sixteen, came to London, lived in a squat in Hackney for a while, bedsits after that, no friends, no family, came to Delphi, and the rest, as they say, is history. Boring. See?

—You trying to spice things up with this? Morrissey held out the magazine.

—Hanswurst gave it to Seeta, she left it in the mess-room and I brought it here.

—For a wank?

—Hardly.

—Hard-on, more like. He turned over a centrespread, but Bohemond couldn't look. —If she was in here now, Chef, it wouldn't be you I'd be giving the massage to.

—If she was in here now, Morrissey, chances are you wouldn't recognize her.

—With an arse *like that?*

Bohemond stared at Morrissey's ankles, didn't dare lift his eyes higher. —But that arse, as you put it, has nothing to do with real life, he said. —Nothing to do with beauty. It's been air-brushed and touched up, the lighting and location have been manipulated. It makes me so sad that most of us seem ignorant of the fact. But then what can we do? Every day we're bombarded with these impossible images, and we run ourselves out of breath trying to keep up with what they dictate, because our lives are dominated by capitalist media.

Morrissey scowled. —You're just sick cos you're not Johnny Depp.

—It's a sign of the times, said Bohemond, and he eased away from the side, bobbing on his back as he looked up at the moon. —The urge we have to be much more than we are, is a sign of decadent times.

. . . so much for new millennium enlightenment. For Bohemond supposed that now, as always during so-called heights of society, the human sense of supremacy only intensified. Subsequently, man made moves to increase his remove from nature: an instinct that stemmed from way back in the MISTS OF TIME as the will to survive. Civilization was simply a negation of pain. The denial of an animalistic existence. With the struggle for everyday subsistence now over, capitalism's dubious gifts of gross wealth and vastly increased leisure time afforded Western man, *and woman*, thousands of hours in which to lounge around their penthouse suites, pondering the true extent of their wretchedness, *and* money enough to get themselves remedied . . .

—Bollocks, said Morrissey.

—I know it's a horrible thought, Morrissey, but history is against us. Take the Romans. After they'd conquered the external world they grew bored and sought out all sorts of sport by turning inwards. Julius Caesar and Hadrian were fair-weather sodomites, Caligula and Commodus part-time transvestites. Elagabalus made himself up as a woman and prostituted himself in brothels. Even went as far as asking his physicians if they could cut a working vagina into his flesh. Nor was Nero just a keen fiddler. As well as masquerading as a woman in labour, a runaway slave, a blind man and a mute, he dressed up in animal skins, crawled on all fours roaring like a lion and mauled the genitals of chained-up Christians.

—*Wow!* What a guy.

—Joseph Conrad said cookbooks of all books are above moral reproach as they have no other purpose than to increase the happiness of mankind. If only the same could be said of the magazine you're reading right now.

—Bit of imagination and you can be anyone you want. That's cool.

Bohemond sighed. —Imagination cannot make fools wise, but it makes them happy, as against reason, which only makes its friends wretched: one covers them with glory, the other with shame.

—Shite.

—Pascal.

—You need a shag.

—Sometimes I think . . .

—Someone like this. He held up another picture, but Bohemond averted his eyes.

—All of the women in that paper are like the characters in Faulkner's stories: pure fiction that people mistake for the real thing.

—Oh come on . . . what about Faulkner tonight though, eh? That guy Roosevelt . . . they don't make em like that any more. He must've been *so* bitter.

—Faulkner saddens me. He despises everyone. That's why his stories are so hateful. I'm not sure it's a coincidence that he chooses to tell a grisly morality tale about a black man and his white muse just as Hermione and Paris announce the date of their wedding.

—Sure, all that shit about enchanted forests and gold birds is just him spinning a line. But the rest? *Christ.* Even if it didn't happen to him, you only have to *look* at the guy to know he knows some fucker it *did* happen to.

—You think there's some truth in it then?

97

—*Totally*.

A flash of fur. Echoes of voices at the top of the stairwell. —Are you . . . familiar with the scent of lavender?

—Am I *what*?

—No . . . nothing. Forget it.

Morrissey slung *Vogue* onto the floor and slunk off into the bedroom. Bohemond swam to the side, glancing at the magazine. It'd fallen open, face-down. Something gleamed between the spread-eagled pages: an envelope, ripped open along one edge. He picked it up. Held it towards the moonlight. All blank; a dark thread of handwritten script just visible on the paper folded inside. —*Morrissey*.

—*What?*

—There's a letter inside the magazine. Is it yours?

Morrissey skipped back into the bathroom. Snatched the envelope from Bohemond's hand.

—No, *wait*. It might be private.

—Good. He leaned away from the water, face soon filled with a grin. —*Holy* . . . Listen to this:

I won't pretend I know how you're feeling but don't think I'm not suffering too. This is the hardest thing I've ever had to do. You've become a big part of me – no joke when I say you made me whole – so this is something like cutting out my heart.

The world just looked so different when I was with you. Like I'd been blundering along in black and white all my life, you showed up, and suddenly it was all in colour. Some days I didn't even like to call it love. It seemed too common a name because the way you made me feel was unique. Sorry, I'm talking past tense. But believe me, nothing has changed as far as how I feel about you goes. It's not like I can just switch off. Not like I can ever forget.

Even so there are things I need to do and to do them I have to let go of you. I know it's the right thing, but saying so still kills me and I honestly don't know if I can come through this in one piece.

I'm going to miss you so much. The way you lit up when we talked. The way your eyes betrayed all that longing. The way my nerve endings sang whenever you touched me. The way my body ached for you. Everything up until then was just fucking; good enough but you get bored always going for gold. You showed me that there's so much more to aim for: the little things, which build and build until it's impossible to resist. Fingers and wrists, the skin between my toes, the backs of my knees, hip bones and elbows, armpits and earlobes, the little pocket behind my collarbone.

All those hours spent just kissing.

I'll miss the way you lay on your belly with your hair pulled forward over a shoulder and allowed me to explore you. Starting at your ankles, over your calves, the backs of your knees and thighs and on to where the spine divides the small of your back, that little dark dip at the top of your hips where the fit of my hand is just perfect. I'll miss the way that gazing at the inclines of your body makes me think of watching the sea swell from a faraway clifftop. It's like leaning back, looking at the stars and knowing I'm going up there.

I'll miss the way your skin makes mine look golden, and the way that mine makes yours look bronze. I'll miss travelling home at night with the smell of you still warm on my top lip. I'll miss how, when I get round to going down, you go limp and giggle about being blown. I'll miss how you start with a single finger and finish with a fist.

I know these things have been said thousands of times by thousands of people over thousands of years but it's all brand-new to me. The disappointment is that when you're as switched on as this, everything you say sounds as if it's come straight out of some clichéd movie. I didn't know it was possible to feel this way and so, you see, I'm a little unprepared.

I know that it'll never ever be like this ever again but in a way I don't mind because I've been lucky enough to taste something most people don't even get a whiff of in hundreds of lifetimes.

It seems a contradiction to say that all that love isn't enough, but the truth is we can never give me everything I need. The prospect of spending the rest of my life with you truly dizzies me with delight, but there'd always be that doubt. Circumstances we have no control over and still I feel guilty.

Maybe I just don't deserve you yet.

All my love.

Always.

Bohemond looked up. His guts and heart rumbled and fluttered at the mention of top lips and fists, all those hours spent just kissing. But the vertigo gave way to near-vomiting when he supposed the words might be Hanswurst's.

—*Mental*, said Morrissey. —Whose is it?

—Seeta was reading the magazine, but I think Hanswurst bought it.

—Hanswurst never wrote *this*.

—For a moment I thought he might have, but then, if you wrote such a letter, sealed it in an envelope and had second thoughts, you'd throw it in the bin or burn it. You wouldn't re-open it like that. Besides, God bless him, the proclamations of love are far too poetic for Hanswurst.

—OK Sherlock, but no way did anyone send this to him. I mean 'Gazing at the inclines of your body makes me think of watching the sea swell from a faraway

100

clifftop. It's like *leaning back, looking at the stars and knowing I'm going up there.'* Ha!

—Do you recognize the writing?

—Can't even tell if it's a guy or a girl's. You? He held out the paper.

—I'd rather not.

—But you just listened to me *read it out.*

—Morrissey.

—Take it.

—All right, hold it up.

—Fuck you, *hold it up. Take it.*

—I'll get it wet.

—Prick. Morrissey sat down on the side, his legs dangling in the water. —Come on.

Bohemond didn't recognize the handwriting, but then, if the letter had been penned by any of the staff they would surely have disguised their style. Not that he'd be any the wiser if they hadn't; beyond the occasional scribbled note or Post-it, there wasn't much call for the written word in Delphi. He scanned the lines for any telltale turns of phrase. Nothing surfaced; the identity of the writer buried under borrowed prose.

—I think it's Seeta's, said Morrissey, eyes darting back over the page. —It's definitely not Hanswurst's. And the moods she's been in lately. Could be some big cock's given her the old heave-ho and she can't handle it.

—*My God* . . . the day's conversation came back to him, — . . . you're right.

—Yeah, it would explain why she spent the night with you.

—How do you know that?

—You *blabbed.* Remember? Morrissey waved a finger and grinned. —You wanted me to think you'd seduced her.

101

It'd happened in the heat of the moment: Bohemond bickering with Morrissey about who he'd bedded, letting slip the secret of a night spent with Seeta, because he couldn't stand to have his manhood mocked. When Morrissey threatened to check the details, he'd been forced to confess that she'd come to him on the run from her father. That she'd slept in his bed while he dozed on the sofa. Whatever, by telling Morrissey he'd betrayed Seeta's trust. —I can't *believe* you threw that in her face this morning, he said.

—Has she said yet why her dad kicked her out?

—No.

Morrissey glanced at the letter and smiled. —I don't think I'd give a toss if I found out my daughter was having an affair with another bird's bloke. I'd be like, *Go on girl*, get stuck in, it's not like he's married.

—An affair? Who with?

—Paris.

Shock robbed Bohemond of buoyancy, he sank and resurfaced, snorting.

—I thought you'd like that, said Morrissey.

—You're not serious.

—You heard her laying into him today. And I heard her mouthing off about him to Loretta just before that.

Toes tingling, throat raw, Bohemond saw the way to Hermione unbolted. Already so many omens. —You know this for sure?

Morrissey grinned. —Hermione and Paris on the rocks is all your Christmases come at once, isn't it? But you should've shagged her ages ago. Like everyone else.

—*What?*

—Hermione's a *slag*. No wonder Paris had a fling with Seeta, when his fucking bird's been doing the rounds.

Bohemond backed away shaking his head.

—She *puts out*, Bo. Honest. Didn't she try it on with you? She tried it on with me . . . and the waiters . . . and . . .

—*Enough.*

Morrissey scrambled to his feet and trotted halfway around the banks, following Bohemond's drift to the middle. —*It's true.* She was up for sucking me off – pants down, dick out, everything.

—Liar! You would have said something before now. Hermione's the one who's been cheated in all of this!

He waved his arms, laughing out loud. —All right. Serious. Unless Paris has turned into a right ponce, there's no way he wrote that letter. What was it? . . . *watching the sea swell from a faraway clifftop* . . . ? *Piss off.*

Clouds rolled over the moon, white light winking on the water.

—But then maybe, said Morrissey, —he got some twat to write it for him.

—A Cyrano de Bergerac!

—He can be a devious bastard.

—You think that's it?

—I reckon he got sick of Hermione going AWOL. Got it on with Seeta one night for a laugh. Kept getting it on, by the sounds of it, and before he knows it the whole thing's out of hand. Hermione finds out, gets jealous and says, Truce. Let's both stop fucking about and get married. Paris is like, Great. Game over, Seeta, I'm marrying Hermione. And Seeta just fucking flips out. She's not the most stable person in the world.

—You can't believe Hermione knows about Paris and Seeta.

—That'd be a kick in the balls for you, wouldn't it?

—She *can't* know.

—Nah . . . probably not. She's having these sneaky snogs with the staff in here. Doesn't think it's a big deal. If Paris is in deep as this letter makes out, and she knew, they'd be getting divorced, not married.

—So, now . . . you're saying he *did* write the letter.

—Who knows. Could be he changes his act depending on whose knickers he wants into: dirt for dogs and ice-cream for angels. You know how he got it on with Hermione.

—At college, wasn't it?

—Paris was never at college. He was a roofer. And he's on a roof near Baker Street, sat up there in the scaffold having lunch with his mates, when this double-decker stops right in front of him and there's Hermione on the top deck, writing something down on a piece of paper she's got spread out on the back of a box of chips. She looks up, sees Paris and they both just go BANG! Love at first sight. Her pen goes through the top of the box, chips spill everywhere. Paris almost falls off the scaffold. He shouts to the foreman to give him the afternoon off, but the foreman's like, no way. So they argue and in the heat of the moment Paris grabs an eclair out his mate's lunch box and lobs it at Hermione's bus as it pulls away. Cream sprays all over the back window. Foreman threatens to fire him. Fuck you, says Paris. Two hours later he's out of a job. So he's on his way home right, walking past Aldwych where some buses are parked up, and guess what? One of them's got cream splashed over the back of it. He gets on. There's a cleaner on board with a seethrough bin bag full of shit. Paris recognizes the chip box with the hole in it. He fishes it out the bag, and there's bits of a letter, half a phone number and a whole phone number etched into the top of the box where the pen's been pressed down on it. He doesn't know who she was writing to, but takes it for a sign. So he phones the whole number, and some guy at a club answers, and Paris is like, I think someone from there left something on a bus. And he describes the girl he saw, and the guy on the other end goes, Oh yeah that sounds like Hermione. So Paris gets the address, goes down, waits till she comes in and sweeps her off her feet, or so he says.

Bohemond's head felt cold. —I've never heard that story before, he said. —It's obvious to me now that Paris is more than capable of writing a letter like this.

—Fucking *right*.

—But I don't believe for one minute that Hermione has had dealings with you or anyone else, other than him.

—Think about it though . . . if she has, you'd definitely be in with a chance . . .

—Oh tell me honestly . . . Did you?

—Maybe . . .

—Morrissey . . .

—Whatever.

—Hermione's my oldest friend. I can't stand by and watch her humiliated. I'm going to have to tell her about Seeta and Paris.

—But you're not even sure, you dozy prick!

Bohemond closed his eyes and tipped onto his back again. —Actually I'm worried that Seeta may not be the only one.

—Say again.

—Paris climbed in through my bedroom window yesterday morning.

—*No.*

—With some floozy. They were both quite drunk.

God knows what they'd been up to, or what they were going on to do.

Morrissey skipped along the bank clapping his hands. —*Brilliant!*

—When I told Hermione what happened, she looked as though I'd slapped her across the face.

—What the *fuck* did you do that for?

—Morrissey, she's getting married in six months. If Paris is being unfaithful, she should know.

—But you're just gonna . . . *ah shit*. Suddenly serious he said: —If you go spreading crap you're not sure about, you'll never get in her knickers. She'll just think you're stirring stuff up between her and Paris. You've got to do it properly.

—I told you she's my *oldest friend*, and yes I love her, but I'm not—

—You know what you should do, right? Forge . . . he started giggling, tongue between his teeth. —. . . *forge* another two letters. Actually, it's probably best to print them. Send one to Paris and one to Seeta with a dead simple message saying something like, We have to meet up and talk about you and me and *H*. Name a time, and place well away from here, sign one of the letters with a *P* the other with an *S* . . . very discreet . . . then go and lie in wait. It says in this letter here it's over, but the amount of passion in it, and the *timing*, there's no way they'll resist.

—What are you *saying*?

—Serious, right. If they don't turn up there's nothing going on. If one of them does, there's *probably* something going on. If both of them turn up, you'll be able to tell, yes or no, in two seconds. Then you can do what you like. I'd take a camera, cos if they go off together you'll want proof. But if you aren't that hard-core, wait till the next day and go for Seeta, cos she's what? Twenty-one? And she'll swallow this shit whole. You tell her you know all about it, and pressure her, as reasonably as possible, to do the *honest thing*, marriage is sacred and that, blah blah blah. And the ultimate would be to somehow get her to own up to Hermione, *while you're there . . . ha, ha . . .* acting as the counsellor, the fucking . . . concerned *friend*! . . . Racked by another fit of laughter, he crashed amongst the pot plants.

Bohemond swung upright, treading water. —I can't believe you . . .

Morrissey pulled himself clear of the tiny tropical forest, his shorts spattered with soil. —Women are funny, he said. —Hormones and stuff. Make the right move and Hermione'd even fuck a beached whale like you.

—Please . . . stop laughing at me.

—It's *just* . . . the thought of you getting off with Hermione . . . !

—Stop *laughing* at me.

Morrissey wiped his mouth and eyes on a bicep. —But it would be *brilliant*. A couple of rounds with you and she'd think twice about going AWOL again . . . you'd fucking *flatten her* . . .

—She has never *been* AWOL!

—I just told you, she tried to get off with me.

—Lies!

—So how come I know she's got a star-shaped scar on her arse?

Bohemond allowed himself to sink; slow to the surface once his feet brushed the bottom. Water veiled his tears as he broke for air, but there was nothing to hide his hoarseness. —The world cannot be this bleak.

—Fuck off.

—*Morrissey*.
—What?
—You're lying.
—Toughen up, for fuck's sake, he said, and spat his bubblegum into the bathwater.

golden game

In which a beautiful tune yields peculiar riches.

Bohemond was woken by music. Sleepy-eyed, he peered against the gloom, waiting for Paris to leap out from behind the curtains, until he realized the sound was coming from the dry store.

It was still dark. The grandfather clock showed ten past four.

He kicked back the bedclothes and tipped onto his feet. Grabbed his dressing gown as he made for the door. A draught swept up the hall and under his sweat-soaked pyjamas. One hand clamped on his collar, he tried to tiptoe down the stairs.

Though the tune died out as he crept through the restaurant, it leaped to life in the corridor by the kitchen, and was almost deafening in the dry store. The musician was a trapped bird. Plump, plumed, glowing gold, it bobbed and wove around the glass-domed ceiling, wings chiming like the keys of a glockenspiel and sparks arcing into the air whenever it flapped against the window panes and frames. Over the years Bohemond had found all kinds of curious creatures in Delphi's dry store, but he'd never seen or heard anything quite like this.

Worried that switching on the light might startle it into any one of a hundred suicidal manoeuvres, Bohemond made do with moonlight. He tightened his belt and began scaling the stairs.

Forty feet high, the dry store was Delphi's tower. Three tiers of woodplanked gangways circled its walls, each allowing access to shelves built into the brickwork. The first level carried pasta and pulses, fruit and vegetables, whilst the second overflowed with herbs and spices, railings hanging with game. The third floor was more or less a hanging garden, its English ivy and Dutchman's pipe wreathing the steps and railings almost to the ground, which itself was crowded with bottles of oil, and boxes of foil, cling film, greaseproof paper, bags of flour and a mini mountain of tins and jars.

When Bohemond reached the top level ten minutes later he sat down, out of breath, shielding his face from showering sparks. The tiny brands stung his wrists and fingers even as the melancholy melody moved him to the brink of tears. On hands and knees he made his way to an array of brass handles mounted on the wall and wound the one that opened the nearest window. As the bird escaped, its wing clipped the frame and sent a brilliant splinter singing down the drop. Whatever it was tinkled to a landing on the tiled floor, pealing through a full pentatonic scale before it quivered to a stop. Bohemond gaped between the railings. The splintered thing glimmered, highlit by the hall lights. Window wound shut, he slowly thundered down the stairs, squinting over the banister every few steps. But it wasn't until he reached the final flight that he realized what the bird had left behind. He shuffled across the floor and picked the trinket up, smiled at the design and disconcerting weight of a solid gold feather.

heart and arteries

slaughtered lamb and slander

On love, hate and Turkish wedding soup.

Innocent leaned forward scanning the chessboard,
fingers pinching the ears of a black knight. Satisfied
that his position was impregnable, he let go of the
piece and poured himself more wine. Bohemond
closed one eye and nodded – he was a far greater
tactician, but Innocent had a flair that unsettled him.
They played in Bohemond's bedroom every Sunday
morning before lunch, Innocent aiding his concentration with at least one glass of claret, while
Bohemond shovelled his way through a few pints of
ice-cream.

—Can I ask you something, Innocent?

—You would like to concede defeat. He sat back. —I
accept.

—I admit, there's a Gallic quality in the warlike way
you have around the board. You manoeuvre and strike
like a latter-day Napoleon . . .

—Don't insult me. Your question.

—You won't laugh.

—I have been known to laugh, on occasion. But from your expression I don't think that will happen.

—OK . . . all right. Bohemond drew breath. —Do you believe in ghosts?

—In ghosts? Innocent's brow twitched. —No. Once you are gone, you are gone. There is nothing else. Why?

Bohemond retold Faulkner's story, went over his recent visions of fur and lavender, and finished by handing Innocent the feather he'd found the night before.

—Faulkner, said Innocent, —is a bigger dreamer even than you. These things he talks of that you have seen and heard and smelled around Delphi are normal things turned into the telling of his story. But because he has planted his little seed in your head, your imagination runs away with you. Half of the footsteps you heard running down the stairs were his. You heard his voice. It is my guess that the person with him, the lavender carrier, was the person you saw in the bar in the fur coat: one of his lady-friends. Perhaps he is basing his story on things that she has done in the past, with him, or with any or all of the men in the band. Perhaps not. He smiled. —If she is real, that would make her older even than me.

—Sixty-four's hardly old.

—Sixty-eight.

—Still.

—So this woman with Faulkner was older than me?

—She ran too fast for that.

—And so you think she was a ghost? Faulkner was running with a ghost?

—I . . .

—Another thing is that Faulkner's story happened in America, but these things you told me about are here in London.

—So what about the feather you're holding right now?

Innocent wafted it under his nose and handed it back. —This, I cannot explain.

—Well, there you go.

—*Bohemond?*

—But just for a moment, Innocent, imagine: *true* love in the face of tragedy. Forcibly separated from your loved one, your entire life is given over to the search. You die, of grief perhaps, but what with all that passion unconsummated, your spirit, or ghost, cannot rest until it finds its other half.

—Fairy tales.

—But love drove some of the greatest men in history to acts worthy of gods. It made heroes of cowards. What's to say it wouldn't keep a soul from rest?

—Can you imagine such a love?

—You know I can.

Innocent lowered his voice and leaned across the table, careful of the chess set. —*Bohemond*, Hermione is going to marry Paris.

—But sometimes . . .

—She does not love you.

—She could.

—Only as a friend.

—If she knew what was happening . . .

—What do you mean?

Bohemond grew still. —I can't be sure . . . Who knows though, maybe it won't come to some revelation I have no real control over . . . Perhaps one day my love'll change me . . . drive me on to some great deed that wins her.

117

—Are you planning something to make this wedding a disaster?

—No . . . *no*.

—Then what is this deed?

—All I'm saying is, perhaps love can free me of this thing I've become.

—But Bohemond, you're *beautiful*. You have nothing to prove.

—Innocent, I have *everything* to prove. Just last week . . . you were there . . . you saw it all. The mother who came into the kitchen with her little girl, to say how much she'd enjoyed her meal. Soon as she sees me, this utterly mystified, vaguely horrified expression creeps across her face. The child . . . you remember? Mummy, is that a lady or a man? And mummy smiles, tells her daughter not to be so silly. But I could see, she *didn't know*. Then on Friday night, Paris and some woman *in a dress* climbed up to my bedroom window, for God's sake. I could never do *anything* like that.

—Wait, wait. Paris climbed in through your window *with a woman*?

—. . . I prayed for a sign that would tell me whether or not my love for Hermione would remain unrequited . . . No sooner had the prayer left my lips, or rather my pen, than Paris climbed in through my window accompanied by a woman with whom he seemed more than a little familiar.

—*Oh Bohemond* . . . Innocent drew back, smiling, his face quick to cloud —Don't you think that if Paris did something so obvious like climbing up the walls of Delphi with this friend, it is very likely that she is a friend of Hermione too? *Think* . . . he was trying to get *into* the building, not out . . .

—I didn't . . .

—You told Hermione, yes? What did she say?

—She looked hurt.

—That look could have been many things.

—Maybe you're right . . . *But his coming into my room set off a chain of events that* . . .

—That what . . . ? Bohemond, you look so . . . *strange*. Are you ill?

—You won't believe it.

—Believe what?

—Paris is having an affair with Seeta.

—*Seeta?* Innocent puffed his cheeks, rolled his eyes. —*No*. You know this *for sure*?

—Incredible things are happening, Innocent. Suddenly I feel as if my life is taking on some meaning. First my prayer, then Paris climbs through my window, then the voices on the stairs, the lavender, the woman in the bar. I was ready to dismiss Faulkner's fairy tale as some kind of sick joke. But, now, after the gold bird and *this feather*, the things he said are starting to resonate with me. *Now*, I almost feel as if, last night, he was talking *about* me, even *to* me. Telling me not to give up.

—Stop! *Stop*. Look at yourself. *Listen* to yourself. *Seeta having an affair with Paris? Ghosts*. You sound half-mad. Put these foolish fairy tales out of your mind. Put Hermione out of your mind. For God's sake.

—*Christ . . . I just . . . ffff!*

—*Bohemond*.

He slapped a hand against his forehead, squeezed his eyes tight shut. —I . . . *fffff!*

Innocent reached out, gripped Bohemond's elbow, shook loose the hand that he'd moved down over his face. —Bohemond, *please*, he whispered. —You're scaring me.

Bohemond threw back his head and wiped his eyes,

119

even managed a laugh of sorts. —Have to be careful or my mascara will run.

—My God . . . you must listen. *Listen* to me. The world has more variety than you think. You must learn to love yourself. That make-up on your face doesn't make you any less of a man than Paris. Your mistake . . . is you think Hermione is the only one for you. You are *wrong*, and perhaps deep down you know you are wrong. But still you wait and wait until your confidence is at nothing, never saying anything because it is the easiest thing to do. *Act*. Forget Hermione. Be out there looking for someone else. When you find the right person all these things you hate about yourself will fall away. Your lover will be able to see the real you and because of that, *you* will be able to too.

—No-one will ever see the *real me*.

—I just told you, Bohemond: you're *beautiful*.

—A Michelangelo.

Innocent pulled away, sorrow in his blinks and the roll of his head. —I hate it when you talk in this way. OK, you do not look like a famous statue, but neither do I, and no-one I know. And these great historical men you talk about, perhaps it is true that love made them do extraordinary things, but that does not necessarily make them extraordinary men; extraordinary as human beings. You mentioned Napoleon before. A so-called great Frenchman, but I am sure he was nothing much next to you.

—Oh, he was much more than me. The day after his first night with Joséphine, his future wife, he wrote:

I awake to find myself all filled with you. The heady delectation of yesternight has whipped my wit and reason into violent agitation. Beautiful and peerless Joséphine, with-

120

out equal in Heaven or on Earth, what have you done to my heart?

Soon I will be with you again. Until then a thousand kisses, mio dolce amor: but please, do not give me any in return for they set my blood on fire.

—OK. *Enough!* Innocent rapped his queen on the chessboard. —Stop!

—He wrote those words in Paris, in 1795, at the age of twenty-six. And I'm sure you recognize the fervour found in other letters. For instance: 'I love you more with every waking second.' Or, 'If I make from you with all the swiftness of a raging Rhône, it is only because I am hurrying towards the moment I can be with you again.' Or the more fearsome, 'Were I to learn that my love for you had ever been unrequited, I would tear out my heart with my teeth—'

—Stop! I said *stop*! Innocent's lip curled, eyes wild.

Bohemond jittered, tugged the inhaler from his pocket, swallowed two shots. Innocent shook his head, watched the tension ebb, listened carefully to the high sighs of Bohemond's settling breath. —You will drive yourself *mad* with this, he said.

—I only meant . . . said Bohemond, —. . . that love is at the source of Napolean's greatest exploits . . . Deeds of diplomacy and empire, all proof of his passion . . . The promise of being in Joséphine's arms once again spurring him on to even greater achievements.

—They were divorced though, weren't they? Napoleon and Joséphine?

—She was unfaithful.

—I wonder why?

Bohemond sighed.

—How long were they married?

—Fourteen years.

—And he was always the perfect husband?

—He grew frustrated . . . because she didn't bear him a son.

—*You see?* Just because this man did great things, and I for one do not think starting wars is great, that does not mean he was a great person. *You* are great. A great friend, and a great chef. A great human being. Beside you, most of the people I know, including myself, are simply average.

Bohemond cradled his head in a hand. Closed his eyes. —But you're not average. How can a man who experienced love like you did be average?

—My wife?

—If I am a great chef, it's only because I threw myself into this profession for lack of love. If someone had loved me the way you and your wife loved one another, I might not be so great, but I'd feel worth something.

Innocent kneaded the bridge of his nose, the pinkishness in his fingers forced white.

At last Bohemond looked up, encouraged the confession he knew was coming. —It was true love. The real thing.

—Sara. I met her here, in England. We were just children. When I was only two years old, my mother fled here with me from Poland. This was three years before the Second World War began but still, things in Europe were getting very bad. She had lived in a small town called Zyrardow with my father who was a doctor. One day he went on business to a village, Przytyk, a few miles to the south saying he would be back the next evening. He was gone four days when my mother heard news of trouble in Przytyk. Polish peasants had attacked the small Jewish community there. People had been tortured, some were killed, for

122

no other reason than that they were Jews or that their parents or grandparents had been Jews. A week passed, my father didn't return, and of course, in times like that, my mother was fearing the worst. I don't blame her for running away. Some would have stayed and waited. But deep down she knew that she would never see my father again and that Zyrardow would not be safe for ever. So she fled with me. I don't remember anything about it. But she loved to tell me of how we were smuggled from Poland into Germany strapped underneath a horse and cart.

After a short time in Holland we got to England, where my mother found work as a housemaid at a hotel in Torquay. There were other Poles there and over the next years more would come. Sara arrived in the autumn of 1940. I was only six but I remember seeing her for the first time like it was only a moment ago. It was dusk, with the trees and buildings covered in the syrup-coloured sunlight you only get at that time of year. She was with her mother and father, standing between them, holding their hands, dressed in a woollen coat that made her body look far too big for her legs, especially as she was wearing stockings and little leather boots. She had a yellow satchel over her shoulder, and a red wool cap with red wool mittens. All I could properly see was her face and it seemed to me, back then, as a boy of six, like the face of an angel. Don't think I am exaggerating when I say that her skin was as pure and white as snow. Her eyes were like yours, like sapphires, and a little rosy in her cheeks and lips. But what really made my heart burn was her hair. It came down from under the cap, covering her ears, and it was red. And I don't mean red the way people mean it now when they talk of redheads and the colour they mean is really copper or ginger. I mean red like wine or blood or the embers of a fire. Red so deep that sometimes it looks black. I grew up a little that day.

At first she was nervous at being in a strange place and so, in the first months, she was very quiet. Soon though she opened up like a flower and we became great friends. We explored the countryside around the hotel. Made maps so that it became our own world. We buried treasure and went hunting for ghosts. Guarded the coast against German invaders. We found a lake with a boat and sometimes we'd row out to a little island in the middle. There were some ruins there that Sara said had been a tower where a beautiful princess was imprisoned hundreds of years ago. Every time we walked back to the boat she would hold my hand. Once, we built a shelter with rocks and wood and spent the night there eating food that we stole from the kitchen. We went back home at five o'clock the next morning because it was too cold, only to find our parents out of bed, sick with worry. They didn't allow us out to play again for another month. Can you imagine how bad that was for us? Every day up until then we had spent together and then, for one whole month, only seeing each other from a distance. It is from this that I got my name. It was the first thing Sara said to me when we were back together. I hope they treated you well my little innocent.

One day her father told us that they would all be going back home soon because the war was over. I remember Sara watching him walk away and when she turned back to me her eyes were full of tears. She took me by the hand, which she only ever did on the island in the lake, and led me down to the shelter. She said that we should spend an hour every day until she left, trying to talk to each other without speaking because writing letters would never be enough, and that we should also practise not breathing as our hearts were going to break. Then she kissed me for the first time.

The day she left I cried and then every day at the same time for a year. I hated her for leaving me. I hated her. I hated her again too, years later and many years after we had been reunited, because she died without me by her side. Without saying goodbye.

Bohemond gazed at the ground. He'd heard this story many times before, but late at night in the mess-room after marathon shifts and stiff drinks. This was a Sunday morning and Innocent had hardly touched one glass of wine. The recent talk of weddings and romance should have been a source of joy, instead it seemed to be kindling all kinds of sorrow.

—Does that sound strange to you? asked Innocent. —That I could hate this woman I loved so much?

—It makes perfect sense, said Bohemond. —Love and hate are both passions. Halves of the same response. But sometimes we delude ourselves and project. We think we hate our loved ones when in fact we hate ourselves for what seems like stupidity and gullibility. For having allowed ourselves to love so much.

Innocent smiled.

—It's true, and in some ways it's an exciting fact of life: just how helpless we can be when a beautiful woman walks into our lives. There's a tale from *The Thousand and One Nights* about a woman whose husband is a traveller. One day he goes away, a year passes and there's no news of him. His wife, whom we'll call Safiye, waits another year, and yet another, but still he doesn't show up, and the thing is, she's very beautiful, so it's not long before the usual rich and wealthy suitors are knocking at the door. In the end she marries a handsome youth called Mahmut. He's younger than she is, a little hot-headed maybe, and he gets himself into some pretty nasty arguments. One of these snowballs into a full-blown fight and, unfortunately for him, his enemies report his conduct to the governor who has him thrown into jail.

As soon as Safiye hears of what happened, she puts on her best clothes and hurries to the house of the governor with a written plea that says, The young man you have in prison is my brother and protector. Those who accused him are false witnesses. Please have mercy on us both and release him.

As I said, Safiye is incredibly beautiful and the governor falls in love with her immediately. He says, If you go and wait for me in my harem, I'll write an order for your brother's release and bring it to you.

But Safiye, being wise to the ways of men says, I'm afraid that custom does not permit me to enter a stranger's house, but you are quite welcome at my house.

Very well, says the governor. Expect me there this evening.

So she bows out and runs on to the house of the magistrate, where she makes the same plea.

As soon as the magistrate lays eyes on her his jaw drops. Go to my harem, he says, and I'll come to you presently with an order for your brother's release.

Please sir, she says, but perhaps it would be better if you brought it to me at my house this evening, where there's less chance we'll be disturbed.

Very well, says the magistrate. Until then.

And she runs on to the vizier's house.

Like the governor and the magistrate, it's all the vizier can do to stop himself from falling to his knees at the sight of Safiye. But unlike the governor and the magistrate he's somewhat more to the point. He says, Come to bed with me for a couple of hours and I'll see what I can do.

Safiye laughs. Why not come to my house this evening and give me everything you've got.

Very well, says the vizier. Can't wait.

From there Safiye makes her way to the royal palace where she seeks an audience with the sultan himself.

The sultan may be a king but he's still a man and as soon as he lays eyes on Safiye he is all but overcome. I will bring the governor here and order him to release your brother, he says. But as repayment you will spend the night with me.

Your majesty, says Safiye, one such as I could never disobey a king and I take your invitation as a sign of favour, but you would do me an even greater honour by visiting my house this evening.

So be it, says the sultan.

Safiye hurries off to the workshop of the city's finest carpenter and asks him how much it will cost for a large cupboard with four compartments, one above the other, each with its own lock and key.

The carpenter looks her up and down and says, Four dinars, but if you come through the back shop with me for a few moments, I'll do it for cheap.

Ah, says Safiye, I think it might be better if you came around to my house this evening, and silly me, I've just remembered I'll need five compartments in this cupboard not just four.

As you wish, says the carpenter and he sets to work. Safiye waits until the job is finished, pays the carpenter and has a porter cart the huge chest to her house.

After that she looks out some unfashionable clothes and has them dyed odd colours.

As the evening approaches she changes into her most revealing silks and robes, lights candles and incense, and decks the place with flowers and fruit.

The magistrate is the first to arrive. No sooner is he in the door than he is upon Safiye, kissing her neck, licking her lips, working up a sweat, virtually on the point of penetration when she says, You must be hot. Take off your clothes and turban and get into this lightweight shirt and hat.

So he gets into this ridiculous yellow robe and purple cap, and he's ready to give Safiye the time of her life when there's a knock at the door.

Oh by Allah, says Safiye, that must be my husband.

The magistrate, who knows he's in danger of having more than his head lopped off, flaps around the room like a frightened chicken, crying, Oh, what am I to do?

Quick, says Safiye. Hide in this cupboard until I can get rid of him.

The frightened magistrate crawls into the bottom compartment of the cupboard and she locks the door behind him.

As you may have guessed, it was the governor at the door.

My love, says Safiye. Come in, make this house your own. Make me your own. Take off your clothes and put on this nightshirt.

Like a maniac, he leaps out of his clothes into the shocking pink nightshirt that she holds out for him. As he dresses, she ties a polka-dot scarf around his head.

Now, he says. Let me lose myself in you.

Ah ah, says Safiye. First you must sign the order releasing my brother from prison.

The governor does as he's told of course. Safiye lays hands on him and whispers, in quite devilish detail, how she intends to pleasure him. The dirty talk works him up into a terrible frenzy. He pushes her onto the bed and is literally on the point of having his wicked way when there's a knock at the door.

Oh Allah! says Safiye. That must be my husband. Quick, you must hide in this cupboard until I can get rid of him.

The terrified governor climbs into the second compartment of the cupboard and the door is locked behind him.

The third visitor is the vizier.

Safiye manages to get him into an orange dress and silver pointed hat. But no sooner does he touch her than the sultan knocks at the door.

By Allah, she screams. That must be my husband, and she locks the vizier in the third compartment of the cupboard.

When the sultan comes in she says, Lord, I am your slave. Here to grant your every wish on condition that you grant me but one wish.

Name it, says the sultan.

That you undress before me and put on this robe and hat. In this way my arousal will be doubled and so will your pleasure.

He undresses and puts on a tattered grey shirt and a cap made of feathers.

As with the others a fierce knock at the door sends him clambering into the fourth compartment.

It's the carpenter. Safiye yells at him that the top compartment of the cupboard is too small and the carpenter says, Why you silly slut, I'm a master craftsman. That top compartment is the same size as all the others and could hold a man four times my size.

Oh really? says Safiye.

Of course. Watch. The little man climbs up to the

top compartment and when he's inside Safiye locks the door.

She takes the governor's order to the jail, gets Mahmut released and they ride away, never to be seen again.

But what of the five men left in the cupboard? Well, they kept quiet, not daring to utter a word for three days. In the end the carpenter just couldn't hold his water and he pissed long and hard, soaking the sultan in the compartment underneath. The sultan in his turn pissed on the vizier, the vizier on the governor and the governor on the magistrate who was in fact the first to speak. Oh woe, he cried, I can't take any more of this.

When the governor recognized the magistrate's voice, his shame abated a little and he spoke. Allah curse that whore!

The vizier, recognizing the voices of the other two, said, I can't believe this. She has locked us, the most senior executives of the kingdom, in a cupboard! Thank Allah she did not ensnare the sultan also.

Be still, muttered the sultan. For I am imprisoned here too.

I feel most foolish of all, moaned the carpenter. For it was I who made this cupboard for her with my own hands.

Now, the neighbours had noticed that the house was quiet and they grew very suspicious. After some debate they broke down the door and you can imagine their horror at being confronted by a chest that rumbled with the pleas of starving men.

What sorcery is this? they yelled. The cupboard is haunted by an evil jinnee. We should burn it to the ground.

Being of a quicker wit than the others, the vizier

recited certain verses of the Koran and, as a result, the mob drew nearer, doubtful that an evil spirit could speak such holy words. Once they were close enough, the vizier described what had happened, and as soon as they became aware of the true course of events, the neighbours broke open the locks. All five piss-soaked men crawled out of the cupboard, four of them in outlandish costumes. And when they saw each other they could do nothing but laugh and curse their own frailties.

Innocent was smiling, eyes lowered, slightly glazed. —I think of those two lovers riding away and that maybe it will not be long before you are one of them.

Bohemond sighed.

—You should bewitch someone with one of your dishes. The same thing you are doing with Paris and Hermione, you should do with the woman of your dreams. I promise you, she will not be able to resist you once she tastes something that you have put your heart and soul into.

—Not a bad idea, but it'd be nice to think I wouldn't have to bewitch anyone.

—I'm sorry. I didn't mean . . .

—I know . . . On that subject though, I'm still trying to decide on a second course for the wedding dinner.

—Well, said Innocent, —I may have an idea about that.

—Oh? Bohemond froze. His blood lifted and flickered.

—Hermione's mother is definitely Turkish?

—Yes.

Innocent rubbed his wrists together, ardour inflamed. —The Turkish have a dish they call dügün çorbasi which is wedding soup. I think this is how we should start.

—And what about the fish-based antipasto we already discussed?

—There was no firm decision on that. Besides, we can always have fish for the second course.

Bohemond tried to hold back but despite everything that had been said, panic hardened his heart. —Would you stop that, for God's sake! It drives me mad.

—Stop what?

—Rubbing your wrists together. You do it whenever you're anxious or excited, but it just looks as if you're *fawning*.

Innocent looked up, all doe-eyed dismay that passed in a flash.

—I'm sorry, said Bohemond. —I'm sorry . . . it's just I've put a lot of thought into how this meal ought to progress. I mean, what about the points I made about olive oil?

—Good points . . . Innocent rallied, but the glitter in his voice was gone. —. . . although . . . what is there to stop us using olive oil in an Italian second or third course?

—I thought it would be more appropriate to have olive oil in the first course as a kind of figurative anchoring. Remember: immovability, constancy, inviolability, peace, tolerance and regeneration?

—You're right. As always. We should do it your way.

Bohemond faltered. —What were you going to say?

Innocent waved a hand over the chessboard. —It's your move.

—Come on, Innocent.

He kept his eyes low, murmuring in monotone. —I was going to say, I understand your reasons for olive oil in the first course, but it too needs to have a foundation and so I think it could be better to start with a Turkish dish, since Turkey is a place where east and west meet in culture as well as geography. Some say it's where civilization began. In a way, it is a place that Hermione and Paris's ancestors have in common.

—What are the ingredients of this wedding soup? Bohemond raised his hands, lurched forwards and rumbled to his feet.

—Boneless lamb stew meat, lamb soup bones, water, onion, carrot, salt, black pepper, fresh butter, flour, egg yolks, lemon juice, melted butter and paprika.

Bohemond circled the table, eyes closed by the sixth lap, words tumbling, coming quick, as he worked through the sacrificial symbolism of Lamb; the instant of its death marking the ending inherent in every new beginning – new lives, new love – the prime meat, a metaphorical manifestation of bride and groom sharing the very best of themselves. And on and on he went, beyond the pepper and paprika, two spices which, along with cinnamon, cloves, cardamom, ginger and saffron, were, for hundreds of years, at the root of the uneasy peace between east and west, forming as they did, the basis of the spice trade. Returning crusaders, believe it or not, their palates expanded by exposure to piquant eastern foodstuffs, re-kindled European delight in spices. Yes, *re-kindled*, for sure the Romans had bartered with Arabs, Egyptians, Indians and even the Chinese a thousand years before. In fact, such was the Roman zest for zip, their spice expense tipped the economy irretrievably, did, in part, precipitate the disintegration of their empire. The pepper and paprika in Innocent's Turkish wedding soup embodied centuries of cross-cultural fertilization. A Eurasian exchange to replace a legacy of hate. What better way to consummate the love between Paris and Hermione? A pinch of salt? Purifying preservative. Subject of taxes. Currency in Tibet during the reign of Kublai Khan.

Loosely speaking, honey could be used in place of sugar, margarine instead of butter, but salt had no substitute. Its value and durability made it the perfect basis for the invocation of oaths – when God made his covenant with the Jews, for instance, it was one of salt.

—As for all that butter, he said, —I think it might be better left until later. For the time being though: intimacy, unity, durability, tolerance and promise. I think this soup would make a grand opening. He sat down again, at once ashamed and overjoyed that Innocent's Turkish wedding soup was an even better way for him to begin his seduction of Hermione. —So tell me, how is it made? This dügün çorbasi?

Innocent gazed at him, his water-spoiled eyes so brittle a blue as to be almost colourless, but the depth of expression was glaring. One sip of wine, he smacked his lips and began to recite the steps of the recipe.

Bohemond leaned back listening, Innocent, his 68-year-old sous-chef, looking at him in the way he wished Hermione would; how she had done, only once, years before, on the night she fell through his window.

When Innocent started work at Delphi, his wife had been dead for six months, but time only intensified his misery. On feast days and birthdays especially, the kitchen and cooking came second to his suffering. He'd curl up mid-shift in a corner of the mess-room. Sometimes he'd slump to the floor while slicing – his fingers, palms, wrists and forearms ringed with ruddy weals and half-healed piercings, tokens of tumbling cleavers and knives. He always ruined soup stocks, overdid rare cuts, deflated self-raisers and used too much salt.

On good days, he was easily the most gifted gourmet Bohemond had ever worked with, and so he bore with him, always on hand to bolster his spirits with herbal cocktails and vodka shots, late-night chats and games of chess; the old Pole's life steadily fed back to him through the cool compassion of the French head chef.

Innocent responded, slowly unfolding as Bohemond bridged the void and became the new object of his affection. At first, tearful confessions that his peccadilloes were the same as those of Innocent's dead wife, spooked him into retreat. But finally, flattered by the fact that he gratified a deep-seated need, his struggling ceased.

Occasionally though, he'd blow it. Like today.

During his early months at Delphi, Innocent rubbed his wrists raw. Bohemond found out that it was a nervous habit dating back to the weeks he spent by his dying wife's bedside. Whenever he rubbed now, it was for comfort, a conjuring of her memory that everyone recognized. Bohemond had shown no mercy, because even though he knew how important it was for Innocent to make a concrete contribution to this wedding, his obsession had got the better of him. He'd lashed out because culinary creativity was his sole gift, his only weapon in the holy war for Hermione. Everything else about him was packaging. A ton of garbage.

But whatever Bohemond felt about himself, the way Innocent felt about him made what he had said unforgivable and unforgivably stupid. Stupid because when Innocent looked at him, the way he was doing right now, Bohemond was perhaps as close as he would ever come to feeling truly loved.

He gripped the gold feather in his pocket, gasped as the stem skewered his thumb. Innocent smiled as he spoke, mistaking the feeble expletive for a cry of encouragement, while Bohemond bit his lip, woozy at the build-up of blood.

TURKISH WEDDING SOUP

Put lamb meat and soup bones in a large pot and add water, onion and carrot. Bring to a simmer, skimming whenever necessary. Salt and pepper to taste, cover and simmer very gently for a further ninety minutes until the meat is tender.

Remove the bones. Take out the boiled meat and cut into smallish pieces. Strain the stock, return it to the pot and let it simmer gently.

Melt butter in a large pan and stir in flour. Cook gently for two minutes but don't let it colour. Gradually add the hot stock, stirring constantly. When smooth and bubbling, let it simmer gently.

Separate the egg yolks from the whites. Beat the yolks and add the lemon juice, but hold a little back. Beat in a little of the thickened stock and add this mixture to the soup. Stir over a gentle heat and add the lamb meat. Keep stirring all the time until the egg is cooked. Adjust the flavour with the remaining lemon juice and add more salt if necessary.

Combine the melted butter and paprika. Serve soup in deep bowls, and pour a little butter and paprika mixture into the centre as a garnish.

lavender

In which Bohemond receives a surprise invitation
and sees another ghost.

At the end of the evening shift, Bohemond retired to
the mess-room feeling Innocent hadn't fully forgiven
him. They'd circled each other all day, hardly speaking, the old Pole still smarting despite the head chef's
concession to his request for Turkish wedding soup.

The door swung open and Seeta trudged in. She
slumped onto the stool beside him, hooked an arm
around his and rested her head on his bicep. Hot spots
blossomed all over Bohemond's body. —*Tired?*

Seeta nodded, her chin digging into him. —You?

—So so. He glanced through the laundry towards the
kitchen. —Are you feeling better today?

—Bit . . . Went out last night after we finished. Got
smashed. Friends of mine running naked up Shaftes-
bury Avenue. I called home, but it was a mistake.
Woke the whole house. I was pissed and . . . my dad
started crying . . . he does that . . . when he can't get
his own way . . . Shit, yeah, but it made me feel better
. . . Does that sound bad?

—It's understandable.

—Morrissey's been really friendly today too . . . Kind of creepy, but I couldn't resist the novelty . . .

—That's some novelty.

—Worst thing, is my sister: I miss her so much.

—And I'm sure she misses you.

—Yeah . . .

—. . . Remember, if there's anything you want to talk about . . .

—I know. She patted his wrist. —Thanks.

—I was worried about you yesterday . . . Sounded like you wanted Paris's head on a plate.

She took a breath, held it, tensed as she let it go. —Listen, Chef . . . a friend of mine's got his birthday on New Year's Eve, and a bunch of us are going to go out. I was wondering if you'd like to come with me.

—*Me?* Bohemond gasped, all stealth shattered. Heat seeped through his clothes. He tried to ease away but Seeta had too fast a hold. —Haven't you got anyone else to go with?

—Don't be like that, she said, nudging him with her shoulder. —I want to go with you.

—*Really?*

—Don't sound so surprised. It'll be drinks in Covent Garden and then on to a club in Clerkenwell.

—A club? He wiped a damp palm on his thigh. —Seeta, I'd love to go with you, but I'm not sure I can.

—Why not?

—I don't want to show you up in front of your friends.

—Bollocks.

—I'm not the world's greatest socialite.

—You'll be in good company then. She yawned, wavering to her feet. —Are you up for it?

He sniffed, not quite knowing what to say. —You're not at all happy just now, are you?

—You and me both.

—Have you spoken to your . . . boyfriend?

—Oh . . . that's all fucked up too. Platonic bollocks. But hey, I'm *young* and hard as nails.

—Would you have him back?

They looked at one another, eyes searching, both silent. Broke into smiles at the same time.

—OK, said Bohemond. —I'll come.

Seeta kissed him on the cheek, heaved herself away from the table and waved goodbye as she wandered out.

Bohemond bit his tongue to keep himself from calling her back. A button popped from his trousers as he stood up. The waistline slipped quickly, but he gripped it before it dipped past his crotch and hitched it up over his hips, leaned a shoulder against the light switch. Gloom threw the view from the window into sharp relief. Someone had left the back lot door open. He strode outside, mumbling admonishments, snow spilling over the rims of his moccasins.

Tower Bridge was raised to allow a fleet of ornamental floats passage downriver. Bohemond stopped to watch, following the gleam in the gaps between houses as each launch slipped out of sight. Some were manned, others abandoned – giant swans, ducks, puffins, gulls, mini-submarines and tiny liners. And one as high as the bridge road itself: three flaming lovehearts on a vast brass barge.

A woman in a fur coat flickered past on Shad Thames. Strands of blonde hair swept back over her hood, the fragrance of lavender slow to follow, but so solid when it did it almost knocked Bohemond on his back. —Devoted, he said, and bounded down to the end of the street to find the woman gone – not a single footprint on the spread of freshly fallen snow. Whoever she was, she'd passed so swiftly that her feet hadn't touched the ground.

cherries

Outlawed love.

Half-crippled by a head full of lavender, bewildered by the gold feather in his pocket, Bohemond staggered into the foyer and stumbled upstairs, only to tumble onto the first floor at the sound of Hermione's screams rising above the dull thunder of overturned furniture. The landing damaged his ankle. Yanked the workpants down to his knees. He rolled over, grappling for the waistband, surged back onto his feet and rapped on the flat door.

Paris answered almost immediately, jaw set, nostrils flaring. —What?

—What's going on?

—*What!*

—Where's Hermione?

—*WHAT!*

—What do you mean, what? I heard Hermione screaming.

—Fuck off.

—Paris.

—Fuck off!

He swayed left then right, dancing to catch sight of Hermione but the light was too dim and Paris tracked his movements, blocking the view. —If you've hurt her.

—Threaten me and I will knock you out. I will knock you out.

—Hermione. Bohemond tried to stem a sweat over the pain in his ankle. The fingers tangled in the waistband of his workpants began to cramp. —*Hermione?*

A small voice drifted out of the dark: —Yeah?

Paris smiled and turned towards the rustle of footsteps, his grin broadening as Hermione crept up beside him. She looked into Bohemond's eyes, no inkling of anger or distress.

—I heard you screaming.

—It's nothing, she said. —Nothing new anyway.

—Are you sure?

—Domestic.

—Yeah, said Paris. —*Domestic!* He swung the door, but Hermione blocked it with a foot. —The *fuck*? he spat, and raised a clenched fist to within an inch of her chin.

—I'll be in in a minute, she said, nodding towards the living room.

Slowly straightening his fingers into a gun shape, Paris aimed at Bohemond's head and said, —Boom.

—Doubt it. Hermione folded her arms and shifted in front of him, glancing over her shoulder as he swaggered back into the flat.

Bohemond blew out. —Why do you do it?

—He's not all bad.

—I can't watch you go through this again, Hermione.

She held her head in her hands. Brushed the hair back over her ears.

—If he touches you.

—Oh, Bohemond, if he touches me what? *What?*

—You could have anyone you want.

—Well . . . maybe I'll be back on the market soon.

—*Oh Christ!* Suddenly bumbling, utterly muddled. —Because of *me?* Because of what I said?

—About?

—Jo.

—*Jo?* God, *that little shit?* No. That was nothing.

—It's just when they came into my room the other night, Hermione, they seemed so . . .

—Paris was playing you, Bo. He knew you'd come running to me. That's what he does, – what he's always done – he plays games. Sometimes they're harmless. Sometimes they hurt.

—*Games? Why?*

—Classic boy-man. Immature, insecure. Like he needs to push and push to see how much I love him.

—And what happens if one of these *games* gets serious? How can you be sure he hasn't cheated on you?

—*I can't.* I just . . . have to trust him.

—And what would you do if you found out he had been unfaithful?

—I'd run away . . . Hermione gazed up at him, cherry scent and softness, almost lost-looking; —. . . with you.

Bohemond slumped against the doorpost, blood buzzing in his throat and shoulders.

—Are you serious?

—Why not?

—*With me?*

Hermione glanced back along the hall. —Can't think of anyone I'd rather do a runner with.

—And the wedding?

—If I found out he'd cheated on me . . . She looked him up and down. Shrugged.

—When I heard you arguing . . . Bohemond held a hand over his heaving chest, hardly able to speak —. . . I thought it was because you'd found out he *had* been unfaithful with Jo, or . . . someone else.

—No. It was cos I was in a chatroom on the internet. He was watching TV, trying not to let it get to him. But he couldn't handle it. He comes over to the computer, sees I'm cavorting with Black Cock Rapist and his ten-inch strap-on dildo – probably some skinny white kid in the wilds of Idaho – and he just loses it.

—You did *what*?

—Don't look so shocked. It was just a bit of fun.

—*Virtual sex?*

—*So?* It's not the real thing, is it?

—He's not enough for you, Hermione.

Her eyes sparkled as she looked away.

—And a moment ago . . . you said you might be . . . *Oh God what did you say . . . ?* He bounced up and down searching for the words, puffing, panting, sweat and fat squelching in his shoes. —. . . *back on the market*.

—Yeah well, I thought . . . something was on the cards . . . She nudged the doormat with her foot. —. . . Anyway I was wrong . . . but I got the fright of my life. And now . . . things don't look quite so rosy.

And suddenly the words out there, in the air, tongue twittering utterly independent of his will. —Anything to do with Seeta!

Hermione's features stuttered down to a frown, flashed blank with wonder and lightened to a half-smile that died. —What's that smell? she said. —Lavender or something. Is it you?

Bohemond sniffed and shifted, chased the change in direction, struggled to regain his composure. —You can *smell* that?

—What is it?

—I keep seeing . . . he re-twisted the workpants waistband, —this woman.

—You've been seeing someone? Hermione's voice swooped, but she looked all undone.

—No, no, not like that. Just daydreams. He took the gold feather out of his pocket and handed it to her, stepping back as the hallway filled with firelight, and he filled up with memories of outlawed love. Love worth pursuing with all his heart. —Were you serious about running away with me?

She gave the feather back to him and seemed to shrink as the light dried out.

—Speak soon, OK. Goodnight, Bo.

—Hermione.

—Goodnight.

Stock-still, listening, Bohemond heard nothing save the hammering of his heart. He rested his head and the palm of his free hand against the just-closed door, working himself up to breaking it down and punching his weight for once – Paris levelled by his iron fist. As he lay reeling, Bohemond would take Hermione in his arms, climb out the window and shin down the drainpipe to a huge blue Peugeot waiting out back. She'd thank him with a kiss, even as he carried her, but there'd be something on her tongue, just a roughness at first, hot, hard and metallic, growing until its weight, coupled with all the sucking, set it free and he'd find a key rattling around inside his mouth, a key that'd fit the car doors, and they'd curl up on the heated back seat as the wheels sped them out of the city, through the Channel Tunnel, all the way to an old château at the southernmost tip of Bordeaux, where Bohemond would soothe his beloved's wounds with white willow poultices, soap and soak her beautiful skin in his hallowed bathwater, seduce her with his most sumptuous dishes until she was fat enough to fuck him.

On the other hand, maybe he'd just do what he did best, creep quietly off to bed and bad dreams.

Upstairs in his room, candles lit, he stripped off and lingered in front of the mirror.

heart and arteries

In which Bohemond questions his mettle, and readies
himself for redemption.

Hanswurst called Bohemond *Fats* to his face, but it
was *Tits* behind his back. If Paris was drunk, he'd often
beg the head chef for a suck on his cherries, while Lili
had made him gifts of lace lingerie.

In truth, Bohemond's boobs were big enough that
he'd once toyed with the idea of a bodice. He didn't
balloon like a *Baywatch* lifesaver, but had enough of a
bust to rival one of Renoir's bathers or Rubens's nudes.
The problem was that while these peach-skinned
nymphs still ignited the viewer's desire to clutch at
their voluptuousness, a glimpse of Bohemond's black
bosom pretty much crushed any potential cupidity.
The babes in Rubens's wood were deeply female
whereas the head chef was dreadfully effeminate.

He closed his eyes, caressed his breasts – felt heavyweight crests of a heaving sea, twin peninsulas rising
from the horizon, plump new worlds ready for the
ravishing. But when he opened his eyes, despite the
candlelight, his boobs had all the bounty and bounce

of an overmilked blancmange. He didn't want a pair of exocet pectorals. Just a bust that reflected his best. But at best, his breast was beguiling, for it hid a heart and arteries that thundered with quite masculine passions.

The love letter lay open on the dresser alongside his unfinished farewell. He picked up both and limped into the bathroom, cursing his ankle, sucking on his feather-fucked thumb, still numbed by the blow of Hermione's proposal. Bohemond ready to risk a lynching for love.

He opened the toilet bowl. Couldn't resist reading through the love letter as he sat pissing. Sure now that these affirmations *were* the source of Seeta's sadness, the reason why she'd asked him on a date, he prayed that her request and the letter were connected to Hermione's suggestion that he and she elope . . .

She'd said she might be *back on the market* . . . and what else . . . *I thought something was on the cards. I was wrong and now things don't look quite so rosy* . . . In the fourteen years Bohemond had known her, he'd never seen Hermione look so wounded, so confused, as she had when he'd blabbed Seeta's name . . . and here was why . . . Hermione had confronted Paris with her suspicion that he and Seeta had been having an affair, and he'd crushed her with false moral indignation. Given her an ultimatum . . . *If you ever suspect me of being unfaithful ever again, we're finished!* Things weren't looking *so rosy* because, now, Hermione was living under a cloud, afraid that Paris might call off the wedding. A lifetime of abusive relationships had killed her conviction that she deserved better. She was an emotional prisoner, reduced to having virtual sex on the internet. She needed to be saved, because she didn't know how to save herself. And tonight, *at last*, she'd made a tentative cry for help.

Bohemond reached round and wiped himself with the farewell note, even smiled as he flushed it, muttering, —You must learn to love yourself.

One last look in the dresser mirror, he snuffed the candles and bounced into bed.

virgin milk

In which Bohemond begins to appreciate his place
in the scheme of things.

Five days later, at the end of the evening shift,
Morrissey bullied Bohemond out onto the back lot.
Giggling, gasping, he lit up a cigarette and danced
like a dervish in the snow. —*Fucking top fucking top
fucking top*.

   —Morrissey?

   —I fucking did it, didn't I? And it was *beautiful*.

   —Did what?

He stopped hopping, started panting, laughing, and
drew on his cigarette. —I sent the letters, didn't I?

   —*To . . . Seeta* and . . .

   —*Yes! Yes!* He threw wild punches towards the rooftops. —I fucking nailed them.

Bohemond floundered on his feet. —But I told you
not . . .

   —*Yeah*, yeah, I know what you said. But I knew
what you meant.

   —Good God.

   —Is this all the thanks I get?

—What did you *expect*?

—A fucking hero's welcome. Cigarette clasped between his lips, Morrissey spread his arms and nodded as if drawing applause. —*Caesar. Caesar.*

Bohemond sighed, covered his eyes. —Morrissey . . . what have you *done.*

—Oh, so he wants to know now, does he?

—What happened?

—Listen right . . . they are *so* going out. *Finished?* Hands on hips he glanced away and looked back. —*Finished?* Same again. —*Finished!* They aren't *finished.* It's *Kama*-fucking-*Sutra*, mate.

—You have proof?

He squinted through the mess-room window and strutted out of the pool of light. —I sent those letters, he said, miming the act of typing, fingers wiggling wildly. —*We really need to talk about you, me and H. Meet me Thursday, 8pm, outside Tower Records, at Piccadilly Circus. Not a word until then . . .* I signed one with a *P*, the other with an *S* and put them where they'd be found.

—They . . . *came*?

—Fucking *right* they came. And it was obvious straight away. Seeta was *so* cagey, and fucking Paris, constantly looking over his shoulder. But then something went click and it was all hugging and stuff, and they're off for a night on the town. I was with my mate Cheryl. We tailed them. Got photographs and everything. They don't know Cheryl, see, so she got in close a couple of times. Fucking cracker of them kissing outside Sugar Reef.

—Is that where they went?

—Yeah. Couple of pubs on the way. We lost them though. Bastards. End of the night they hopped in a cab *together.* Cheryl and me got one too. Real cops and

151

robbers stuff. We kept up with them as far as Camden. Last we saw, they were making for Swiss Cottage.

—Swiss Cottage? You know Seeta has a bedsit in Kilburn?

—I told you, it's shag-central. All you've got to do now is choose your moment and wade in. Cheryl's developing the photos. I'll have them for you in a few days.

—This is just . . .

—Jesus *Christ*! Morrissey pointed at the eastern sky. —What's *that*!

Some kind of fiery projectile was soaring towards the north bank. At first Bohemond thought it was a firework, but its flight was far slower, and the sea green tail more flame than glitter, didn't die out.

—It's a fucking UFO! *Shit! And there! Look!*

Another, from the west: a golden low-flying comet; brilliant blue arcs sparkling where its tail mingled with the sea green.

—It's satellites or rockets, right?

—Who knows, said Bohemond. —Satellites . . . Rockets . . . Angels maybe.

—Angels. Yeah. Right.

As the tracers faded and they stood looking up at the stars.

—That'll be on the news tomorrow, said Morrissey. —*Aliens Or Scud Missiles Spotted Over London*. He sucked on his cigarette, and shivered. —Not that you'll be too bothered. You'll probably be on the job with Hermione by then.

Adrift in the blazing wake of the rockets, Bohemond hardly noticed him. —So little light pollution, he said. —You can see the Milky Way. Did you know the ancient Greeks believed it really was milk up there?

—Oh *shit*.

152

—Spilled from Hera's breasts when her husband, Zeus, tried to trick her into suckling the baby Hercules.

—Not interested.

—The milk would've made the boy immortal.

—We were talking about Hermione, for fuck's sake. Wake up . . . you're miles away.

More like light years.

All the quipping about his tits suddenly made sense. Bohemond was beginning to appreciate his place in the cosmos. There, on the back lot, he felt that if he looked up long enough, joining the dots, star to star, he'd discern *himself* spread across the heavens – fat, black and blue-eyed, his long hair glowing like aurora borealis – a new constellation slap-bang in the scheme of things. Sagittarius had his bow and arrows, Libra had her scales, Taurus his horns, Bohemond would have his *bosom*. What could be nobler? Milk fresh from the breast was the stuff of life. Of immortality. A gift of love and compassion, et cetera, et cetera . . . If there were to be any wedding at all, he had no doubts that the Italian-influenced second course of the feast should be the milk-infused baccalà mantecato: cream of cod. Visions strobed across the stratosphere: Hermione licking his nipples, brought to orgasm just through being suckled by him.

—These photographs, Morrissey. If I do use them, it will only be as a last resort. I don't condone what you've done. But your actions have revealed the tr—

—*Seen this?* Morrissey was crouched down, way over at the gate.

—What?

—Snow's melted, he said.

Bohemond bumbled towards him. Saw the reason for all the alarm: the snow at the end of the yard *had*

153

melted, but in a ten-foot deep strip, that ran along the length of the wall.

—This is creepy, said Morrissey. —Bet it was those UFOs. Like crop circles or something. You've got snow everywhere, stops dead, right here, in a *straight line*. And the grass . . . should be soaking . . . he brushed the ground with his fingers, —. . . but it's dry as a fucking *bone*.

—And the gate, said Bohemond, grasping the gold feather in his pocket. —It's not properly closed.

Morrissey jumped up, grabbed the latch, howled and sprang back, flapping his hand. —Bastard! *It's red hot!* What the *fuck's* that about?

Another sign. Flaming angels, miraculously melted snow, and now a scorching door, as hot as that of an oven. Blood up and raging in his veins, Bohemond wondered what mischief his wishes would bring.

meat

In which Faulkner tells the second part of his story.

Christmas Eve, and Faulkner was back onstage.

So me and Roosevelt, we stood there at the bottom of that magic tree, pockets full of gold feathers and we just laughed. Some joke: at least one member of his family was dead and we were wanted men.

We ducked down until dusk when he began to make moves. He told me to stay put while he headed down into Norfolk to check out the contact. Said he'd send someone for me once the coast was clear. I watched him walk off. His steps still cool despite all that flight. Some kind of mettle I don't think I ever possessed. Either that or he was in shock. I sat myself down, back to the trunk, and dozed off.

When I woke it was dark. Same night or not, I couldn't tell. The lowlight slicked up the outline of someone bobbing through the pasture. I panicked and scrambled back into the tree. Figure stopped where I'd been lying, looked up and said, Now why don't you come out of there, Faulkner?

I peered down, trying to make out a face, but I was still a little night blind, so I said, And who the fuck might you be?

Name's Beauregard. Roosevelt sent me. I'm the sucker's gonna send you two to New York. Now how about you come down and we get out of here. This place gives me the creeps.

Beauregard was a baby-faced white boy. Didn't look much over eighteen. He kept pretty tight-lipped on the walk into town; anything I asked him he either ignored or gave a one-word answer to.

We hit the outskirts of Norfolk after an hour or so. Streets lined with trees and big redbrick residences fit for fat white governors. I got the shivers when he led me round to the servants' entrance of one of these grand old mansions.

Don't worry, he said. This is my house. You'll be safe here.

He ushered me through a kitchen full of nigger-cooks and gofers fixing dinner, and on into a silver-crusted drawing room. Roosevelt was there making like lord of the manor, in beige pinstripe pants, a white shirt and matching waistcoat. He was with a cute woman who wore a tweed suit, her silver-streaked haircut streamlined to kiss-curls. She had a kinda heavy set that started round the hands and rippled up the incline of her back. Cool as.

The two of them were sucking on huge Cuban cigars, blowing smoke rings.

Soon as I stepped into that room, Roosevelt laughed out loud and hugged me like a brother. He smelled of soap and sandalwood. His skin was soft. A long shot from the runaway railworker with the weight of the world on his shoulders.

Faulkner, he said, and turned to the woman. I'd like

you to meet a very special friend of mine. This is Blanche.

She held out her hand. How do you do.

Turned out Blanche was Beauregard's mother, the *real* brains *and* brawn behind our great escape. She leaned back, took me all in and said, Don't think me rude, but would you like a bath before dinner?

Two weeks on the run, maybe more – couldn't tell in that tree – I must've stunk.

Bathroom was a palace within a palace: gold moulding, marble floor, brass alcoves and stained glass. Towels were three feet thick apiece. Bath itself big as a boxroom. I spent what felt like a few days soaking in that tub, puffing on those smooth Cubans. Roosevelt came in after I don't know how long and sat down on top of the john.

I'm leavin tomorrow, he said.

What's the plan?

Beauregard's gonna drive me to Cape Henry. His uncle's got a boat down there and he's gonna take me to New York.

How long will I wait before I come join you?

He laughed. No sir. This is where we go our own ways.

No sir it's not. Where the fuck am I going to go? Back to Cherryville?

I'm sure you could find another place to settle easy enough.

I save your neck and this is the thanks I get. After all we've been through.

His head sunk low at that. Why's a guy like you want shit to do with a guy like me anyway? he said. You've seen what happens.

I got nothing better to do and besides, maybe you need someone to look out for you.

He stood up and walked around the end of the bath. Traced a circle in the water with his finger. OK, he said, here's the deal. I sail to New York, get myself an apartment, find a job. Shouldn't take long, I know a few people up there too. I'll send you my address, you come on out, stay at my place till you get yourself into the swing of things, then it's goodbye. We're quits.

Sounds fine, I said. But I'm going to need some new clothes too.

You should speak to Blanche about that. It'll cost.

What did it cost you?

He looked down at the new outfit and said, A few gold feathers. This boat ride to New York'll just about clean me out. Beauregard's uncle's a cool cat, but he likes his cut.

How do you know these regal people anyhow?

He laughed again. Let's just say I helped Blanche out of a tight spot a long time ago and she remembered.

I hung over the edge of the tub. Something you want to tell me about?

He shook his head and strolled out, heels clicking. Steam curling in his wake.

When I got up next day, Roosevelt was gone. Nothing left but a note that said, Stay well.

Over the following weeks I traded gold feathers for new clothes and hospitality. Most of the time I kept myself to myself, holed up in a suite on the second floor, still shitting it about the law or the mob. Blanche wouldn't let me go out except after dark and even then it was through the servants' entrance on an hour-long leash. So there wasn't much to do except eat, read, jack off and sleep.

Letter from Roosevelt arrived about a month after he took off. He'd got himself a job as a piano player in an upstairs joint along Broadway, single room included.

Next morning I gave Blanche a handful of gold feathers, a kiss and a thank you. Beauregard drove me out of town, along the coast. Turned down a lane beside an inlet just short of the Cape.

We got out the car and walked another mile or so inland until we came across a vast silver yacht moored at the riverside. Some mincing middle-aged sailor leaned over the side and called us on board. Introduced himself to me as Vegas. Odd guy. Face made up like a film star's: cracks plastered with some kinda skin tan greasepaint, ultra-bright smile, jet-black hair and blue eyes. I guess he must've froze his neck in some boating accident because his head never moved. Anytime he glanced round or looked up, he'd turn or tilt his body until his gaze was fixed on you. Made him look like a living stiff, and the whites he wore, along with a navy blue officer's jacket and the pipe he smoked, only increased the effect.

Beauregard jumped down as we weighed anchor.

I sat up on deck, spread out across a velvet-cushioned stern. Vegas threw off his jacket and took the wheel. Swung us round the mouth of Chesapeake Bay out into the Atlantic. Day was hot, but the boat worked up a breeze. Sunlight and spray, white clouds, warm winds, Vegas on the bridge, legs spread, pipe-smoking, a swagger in the smiles and raised eyebrows like some upcoming Fifties crooner.

He shouts over, Maybe you'd like to catch us a bit of lunch.

And I'm like, Say what?

We've got some top-class fishing gear and tackle, he says, and points to the cabin. I get up, take a look. He's got a ton of fishing rods racked up there on the roof and what looks like buckets of blood on the ground.

It's bait, he says. You'd hardly need it though; the fish round here bite like they mean it. Why not have a go?

Why not.

The buckets were filled with animal leftovers: heart parts, guts, tongues, the occasional eyeball. I cast off with a pigtail and a monster fish, more like a baby whale, arced out the water, swallowing hook, line and pigtail in mid-air.

I almost got pulled overboard – down on my knees, sliding along the deck. Fought that motherfucking abomination with every ounce. Reeled it in after a half-hour struggle and bashed its brains out with a baseball bat. That's how I spent the rest of the morning: cruising to New York, conquered creatures of the deep piling up all around me, some serious shit too like giant eels, squid, and this yellow thing like a merman with hands instead of fins. I even hooked a swan.

Vegas cooked up some of the fish for lunch. Tossed the rest back into the sea. He set up a table on deck, dressed it with good crystal and silver and we dined like kings in the late afternoon. Heat ruined the black-currant sorbet dessert. I bolted mine, but Vegas sat back and watched his melt.

Boat drifting after dusk, I checked out the leather-bound lounge below, the gauge of the bunk in my luxury cabin.

We moored somewhere off the coast of Maryland that night. Sat up drinking champagne. Vegas lay on his back looking up at the sky while I slouched in the corner, shoulders and arms inflamed with the day's crazy catch.

There were parties in full swing all the way along

the beach. Sand dunes and water spotlit by fireworks, the whole goddamn strand crammed with Catherine-wheels and Roman candles, sparklers and bonfires, and scoring the sky far above, shooting stars and other hardcore bodies like comets with million-coloured tails. Vegas said they were rockets, but I didn't exactly know what he meant. I thought of Roosevelt when three flaming crimson hearts drifted past on a golden barge. Roosevelt and Beatrice.

Next night, I got woken by a commotion on deck. Thought for a moment the mob had caught up with me but the voices were joyous. I found Vegas up there, a single red rose in his mouth, clapping along to a Latino-looking couple strutting through a flamenco. The guy was in some kinda sequinned tuxedo and the girl threw her shapes in a radiant red number. I sat up till dawn, slamming tequilas, rockets passing over-head.

New York City was a fucking letdown after those days on the boat.

Vegas dropped me off at a wharf near Forty-second Street on a rainy Sunday night. I tipped him with a single gold feather; told him if I needed a ride out of town I'd give him a call. He tugged his cap, puffed his pipe and slipped back onto the river.

Didn't take long to find Roosevelt. The joint he was working was on Broadway between Twenty-sixth and Twenty-seventh, a plush speakeasy with a poker room in the back. He was playing piano when I came in, so I sat at the bar, listening, no money for drinks, just a couple of gold feathers rattling in my pocket. The barman kept me in liquors on the house after I told him Roosevelt and me had fought together in the Great War.

I hung out until closing. Roosevelt lurched over once

161

the place was cleared, keeping it cool. He didn't touch me, just nodded. Lit up a cigarette. The panic and angles were gone, dissolved in a new louche look; more like the man he was and not the one I knew.

Sean, he said. This is Faulkner.

Sean the barman bounced a little. We met already. Say Sam, you never told me you fought over in Europe.

Roosevelt peered at me and said, Passchendaele. One muddy motherfucker of a rumble.

We sat in a booth with a bottle of bourbon, other privileged patrons bombed out roundabout.

It's good to see you, I said.

Likewise.

You seem to be taking city life in your stride, Sam.

He laughed again.

Who the fuck is Sam?

It's all a play though, ain't it, he said. Doing as the Romans do. Sam the Piano tryin to get ahead in New York City. It's all too slow though.

You looking for promotion already?

No, I'm just tryin to work up enough blunt to get Bea out here. Plan was I'd sweat my ass off, send money back to her through Blanche and she'd use it to move out here. Thing is, I been here a month already, workin flat out the last couple weeks and I'm fuckin broke. Sure there's a free bed in it and a few free drinks, but the dough's a joke. I get just enough to keep me in beef jerky.

You got any feathers left?

What do you think?

I reached into my pocket. Set the last three on the table. You can have these if you like.

And then what the fuck are you gonna do?

I'm a white man in New York City, for Christ's sake. I'll get a job tomorrow.

He shook his head. At this rate I'm gonna have to whack a millionaire.

Every now and again shit happens that changes your life for ever. Sometimes it seems like next to nothing, signs you might not get wise to until years later. Other times it's stuff that's so in your face you can feel the world turning. When I was with Roosevelt, the little things happened all the time. I mean, you make a choice to hang out with a black man back in those days you gotta be ready for a rough ride. But there were two major deals that pretty much spun me inside-out. The first was the time I helped whack those nigger-hating motherfuckers in Cherryville, South Carolina, and the second, kinda connected to the first, I guess, began that rainy Sunday night as we sat chatting in a classy third-floor speakeasy on Broadway.

The door opened and two police officers swaggered in. No big deal; maybe cause for mild concern, but they looked cool enough and no-one in the joint seemed too bothered. I heard heavy footsteps on the stairwell. Caught a quick whiff of sulphur. The second officer glanced out the door, blinked a couple more times than he needed to and then shuffled aside as the biggest most evil-looking motherfucker of a cop I have ever seen stepped into the bar. He was ten cubits tall, easy, broad as a Bentley, biceps thick as my waist, hands like trenching tools. A killer. Like there was nothing else he could be – every last millionth of DNA geared towards slaughter – and *oh man*, so un-fucking-stoppable. A siege machine, a bone breaker, a *man-mountain*, the very motherfucker you know will never ever go down no matter what.

Roosevelt shifted further along the bench, huddled up and bowed his head. All that South Carolinian Uncle Tom shit come back to roost in a wink.

The cops slung their hats onto the bar, straddled the stools. Sean poured them drinks. He looked real spooked. I made to whisper to Roosevelt, but he shook his head and cursed himself a few times.

Cops got talking. Big one's voice sounded like a landslide. A guy that loaded makes you feel you gotta prove yourself even though you're not in his frame.

City-smart Roosevelt twitching like a Tom and me in the in between, trying to hold down the hormones.

Out of the frying pan into the fire.

Ten minutes in, the big cop got up. He walked around the bar toward the poker room, spotted me watching him and stopped.

Hope you got a permit for that, he said.

I put a hand to my ear. Huh? Whasat?

The other cops turned round as he stepped forward. Up close he looked older. Smell of sulphur was unbearable.

We said, we hope you got a permit for that nigger.

Roosevelt stared at the table. Did the right thing, but I let the liquor I'd had rise and shine. I said, Is that one of your New York City laws?

Damn fucking straight.

Well I don't own this man.

So is that a no?

A no?

You don't got a permit for it?

I guess that would be a no.

He drew the nightstick from his belt, reached over and stroked Roosevelt's chin with the shaft. We think you better crawl back into your hole, he said.

Roosevelt got up and hobbled out the door, the other cops glaring after him.

The ogre glanced at the gold feathers lying on the table and a smile darkened his face. Real evil.

What's that?

Feathers, I said.

May we?

They're all I got.

He picked them up, stuffed them into his pocket and strolled away. God as my witness, his shadow engulfed everything it passed over. Didn't roll or soften with the change in light, just kind of hung beside him like a pitchblack twin, swallowing floorspace, tables, even people.

Times like that, you don't do much more than watch.

The first few verses of Mark chapter five end an account of how Jesus sails over the sea into the land of the Gadarenes and exorcizes some nutcase with a head fulla devils. When the good lord asks this lunatic who he is, he replies, My name is Legion: for we are many. The monster cop in the speakeasy was known as Legion not just because his body was home to the hordes of Hell, but cos when Christ drove the fiends outta that motherfucker they flew into the fields and possessed a herd of swine that, very quickly, went very very crazy and threw themselves off a cliff. Legion was nothing if not a demon pig.

Some of the Hungarians and Romanians I got to know called him Tepes, or The Impaler, after Vlad Dracula, the bloodthirsty medieval prince Bram Stoker based his somewhat lighter-weight Dracula on.

This guy ruled a small Romanian province called Wallachia at around the same time as Constantinople fell to the Turks, and when he wasn't driving the infidel back across the Bosphorus, he was butchering Germans, Hungarians, Jews, Gypsies, Catholics, Muslims and heretics. He sliced, flayed, burned and boiled, most of these motherfuckers alive. Favourite trick was impalement. Men, women and children, skewered through the navel, through the heart, through the ass, the balls, the cunt and the head. He stuck those poor peasants with big wood stakes and raised them up like Christmas tree fairies. Oddly enough, the sick fuck was passionate about law and order. Couldn't stand to have the rules broken. Set his subjects all kinds of tests, with impalement as the prize for failure.

Legion shared that love of justice. Though truth be told, the things he did to enforce it made Vlad's exploits seem like a day at the beach. Sure he impaled prisoners of every ethnic description but instead of wood stakes, he used his bare hands. You've heard all the classic Hollywood big talk, like, *I'm gonna shove this gun so far up your ass, it'll come out your mouth and then I'll blow your fucking brains out.* But Legion was the guy that really did that shit. Stories about him playing prisoners like glove puppets. Nailing motherfuckers to the wall. Splitting them in two. Ripping heads off and shitting in the hole. He loved the humiliation. Got off on agony. He'd pull in a handful of suspects, lock them in a cell without food. Sometime later, maybe days, he'd come in and take one of the marks down to the basement where he'd help them breathe their last. Dungeon was in easy earshot of the cells and as Legion ripped those motherfuckers apart he screamed out the sounds of struggle Batman-and-Robin-style. Got so every fucking hood in New York City knew what these words stood for. POW! and whoever he had his hands on was getting fisted. SKRAAK! Teeth shattered, legs snapped back at the knee-joint, necks and ankles broken, spine uprooted. THUNK! meant a fucking, pure and simple. SHEEYAATCH! Back, chest, arms, legs, head and hands, skinned. KERRRUNCH! Fingers, toes, noses, ears, tongues, balls, cocks, clits, flaps and tits chewed off. GULK! and he'd have some poor motherfucker chained to a bench, sliced open, clavicle to coccyx, and be rummaging around inside their guts, pinching and pummelling different organs so they'd shit, piss, puke or scream depending on what part of their entrails was being fucked with. The clincher was KROOOM! which meant he'd bent and rent some motherfucker so out of shape he'd managed to suffocate them by sticking their head up their own ass.

That first night I saw Legion he was collecting protection money. He ran a racket the length and breadth of what had been the Tenderloin and the last Sunday of each month, he went round every den in the precinct looking to collect. No-one ever held out on him.

It wasn't long before I grew used to the rhythm of the city. I shared Roosevelt's room two weeks before I got myself a spot playing drums with Ray 'Baby Face' Rico and the Blueboys, an all-white uptown ragtime outfit. Jazz was starting to break bigtime; every pale-face in the Union jumping on board, taking credit for music that niggers all over the world had been playing for centuries.

I hung out with Roosevelt whenever I could. Got so he dropped his defences a little. Sometimes he welcomed me with open arms. After a while, he introduced me to a few of his acquaintances; one of them a teenage goddess called Blossom. She was a half-blood Latino, but blonde. Long legs and lashes, lips, hips and cool green eyes. I fell headfirst into that one. She cut it as a waitress and occasional dancer in a mid-town ballroom called The Golden Fleece, and I spent a lot of time hanging out there.

Whenever me and Roosevelt went along to watch the cancan marathons and backroom stripshows, Blossom always made a point of serving us drinks or playing tease. I asked her five separate times before she agreed to go on a date. After that I saw her almost every day.

With money tight, me and Roosevelt got a badger rap going with her. She'd lure some married country gentleman up to her room, roll around with him a little, before me or Roosevelt bust in, sometimes with a dummy gun, playing the outraged spouse. We'd railroad or blackmail the mark into giving up a chunk of his earnings. Took a couple of lawyers for a small fortune once. But mostly it was regular guys with regular jobs that paid regular pay.

Pretty good days, but all the time I spent with Blossom drove Roosevelt into a real blue period. He'd been sending cash to Beatrice through Blanche but since he got paid a pittance, it didn't mount up like he wanted, and he couldn't seem to get a job that'd pay any better anywhere else. I would've given him every last cent I had if I thought it would've made any difference. But the kinda money he was talking about, no drummer in any jazz band on the planet could've helped him. Wasn't much else to do but watch him get desperate.

Christmas Eve of that first year, I was full of rum at a Fleece party when he told me he had a plan.

Faulkner, he said, I know I owe you already, but I'm afraid I gotta ask you for another favour.

I was drunk, it was Christmas Eve. No problem, I said.

Before you yell, just hear me out, OK.

I'm listening.

In this day and age, niggers like me is pretty much never gonna get what they want. But there's some things it's every human bein's God-given right to get their hands on. Like love. Everyone should know what it's like to be loved, and I ain't talkin about the love between a mother and her son. I'm talkin about the kind of love goes on between a man and a woman. The stuff that stops you in your tracks, turns you inside-out, messes with your heart so you can't eat or sleep. Stuff that once you get a taste of it you'd rather die than never feel that way again. Faulkner, all I wanna be is free to love someone who loves me. I wanna be with Beatrice. It's drivin me outta my mind, bein here without her. It's *Christmas*, Goddamnit. I should be celebrating. Look at these motherfuckers in here. Everybody partyin with the ones they love and all I got is cold bones cos I got the hots for a white woman. Man, if I never see her again, then my brother maybe my whole goddamned family all died for nuthin. I'll have lost everything.

I heard that, loud and clear. What's your plan? I asked.

Ain't for the faint-hearted, that's for sure.

Shoot.

OK. As you know, Legion gets rich once a month. But what you don't know is that he stashes the dough in a locker in a safe house on the Upper West Side. The place is on the waterfront. It's rundown, unguarded, always deserted, and I think that's just the way Legion likes it. He checks the goldmine out twice a day – twelve in the afternoon and twelve midnight. Keeps the key to the locker on a chain round his neck. Never takes it off. Now here's the deal. We get some brave and willin pro, someone we can trust, to take a shine to him, butter him up over the next couple of

169

months and get into his bed. She spikes his liquor with dope one particular night and once he's out for the count she takes the key off the chain and brings it, along with the keys to Legion's apartment, down to us in the street. The babe hides out and keeps watch, so in the very unlikely event that Legion wakes up, she's got a head start. If she ain't there to meet us when we get back, that's our sign that all is not well. We take the key to a late-night cutter, get it copied, and since I'm the one who's callin in all the favours here, I'm gonna fix that key back round Legion's neck myself. All you gotta do is be ready. Whole trip, cut and trick shouldn't take more than fifteen minutes. After that, the big heat's off. But it's real important that key goes back, cos if he does wake up and finds it gone you can bet he'll sniff us out before sun-up and slow-roast us all for breakfast. I gotta tell ya though, chances of him waking's non-existent. The dope I got in mind, he'll sleep the whole fuckin week away. We go open the locker, take the cash and then make for the Hudson docks where we board a liner called the *Columbus*, that'll take us all the way to England. Friend of mine can get us places in the band that plays on the ship. All I gotta do is give him the word. It's gonna be sweet. How about it?

I thought he was out of his mind. I said, You're gonna to try to pull a fast one on *Legion* and you want me to help you?

Cash he screws outta my joint is cash that would otherwise be goin into my pocket and bringin Bea to me. I'm just gonna take what's mine.

You're *crazy*.

And you're a white motherfucker that never wanted for anything.

Blossom swept round the table and sat on my lap.

She put her arms around my neck. Kissed me.

Roosevelt honey, she said. You mind if I borrow this body for a few minutes.

He just glared in the other direction. Looked just about as pissed-off as it's possible to be.

Blossom hooked a finger under my collar, slid to her feet and led me through a door to a room full of cubicles. She spun me into one of them, sat me down and straddled me as she drew the curtain. Rockets shot past the skylight above her head. Tails sparkling in the snowstorm. She cupped my face in her hands, pulled my head to her breast. Weight coming down through her crotch, on top of my crotch. Her fingers met round my neck, thumbs crossed over my windpipe, squeezing the breath out of me and she was sighing. I slid my hands under her skirt, grabbed her ass, all that weight coming down on me doubled up. Blossom, my green-eyed Latino blonde and those sighs like smiles. It's all yours, she said. All yours. Marry me.

I knew it was coming. Felt like the time. Christmas Eve off Broadway. Rockets passing overhead.

A breeze purled the curtain. I caught sight of Roosevelt sitting at the table, waiting for Beatrice.

Blossom reached back, put her hands on top of mine.

I said, I'll marry you on one condition.

What's that? *What's that?*

That you help a good friend of mine out of a tight spot.

What friend?

I'll tell you later, I said and rolled her over.

I told her on Christmas day. All about me and Roosevelt and Beatrice, about Roosevelt's plan. Asked her if she'd be the one to woo Legion, dope him up and

171

get the key. It wasn't easy, but it's like Roosevelt said, every regular motherfucker on earth has a right to love and be loved, regardless. Who the fuck am I to stand in the way of that kinda karma?

Blossom didn't see it that way. She kicked up a real stink. Couldn't believe what I was asking her to do. I said, I'm sorry but I don't know anyone with your kinda nerve and there's no-one else I can trust. Besides, what's the big deal. You've made moves on plenty of other guys. Yeah, she says, but that's not the point. The point is, you've put a price on us getting married. One that might get me killed. How could you do that? Baby, I said, me and Roosevelt go back a-ways. He might not know it, but he needs me. Until he's out of the woods, there's no way I'm gonna get hitched. It'd be like rubbing his nose in it. *Jesus fucking Christ*, she says. Who's getting married here? You and *me* or you and *him*? Believe me, baby, I said, I wanna be with you but some things just go way beyond what you or I want. Some things are more important than a damn wedding.

She took off in a spray of smashing glass. Christmas dinner cut short.

Blossom got the best of me every day for two months before she came round to the idea. Plan was Roosevelt'd get her a place on the ship too and we'd get married onboard or in England. She always said she'd go out on a limb for him any day of the week whether we got married or not, so why didn't we just tie the knot, and I think she meant it. But I had to be sure. If she wanted to be with me as much as I wanted to be with her, she'd make damn sure Legion was flat on his back while Roosevelt and me got our hands on his hoard. She knew that devil already – motherfucker got paid by the Fleece too – but he didn't rattle her much.

Sure, she said, Legion's a killer but same as every man, he's got soft spots. That's cool, I said. Do whatever you gotta do, only don't let him fuck you. A guy that size fucks you, whoever you are, you're gonna wind up with a bust pelvis at best. At worst you're looking at giving birth to the anti-Christ.

First time Blossom made a move on Legion, I was there. We were drinking in the Fleece one Sunday night in February when he lumbered in with his two cop buddies. As they sat themselves at the bar Blossom kissed me and broke into some new dance routine. It was a quiet night, no music, only a handful of people in the place and my Latino queen cooking up these eastern moves. I'd never seen a dance like it. Usually it was second-hand cancan or some other cheap smut, but this was beautiful. Long limbs and lipstick. Could've been rapture in her glances, like she'd been practising behind my back. Something I'd never seen, unwrapped for a monster cop.

Legion watched her over his shoulder, kinda bemused, then turned all the way around. Blossom swung closer to him, passed by and doubled back. Looked like a fairy fluttering round a gargoyle; his threads and face lit up with all the glitter. She stopped right beside him and his head jolted like he suddenly woke up. He said nothing, just started clapping, the other cops, cigarettes wedged in the corners of their crooked fucking mouths, following the leader.

Blossom curtsied, came on cool. Legion called for more drinks. I sat watching the first act, listening to the wordplay. Got closed out when Blossom stretched up on tiptoe to whisper something in Legion's ear. Her arm slipped around his neck and his hand came to rest on the small of her back. Could easily have circled her waist and squeezed the life out of her.

As he made to leave, he brushed Blossom's cheek with the back of his hand. She gripped one of his fingers, held it to her face.

That's how it began and it all just upped from there. Got so Legion was with Blossom most nights he could spare the time. I lay low mostly. Kept out of the way. But whenever I saw them together, the monster cop seemed almost human. Felt very fucking wrong, a guy that size, that ugly and with that rep being so gentle.

Blossom started getting a real kick out of hanging with him – always on the list for restaurants, clubs, the theatre, the cinema, and any time they wanted, a motherfucking opera box all to themselves.

Nights I got with her she was whacked. Might've been my imagination but the way she came on with me those few weeks, I guess what I had to offer pretty much paled beside the bellyful of culture she got out of that fucking cop. Some nights I'd get a sermon on how Legion wasn't bad as all that. How maybe he was just misunderstood. I knew then the time was getting close to make a move.

I kept Roosevelt posted with what was going on. Meanwhile he made sure everything else was kosher. He fixed up a key-cutter, a car and enough potent Chinese dope to fell a herd of elephants. Got the boat-band suits too: shimmering silver numbers. We gonna sail the high seas in style, he said.

Wasn't long before Legion was inviting Blossom back to his apartment. Not long before they were making out. She'd come home, thighs blueblack with bruises, red-rimmed fingerprints all over her arms, ass and back. Fucking teeth marks like Great White bites messing up her honey-coloured stomach. But she didn't seem to mind. She'd come to me, show off her wounds and sigh like she was miles away. Times I fucked her she just wasn't there. Two weeks to go before the *Columbus* sailed, all this shit really started getting to me.

She limped in, three o'clock one morning. I was still awake, waiting. I said, What happened to you that you're walking like a crab?

Nothing.

You been with Legion?

Where else?

Did he fuck you?

What?

You walking like that. I just wondered. Did he fuck you?

She turned around, tired-looking, but still glowing. It's like you said, she said. If he fucked me I'd be dead.

So he didn't fuck you.

No, but he did do a whole lot of other stuff you wouldn't believe.

Like what I wouldn't believe?

Put it this way, Faulkner. A man who speaks five languages fluently, who loves Verdi, Chekhov, Mozart, Monet *and* Valentino is going to know at least a little about lots of other things.

I don't like it, Blossom. The way you talk about him. The way you're so, Hey look! about how he's got you all bit up and covered in pawprints. I'm starting to wonder if you wanna go through with this. If you wanna be with me any more.

Have you *forgotten*? I'm doing this for you. For *us*.

Sometimes it doesn't seem like it.

You lousy fuck! It was your idea.

Don't you throw that shit back in my face. I'm trying to do the right thing here. Never seemed like a good idea but then we don't have a whole lot of choices, do we?

What about doing the right thing by me?

I told you, I will, just as soon as all this is over.

She rushed out. Came back in five minutes later, cooler, calmer, slunk down onto the bed and kissed me. I've seen the key, she said. Biggest key I ever saw, and it really is on a chain round his neck. Whenever I ask him, What's that key for, all he does is smile and say, It's the key to my heart.

Don't you go soft on me, Blossom, I said. Don't you go soft on me now. Cos you know, we're gonna break his motherfucking heart in two.

The night of the heist I had a late show with Baby Face and the Blueboys in a downtown brownstone. We got in a ruckus with some sailors. A set-to that snowballed until every motherfucker in the joint had jumped into the rumble. Baby Face took a bottle on the back of the head. Austrian aristocrat got his finger bit off. Sea dogs got nasty. Carved us up with cutlasses. Captain pulled a gun and popped a bargirl in the gut. Fire broke out in the poker room. I ran out into the street where Roosevelt was waiting in a champagne and caramel Cadillac. Hopped onto the back seat, slouched out, as he took off.

We cruised up the West Side, killing time, came about in Harlem and swung a slow way down East. Neither of us said much. Nerves I guess.

We stopped on East Forty-ninth, not far from St Bartholomew's Church. Roosevelt pointed to a third floor apartment across the road. Dim light shining in the window. Shadows swaying.

That's Legion's den, he said.

I nodded.

Don't it bother you none?

Don't what bother me?

The fact that he's in there with your woman.

I pulled away from the window. Of course it fucking bothers me.

So why let her do it?

Who else do we know with the kind of nerve it takes to carry a thing like this off? Who the fuck else can we trust?

He shook his head. I wouldn't let any woman of mine be up in there with him, that's for sure.

So you'd rather go without ever seeing Beatrice again?

Faulkner, don't think I'm not grateful. Way things is goin I'm gonna be in debt to you and Blossom for the rest of my days. It's just this is one heavy call.

Well, she said she'd do this for you any day of the week. She's in there of her own free will.

He ducked down. Oh. *Oh*.

I looked up at the tenement. The light was out.

Roosevelt grunted. What time is it?

Three thirty.

I guess this is it.

I got out the car, walked across the road. Blossom opened the window, blew me a kiss and disappeared. Came back, bowed under the weight of something cradled in her arms. It was the motherfucking key. She leaned over the ledge and let it drop to the sidewalk, but it bust through the paving and stood upright like a signpost. The shaft was shin-sized and the teeth big as my feet. Took me and Roosevelt five minutes to uproot it.

Blossom stayed in the shadows by the window as we worked.

Once we were done I signalled to her to come down, but she shook her head. Sounded real distant, whispering, I can't find the keys to the apartment. If I come out we're gonna have to break back in.

177

So wedge the doors open or come down the fire escape, I said.

Doors is too risky, someone might see or close em, and the fire escape window's locked. When you come back, I'll come down let you in, then we'll all leave together. She glanced round to check if the giant was still under. Don't worry about me, looks like he ain't never gonna wake ever again.

Blossom!

A finger over her lips, she slipped back into the room.

I didn't like it. Didn't like it one bit. But it wasn't any kinda time to argue. We hefted the key into the car and took off.

The cutter was back in Harlem. We drove up there, really starting to buzz, but all the smiles stopped when he saw the key. What the fuck is this, he said. Some kind of a *joke*? You wake me up in the middle of the night for what? For *this*? I'm a key-cutter for Chrissakes, not a shipbuilder.

We jumped back in the car with a real fucking problem – we'd have to use the original key. I wanted to go get Blossom and then go get the money, but Roosevelt was real desperate. Only thing on his mind right then was Beatrice. He wanted to go get the money *then* go back for Blossom. Said anything else was wasting time especially since we were nearer the Upper West Side than we were Legion's Midtown East apartment.

So what the fuck happens if we get waylaid down at the safe house and Legion wakes up? I said. I don't care what Blossom does to distract him, no way is he gonna miss a key like this.

Fucking Christ, Faulkner, I told you, no mother-fucker on *earth* is gonna wake up with the dope he's had.

If that's so, what's the problem with going to get Blossom right now?

The more time we waste the more chance we got of gettin caught. If Blossom smells any kinda trouble, she's got the sense to bail out. She'll do what she has to.

Yeah, but then how the fuck's she gonna find us?

Man, she goes down to the docks and gets on the *only* motherfuckin ship called the *Columbus*!

And what if she can't? What if we can't? Anything could happen! You aren't thinking straight, Roosevelt! I mean, Jesus, we're talking about the woman I love here. I can't just abandon her.

Oh, yeah, I forgot: you must love her a whole lot to let her play bait in a trick like this.

I bashed his face with a fist right then, but he came up all hands and feet, hooked me in the mouth with a heel, trampled my throat and shoulders. Car swung to the side, bounced onto the kerb, coasting as we tussled. My door opened, swung closed, fingers jammed in the hinge. I spilled out backwards. Fireworks when my head rapped the road. I heard footsteps, saw Roosevelt coming towards me, big motherfucking snarl on, but the steps weren't his. Cop whacked him on the crown with a nightstick. The blow sounded like broken coconut. Wasn't Legion, just some regular nigger-hating cocksucker thought he saw a white man in trouble. He hit him again. I rammed him from the back, smashed him face first against the wall, his black cap skewing off like a discus. Roosevelt grabbed the stick reeling and squealing. We've got to go, I said. We wasted too much time on this shit already. Cop tried to crawl away, but Roosevelt pinned him and broke the motherfucker up. We threw the ruined body in the Caddie trunk and I spun us the fuck out of there.

Roosevelt went crazy; blood streaming down his face, wide-eyed, yelling. Motherfucker! Motherfucker! What the fuck we gonna do now?

First we go get Blossom, I said. Then we go get the money. Then we figure out what to do with the motherfucker in the trunk.

My heart popped as we swung on to Legion's street. The window light was back on. Drapes had been ripped down. No sign of Blossom. I hauled up outside the tenement, grabbed the crushed cop's nightstick, ran at the door. Motherfucker was locked. Roosevelt wasn't any good to me then; still in the car, head in his hands.

Round the corner of the block, I ducked down the first alley, counting houses, raced up the fifteenth fire escape and crouched down outside the third-floor window. The light from the front room spilled into the hall. Died out by the time it reached me. I held in my wind. Listened. Place was dead. Window wasn't locked but the frame was too hot to touch. I slid it open, using the sleeve of my jacket as an oven glove and stepped down onto the floor.

The whole joint stank of sulphur, sweat, heated sweetness. No room for breathing, like even the fucking air didn't want to be in there. I crept up the hall, the soles of my shoes tacking to the floor it was so hot. Pushed the first door I came to. Room was completely empty. I passed a kitchen on the right. Glimpsed something slip into a shaft under the sink. At first I thought it was an outsize rat but the back and tail were scaly. I waited for the sound to die down, carried on. Only other room was the one with the light. Blood boiling, nightstick slipping in my grip, I leaned around the doorpost.

Not good.

Shit like I'd never seen. The walls were charred, still smouldering. Red paintwork blistered higher up. A bed the size of our Cadillac was upturned against an armchair, a hole the width of a steering wheel burned through the mattress. Tracks of blood, black knots of shit and gristle smeared along the wooden floor. Bloody bare footprints climbing the walls. Footprints on the fucking *ceiling*. Heat and stench were unbearable. Not a mother-fucking sign of Blossom. Wound up I pulled that little corner of Hell apart looking for her. Hurt bad thinking the blood and guts might be hers. I scrambled back down the fire escape out into the street, the palms of both hands burned loose.

Legion had Blossom with him if she wasn't dead already. First place that motherfucker would head for was the safe house to check out the stash and wait for us. Roosevelt wanted Beatrice and I wanted Blossom. No choice. I got back into the car and headed for the Upper West Side. Told Roosevelt about what I'd seen in Legion's apartment. He just shook his bloody head and said, We gonna go out fighting now.

All quiet down at the safe house. No people, no cars, no sign of any cops. Legion didn't really have anything on us and he couldn't risk anyone, especially not other cops, finding out about the stash. If he was here, the only other soul with him was Blossom.

Roosevelt got out the car, carrying the giant key and a suitcase for the stash. I followed with the nightstick and a suitcase of my own. Safe house didn't have a door, just a long dark yawning hallway. I switched on the Caddie lights. Yellow beams splashed down the corridor. Sure it was like a fucking invitation to the whole of Manhattan, but we were desperate. Both of us with everything to lose. Roosevelt squeezed my hand as we entered. Split up, he said. If I find anything I'll let you know.

He took a stairway that curved up to the left. I kept right on down the hallway. There were doors either side quite a way on. All of them locked. None of them with keyholes like the one we were looking for. Corridor sloped down into darkness. Air grew hotter. Hints of sulphur sifting. I couldn't get those scorched walls and bloody footprints out of my mind. Couldn't stop thinking I'd as good as killed Blossom with my own hands. And then the lights went out. I almost puked. More scared then than I have ever been in my life. I fumbled for matches in my pocket. Lit one. Roosevelt's voice rose out of the glow. Faulkner! Faulkner!

He must've been real excited or real afraid, shouting out in a place like that. I gripped the nightstick and clanked back up the corridor, feeling my way, guided by the far-off lights of New Jersey. Skin slipped off of both melted palms. Dust, grit and splinters working up a rage.

Lights on the landing at the top of the stairs. I scrambled up and fell back on my ass when I found a twenty-foot-high door opened on a glittering hoard: gold coin, diamonds, jewels, millions of bills and there on the ground by my feet, one of my gold feathers. A voice like a landslide said, Howdy, and Legion lunged out of the shadows, grabbed me by the throat, lifted me off the ground. The nightstick spun out of my hand. Fucking fingers melting my neck. I couldn't make out his face. Couldn't make out anything. Choking to death. He held me up like I was a little doll, carried me through the doorway and over the golden mountain.

Fucker gave me a real good throttling. I tried to punch, kick, but my hands and feet wouldn't reach him. Close to blacking out when he threw me down into a chair and ripped off my clothes. Bound me with rope before I knew where I was.

First thing I saw was Roosevelt. He was naked too, tied to another chair opposite. The room was stone floored and walled. Lit by a single bulb. A sink on the wall to my left but that was all.

Are you OK?

Roosevelt tried to speak but couldn't. He spat and nodded.

Legion stepped out from behind me. Sweet, he said.

Sick fuck. He was wearing his regulation boots, pants and hat, but he was shirtless. His torso was tanned and weathered – same kind of sagging leathery look as those Iron Age motherfuckers they dig out of peat bogs every once in a while – oiled up like a Greek wrestler's.

He started on a slow-motion workout in the middle of the floor – hamstrings, ligaments, biceps, abdomen and back – made sure we got a good idea of just how far he could go. A huge motherfucker of a man, limbering up before he crushed us.

The rustle of hair in his armpits as he tensed and stretched, the nightstick sheathed in his belt, more of a club, scraping against the ground whenever he swung low. And that shadow – pitch-black twin, lagging behind his movements – with a sound all its own.

I couldn't see a way out.

Legion walked around the back of Roosevelt's chair and lifted him above his head. He strutted around the room a few times like a giant slave carrying a king's litter, then launched everything into the air. Roosevelt's face took the full force of the landing –

nose and cheekbones broke, neck fucked, blood
flashed out in a star shape. Roosevelt still tied to the
chair, face mushed against the ground, snorting like a
fucking racehorse. Monster cop dropped down until
their heads were level. Cranked his way through one
hundred and fifty press-ups, counting every one.

I was screaming all the way. All the fucking way, but
Legion kept pumping.

He flexed his biceps when he finished, pulled
Roosevelt upright and lit a match under his nose.
Roast his fucking nose just after he broke it. Roosevelt
screaming, me screaming, Legion frowning. He hurts,
he said. He hurts.

When Roosevelt's snuffling blew out the match,
Legion swung around behind him, hooked two fingers
up his bloody nostrils and hauled back with all his
weight, grinding the already splintered bone.

Roosevelt wept.

You get the fuck away from him, you *motherfucker*!

Cop just glared at me. You're Blossom's sweetheart,
right? You should see what we done to her. He closed
his eyes. You gotta see it.

He lifted Roosevelt off the ground by the ears and bit
the bridge of his nose.

I screamed above more screaming. What the fuck
have you done with Blossom!

Roosevelt landed on his face again as Legion let him
go and strolled towards me. He put his arm around my
neck. Skin was fucking scorching. Burned me up.
Burns all over. Got his lips right in at my ear. Fucking
lips grilling my ear and he says, We're gonna make
broads outta botha yous, just like we made your sweetheart into a man.

He pulled me closer, wormed his freak tongue into
my earhole, screwed a finger so far into my bellybutton

the knot nuzzled my spine. Somehow managed to pulp my balls with the same hand, a white-hot shock made me spray grey puke all over his shoulder. Motherfucker made me puke a second time and tried to kiss me. Then he rolled off into a handstand. Kept it up, legs in the air, counting down sixty seconds. When he kicked back onto his feet, he pulled a knife out a side pocket of his pants, and, no fucking ceremony, sliced off both Roosevelt's nipples. See ya later, he said, and carried that sobbing Negro by the neck into the room next door.

I strained at those ropes like a motherfucker. Got one hand free when the screaming started. Roosevelt's voice, growing hoarse against Legion's roar. POW! POW! Only Legion left by the time I got my other hand free. SHEEYAATCH! KERRRUNCH!

Another quieter voice scared the shit out of me. For the love of Jesus, what's going on here?

It was the broken cop we'd stuffed in the Caddie trunk. He crept into the room, gun in hand, but he was in a bad way. Roosevelt and me had made quite a mess of him.

There's a murder going on in that room there, I said.

You stay right where you are, he said, limping towards the door.

I got my other hand free. Caught up with him as the shooting started. Saw Legion charging with his club. His arm slicked beetroot-red to the elbow. Took six bullets in the head and heart to down him, but the momentum carried him forwards, an avalanche of outsize arms and legs that crushed me and the bust-up officer against the wall. I landed right, got myself out from under there real quick, but both cops were ruined.

Roosevelt sat slumped against the wall, blue-black

blood pooling between his spread legs. He had three toes and one finger missing, no nipples, thick strips of flesh ripped from his thighs and not much left of a nose. I helped him to his feet, dragged us both into the hallway. All I could think of, even then, was Blossom, and all Roosevelt could say was, Money, get the money, words bursting over his lips in blood bubbles.

Somehow I found my way back to the stash. My clothes were scattered there along with the night-stick and suitcase. I gave Roosevelt my coat, and that nonchalant nigger, with his fucked fingers and no nose, smoked one of my cigarettes as I scrambled round on my hands and knees scooping as much booty as I could manage.

We tumbled down a different set of stairs. No sign of Blossom anywhere. No sense of her. I tried to comfort myself that even if she was dead, I'd done the decent thing, but that fucker just wouldn't stick.

A hundred half-lit passages later, we came back upon the torture chamber. Roosevelt grabbed my arm, still swooning, and said, I'm gonna pay that cop my last respects.

No way, I said, we've got to get out of here. Got to make it to the *Columbus* before sun-up.

He pulled away from me. Nothing I could do but follow him through the blood-, piss- and puke-stained first room. The Caddie-trunk cop was in the second, curled up fucked on the floor.

Legion was gone.

Roosevelt let out a low moan. Fear and agony. I was about ready to die.

We lunged out. Another half-hour of darkness and dread before we found an exit. The car was where we'd left it. Dash was mostly melted along with the wheel and driver seat. Familiar stench of sulphur. Loot on the back seat, cos the cop had blasted his way out the trunk with the handgun, I spun us out of there, speeding all the way down to the docks. Parked in some lot. We got changed into our glitter band suits where we sat. I cleaned Roosevelt up with my civilian shirt and mouthfuls of spit. Wasn't much I could do with his nose in the end, and he was going to have to keep his bad hand out of sight.

We bailed with the suitcase full of loot, I looked in through the window, checking for anything we forgot. Nothing left but a pool of blood where Roosevelt'd been sitting.

I don't know what we looked like boarding that ship at six o'clock in the morning, but KC, Roosevelt's contact, didn't seem too bothered. He showed us to a double room below decks. Real luxury compared with the dives we'd stayed in in the city.

Roosevelt crashed out on the bed while I took a shower. Was drying myself when there was a knock at the door. I tied the towel round my waist and limped into the room. Roosevelt was holding the door open for someone; a silhouette stepping out of the sunlight. My heart stopped. Blocked my throat. It was Blossom, looking more like eighty than eighteen, but still Blossom. I ran at her and she collapsed into my arms, bashing all three of us back onto the bed. Every one of us fucked way up, but right then, laughing out loud.

Things even the most common souls will do for love.

Faulkner leaned back, basking in the spotlight. He unclipped the microphone, jumped into the air and when his feet hit the ground the band launched into a heavyweight cover of Swans' 'Cop'.

belly and entrails

belly and entrails

In which Bohemond contemplates the constitution of his corpulence and accepts a deadly gift.

—Fuck's sake man, if you get any bigger I'm going to have to invest in a set of mountaineering tools.

Bohemond lay naked, face-down on his bed, rocking gently as Morrissey clawed a way up to the summit of his back. He crashed out in the valley between the head chef's shoulderblades. Plucked a pack of Silk Cut from his shorts' pocket.

Tongue, teeth and lips tangling with quilt cover, Bohemond mumbled, —Don't even think about it, Morrissey. I don't pay you to smoke. You're here to give me a massage.

Morrissey stropped. He threw the cigarettes onto the floor, rolled around onto his knees and attacked the eternal tundra of Bohemond's blubber, whacking at the fat with his hands and feet, kneading the neck, digging deep for the vertebrae, every manoeuvre reminiscent of a more desperate act. As for Bohemond, his submission was spoiled by the anxiety that Morrissey's heels and fists felt that bit more distant,

191

much less threatening. This kind of flagellation was no longer penance enough. He was just too huge. Nothing left to save him but love.

Fifteen minutes later Morrissey collapsed onto the vast expanse of Bohemond's back, rested his head against the pillow of his buttocks and said: —Right: Seeta. What're you going to do?

—I'm going to the party and at some point I'll ask her about Paris.

—Wait till she's drunk, and *bang*.

—I don't want to run the risk of embarrassing her here in Delphi.

—You just going to embarrass her in front of her other friends instead.

—All I want is the truth.

—You know the truth. Best thing you can do is play concerned. Get her to admit to Hermione that she's been at it, but still make her believe you're doing what's best for her, watch as Hermione and Paris fall apart, and lie back and wait for your rebound-thankyou-shag.

—I just want to protect her from humiliation. Paris falls so short of her, she's been having virtual sex on the internet.

Morrissey spun onto his front, swung around and hung his head over Bohemond's shoulder. —*No way!*

—I wasn't going to tell you, but things are starting to make so much more sense.

—*Ooh* . . . she's fucking deep, Hermione. Bohemond felt Morrissey shake his head. —Deep and dark. Stuff you wouldn't want to get into.

—You know she was in an abusive relationship?

—*See?* Damaged goods.

—The first time I saw her she was living with her boyfriend in the flat above my bedsit. They fought all the time. Seemed like my ceiling was always rumbling. Then I'd see her in the street and she'd look so lonely. So *innocent*.

—Fff! *Piss off.*

—Look hard and you'll see a great deal of vulnerability, Morrissey. I hate to say it, but I've always felt that life has, in some sense, betrayed her, just as it's betrayed me. And now she's with Paris because, behind all the breeziness, she doesn't think she deserves any better.

—Listen to you! *Hermione's been betrayed by life.* She's vulnerable, she's innocent, she's this, she's that! *No-one's* innocent! She can have anything she wants. She *gets* whatever she wants. She's gorgeous. She's got money. Last thing she needs is a sad case like you trying to protect her.

—All the good looks and riches in the world are no substitute for love.

—Crap. You're making her sound like she's a child, or something. *I told you*, she tried to get it on with me in the bar. It's just fucking women batting their eyelids and wiggling their arses and getting their own way out of it.

—I only mean that Hermione and I are two of a kind. We've had similar troubles.

—Wank, wank, wank, wank, wank.

—It's the truth.

—You're full of more shit than Hanswurst. Morrissey rolled over, sliding down Bohemond's back until his head became wedged against a shoulderblade. —And believe me, he's full of it.

—God, what now?

—Last night, said Morrissey, —after we finished, Christmas spirit and that, I went back to his bit with him. We got some wine and whiskey, thought we'd make a night of it watching some of his videos. He's got tons: bit of snuff, bestiality, blah blah blah. But anyway . . . and this is proof he's an evil bastard . . . he brings out this one video, and says, This is going to knock your socks off. I just got it in today from up the river. He puts it on and I promise you, you've never seen anyone turn so pale so quick. There's two guys on the screen blowing each other, and Hanswurst, fuck, he looks like he's seen a ghost. He puked all over the carpet. But it was *black*. His puke. Black with little yellow lumps. And I *promise* you, there was something splashing about in it. This thing like a tadpole or a newt or something. Something living anyway. It had *tiny little legs on it*! Came out his fucking *mouth*!

Bohemond grimaced. —He didn't get that out of my kitchen.

—For fuck's sake, it was living. It had *legs* on it!

—I'm sure it did, Morrissey. You should've had a look in his fridge.

—You going to heal all society's ills with one wave of a spatula?

—Our stomach is our body's kitchen.

—Yeah, right.

—William Vaughan, *Directions for Health, Natural and Artificial*, London, 1626.

—So . . . ?

—So Hanswurst is a bad chef. Would you fetch my clothes now, please?

Morrissey vaulted onto the floor and darted behind the dresser. Slow to bowl onto his feet, Bohemond took a long look in the mirror.

His belly glimmered like a misty still of Jupiter.

And that killed him.

It killed him because there was something very pure indeed beating underneath those fathoms of flesh. A current that coursed his core, his wick, his set and essence, the mighty leitmotif found in Cellini's *Perseus* and Donatello's *David*. Yet, whatever it was, that dreaming seed, it had been misplaced, or incorrigibly bound up with how he was bound up, all form and no demonstrable content, the head chef left with the petulance and protuberance, none of the exuberance, nonchalance or youth.

The idea was that the candlelight might soften suggestion. Spark a daydreamed shift of fatty matter in the shadows. But his imagination wouldn't accommodate that depth of pure fantasy. Gluttony engulfed the God-given range of his frame. It spread him out like salmon paste and swallowed him like quicksand.

On one hand he was in illustrious company, strolling the heights with Balzac who once brunched on a hundred Ostend oysters, twelve pré-salé mutton cutlets, a duckling with turnips, a brace of roast partridges and a sole normande, not to mention a selection of soups and fruits; with Zola who claimed his appetite was the only thing that mattered to him; Vitellius Caesar, Marlon Brando, Orson Welles, and a hundred others. But these were men of action – bruisers like Roosevelt – the food they consumed fuel or reward for noble endeavour. Whereas food was the *object* of most of Bohemond's efforts.

The rear view was only slightly less cruel. He hugged himself, eyeing the birthmark beneath his shoulderblade, the one that seemed to shrink day by day, its contraction having less to do with *it* than it had to do with *him*. Just over a month ago, in this very embrace, he'd been able to see four fingers one knuckle deep pressing into the flesh on either side of his back. Now there were only three fingertips on one side – Bohemond in the throes of an unwanted pregnancy. He let go of himself. Knots of real grief tightening in his chest. —You must learn to love yourself, he said.

And in truth, there was much to love. He wasn't like Hanswurst – an evil bastard with worms and spiders crawling around inside his belly. His body's kitchen brimmed with sumptuous ingredients. After all, his breath smelled of buttermilk, and his blood was sweet as blackjack, his spit smacked of satsuma, and his sperm of silverside, his sweat reeked of peaches and his tears of toso, his piss whiffed of pistachio and his shit stank of saffron, while his farts, funnily enough, had the fragrance of freshly baked focaccia. It stood to reason that if what Morrissey had suggested were true, if a person's outward disposition was a reflection and projection of their intestinal temperament, then his guts were good as gold.

He'd prove that tonight with Seeta.

—Is all this stuff from that Ali? Morrissey laid a gold shirt, a brown suede waistcoat and black trousers on the bed.

—That's *Eli*, said Bohemond, —and yes it is.

He was a friend of Hermione's father – an Italian dressmaker with a cutting room in the basement of his Covent Garden shop – who made Bohemond clothes in exchange for free meals and home deliveries.

—You might want these as well. He handed Bohemond a brown paper bag.

—What's this?

—Photographs of the happy couple out on the town.

—*Oh God*. Bohemond's naked body suddenly submerged under a wave of sweat. —You *did* do it.

—You think I was lying?

—I don't know if I can take these.

—Those are the best ones.

—As a last resort . . .

196

Morrissey nodded. —I'd fire straight in with them, but it depends what you're after.

Stupefied, Bohemond almost floated into his clothes. The man in the mirror made him smile, mostly because he looked so much better dressed than undressed. Hands spread wide, he beamed, nearly speechless, Morrissey nodding at his side.

ambrosia

Several confessions and a moment of madness.

Seeta was already waiting in the foyer when Bohemond came down the stairs. She was wearing a red leather jacket, with black leather trousers, a gold satchel strapped to her back. Undone hair spread over her shoulders. Flecks of glitter at the corners of her eyes. Her smiles slowed Bohemond down, momentarily mellowing his own too-eager misgivings. —You look wonderful, he said.

—You too.

A black cab crawled past the window.

—Ready? Seeta hugged Bohemond's arm.

He sucked in but the air wouldn't go down, so he nodded.

She tugged him out into the street, fighting for balance as he reeled and teetered, suspicious of the slush. Bohemond opened the cab door, Seeta slid inside, held out a hand to steady him as he stepped up, but his great weight rocked the chassis, knocking her against the window. By the third attempt he managed to force his way in – Seeta gripping his lapels, hauling with all her weight, catapulted into the corner as he splashed across the back seat. Arms and legs awry, Bohemond lay panting. The slush-spattered hems of either trouser-leg clung to his ankles. Strands of hair plastered his brow and curled around corners of his mouth. Three puffs of Ventolin set him trembling. Seeta closed the door and opened one of the spring-shut seats. She sat down. Patted his knee. Gave him a smile that her pity twisted.

Black cabs weren't built for bodies like Bohemond's, and this one sounded more like a snowplough when it took off, its shafts or axles not quite robust enough, carving gutters in the asphalt. Shifting to the window opposite Seeta certainly killed the racket, but the whole cab slanted to his starboard. He brushed hair out of his mouth. Put the inhaler in his pocket. Seeta let his fluster fade to just fussing. Kept quiet as he began to relax.

—I'm sorry, Seeta.

—Are you OK now?

—Fine. You?

—Just freezing. She leaned forwards and flicked the fan switch. A short while of silence as she sat back and studied him. —It's funny, she said at last, —but whenever I see you outside of the restaurant you look a lot smaller or something. Younger too.

—I'm not as old as you think.

—No?

—Believe me.

—I've thought about this before, you know.

—Go on.

—Forty-five.

Bohemond chortled. —Try ten years younger, and then some.

—No way.

—Yes way.

—You're in your thirties?

—Only just.

—So how come you lecture us all like a senior citizen?

He felt her delight and couldn't help melting. Whatever the mess, she was one of the three best friends he'd ever had. —I used to be a bit of a goth, he said. —So I've had lots of practice at talking all kinds of esoteric tosh with what seems like the utmost authority.

Seeta's grin had frozen. —*You used to be a goth?*

—I thought that might be a little before your time.

—A *goth*. Like those old Duran Duran fans, but all in black with make-up and stuff and songs about corpses?

—Not a full blown Sisters of Mercy goth . . . And anyway, it sort of happened by accident.

—How the fuck do you become a *goth* by accident?

—When I first came to England, said Bohemond, curling his fingers into fists, —I hitched lifts all the way from the convent. A truck driver picked me up on the outskirts of Orléans along with a young English couple, Paul and Rosie, and brought us all over. When we reached London, Rosie invited me to stay with them until I got myself organized. So I wound up in a derelict Victorian block in Hackney that the two of them squatted with some friends.

—No way.

—It was through them I was exposed to all the goth stuff, and I suppose I embraced it mainly to fit in. Don't get me wrong, I loved the music and the look; I still love the music. But first and foremost I just wanted to find another home and live some kind of a life.

—Dark horse.

—You and Hermione are the only people who know.

—Can't believe it.

—I dressed all in black and wore make-up, but I liked Joy Division, Dead Can Dance, more *gothic* than goth really. Thing was, though, I didn't really possess the classic pale-skinned and waif-like look necessary. I looked like a fool and everyone must've thought so.

—Doubt it, Bohemond.

—Well don't. A block full of nubile nymphomaniacs, hormones steaming, but not one of them gave me a second glance. The most they'd ever do was cry on my shoulder about some failing relationship . . . And it was always the girls who'd come . . . always the girls.

—Unlucky.

—The very women who came to my bed in the dead of night to reveal their innermost were the very women who often only a moment before had been revealing their outermost to some effeminate goth boy in a dark corner of the tenement. And they would talk with me, Seeta, as if I were above these things; as if I'd be totally unaffected by their tales of blood and lust. But I was young too . . . Subject to the same appetites and desires.

—Sounds like Hell, she said. —How long were you in there?

—I lasted about a year. Couldn't bear it in the end. It was the first time I realized that I was different. So often, in my room, so close to kissing, and in the same breath being asked if I didn't prefer Bob Marley or James Brown over Echo and the Bunnymen.

—The Eighties, Seeta sighed. —What a waste of fucking time.

—I moved to a bedsit in Brixton. But being on my own was worse than not being wanted. One morning, I just . . . stayed in bed. Didn't get up until Hermione fell through my window more than a month later.

—You're bullshitting me!

—That's how we met. She was going through all sorts of trouble with her boyfriend at the time. Bad enough, would you believe, that she climbed out of one of the windows of their second-floor flat at three o'clock in the morning to escape him.

—*Hermione?* And she fell?

—Straight through my skylight.

—I had no idea.

—It was a long time ago.

—How long?

—Nearly fifteen years.

—Jesus . . . I was six.

—Luckily the junk on my floor broke her fall. She saw me lying down, the state I was in, and, not sparing a thought for herself, hauled me out of bed and into the shower. I remember watching her undress, no embarrassment or coyness, just the clothes peeled off and scattered: the silver-glitter one-piece, like a suit of armour, the miniskirt and pink day-glo trainers. Even in that semi-sensible, half-starved state, I was amazed that someone who'd just fallen through my roof could be so cool.

—Ice-cool back then too?

—Oh yes.

—Super-detached Hermione . . . And you showered . . . together?

—I remember how the water round our feet rusted up with blood when she climbed in . . . How after she washed herself, she washed me. I can't tell you how that made me feel . . . her hands, Seeta, soft as . . . *oh* . . . Thinking about it now, all these years on, I still fill up . . .

—Then what?

—Nothing. Just a single look from her that said it all. Then she left.

—What kind of a look?

—If I told you, you'd think I was being pretentious.

—*You?* Pretentious?

Bohemond paused. —It was the look I'd been waiting for all my life. And it's the one I hope to be the focus of again before too long.

—From Hermione?

—Hermione's getting married to Paris.

—So I hear.

—That said, we're closer now than we ever were. When she left that first time I didn't see her for another year. She phoned occasionally, but she never wrote. When I did see her, it was only for a few days and then there was a gap of two years. That's how it went at first. On and off. I wrote to her. Kept her up to date with what I was doing. Then one summer she turned up and offered me a job as a chef at Delphi.

—The way you talk about her, Bohemond . . . Seeta shook her head gently; —. . . your eyes go funny and your voice kind of creeps off.

—. . . It was just that look she gave me, Seeta. It woke me up.

—You're in love with her, aren't you?

—I told you, he said, his voice weakening, —Hermione's with Paris now.

—So?

—So she's off-limits.

—That doesn't mean you can't be in love with her.

—I know. He looked away. —I know.

As Seeta gazed out the window again, she murmured, —What do you think of the two of them getting married, really?

203

Bohemond braced himself. —Can I be honest with you?

—*Yikes* . . .

—You remember what I said about Hermione being able to see things in Paris that we couldn't?

—Yeah.

—Well . . . he fixed his eyes upon Seeta's, —. . . I think there are things she *hasn't* been able to see, too.

—Like wh—

—For some reason . . . and you have to understand, I'm not passing judgement . . . people change and no-one's to blame for that . . . I mean *I* don't feel the same way I did even a month ago, so you see even in that short time you could say I'm a different person, and what I mean by that is, it's not black and white, not simply about right and wrong, but at the same time, I can't stand back and let . . .

—Bohemond, get to the point.

—Oh . . . deep breath, a split-second blackout, dazed, disoriented, —. . . I think Paris is having an affair.

A single solemn nod, Seeta glared at the ground, her jaw rippling.

—I'm not making any accusations, Seeta, it's all down to circumstance, fate, no-one's to blame . . . Hermione's at a vulnerable time in her life . . . abusive relationships have sapped her confidence, *not that* Paris is in any way abusive, I meant the boyfriend she lived with above my bedsit, other men she's been with, but like I said I'm not pointing the finger, it's simply a question of circumstance, things being the way they're supposed to be, and all I'm trying to do is the right thing, because I don't want to see Hermione hurt or humiliated, and I know no-one would do that on purpose, but because I love her, *as a friend*, because

204

she means everything to me, absolutely *everything*, which isn't to say I don't love you too, but that shower changed my life, it was the most beautiful moment of my life so far, and believe me, this is a life in need of . . .

Seeta leaned back, her voice just short of a whisper.

—You're *completely* obsessed.

—*But if you could've seen the look she gave me, or if you'd ever heard Innocent talk about his life with Sara his wife, you'd understand . . . Even Faulkner . . .*

—*Christ*, you really *are* in love with her, aren't you?

He coughed, passions racing, overtaking him.

—Aren't you?

—All I'm trying to do is protect her.

—You go *on* and *on* about true love, but if it's anything like you say, who needs it. *Look* at you, Chef. I'm sorry but you're a fucking mess, what with your fairy tales and everything . . . And as for Innocent, a fat lot of good true love has done him. The man's a *wreck*.

—But if you can imagine how it must feel, said Bohemond, —to love someone with all your heart – until you think it is impossible to love them any more – and yet know they love you just as much, it stands to reason that if you love like Innocent did, when it slips away you're changed for ever.

—You're making him sound like Peter-effing Pan.

—But it's true. When Sara went back to Poland he lost touch, but he never forgot her . . . Sixteen years old, living in Holland, he went looking for her . . . Two weeks he searched the length and breadth of Poland and nothing . . . so he jumped on a freight train and started making his way back.

—Told you he's mad.

—But wait. He woke next morning, found the train stopped at a small town in the mountains and got off to

205

stretch his legs. As he wandered around he heard a choir, tracked the sound down to an old synagogue and sat on the steps so hypnotized by the song that he found himself able to distinguish between each of the voices, which believe it or not seemed to take on seraphic form.

—They *what*?

—Imagine, Seeta, day dawning and poor old Innocent lying on the steps of a mountain church, practically wiping the sleep out of his eyes and these voices appearing to him as angels.

—Ah *Christ* . . .

—And they had faces, one of which he recognized as Sara's. He ran into the church and spotted her red hair immediately. She was one of the sopranos. And that's how they were reunited.

Seeta grimaced. —And did you have angels fluttering around your head too, after this look Hermione gave you?

—Nothing so vivid. It was as I said: just a quick glimpse of Paradise. He gazed out across docks, open-mouthed, blinking softly. —I often wonder . . . had it not been for that look all those years ago, whether I'd still be here.

wings

In which Bohemond survives two explosions and saves an angel.

Packed houses always brought to Bohemond's acute attention just how far his body, particularly his belly, preceded him. At such times the discrepancy between where he was and where he felt himself to be caused no end of injury.

As soon as she saw them, Seeta screamed and surged at her friends. Bohemond twitched as she slipped between people, his mouth watering at a vision of himself ferried along on her coat-tails, making reins of her hair. He bolted back a pint of rising bile and followed on, trying to ignore fitful resistance – his belly buffeted by elbows and shoulders. Bag straps snagged on his fingers and heels. Stocky young men squared up to his shoulder-blades over spilled pints and crushed feet. Just shuffling, as he was, made him moving epicentre of a domino effect that knocked those nearest off-balance, damage increasing in amplitude towards outlying reaches of the room where canoodling couples hidden under lintels were bulldozed onto one another – the fruits of butterfly-light flirtation butchered by cigarette burns, chipped teeth and cruel wineglass wounds.

The first person Seeta kissed, a beautiful Oceanian boy, whispered in her ear. Bohemond caught every word. *Who's the medieval drag queen?* was hardly the worst slur he'd ever heard, but chasing the million muttered nigger quips and fat ass remarks he'd borne over the last ninety seconds, not to mention the playful slap and gasp it'd elicited from Seeta, it was enough to make him wish he'd never come. He wobbled to a halt, worn out by all the clowning and livid looks, the weight of poorly chosen clothes, hot lights grilling the back of his neck, seizures in the vicinity of his kidneys. Ninety fucking seconds and already he was pining for far-off places.

He waded towards the bay windows and stepped out onto the balcony overlooking the square. A warm westerly wind smothered some of his resentment. City-lit sky cluttered with cloud. New Year's Eve. —Love yourself, he muttered. —Do what you came to do.

His gut rumbled, a tiny flood forced by the fragrance of candyfloss and hotdogs, by the reek of commercial kitchens crammed into all corners of the district. Every restaurant had its own smell and those clustered around Covent Garden stank of overblown ambition and second-rate standards: too little puff in the feuilletage, too much butter in the hard sauce, over-egged jaunemange, underdone tongue, the musk of rotting dolcelatte and wet nectarines.

A mime on a two-storey monocycle juggled flaming clubs in front of St Paul's Church. The brands twirled high above the heads of the gathered crowd, and on a count of three exploded. Bohemond ducked under a roaring umbrella of fire, glimpsed its white light winking brilliantly on the faces down below. A garland of smoke hung in the air above the church clock. Fingers pointed and mouths rounded as a flock of what looked like flamingos swept out of its depths and soared over the southside roofs towards Charing Cross.

Suddenly Seeta was upon him, hands tangled in his hair, a blur of pouting painted lips quick clue to a kiss that slid from the corner of his mouth and smooched along his jowl, finishing off as a whisper that wet the shell of his ear. —You're just fucking brilliant, she said. —Obsessive ex-goth or not, I love you.

He pulled himself away, managed a smile.

As the birds disappeared and applause petered out, the breeze brought promise of fresh pandemonium: distant drums and fanfares slowly solidifying until the square was overrun by a pageant of outsize cuddly toys. Huge-headed teddy bears, lions, racoons, monkeys and wolves bounced around, waving and dancing, and at the tail end, divorced from the main, moving in another direction, a giant black cat swaggered on stilts.

—Jesus Christ, said Seeta, bent over the rail of the balcony. —What is this?

Everything had to be said. And right now. —I found something, Seeta . . . which I think perhaps belongs to you.

—Oh yeah. She turned around, her smile fading as she gaped at the envelope he held in a trembling hand. —Right . . . what is it?

—You don't know?

—A letter?

—I found it in the magazine you were reading a few weekends ago.

—What magazine?

—I was . . . simply leafing through it and this dropped out.

She glanced at the people standing beside them. —Did it really?

—I thought it might belong to you.

—OK. If you found it way back then and thought it was mine, why didn't you bring it to me before now?

—I forgot all about it.

—Have you read it?

Bohemond's neck prickled.

—Well?

He took the appearance of a giant cuddly snake as a sign. —No.

—Give us a look.

—It might be personal.

—Probably a shopping list.

—You haven't even told me if it's yours or not.

—How do you know it's not some ad from the magazine?

—I *don't* know, said Bohemond.

—So have a look.

He squeezed the envelope open and peeked at the folded page. —Definitely handwritten.

—That doesn't mean *anything*, Seeta sighed, her breath breaking up. They do shit like that all the time: ads that're supposed to look like private letters. Open it.

—I . . .

She plucked the letter out of his grasp and turned away again. Bohemond didn't make a move. Gripped the rail until his toes curled.

A man was attacking a phone box at the corner of the square. He dashed the handset against the console. Threw himself into drop kicks and head butts. Someone thrashed the windows with a baseball bat, glass splinters showering down on the heads of fluffy crocodiles. The box rocked like the taxi cab Bohemond had almost capsized and he rolled his eyes at the recollection, a couple kissing on a nearby rooftop wheeling into his field of vision.

—You thought I wrote this? Seeta had finished reading and flashed something like a smile – all shine and no delight.

—I thought someone wrote it to you.

Her eyes darkened. —You liar.

Bohemond hobbled back. The moment misjudged.

—You said you hadn't read it.

—I'm worried about you, Seeta. I thought this letter might have something to do with how upset you've been. Something to do with you inviting me to this party.

—*For fuck's sake*, she hissed, —how self-obsessed can you *be*? I invited you here because I wanted to come with you, not because I've got no-one else to go with. And that's no excuse. If you thought this letter was mine, *no way* should you have read it.

—It is yours . . . isn't it?

—Course it's *fucking* mine. She leaned against the rail, shaking with rage.

—Seeta, *please*, calm down.

—I'm not angry with you . . . I'm not angry with you.

—I'm just trying to do the right thing.

—Reading my private mail?

—I'm only trying to protect Hermione.

Seeta slowed down, dumbfounded. —You what?

—I know . . . about you . . . and Paris.

—About *me and Paris*?

—Please don't deny it. I can see by the look on your face that you know what I'm talking about. But as I said in the taxi, I'm not here to make accusations.

—What are you *talking* about?

211

—I know that you and he have been having an affair. That this letter is from him.

—Did *he* tell you that?

—No I . . . found out.

—I can't believe I'm hearing this. *How?* How did you find out?

—The letter.

—And I'm fucking telling you it's *not from him*!

—And Morrissey saw you.

—He what?

—Look, Seeta . . . let me help you.

—What did he see?

—There's a chance we can sort out all of this without anyone getting hurt.

—What did he *see*?

—You and Paris . . . together in the West End.

—Bollocks!

—He *did*.

—That *fucking little prick*! That fucking, shit-stirring, little *prick*!

—Seeta, *please* . . . calm down.

—*Don't tell me to calm down!* You're all so *fucking* . . . she raised her hands and spun a half-circle, snarling, —. . . *self righteous!* Fucking two-faced little *bastard*. Liar!

The men behind her rumbled.

—Seeta, it's not a lie.

—You're taking his word over *mine*?

—Please don't deny it.

—Are you?

—*Seeta?*

—Cos I'll fucking cut you off, Chef. I'll cut you dead. I can't *believe* you'd take his word over mine. That little shit-stirring . . . *cunt*!

Bohemond's strength melted. —You've been under a

212

lot of pressure . . . I understand you're upset . . .

—*Chef . . . Chef* . . . she waved her hands in the air.
—Let's just get this over with right now. Are you taking
his word over mine? Cos if you are, you and me are
finished. As friends . . . we're finished.

—Seeta, don't make me . . .

—I'm pissed off about it, but at the end of the day, I
don't give a shit if you think me and Paris are going
out. Same with you reading my letter. But if you're
taking the word of that fucking *wanker* over mine . . .

—But Seeta . . . I've got proof.

—*Proof?* Of *what?* All you've got is *bullshit!*

—No. He took the photographs from his pocket,
Seeta snatched them from him. She ripped open the
bag and, head shaking, weighed each one in her hand.
Bohemond reached out when he saw the tears rolling
down her cheeks, but she jerked back, frantically wiping her face. —Who took these?

—Morrissey.

—Did he . . . send the letters? The ones that got us to
meet up. Outside Tower.

Bohemond nodded.

—Did you *know?*

—He . . . said he might send something . . . but I told
him not to.

—But you still brought these here.

—Seeta, listen . . .

—That's some obsession, Chef.

—I told . . .

She leaped at him, slapping, punching, kicking,
crushing the photographs into his face. —First my
dad! And now this! You bastard! You bastard! YOU
BASTARD! YOU CUNT! YOU CUNT! YOU CUNT!
YOU CUNT!

Bohemond's eyes clouded over. He buckled as the

213

men behind Seeta rushed him. They twisted his arm behind his back, frog-marched him through the pub, practically threw him down the stairs. The impact of the landing bounced him up onto his feet and sent him in a southerly direction. Shaken but unscathed, he brushed himself down and wobbled on. If he had to sacrifice his friendship with Seeta to win Hermione, so be it. She'd lost it. Got it all wrong. Despite his failings, Morrissey was right: Seeta *was* a firebrand. Some kind of crazy. All Bohemond wanted was the best for every-one. Hadn't deserved the browbeating she'd given him. And to be ejected by those idiots, none of whom knew the *weight* of the situation. At least now he knew the truth.

He flagged a cab on the Strand and rode to the southern end of Tower Bridge. The air there was cooler. Pavements packed in ice. The steps descending to the quarter, treacherous. He turned away from the road home. Swung wide along the riverside. The quay was deserted, but the restaurants were full; dull rumour and drizzly windows slashed by a clear blast of cooking, music, voices, glass and silver glimmering as he passed an open door. Three waiters smoking cigars, squatted around an outdoor table. A fourth, in a feather boa, serenaded them with Solex songs.

Bohemond sat down on a bench facing the river, flashed back to how Seeta had attacked him, and burst into tears. The hurt and *hate* etched on her face. Her tiny ineffectual fists. For a moment he wished he'd crumbled under them. Given her the satisfaction of smashing his head in, of making absolutely *nothing* of him. But then again, that she hadn't come quietly was simply part of the karma. Another test in Bohemond's quest for Hermione's heart.

His moment of clarity was shattered by the sound of

footsteps clattering along Shad Thames, booming in the chasm of Maggie Blake's Cause, echoing against the windows of the waterfront restaurants. Lili and Mr Lewis were sprinting towards him, suit ties streaming over their shoulders. Bohemond stood up and began to hurry away but Lili hissed, —No! Bo! Wait!

He stopped and dabbed his eyes. Steeled himself against the prospect of snowballing shit.

Mr Lewis reached him first, huffing and heaving. —Holy heart attack, fatman, you and me are gonna have to go to the gym. Nice outfit, though.

Lili trotted up behind him, head and eyes darting as he slackened to a trot. —Have you seen anyone come along this way?

Bohemond backed up a step. —No.

—A blonde in a fur coat.

—No.

—I bet you haven't.

—I haven't.

Lili stooped. —Positive?

—Actually, I saw someone of that description some days ago.

—*Days ago?* You silly chocolate sausage.

Head bowed, Bohemond kept out of eye contact. —Not tonight. No.

—Well, if you do see her, shout out and let us know. OK? OK?

—Whatever you say.

Mr Lewis patted Lili on the back. —C'mon, he muttered. —Faulkner's going to be *so* pissed off.

They ran off, Bohemond blundering in their wake. He turned in the opposite direction on Shad Thames and crossed over on to Curlew Street, drifting past the ruined factory that hung over the corner. It was really nothing more than a crumbling façade. Its floor a power-drilled crater that plunged many metres below street level. He peeked through a gap in the barricaded doorway, and stumbled, stunned by a pair of slender white hands hooked over the last window ledge: seven luminous blue nails, the eighth – smallest on the left hand – missing, just a smooth nub at the first knuckle where the finger had been severed. The thumbs were angled back out of sight.

Slowly, ever so slowly, he leaned over the ledge, straining for a glimpse of whoever was hanging down the other side. —Are you all right?

No answer. He saw swirling strands of blonde hair, a glint of fake white fur before the scent of lavender forced his eyes closed. It could only have been the girl Lili and Mr Lewis were looking for. She'd climbed through one of the windows hoping to elude them in gloomy rooms, but hadn't reckoned on the lack of floorboards.

Bohemond glanced up and down the road. —Are you OK?

—*Fuck off!*

He jiggled back. —I'm not going to hurt you.

Silence.

—I'm alone. Lili and Mr Lewis have gone.

Still nothing. Voices curled from around the block.

—Oh God. It sounds like they're coming back. If you stay like that they'll find you . . . Please. If I was one of them I'd have grabbed you by now.

—And who might you be?

Bohemond's heart boomed. —My name's Bohemond, he said. —I'm a chef.

Streetlight brushed the paleness of a face cocked back in the darkness. —Well, Boomer, are you going get me out of here or not?

Her fingers were too cold, but as soon as he gripped

them she came floating up like a kite, blonde hair spilling across the sky. Bohemond beamed as she sailed out into the street, held tight, frightened that her weightlessness might take her out of reach. She descended, watching him all the while, and right then, with the New Year only moments away, deposits of frost and cumulus cloud, she was the most beautiful woman he'd ever seen.

—Thanks, she said, as her feet padded against the ground.

—No problem, he whispered, his vision swimming.

—I seem to attract fallen women. Or falling women anyway.

But she was already at the end of the crescent. One look over her shoulder as she slipped around the corner.

Bohemond lifted both hands over his nose, filling his lungs with lavender, waiting for the midnight bells – a sure sign that he'd done the right thing and wouldn't be forgotten – but the cold drove him on up the street.

red hot hands

Two lessons in longing.

Hermione's door was open. Golden in the glow of a single table lamp, she was sitting on the living-room floor with her back to the couch.

—*Hermione?*

She looked up.

—Where's Paris?

—Guess.

—I wouldn't have a clue.

—That's right.

—But it's New Year's *Eve*.

—Looks like we've both been jilted: I thought you and Seeta were going to make a night of it.

He glanced down at his damp trousers, the velvet shirt and suede waistcoat straining against his stomach.

—Come in, she said fingering the half-empty wine-glass on her lap.

Bohemond walked up the hall, into the living room and carefully lowered himself onto the floor beside her.

—*Poo* . . . you been seeing that woman again?

—What?

—Lavender man.

Only just able to recall the girl's face, the blue nails and weightlessness still vivid, he smiled and shrugged.

—Suits you.

—You wouldn't believe me if I told you.

She hummed, absence in her glances.

—Are you OK?

—No.

—It's Paris, isn't it?

—Partly.

—Why do you let him do this to you?

—Bohemond.

—I can't watch you being destroyed by yet another abusive relationship.

—I'm the one who messed up.

—It's not your fault, Hermione.

A long pause punctured by pealing bells, the distant litter of voices roaring, car horns and crackling fireworks. —Happy New Year, she said, and stretched out her arms. Bohemond watched her glide across him, bolting blood and near-delirium as she kissed him full on the mouth. He brought his hand up, her hair like a breeze on his fingers, and through some smooth move that he couldn't quite fathom she was sitting on his lap, cushioned by his belly, her head resting in the hollow of his neck. She brushed the back of a hand against his face, cherry scent sifting as she spoke. —You've got lipstick on you.

He tried to say, Seeta, but everything was obliterated by breathlessness.

Hermione shifted, her weight closing on Bohemond's crotch, prising apart his thighs. —What?

—I said, it was Seeta.

219

—She was on form then?

—Quite the opposite.

—Oh?

One, two, three. —Hermione, I found a letter.

—So?

—It was inside one of Hanswurst's magazines. It wasn't signed and I didn't recognize the handwriting. I feel awful about reading it, but—

—What did it say?

—I love you, more than I've ever loved anyone in my life, but because of circumstances beyond my control we have to split.

—It was Seeta's?

—Yes.

—Was she upset?

—Wouldn't you be?

She lifted her head and gazed at him, a long look that kept going. —You know, don't you?

Eyes wide, heart in his mouth: —*Hermione.*

—Are you surprised?

—*You knew all this time and didn't say anything.*

—I'm sorry, Bohemond.

—You've got no reason to feel ashamed, Hermione. I told you, it's not your fault.

—I always expected you'd say something like that.

—You sound as if you've known for a long time.

—For ever, she smiled. —It's not the sort of thing I feel like screaming from the rooftops, though. This thing with Seeta goes back to the night the fox jumped out of the mess-room garden?

—Hermione, *please* . . . Paris is no good for you. Leave him . . .

—You think I should?

—You deserve so much more.

She paused again. Minutes passing. Then slowly, —I

want to get married, I really do, but . . . I don't think I
love Paris any more.

—After what's happened with Seeta, I'm not surprised.

—I know you've never liked him.

—He walks all over you.

—But I've known him for ages and he's nowhere
near as bad as everyone makes out. I just want to settle
down, buy a house, have kids, real kids, with a real
husband.

—And I want the same things, but with someone I
love and who loves me.

—Can you imagine? Hermione ducked back down
against Bohemond's chest and, shortening the cycles of
her breathing to match his, fastened her arms more
tightly around him.

—What?

—You, me and a houseful of kids?

His toes, nose and fingers twitched. His tongue
turned somersaults.

—If you're anything like you are in here . . . she said
. . . —it'd be totally relaxed. Hassle-free. Everything
now is just so . . . *complicated*: Seeta and Paris, the
wedding, this place . . . I need to get away . . . get my
head together. How about it, Bo? We take off for a
while. Anywhere, I don't care. If it's any good, we don't
need to come back.

Fourteen years of wishing, and *at last* she was sat in
his lap, giving in to all the good. —So you *were* serious
about running away with me.

—Totally.

—I can't . . . believe it.

—What's to not believe?

—You? And me?

—It's got a ring to it.

221

—But where will we go?

—Where do you want to go?

—I'd follow you to the ends of the earth.

She kissed his breast through the damp fabric of his shirt.

—We could go now.

—Bohemond, it's New Year's Day. We'd get as far as the Bridge.

—Then when?

Hermione sat up, held his face in her hands. —Are you *sure* you want to do this?

—I've never been so sure of anything in all my life.

—I'm serious.

—If you could see yourself right now . . . the way your eyes are searching mine . . . and if you knew how long I'd been waiting for just such a look, you'd know that I am too.

—All right then. She let go of his face. Trailed her fingers through his hair. —I'm going to go and stay with a friend for a couple of days. I'll meet you on the third, at six o'clock, by the Tube, inside Liverpool Street station.

—What should I bring?

—The way I feel now, *right now*, I'm not coming back. So maybe you should bring everything.

—You really want me with you?

—. . . The night I fell through your window kind of changed my life. But . . . at the time I couldn't see it. I've spent too long ignoring all kinds of stuff that's just staring me in the face. I fell *two floors* for Christ's sake . . . I should be dead. But no, here I am, cos of you. It sounds mad, but . . . honestly . . . I think we were meant to meet. You've no idea how *warm* having you round here makes me feel. You've got a calmness of spirit or something. Like you're an old soul . . . just . . . totally *sussed*. I only wish I'd realized sooner.

Bohemond was choked. *Déjà vu* or dreams come true, he wasn't sure. —What if you change your mind?

She held his head in her hands again and kissed each closed eye. Toppled three empty wine bottles with outstretched legs as she tucked herself back into his embrace. Bohemond froze, not knowing what else to say, sweating even as the room cooled and he could see steam curling off his clothes. They sat like that a long time, not talking; Hermione's breathing deepening, her weight changing as she began to doze off, Bohemond, strung out, wondering whether he'd die of exposure before he had a chance to hear her full-blown declaration of love.

Though Bohemond woke to find Hermione gone, the joy in his heart was molten. He threw off the sheets with which she'd covered him, made sure she was in bed, and headed downstairs for a celebratory glass of champagne.

The mess-room light was on. Paris slumped over the table.

—Aw, Jesus, Bo, man.

Bohemond quashed a pinch of rage and guilt. —You're drunk.

—Weird shit tonight.

—So what's new?

He swayed to the side. —Have a seat.

—Hermione's upset, Paris.

—Sit.

—I'd rather stand. Where were you?

Paris ran a hand over his brow. —I was out with H for a New Year drink, but we got in a ruckus over the dress she had on. Chill, I said, wedding's not till the summer, and she stomps off. But I wasn't going to let it spoil my night. I wandered round for a while. Couple of other bars. Nothing much happening so I jumped on the last Tube at Embankment.

I'm sitting in the front carriage, right, it's totally empty, and some *guy* comes out the door that goes to the driver cab, y'know the one that has the Do Not Open Except In An Emergency on it. Fucking *massive* guy. Nothing like a driver. He's wearing this Gucci suit, carrying a big wallet, kinda Fonz-style hairdo, big grey ice-cream quiff. And fuck, I say it twice, but he was *giant*. Biggest, broadest guy I've ever seen, bent over just to fit on the fucking train. The carriage is empty, but he sits down right next to me. And this Godzilla guy, white guy, says in American, You and me bubba, we gotta stick together. And I say, Who's got to stick together? and he says, Us niggers. And I'm like, What did you say? And he says, You heard. Fair enough, I says. But Bo, he fucking stank. Clothes, manicure, gold Rolex, and he smells like a sewer.

After a while, he says, You wanna make some money? I'm still feeling a bit pissed-off with H, and even though this guy's creepy he's not intimidating or nothing, so I says, How much? He opens up the wallet and I know now there was over a grand in there. What's the catch, I say, and he's like, I locked myself out my apartment, all you gotta do is climb in through my window and open the door for me. And I say, Fuck yeah, this I can do, but why so much for one fucking key? And he says, Cos it's the key to my motherfucking heart.

So we get off eventually, I forget the station, and his place is about five minutes' walk away. We get to this block and he points up at a window. I'll give you a lift up, he says, it should be open. And you will never believe it, but he lifts me off the ground like I'm a fucking Barbie doll. One minute it's terra-fucking-firma, next it's I'm Mandy, fly me. I'm up there jimmying this window, and he's on the ground like a circus strongman, with me standing on the palms of his hands, and he says, You're a friend of Faulkner's, huh? And I'm like, How do you know Faulkner? Oh, he says, Me and Faulkner go back a long long way. And that's when I started to feel the soles of my feet getting warm. Window's stiff, I'm giving it everything I've got, and he's off about how he met Faulkner in New York years ago. But I'm hardly listening because, now it's like my feet is *frying*. In the end I get the window open and get inside, but fuck the room smells worse than he does. Can't hardly breathe. Got my hand over my nose looking for the key. He said it's on a ring on the bedpost, but it's taking me a while to get used to the dark, and my feet's sticking to the fucking floor, and the *smell. Uh!* I found it in the end. Right enough it was on a keyring hanging on the bedpost. Thing was, it was the size of a fucking *traffic cone*. Weighed a ton. Took me ages to get it down the stairs, with my feet sticking to the ground, and the steps seeming like they're never going to end. Like shifting a piano. When I got out the sky was light, like morning, and the Fonz was standing there in his Guccis. Thanks, he says, and picks up the key like you or me would pick up a fucking matchstick. No problem, I say, What about my money. He hands me the wallet and says, There's a little something in there for Faulkner too. Tell him I'll drop by sometime. I didn't wait around, Bo. I just got the fuck out of there. Didn't stop moving until I got back here. Tell me it was the fucking Devil I was with tonight and I'd believe you.

Paris reached down to the floor and slung his shoes

up onto the tabletop. The soles curved violently around the width like moulded handgrips, palm lines imprinted in the reset rubber. Huge grooves, thick enough for giant fingers, notched the sides. Strips of red leather scorched black stretched up to the tongues.

—Bastard melted my fucking shoes, man. Two hundred and fifty quid.

—Christ . . . How did that happen?

—It's like I said: Fonz melted them with his bare hands.

—Rubbish.

—Fuck's sake, his fingerprints is in the rubber! *Look!*

Bohemond took the shoe in his hand. A new looseness welling in his chest when he smelled the sulphurous scent.

—Is that or is that not fingerprints?

—This is another twisted scheme you've cooked up to get back into Hermione's good books. She told me about the games you play.

—Fuck off.

—So you haven't seen Faulkner's stage-show of late?

—Haven't seen him in months.

—You've created this little vignette around Faulkner's fairy tales as a means of buying Hermione back. It's pathetic, Paris.

—I'd ruin a two hundred quid pair of shoes for a *shag*?

—You might.

—You calling me a liar?

—I'm saying you should leave Hermione alone.

—Fuck you, man! Fuck you! I'm so sick of this. Everybody so ready to believe Paris is throwing his weight around cos he's the one screwing the boss. You're all just fucking jealous.

—Including Seeta?

—What did you say?

—That maybe Seeta has more reason to be jealous of Hermione than most.

—Fuck you!

—You didn't write her that letter, then?

—What *letter*?

—As I thought. Bohemond pulled away. —You've already lost her, you know.

—Hermione? *To you?*

He held back, way too jubilant to be really angry, but desperate to score points; desperate to share his news with anyone who'd listen. —Perhaps, he said.

—Keep wanking, you smug cunt, not that you'd be able to reach round that fucking gut.

—You should tell Faulkner about what happened to you tonight. I'm sure he'd be very interested to hear your story.

—Fuck him. I lost a pair of shoes because of him.

Bohemond stepped into the laundry. —By the way, what about the present you were told to pass on to him?

—I did the time, it's mine. Besides, it might be worth something.

—That's convenient. I don't suppose you've got this mystery gift to hand, have you?

Paris shook his head, rifled through both pockets, and skimmed a solid gold feather across the table.

juice

In which Faulkner tells the third part of his story.

Faulkner took to the stage again two nights later.

When Blossom collapsed into our cabin looking like a corpse that'd been keel-hauled through Hell, all thoughts of marriage, wedded bliss, kids and shit, all that flew right out the fucking window. After all I'd been through, I wanted to fall into the arms of my honey-skinned Latino queen. Take what was mine. But the ghoul that came knocking on my door that morning was no kind of prize at all. I felt like I'd been set up. Cheated out of a once-in-a-lifetime win. Sounds harsh, I know, but the clincher in all this was that it was *her* that'd ruined the whole score by getting in too deep in the first place. I warned her when we started this thing not to let Legion get close, but all I got was mouth and attitude. Now she was burned and broken and spoiled. She'd brought a world of hurt down on her own head. Dropped me and Roosevelt in it. Almost got us killed. Roosevelt fucked up for life. If she thought I was about to take vows on the back of that kind of betrayal, booty or no fucking booty, she had another thing coming.

First couple of days on the boat, she and Roosevelt stayed in bed. Him curled up with his guts all ruptured, missing nipples and fingertips, and her pretty much fucked everywhichway. I covered for Roosevelt until he was well enough to limp. Blossom lay low a whole day more. She slept most of the time. Wouldn't eat. Didn't say much either until she was able to walk and then she let rip.

Good nights, the band played out on deck. There was a dancefloor behind the swimming pool in the shadow of the aft smokestack and every motherfucker who could throw any kinda shape came out to swing in the starlight.

First night Blossom was up and at it, she was there to watch us play. Sitting by the stage, wrapped up in a shawl, she looked like a grandmother. I took a seat with her once we'd done half a set. Soon as I sat down, she grabbed my hand and said, How's my husband-to-be?

She knew something was up. She knew something was up soon as she started trying to play me off against that motherfucking monster cop. The hand-holding and spouse speech was meant to force all the shit I hadn't said out in the open. And it worked.

Things've changed, Blossom.

What things?

I can't marry you any more.

She pulled her hand away. Eyes looked real kind of misty. But I thought we had a deal, she said.

We had a deal before you fucked things up. Before you gave the game away and almost got us killed.

Before I almost got *you* killed? Have you seen the state I'm in?

Yeah, and whose fault is that?

You're fucking *unbelievable*.

I told you not to let that cop get in your head. But you came back to me those nights, all bit up with love bruises, talking loud about his style, living the high life and making out like you could handle it. You fell for him, Blossom. Pure and simple. Gave the whole god-damned game away while you were giving him eyes. Giving him head, for all I know.

Oh, Faulkner. You've no idea how out of your depth you were, trying to take him on. You don't know what you got into. Don't know what he was like. I saw things you wouldn't believe.

Wrong. I saw Legion take six slugs in the chest. Saw him go down. Thought he was dead. But when I went back to check on him a half-hour later, he's gone. Now that don't surprise me. Not one bit. At Wounded Knee, I saw men walk off the field with holes enough to kill an army. It ain't just that Legion's built like a fucking cathedral; he's full of hate. Not much I know of can douse a heat like that. Nothing like true love or pure hate to keep a man going. Emotions clean as that'll drive a motherfucker across continents. Across time. That's why Roosevelt's still alive. Why I wouldn't be surprised if Legion turned up on this very boat and dragged us all to Hell. So don't try to tell me I don't know what I got us into. There are more things in Heaven and Earth than you could fucking dream.

I'd gotten to her. She was crying. Said, You fat-headed asshole. So you saw some guys bloodied in a rumble in the Wild West. Big deal. You still ain't got no idea what *I* was up against, night after night. No idea what *I* went through, for you.

Well, if it was anything like the shit Legion put Roosevelt through, I'd be real surprised.

She shook her little fists at that. *Roosevelt. Roosevelt. Roosevelt.* All I keep hearing is Roosevelt. It's like I said back on the Island, it was him you had the hots for all along. Him you shoulda promised to marry. Not me. After what I been through for you, all the plans we made, all your promises, after all that, this little guys' club you got going on with Roosevelt, it's like you're sticking a knife in me, Faulkner, and Heaven knows I don't feel like I got much time left.

That hurt. Hey, I said, Don't you go talking like that. We're all gonna come through this thing in one piece. OK?

That night, she said, when I threw you the key from Legion's window . . . She tailed off, keeping real low.

I reached out, held onto her arm. What about it?

That *wasn't me.*

What?

It was Legion.

What do you mean, *it was Legion*? I saw you up there.

She shook her head. Wouldn't look at me.

Blossom. I saw you up there.

I don't know who you *think* you saw, Faulkner, but it sure as Hell wasn't me. I was handcuffed to the bed with a gag stuffed in my mouth. I could hear your voice. Damn near snapped my wrists trying to get free and jump down to you. I heard you shout. *Blossom! Blossom!* Broke my heart.

I let go of her. I know you ain't well, Blossom, but this shit is sick in the head.

That's what I'm trying to tell you, Faulkner. You don't know what you're dealing with. You saw for yourself: Legion walked away after he took six bullets. Now, you can make sense of that anywhichway you please, with your bullshit war stories or whatever, just don't ask me to go along with it. This is as bad as it gets.

Baloney. It's a fucking fairy-story to get you off the hook. You sure you didn't take some of that Chinese dope Roosevelt gave you?

I did it for you, Faulkner.

Don't you give me that crap, Blossom.

It was all for you.

Don't make me walk out on you right now. Don't make me. You trying to tell me that you weren't in love with that nigger-hating cocksucker? That you didn't give us to him on a fucking plate. How the fuck did he know we were coming if you didn't tell him, Blossom? Huh? How did he know? You gonna tell me he was a fucking *mind reader* next, ah?

Faulkner. You gotta believe me . . . that cop. Jesus, that man, he's the *Devil*.

Ah please. *Please*. Enough already.

You've no idea what he did to me.

So tell me. Come on, Blossom. Tell me.

She looked into the sky. There were rockets up there.

Tell me, I said.

No dice. She got up and walked away without a word. Didn't feel good at all. I knew I'd been hard, but man, I wasn't the same easygoing kinda guy I was back on Manhattan. Even as I was sitting there saying those words it was like they were coming out some other meaner motherfucker's mouth. Everything was just fucked-up.

Roosevelt came up behind me. He'd watched the whole thing from the other side of the stage. You gonna go after her, or am I? he said.

Let her go. She'll cool down.

I went looking for her after we'd finished playing. No

sign of her in our cabin. All her clothes and shit, everything was gone. Nothing to suggest she'd been there at all; not even a whiff of perfume. I never saw her again.

I like to think she shacked up with one of the crew, or some rich European sugardaddy, and lay low until she was far far away. Course, there's always the possibility that she jumped overboard; much as I hate to admit it, there's a little part of me, even now, that thinks I spent ten minutes, on board the *Columbus*, talking to a ghost.

Boat docked in Southampton. Roosevelt and me hopped on a train to London, still lumbering with the suitcase full of stash. We hit the smoke around dinnertime. Stayed in a hotel near Paddington the first few nights. A real sweet suite.

London was cool. Too cool. Took me while to get used to the climate. The weather *and* how chilled-out folk seemed to be about the whole race thing. Sure, there were fuck-ups here and there, but still, nothing like the near-lynching we got in Cherryville, South Carolina.

Roosevelt did good. Called in all his contacts and they came up trumps. We ended up working for a cigar-smoking city gent going by the name Livingstone. Turned out he was a friend of Blanche's. Some guilt-ridden colonial only too happy to help out. He saw to it we got a regal apartment off Holborn, ringside seats and peaches. All we had to do was run visiting dignitaries round town, perform the occasional favour. Small price.

Every night we were onboard the *Columbus*, Roosevelt'd wake up half-hysterical, screaming some shit or other. Got worse in London. Just lights in his head going out as he dealt with disaster. He took to carrying a machete inside his coat whenever he went out. Sometimes slept with the motherfucking thing under his pillow.

We passed off the rest of the year living like kings pretty much. But then I reckon we were due some. Roosevelt wrote a lot of letters during that time. Pulled in a few too. He hardly ever mentioned Beatrice, but I reckon most of the letters he wrote he sent to her and that she wrote most of the ones he got.

Shit seemed to take a long time to pull together. All the writing and receiving stopped come winter. Round spring Roosevelt started going AWOL. Days on end, I'd see no sign of him. Didn't know what was going down at first. Whenever I asked him where he'd been at, all he'd ever say was, Someone's comin to dinner.

Things spun out of control. I got pulled into all sorts of shit. Roosevelt changed some. Became kinda sullen, temperamental, violent. He was off a lot of the time, taking scalps, and if I wasn't covering his back on some ugly deal, I was covering for him at work. Got so it looked as if we'd have to leave town for a while, but he wouldn't do it. I told you, he said, Someone's comin to dinner.

We wasted the slow bake of summer tucked under-ground, suffocating at poker parties. Roosevelt and me, blissed out on strippers and below-the-table fellatio. I knew then we shoulda been diving in the Med, or hot air ballooning over African savannah, shit, skiing in the Alps. But no. Against my better judgement, Roosevelt insisted we stay in the city and play cards. He fancied himself as some kinda hustler. But he didn't have the head for heights. Couldn't tell when he was being hustled. You'd watch his cool slip, the skin rippling along his jawbone, a quick hint that he

was gonna erupt and you'd be thinking oh fuck, looking round, sizing up the opposition, the best escape
route, who to hit first and how. We got caught on the
hop, in Clapham, one night. Seven guys, kung fu,
chicken ju-jitsu and all that shit. They tied us up and
slapped their Hong Kong Phooey on us. Hours of fist
and foot technique. The Empty Hand. Divine Wind. I
woke up sore from that tussle. Bust ribs and knuckles.
Ruptured fucking gonads. Roosevelt went back with a
crew about a week later and took an eye and a tooth
from each one of those ninja motherfuckers. That was
the way he played. Tit for tat.

Times the hustle was smooth, there was always
some other fix that nigger was getting into. He could
never just walk. If you offered him the choice between
a pot of gold on his lap and one in a mined cesspit,
guaranteed, every time, he'd dive to the bottom of the
booby-trapped shit pool.

He browned off some German cleric over blackjack
in a Soho cellar one night. Arrogant Teuton was still
in his dog collar, muttering Mea culpa. Amen, said
Roosevelt and cleaned him out for every last relic.
But the priest was a bad loser. He pulled a knife on
us. Roosevelt pulled the machete and we bowed out
whistling with the dough.

We rolled on to the streets, wired after the win and
shunted through Covent Garden. It was getting late –
early Sunday morning – but Roosevelt showed no signs
of slowing, all high five and big mouth. Juicy scores
always got him talking immortal. Always gave him a
sore appetite.

He pulled me over at a fast-food bunker, brandishing
the wedge of hustled cash. I feel like one sacrilegious
mofo, he said. Like my man Vitellius Caesar. Now
that's one hungry sonofabitch. Invites himself to

dinner and eats motherfuckers out of house and home. Snatches cake and meat hot offof the sacrificial altar. Ain't nuthin you can do but kiss ass cos this guy is the Emperor of the Known World. Rex. That's how I feel.

This was Roosevelt; on his way to Heaven, already making like a God. He turned to the old Chinese guy in the booth and said in way too loud a voice, Bring me pike livers and peacock brains, flamingo tongues and lamprey milt.

Some halfcaste Latino pimp in a wide-cut pinstripe stepped out of the shadows. Champagne Crombie draped over his shoulders like a cloak, he swaggered on the spot as he chewed down the last of a hotdog, and in this hyena kinda voice says: Guy who flashes all that money around is looking for a slap. Roosevelt didn't take his eyes offof the Chinaman. I stepped forward, ready to rumble. The spic moved closer. His play threw me. The guy was bigger than either of us but we were two and he was one. I couldn't see his backup. Couldn't see a shooter. You want some action, ah? Big shot? Like that? He nodded at a blood-red convertible with chrome spoilers thick as a man's waist parked on the faraway kerb. Someone long and blonde in the back seat. Like that? He motioned at whoever it was to come on over.

A hard-bodied goddess stepped out of the car in a white, low-cut, hip-hugging dress. She swayed towards us with this ancient kinda suss, like she'd seduced too many Pharaohs or gotten bored with jilting princes. Her hair flared in a gold stream. Platforms slapping the asphalt. Bright blue fingernails and waves of lavender. Jesus Christ but she was beautiful. A weary angel. No joke. Made me feel too fucking human.

The Cuban dabbed at his mouth with a handkerchief as she catwalked up to him. He slipped an arm behind

236

her back and pulled her into a kiss, her arms hanging limp as she gave in – the two of them swooning in the clinch like flamenco dancers. When he pulled away, his lips were smeared with lipstick, a silver thread of spit glinting for a second between her chin and his hung-out tongue. He grinned like a Cheshire cat and pointed at his teeth. They were all gold. You want some of this fucking action, huh? You nigger big shot?

I looked around. The corner was quiet, out of the way. Something about this whole thing smelled funny.

The spic rubbed the girl's belly with a heavily jewelled hand. Hey big shot, I'm talking to you.

Roosevelt didn't flinch. He just bit his lip and I stood back. There was no code with that cat. No circling or backchat. Just the odd twitch or buzzword. He reached inside his coat, swung into a pirouette and whacked the Cuban's nose with the flat of the machete. The bridge split first crack. Blood striped the bitch's dress like a necklace. She tottered back tutting at the stained silk and the spic crumpled like a fan. Girl didn't scream. Nothing like that. Just blew out and rolled her big baby-blue eyes.

The spic curled up on the ground, groaning. Roosevelt stomped him – kicked ribs booming like a bass drum, head bouncing offa the road. I stood on his throat, listened to him choke on half-digested hotdog. A minute or so of that shit and he blacked out.

Roosevelt grabbed one of the Cuban heels in both hands and dragged that coffee-coloured fop into a courtyard a few feet along the street. I pushed his woman after them.

We propped the pimp against the wall by a stone stairway. I had one hand on him, the other dug into the girl's arm, but she wasn't making any moves. She seemed more interested in getting a better look.

Roosevelt squatted with the machete. Real careful of the coat, he sawed through the spic's suit and shirt, placed the knifepoint at the bared junction of collarbone and shoulder-joint, linked hands around the handle, and leaned forward pushing at the blade until the skin stretched under pressure. He looked up and I shrugged trying not to smile as he brought his full weight to bear. Kebab, he said, and pinned that spic motherfucker to the wall. The sucker's eyes snapped open. I stood on his fingers. Roosevelt throttled him with a free hand. Fucking cocoa kid rasping like a meat grinder, teeth turning brownish with blood, eyes rattling like pinballs. The girl drew breath. Big open-mouth smile. Squealed when I kicked the Cuban in the face. His head slumped forward. The body sagged. Roosevelt's stranglehold and the machete skewer fastening him upright.

I strolled back to the sidewalk to keep a lookout. Lit up a cigarette. Couldn't see much: the arc of Roosevelt's back rolling behind the steps, and the girl lit up in the glow from a basement window, watching him work. I don't know what he was doing to the guy but that bloodthirsty bitch loved every minute. Fists over her mouth. All kinds of gasps and half-laughter. I turned every once in a while, melting a little at how wide-eyed she got, like some kid at the circus, astonished, appalled and elated all at the same time. Roosevelt wasn't in any hurry. I once saw him razor-flay some art buyer's legs over an unpaid debt. A handful of us broke into the mark's first-floor apartment. Dragged him out of bed. Tied him face-down on a big old oak dining table. Roosevelt skinned him while we lounged around smoking his cigarettes, listening to his 78s, cooking his food. One of the crew, Valdes, whipped us up a Last Supper. We had chicory and oranges with cheese dressing to start, a main of creamy leek croustade, followed by walnut pie and junket. Roosevelt ate his smeared in blood and meat, then finished off as usual: took an eye and a tooth. Sometimes he'd go for fingers or toes. Big nights he'd even castrate a motherfucker. Axe, razor, kitchen knife, whatever was at hand. It was poetic justice to him. He coveted these little white trinkets like lynching trophies.

I was at the end of my second cigarette when the sound of footsteps filled the alley. Roosevelt was gliding towards me in the pimp's champagne Crombie, a fat Caesar smile splitting his big black face. He tossed the convertible keys in a bloodsoaked hand. The blonde skipped up alongside and lunged at him. I ran at her thinking she was gonna do him some damage, but she flung her arms around his neck, and he whirled her round and round, her feet off the ground. And then they were kissing, hard. Real hard. All tongues and hands. They'd have stripped each other in the street if I hadn't spoke. Man, I said, you two made friends real quick.

Roosevelt frowned at me, but he was smiling too, one arm round the girl's waist. You mean to say, he said, you don't recognize this fine creature.

I shrugged.

He looked at the girl, she looked back at him. Full of fucking rapture.

Faulkner, he said, I'd like you to meet Beatrice.

So this is Faulkner, she said, her voice like the flapping of dove wings. A babbling brook. Angels sighing.

You know there's no way I can thank you for what you've done, she said. I'm in your debt and I think I will be for evermore.

I couldn't speak. Just her being there, with him, turned the months of suffering into some kinda crazy joy that struck me dumb. At last, Roosevelt'd got his hands on his reason for being and, man, she must've felt like diamond. If two people ever looked like halves of the same person, it was them, right there in that alleyway. So obvious that they were meant to be together, even though she seemed a little doped-up.

She sucked his fucked fingers and kissed the scars on his face. I noticed then she had a twin injury: the little finger on her left hand one notch short. Only nine nails shining luminous blue.

We got in the convertible. Roosevelt drove and Bea rode shotgun. I sat in the back. She pulled a black metal box, with a gold padlock, from under her seat and laid it on her lap. Cradled it like a baby. Roosevelt smiled and tapped it with a finger. I knew better than to ask.

We cruised the early-morning city from Piccadilly to Paddington, round Regent's Park, through Finsbury to Bethnal Green. Stopped at dawn, all sprawled out by Marble Key, and watched the sunrise, drive-in-style, over Tower Bridge.

Roosevelt took the Cuban's handkerchief out the Crombie pocket and unfolded it on his lap, chuckling at the glitter of loose gold teeth. He had them melted down sometime later and reset as a wedding ring. True romance doomed from the start because now Bea was Worm's woman and the spic pimp we trashed was Worm's man. You've probably heard of Worm. Big fat evil cocksucking Slovenian motherfucker. The boogieman your folks threaten you with when you're just outta the crib. Look out or Worm's gonna getcha. That Worm. He'd find out what we'd done sooner or later, and when he did, he'd come looking for us. But that's a whole other story.

Faulkner silenced the applause with a finger lifted to his lips, then fanned the band into a stripped-down, hushed-up rendition of Frank Sinatra's 'Luck Be a Lady'.

sweetmeat

sweetmeat

icing

In which Bohemond bids his friends and enemies farewell.

Only Seeta didn't show the day Bohemond made his escape. He cooked from breakfast through to lunch, feeling like a phoney, especially with Innocent. But as far as Bohemond was concerned, every look, every word, every smile, the winks and hugs that passed between them, were disguised goodbyes.

Back in his room, dressed in the best of Eli's specially tailored clothes – horse leather boots, black canvas slacks and a chunky wool jumper – everything he owned or thought worth taking packed into his only suitcase, he sat down at his desk and wrote another five farewells.

Dearest Innocent

I took your advice and have been learning to love myself, no mean feat, but it's paying dividends. Every day of my adult life, given the way I am, the way I look, I've had to live by tenets such as 'what goes around comes around', 'do good and good will come to you', etc, and at long last it seems my efforts are to be rewarded: Hermione has finally opened her heart to me! We kissed! Oh, Innocent, we kissed. I still can't quite believe it. As we sat, on New Year's Morning chatting on the floor of her living room, she told me that she and I were meant to be together. She's taken by what she sees as the calmness of my spirit, the maturity of my soul and even suggested that I saved her life the night she fell through my window. All the while, she looked and sounded so lost, so alone, and believe me I know how that feels. It's one of the reasons why, though I'm still struggling to comprehend the enormity of the situation, it all makes absolute sense.

I know she's engaged to be married but, Innocent, she's not truly in love with Paris. If she were, this wouldn't be happening. He only made her unhappy. All his time spent trying to stoke the fires of jealousy. And yes, I feel guilty, but you know as well as I do that by running away with her like this, I'm helping her escape a lifetime of abuse.

I'm not taking anything for granted. You were right to say that Hermione is not the only one for me. And of course, this may not work out. But I'm going to give it everything I've got. I can't wait another fourteen years. Not for this.

I'll miss you, Innocent; our games of chess, the late-night chats, your ability to conjure all kinds of riches from base materials. Look what you've made of me!

But this is it, my friend. My chance to love like you did. And again, you were right: already I'm seeing things differently; as though I've emerged from a world of dreams. The way I feel about myself is changing. I look in the mirror and, far from hating the person staring back at me, I begin to think that the make-up, the size and shape of me has contributed to who I am – the man Hermione has chosen to be with. At last I understand the sentiments in Napoleon's letters to Joséphine, and thank God such ardour is no longer beyond me!

For ever your friend,

B x

PS. I wish I could say goodbye properly, but you'd only try to stop me, and besides I'm sure I'll be seeing you before too long.

Morrissey

What was it you said? Make the right move and Hermione would even f**k a beached whale like me? I wonder if you ever really thought she'd fall for me just the way I am. Doubtless no. Which is why, when you find out what's happened, you'll probably be more amazed than anyone.

Thanks anyway for continually trying to keep my feet on the ground. I'm sure you meant well.

Bohemond.

Paris

Things have happened this way for a reason. The outcome doesn't mean that either one of us is better than the other. It's all just a question of harmony. I don't hate you, Paris, although over the years you've given me good cause. In fact I hope one day we can be friends. At present, I think I simply don't understand you. But thank goodness you seem to have found someone who does. Be good to Seeta. She's one of a kind and deserves the world.

Bohemond.

Dear Seeta

I only hope you can forgive me. I never ever meant to hurt you. The way I behaved at New Year was disgusting. Believe it or not, I was trying to do the right thing.

You're special, Seeta. Don't ever forget that. I remember the first time you came into the kitchen, little more than a trainee. How you floored us all with your expertise. How

Innocent had tears in his eyes when he tasted the first birthday cake you baked for him. I'll never forget how you've been with me: always generous, always kind, always loyal. There are times that I've felt you and Innocent are the only people in the world who love me.

What I'm trying to say is, despite everything you think of me, you are one of the most beautiful people I know. That Paris has fallen for you comes as no surprise. What man wouldn't? It's no secret that he and I haven't always seen eye to eye, and in that respect I was a little surprised to hear you'd fallen for him. But knowing you, my reservations are simply proof that, as I said to you before Christmas, I don't know the whole Paris. Some people are meant to be together, some aren't. Paris was never meant to be with Hermione. That doesn't make him a bad person. I'm sure those energies which Hermione found most negative in him and could do nothing to tame, meet their perfect foil in you.

I understand now that (true?) love has everything to do with the compatibility of souls, which is why Hermione has asked me to be with her. In a day and age when society places an incredibly high premium on the transitory and the physical (beauty, money, etc), that she could even think of me in this way is nothing short of a miracle. I told you fairy tales could come true. I'm living proof that they do.

I will always love you

Bo xx

PS. I'll be in touch. If there's anything I can do, anything you need, let me know.

Faulkner

No doubt you think me beneath contempt. How many words have passed between us over the years we've been here? One? Two? A grunt? I certainly never thought I'd ever have cause to write to you. But the truth is, the fairy tale you've been telling about Roosevelt and Beatrice has given me the strength to persevere in a matter very close to my heart: as Roosevelt's love for Beatrice overcame all obstacles, so too did my love for Hermione.

I was so influenced by your story that I began to 'see' elements of it in real life: a golden bird, rockets, giant lovehearts on a brass barge, even Beatrice! The most beautiful creature I think I have ever encountered. She looked real enough, but I swear as soon as I touched her she floated up into the sky.

I know how that must sound to you, but I took all of these things as omens, signs that I could succeed. I'm not like Roosevelt, as you well know, though the object of my affection is not at all unlike Beatrice. Your stories gave me the courage to forge ahead, instilled in me the conviction that true love makes all things possible. As you said, 'The things even the most common souls will do for love.'

Strange as it sounds, thank you.

Bohemond (Head Chef of Delphi)

Bohemond folded the letters into envelopes and set them on the floor in front of the door, a welcome to whoever came looking for him first. He shrugged on his sheepskin coat and took one last look in the bathroom. Dark and dolorous, the evergreens and flowers planted around the bath drooped deep into the bowl. —Don't mourn me, he said. —For the first time in too long I feel alive.

Second thoughts brought him back to the envelopes on the floor. He picked up the one made out to Faulkner, ripped it to shreds and threw it in the bin. —Fairy tales, he said, and grabbed his suitcase.

The door left unlocked, Bohemond walked along the hall, down the stairs, past Hermione's flat, and down again to a curiously quiet foyer: no sign of Thom or anyone else, no sounds filtering through from the restaurant – more omens that what he was doing was what he was meant to do. A swift look round, he muttered goodbye and walked out.

lotus

Four flights of fancy.

The day was dark. Drizzle building up. Bohemond rumbled along Tower Bridge, crossed the Hill at the lights, and loped down into the Tube station.

Up until eighteen months ago he'd negotiate the Underground turnstiles with his bottom and his belly, slide through side-on, his softness sluiced between machines. In a rush at Oxford Circus one Sunday, he sped through, head-on, body squashed into a sponge shape as the gates clamped his trunk like a corset. They slid round his gut, massaged his ribs and kidneys. (Nothing happened at his hips because the bones were so deep down.) Both arms held aloft, he lingered, laughing, breathing out as the gates brushed his butt cheeks, breathless by the time he reached the escalator. This was how he imagined the perfect embrace: all encompassing, oblivious of his bulk, but he doubted whether anyone could ever love him enough, and he, certainly, could never love anyone who loved him. The gates would do for the time being and he'd never sidled through side-on since.

Never until now.

A crowded platform made the going slow. Had Bohemond praying that his belly wouldn't bounce anyone onto the tracks. He eased towards the far end, cursing as the westbound train rattled past, its front carriages almost empty, leaving him with commuter-crammed wagons at the rear. The doors opened but only a handful stepped out. Slim people shimmied into the gaps. Huddled tight together, passengers watched him, their faces forming a patchwork portrait of bemusement and disbelief, even spite. Bold stares dared him to climb aboard, but there was no way. Someone thanked God. Others tittered as the doors closed. A boy in a tracksuit flipped him the finger. Bohemond shrugged, said, —You silly sardines, and waddled on.

Bill posters curved up the wall bordering the track – sex magic to arouse decadent desires; to guarantee inflated sales of designer clothes, soaps, scrubs and deodorants, lipsticks, liners and aftershaves, heighteners, lighteners and whiteners, some poor souls succumbing in the long run to the lure of tips, lifts, tucks, implants, resurfacing and sculpture, not to mention the evils of draconian diets and eating disorders. Wonderbra billboards caused automobile accidents in King's Cross for Christ's sake: rush-hour motorists hanging out of their car windows, eyes wide, tongues lolling, while these thrusting busty babes grinned over the din of bashed bumpers and dented wings, broken noses and whiplash.

Not that any of that concerned him now. Well on his way to a better place, Bohemond had already left the city and some of his old self behind. Whereas once he might have wished these women paunches, stretch marks, buck teeth, low foreheads, winter down on their upper lips, or horsehair in their armpits, he now felt something nearer sympathy.

The first real rush hour of the New Year just beginning to hit, Liverpool Street station was overrun. Bohemond sat down on an empty bench tucked away from the main. Hidden from the prying eyes of tourists and teenagers he had a reasonable view of both main entrances and the Underground gates. When Hermione came in she wouldn't see him, but he'd see her. She'd look around, her face at first clouded with doubt, suddenly shining with delight as Bohemond stepped out of the shadows, arms spread wide . . .

Five o'clock. One hour of waiting.

Destinations winked and fluttered across the station timetable. Wherever Hermione decided she wanted to go, Bohemond was ready to follow. He'd even brave a plane journey so long as they flew somewhere warm. Maybe Spain. A sleepy Andalucían village, founded on Roman and Moorish ruins, ringed by high coastal roads with views to Africa. He'd set up another restaurant. Specialize in specialities from around the world. When the villagers finally arrived, beguiled by the scents that wafted down the hill from his kitchen, they'd smile to find the stranger in their midst a fat black blue-eyed Frenchman wearing lipstick. Every day after that they'd come to wine and dine one another, or to sing and dance to the band. Early evenings the old men would take to the terrace over-looking the sea to watch the sunset. As the world turned blue and stars seared through the sky, Bohemond would join them in drinking and dominoes, and they'd toast him by firelight, with tears in their eyes, their daughters and granddaughters dancing on the balconies with their lovers and husbands, all saluting Spain's greatest non-native chef and his beautiful Italian bride.

At five to six the scent of cherry turned his head. He glimpsed Hermione's hairdo, the flared legs of her palazzo pants swishing towards the shopping precinct at the eastern exit. —Hermione! My love! Thank God! I'm here! These words and more erupting from the pit of his throat, symphonic strings stirring in the back of his head, Bohemond grabbed his bag and launched himself into the crowd, mumbling apologies as he thundered forward and folk fell back or fell over and prams capsized and suitcases sprang open and stalls shed their loads, flooding the floor with a hundred different hues of fruit that rolled down into the Underground. He glanced back, his foot hooked on some spur or other, and like always he was falling, sliding as he hit the ground, skidding to a stop against ankles wrapped in palazzo pants. He looked up at the Hermione hairdo. Gagged on his tongue to find a benign and beautiful but definitely male face beaming down at him. Italian or Spanish, almost angelic, the youth held out a hand. —Are you OK?

Bohemond waved him away, jiggled to his feet, brushed himself down. —Sorry. Just a mistake. He snatched his suitcase from the floor and, sucking on Ventolin, limped back towards the bench, growing light-headed as his lungs opened up. Best thing would be to walk around the block. Come back in once he was forgotten. But there was no forgetting him, and anyway, he had to be here when Hermione arrived. She'd be late, of course — fool that he was to have been so impetuous. That's what she was like: nice and easy does it, even at a time like this.

As he sat down again, his eyes closed. He strove to

keep them open but his body, in its state of permanent revolt, wearied by all the angst and action, was ready to doze. When he woke Hermione would be there beside him, just as she would each morning in their home on the Andalucían hilltop.

Bed would be where they'd spend most of their time. Where Hermione would teach him the secrets of love. And she'd need all her powers of persuasion; every night a new ruse or slightly different slant, because Bohemond's prick was more like a clit it was so small and unexploited. He'd given up on masturbation years ago as his burgeoning belly pushed his penis out of reach. Ejaculation itself wasn't beyond him, but the emissions had precious little to do with bliss. Every twenty-eight days, for the last five years, the semen that built up in his balls burst its banks. The first couple of floods caught him unawares and he creamed himself in the kitchen. But he learned to read the signs – moodswings, bingeing – and took to lining his Y-fronts with hand-towels.

Hermione would break the spell and make a man of him. Over a thousand and one nights, each rich with new carnal delights, she'd turn his wimpish dick into an impossible cock. Hot romps to melt down every gram of fat until his head, belly and legs were like Nureyev's. But best of all, at the end of the final lesson, on the thousand and first night, he'd find his liner and lipstick washed away by sweat and kisses.

When Bohemond's eyes opened, one glance at the station clock all but broke his heart: it was midnight. He jumped up, fumbling for change in his pockets, stumbled towards the payphones, stopped. If Paris answered there'd be bloodshed, especially if Hermione was with him, and it was all too possible she was. All too possible that with Bohemond fast asleep, hidden away amongst the station chaos, she'd been unable to find him. After waiting for more than an hour, she'd left to search other parts of London, her fear that Bohemond had never really loved her growing every second. Finally, maybe as far afield as Greenwich, she'd admitted defeat and run back to Paris. Down on her knees, she'd begged him to take her back, promised him she'd play no more games. And Paris, pent-up, desperate to re-make his mark, demanding that she prove how much she loved him, allowed himself to be kissed, stripped, aroused and devoured, all the tease and heat and eventual surrender Hermione had been saving for Bohemond – all the best of the rest of his life – back in Paris's hands.

He swung around and charged through the Underground turnstiles.

sweetmeat

How Bohemond's heart broke and almost mended.

By the time Bohemond reached Delphi he was ready
for Heaven. Ventolin spent, he had no breath left, the
sweat that soaked his clothes so cold it sieved through
flesh and flab and froze his muscles – an agony of
cramp that crept into his legs, his back, his neck, his
head. He had to get to his room, find a spare inhaler,
find Hermione, make another escape.

A letter on the deserted foyer desk:

To Boomer (?) the chef

He snatched at it, blurting, —Jesus Christ! But the
curse clogged his throat and shrivelled his lungs.
Nothing budged. He dropped the suitcase, tripped onto
the stairs, choking on the smell of lavender. When
Hermione stepped out of her office onto the first-floor
landing, his body gave up the ghost: his eyes rolled,
he felt froth coming, the ground giving out. She
scrambled for him, grabbed his hand, swung him up
the last of the steps and shouldered the office door,

hauling him inside. Bohemond's sight crazily hazy, Hermione seemed more of an apparition as she let him go, rushed to her desk, emptied the contents of its drawers onto the floor and tossed him an inhaler fished from the scattered bric-à-brac.

Six puffs and he was near to breathing. —I'm sorry. I'm sorry. I'm sorry.

Hermione coaxed him into his seat. He put the letter in his pocket, coughing as he watched her grab a bottle of pineapple Looza from the fridge. She cracked it open, handed it to him, hovering at his side as he spluttered up to a shallow sip.

—Christ, Bo, what happened to you?

—Thank God you're here. I'm so sorry. I fell asleep at the station. Where's Paris?

She closed the door and switched on the table lamp.

—Is he here?

—Are you drunk?

—Drunk? Hermione, I . . .

She silenced him with a thumb pressed to his nose. —Look, she said, stepping back, the pad of her thumb daubed red.

—Blood?

—You don't remember?

Bohemond drew fingers across his face. They came away streaked red, white and black. Hermione picked a hand-mirror from the junk on the floor. He took it from her, one look at his reflection enough to bring his lungs back to the boil. His face had been made-up with greasepaint. All white around the mouth, he had a Rudolf-red nose and dozens of long black whiskers.

—People . . . he mumbled, — . . . staring at me on the Tube. I thought it was just the usual: fat black blue-eyed drag queen. But I look like . . . the lion from

The Wizard of Oz. He gazed up at her, almost thankful to see that she was trembling, her eyes troubled. —Don't look at me like that, he said and sucked another puff of Ventolin. —That's how Seeta looks at me. Innocent too. Full of pity. Even Eli my dressmaker. Whenever I go to get measured he wrings his hands and cries as though he's at a funeral.

Words stuck in Hermione's mouth. She cleared her throat and began again, but her voice was just as husky. —Are you OK?

—If I seem a little tipsy it's because something in the Ventolin goes straight to my head. —As for this make-up . . . he set the mirror on the table, —. . . while I was waiting for you in the station I fell asleep. I suppose that's why you couldn't find me. Stupid place to sit anyway. I wanted to surprise you when you came in. But the whole day had been so exhausting I couldn't keep from dozing off. Some joker must have done this to me then.

—Bastard, she smiled, rocking back as he swallowed a cough.

—Goodness knows what you see in a fool like me, Hermione. But thank God you see something.

—It's not difficult.

—I'm so relieved you're here. I had visions of you thinking I'd deserted you.

She shifted away from the desk, picking at her nails.
—. . . What?

—About the other night.

—New Year?

—I guess, yeah.

—I'll never forget it as long as I live.

—Bohemond.

—Where did you say Paris is?

—I don't know. He's out again.

259

—Should we go now, then? Wait until tomorrow? I'm ready to do whatever you want.

Hermione came forward, took his hands in hers and knelt between his legs.

Bohemond bristled and sizzled, head to toe. —I don't think I'll ever get used to you, he said. —Your skin is soft as snow.

She rested her cheek on the backs of his fingers. Held his gaze.

—There's that look again. Does this face-paint really make me seem so pathetic?

—Listen, Bohemond, please don't take this the wrong way. She buried her face in his lap. Looked up again. —I love you.

—My God, he gasped, winding a quivering finger through her hair. —How could I take that the wrong way? All my life waiting for you to say those words. All my life.

—You know I love you. Don't you? Love you loads.

—Don't spoil me.

—You deserve it. You're one of the great ones.

—And as soon as we get out of here you'll see how much more there is of me. While I was waiting for you in the station, I was thinking of Spain. How does a hilltop restaurant just across the water from Africa sound?

She sighed and bowed her head.

—Sounds idyllic I know. If only I'd managed to stay awake at the station, we'd be halfway there by now. I'm so sorry I fell asleep. I can't imagine how I'd have felt if I'd walked in and had been unable to find *you*.

—I've *so* fucked up.

—No, I was the one who fell asleep.

—Bohemond, Bohemond. Listen. She inhaled, blinking rapidly, blew out. —You didn't see me at Liverpool Street because I wasn't there.

—I was asleep.

—I know. You said. But I didn't come, Bo.

—Were you waylaid by Paris?

—No . . . I just . . . didn't come. She pulled away from him, stood up and moved to the window. —I didn't come.

Bohemond steadied himself against a corner of the desk. —I don't understand.

—How else can I say it? I wasn't there. I didn't come.

—Didn't or couldn't?

—New Year's Eve, she murmured. —I think we got our wires crossed.

—We *did*?

—OK, *I* got my wires crossed.

They gazed at one another; both wide-eyed, Bohemond open-mouthed. —New Year's Eve felt like the beginning of the rest of my life, he said.

—It's a blur to me, Bohemond. Whiskey and wine. I was celebrating.

—No, you were . . . He broke off, hurt taking hold, desire and despair clashing head-on as the moon emerged from behind a cloud, and, despite the light shed by the table lamp, cast a window-stencilled ray across Hermione's head and chest. —. . . you were drowning your sorrows. Trying to blot out the misery and despair with which that man has filled you.

—But the point is . . . I can't remember much about that night . . . I've been so confused recently. Everything's so . . . *fucked* just now. I've been so stressed. Drinking too much.

—You remember what you said to me?

Hermione slumped back against the wall and, without looking at him, shook her head.

—Don't do this to me, Hermione . . . *please*. You remember I was with you, but can't remember what we said? Yet when I mentioned waiting for you at Liverpool Street you seemed to know what I was talking about.

—OK, I remember bits.

—Which bits?

—Oh don't.

—Do you remember saying that we were meant to meet? How warm having me around here makes you feel? The things about my calmness of spirit? How you wish you'd realized sooner, the love that's been staring you in the face?

—And I meant them all. I'm just not sure . . . her voice tailed away, —what *you* think I meant by them.

Cramp clamped his chest. Sounded like the bells of a thousand cathedrals pealing in his ears. He doubled up, whining through clenched teeth. Hermione lurched towards him, but he stopped her with a raised hand. —I thought we were going to begin a life together.

—Your inhaler. *Bohemond*.

—I was ready to go to Spain . . . Prepared to fly. *On a plane*.

—We were never going to begin a life together. You knew that. All I wanted was to get out of town for a while. Clear my head. *That's all*. Everything around me's got so fucking complicated.

—But you said we might not come back. You asked me to imagine what life would be like were we married. A house full of our children, remember?

—I was *drunk*.

His head listed, drool seeping down his front. —This is another of your games, isn't it? Hermione threatening to elope with a fat black blue-eyed hermaphrodite. What a great way to get back at Paris.

—You know it's not like that. She gasped, —Please, Bohemond, your inhaler. *Breathe!*

—I see tears, Hermione. Perhaps you care about me after all.

—Of course I fucking care about you. But I never gave you any real reason to think . . . She grimaced, bit her nail, turned away, turned back.

—Think what?

—That I'm *in* love with you.

And at last the knot in his heart came undone. Everything fled – his will, his strength, his *spirit* – nothing left to hold up his overweight frame. Hermione rushed him, grabbed the inhaler, and with one arm around his neck forced the nozzle into his mouth. Too weak to resist, Bohemond sucked in, slumped forward and, catching his head in his hands, sighed, a long low note he couldn't stem, —*Oh no! Oh no! Oh no!*

Only slightly less hysterical, Hermione dropped the inhaler and stuttered down onto her knees again. Caressing Bohemond's cheek with her free hand, she fixed her lips to his ear and whispered, —It's not you, it's me.

—Hermione, please. You'll *kill* me. You'll *kill* me.

—You have to believe me.

—I cannot understand why you'd so *torture* the one who loves you more than anyone else.

—What do you want me to say?

—Really?

—Really.

He looked up, cupped her tear-slicked face in his hands and leaned forwards until their foreheads met. —I want you to say: Bohemond, *you're the one that I want*.

Hermione struggled with his weight. Her fingers

snared in his hair, engulfed by his jowls, his neck. One of her thumbs slipped between his lips. —I can't . . . *Oh*, Bohemond . . . I *can't*.

—There were other moments you almost said as much, he muttered. —Not just New Year's Eve. Was it the drink speaking all those times you tempted me?

—No, she said, trying to hug him, his bulk getting the better of her. —When we talked about running away together, I was serious. But I feel the same way about you as I always have. I just . . . changed my mind about running away.

—So why didn't you stop me? Why let me humiliate myself?

—*Bo, we're falling!*

—Perhaps you aren't used to being spoken to like that. Words from the heart. True love. Real passion.

—It might hurt but Paris isn't half the bastard you think he is. He's given me so much. I mean, when we first met I couldn't believe how he made me feel and I still can't. Seriously, it was like I'd been blundering along in black and white all my life, he came along and suddenly everything was in colour.

Bohemond lurched to his feet, his clothes so drenched in sweat they almost dragged him down again. Hermione grabbed his hand, but he was falling away from her, slipping through her fingers, out the door and along the hall, up the stairs into his room, toppling towards the bedside cabinet. He yanked open the drawer and snatched at his copy of Seeta's letter.

Paris. The very mention of his name brought the heavens tumbling. And here was Hell – Hermione's rebuke written down almost word for word: 'Like I'd been blundering along in black and white all my life, you showed up, and suddenly it was all in colour.'

Bohemond collapsed onto the bed, his breath too quick, high-pitched, racing ahead, leading his body not just in revolt but in full-blown mutiny; every ample inch of skin and bone working to overthrow his soul.

Of course Paris might rip off one of Hermione's gems and make it his own – couples traded catchphrases all the time – but a whole letter of such poetry was beyond him. And the idea that he'd had someone ghostwrite for him was just bullshit. More likely he'd close his eyes and ears in the hope his dilemma would disappear. Maybe make a phone call if he was pushed. But he wouldn't write. Not like this. If Hermione had written the letter, its biggest hint – 'I'll miss the way your skin makes mine look golden, and the way that mine makes yours look bronze' – was obviously applicable.

Bohemond swept a swift clip of lesbian love to the back of his mind and read over the last paragraph again: 'The prospect of spending the rest of my life with you truly dizzies me . . . but we can never give me everything I need . . . circumstances we have no control over and still I feel guilty.' Those circumstances were biological. All yin, no yang. Two women unable to satisfy one another in the way a woman and a man found so instinctive. Hermione had mused upon motherhood many times, but Seeta couldn't sate that passion either. And then there were Seeta's blue moods. Whenever she mentioned Hermione her words were always tinged with disappointment, never the resentment she reserved for Paris . . . Their night out in Soho had been some kind of reconciliation – Seeta making peace with Paris because it made Hermione happy – and gay.

Bent double, biting back panic and anguish at how

far Hermione had left him out of her life, at how *Seeta* was the reason she'd been wavering over the wedding, Bohemond stumbled away from the bed. He snatched the four remaining farewell letters from the floor, tore them to pieces and tossed the tatters into the air. A glimpse of his greasepainted face in the mirror, he snarled and swung a punch. Glass smashed. Blood flooded his fist. The blow stopped him dead, but his guts kept going. Vanilla-flavoured vomit gushed out of his mouth, swamped the sideboard, spattered the carpet, soiled his sheepskin coat as he was mid-sprint.

He wound up crumpled on the bathroom floor, eyes to the sky beyond the glass dome where stars waxed wildly, each one becoming a sun, gobbling up the gloom until the entire firmament was on fire. A sigh, a smile, he felt himself lifted, drifting upwards. Rockets blazed the breadth of the inferno. The trails left by their tails spelled out his name. He opened his hands, closed his eyes and gave himself up to the flames.

And there, broken-hearted, lion-faced, sprawled on the floor in the shadow of his toilet bowl, Bohemond might have cast off his mortal coil had not the scent of the letter in his pocket held him captive. All hope of ascending to Heaven finally thwarted, he tugged the envelope out, ripped it open, sat up and slouched against the wall.

The card inside was decorated with a detail of Marc Chagall's *Song of Songs IV*. Bohemond knew the painting well – a winged horse bearing two lovers aloft – its blood-red depth as always crowding his consciousness. He cried out at the marker-penned letters and lavender scent inside.

THANKS!
MAYBE NEXT TIME I'LL FLY YOU HOME
LOVE
B.
XXXXXX

A full-colour recollection of weightlessness. The way the blonde woman had almost flown over his head. She fitted the description of Beatrice, Faulkner's *femme fatale*, Roosevelt's beloved, and this card bore the signature **B.**. He brushed each of the six kisses with the tip of his little finger, wondering how she'd envisaged them: as a sextet of pecks or an afternoon of petting.

As he turned the card over again, the painting ruined his resolve. *Song of Songs* was the 'Song of Solomon', one of the greatest love lyrics ever written. Chagall's composition, based upon that ancient work of art, was itself a tribute to love in all its forms. Why would this woman, whom he'd met only fleetingly, send him such a card? Drenched in romantic meaning – not to mention his blood, sweat and tears – it wasn't the kind of thing one picked up and dispatched without thinking: angels soared up the sides of the sky; the flying horse with its blue mane and gold wings sailed over a bustling city. Bohemond looked closely at the couple riding on its back: a green-faced groom wearing a carmine crown, arms wreathed around his bride whose wedding gown tapered to a flaming comet's tail.

Beatrice had all but flown the night Bohemond found her. He'd spirited her away from trouble, just as the Pegasus in Chagall's painting bore the sweethearts away from the town. But if she thought of Bohemond as the horse and of herself as the bride, who was the green-faced groom? On the other hand, if she saw the horse as a manifestation of the fortune that'd brought them together, then surely the lounging lovers were she and Bohemond leaving the whole world behind.

dough

In which Faulkner tells the fourth part of his story.

The following evening, Faulkner took to the stage, alone.

Some people cause trouble, some attract it, Beatrice did a whole lot of both. Things got fucked up pretty much soon as she got out of South Carolina. Roosevelt had been sending money to Blanche in Norfolk and she'd been making sure it reached Beatrice down in Cherryville. Pockets fulla dough, she walked right out of her folks' house, making like she was going to work and jumped a couple of trains that brought her all the way to Blanche's place. She hid out there three days before Vegas sailed her up to New York. Boat hit some shit or other in the Hudson. Gashed a hole in the hull that sank the motherfucker. Captain of his ship, Vegas went down with it. Beatrice managed to swim ashore with a handful of cash and the clothes she was wearing. She found a hotel that'd accept wet bills and lay low a few days before she boarded the *Columbus*.

KC, Roosevelt's contact, got her a spot serving drinks

in first class and that's when the real shit started. Beatrice was like Roosevelt that way. Always some fucking mess she was getting into.

Last night of the trip she got caught up in a private game of faro. Some of the real regal passengers had cabins all set up. Cabins where everything and anything went. And that night, most of the freaks, strippers, sword-swallowers and shit, laid down their arms to watch this high-stakes game between three guys and a woman. *She* was some Catalan duchess, and two of the guys were uppercrusts from England. But the third guy . . . the third guy was an evil-looking Slovenian. Pencil moustache, ruby-red lips, and boy was he plump. A real obese motherfucker. Bigger than Bohemond. Laid out on a couch like an overgrown slug. *He* was Worm.

Why Worm?

Legend goes that in the early days he was a two-bit hood of homosexual persuasion. Him and his lover, Mikhail, ran the show in a small Slovenian backwater called Izola; small-time crooks with big ideas.

A stranger came by the bar where Worm and his buddy were drinking one wet and windy night; Arab guy on his way to Egypt and the Sudan. The three of them sat up drinking way past bedtime. Come dawn the stranger stood up and said he had to be going. What's the hurry? said Worm. You may as well stay and rest a while, get some sleep before you hit the road. Oh no, says the Arab, not a little drunk by now, I've wasted enough time already. I'm on my way to Egypt. I'm gonna be rich. And he spins them some fairy tale about mountains of dope and diamonds guarded by a lost tribe of women hundreds of miles down the Nile. Well, that was music to Worm's ears. He says, So are you from round there? Is that how you know the way? Aw no, says the stupid motherfucker. I got myself a copy of a map.

Those were the last words ever to come out that Arab's mouth. Worm slashed his throat with a razor. Frisked the body and cut up all the clothes until he found the map hidden in the hollowed-out heel of one of the boots.

Next thing, him and Mikhail got themselves a boat. They sailed all the way down the Adriatic across the Ionian and the Mediterranean, to the Nile Delta, and from there it was down, down, down, into Nubia.

They found the place they were looking for after two weeks' sailing and a week-long trek overground: a city, on the edge of the Nubian Desert. All the stuff the Arab had said about it seemed to be true. From their hiding place, Worm and Mickey couldn't see any men, just beautiful young women of every description. But Worm being Worm, he didn't give a fuck about that. What got his dick hard, apart from the obvious, were the mini-mountains of gold, diamonds and dope he saw on every street corner.

Those two Slavic faggots waited until it was dark before they slipped down towards the city. Stupid motherfuckers shoulda disguised themselves or something. They got spotted straight away. And sure, they were armed with a couple of rifles, but wasn't a whole lot they could do against a host of archers and spear-women. So they gave up their guns and got escorted to the chief broad who had them thrown into some kinda holding chamber where a hundred other guys were already chained up.

Turns out it was breeding season in Amazon land. These men, who came from all over the world, had been picked up, kidnapped, bought, mostly in Cairo, and brought down here for a full-moon orgy. Plan was they'd father the next generation of this all-female race, but soon as the humping was done, they'd get their throats cut.

The Amazons came down to check the studs out and choose a mate for the night. Guards dragged the guys out one by one, some kicking and screaming. Worm and his man hatched a fool plan before they got split up.

So there he was: Worm, at the beginning of his last night on earth, a beautiful broad coming on like a last wish that'd make any other motherfucker think they were on their way to Heaven, but made him feel like he was already in Hell. He let her strip him. Throttled her when she tried to mount him. Then he got dressed, snuck out the window, grabbed a few handfuls of diamonds and dope from the hoard on the corner and bolted into the brush. Town was deserted. Stands to reason. Once yearly night of desire – every woman in the place was indoors getting her rocks off.

Mikhail ran out not long after. Worm signalled to him and they both made a break for it.

Posse caught them kissing in the thicket four days later, about a hundred miles out of town. They dragged them back to the city, nailed Mikhail to a tree, smeared his balls with some sweet-scented sap and watched the ants eat his manhood.

There's two versions of what happened to Worm. One is that those Nubian queens ass-fucked him with a molten poker, Edward II-style – a diabolical parody of the homosexual sex act as some Shakespearean motherfucker might say. The other version, and this was the one that Roosevelt stood by, was that they cut out his heart and locked it up in a box, the very one that Beatrice pulled out from under her seat the night we rescued her from the gold-toothed Cuban. According to Roosevelt she'd literally stolen Worm's heart.

Whatever the truth, Worm survived somehow. The Amazons trussed him up like a dancing bear, made him crawl on all fours so the queen could parade him around the streets and palace gardens. He put up with that shit about a year before he managed to escape. Brass-balled fucker endured a three-hundred-mile trial across the Nubian Desert. Walked on to a German frigate at Port Sudan cool as a December day.

Home again, full of hate, he got a serious crew together, went back down the Nile, overthrew the city – guns and bombs against bows and arrows – and crucified and ass-branded every one of those Amazon bitches in revenge for him and Mikhail. He took all the diamonds and gold and dope, and probably his heart, back to Slovenia, crucified the crew and moved to England where he grew fat offof the pickings.

Why Worm? Well, the sphincter singeing left him with a narrow asshole that wouldn't stretch, so whenever he took a shit it came out looking like a super-long earthworm.

Check the records.

Beatrice shoulda walked away soon as she laid eyes on him, but she played a damn good game of faro. A damn good game. And when she saw these money-fat suckers with no real sense of the art, she couldn't resist. It was her chance to get back some of the booty she'd lost in the Hudson.

She laid down a couple of Spanish doubloons, all she had left of Legion's hoard, and made herself a space at the table.

Worm got his eye on her straight off. Welcomed her with open arms and a bottle of Italian vintage.

Bea struck out well. Played cool hands that bust the party up. The Englishmen bailed out first, both banks broken. Duchess ducked out about an hour later. Worm got cut back to his last hundred. Cabin was rammed by this time: screen stars, senators and safe-crackers, dwarves riding on the shoulders of go-go dancers, all straining for a view of the action.

Round midnight Worm turned. Came back at Bea with sharp cards that rattled her. By one o'clock they were even. By two he was keeping a note of her debt on a tab. Five in the morning, he looks up at her from under those beefsteak eyelids and says, My, my, it looks like you owe me about a half a million pounds sterling.

All Beatrice said was, I hope you're gonna give me a chance to win some back.

Worm shook his head. The streak I'm on, I'm not sure I can be stopped. You should've gone to bed hours ago. However, I'm prepared to cut you a deal.

He clicked his fingers and some lackey brought him a fresh deck of cards.

We only have a few hours left onboard, he said, and correct me if I'm wrong, but I don't think you can raise half a million pounds sterling in such a short amount of time. If we go our own ways when this ship docks, I must have some kind of guarantee that you'll pay me. But I have a feeling that I won't hear from you, that I'll have to come looking for you. It could get very ugly. People might get hurt.

He set the cards on the table, and said, OK, here's the deal. You and me, we're going to cut this pack. The winner will be whichever one of us scores highest. If you win, you walk away. No debt. No heartache. If I win, you're mine. That's to say, if I get a higher card than you, I own you. He pulled a fat lock-knife out his pocket and laid it on the table. If you refuse, he said, I'll have you ripped in half right now.

Beatrice looked him up and down. Didn't doubt for one second that the motherfucker meant it.

Only folks left in the room were Worm's crew and a bunch of sniggering circus freaks. One of them locked the door while another unlocked the knife, grabbed Bea and held the blade to her throat.

Wasn't a whole lot she could do but agree to the terms.

Worm waved the knifeman out the way. Set the cards on the table.

Bea insisted, first time around, she'd do the shuffling and he'd make the cut.

That's how it happened.

He dished up a two of clubs.

Bea smiled.

Worm was sweating.

He shuffled the pack. Burst out laughing when Bea scooped out a two of hearts.

Dead heat, he said. No deal. We play to win. Shuffle.

Bea shuffled.

Worm dug up the king of diamonds.

Every freak motherfucker in that place sighed with delight.

Worm took back the pack, shuffled again, smiling like a fucking crocodile.

Bea pulled out the ace of spades. Jumped out her seat, screaming, I win! I win!

Not so, says Worm, aces low.

That was lights out for Beatrice. Some lumbering Frankenstein clubbed her over the back of the head with a cudgel.

*   *   *

275

Roosevelt was on the dock that morning. I found out later it was the first time he went AWOL. He drove down to Southampton to meet Beatrice off the *Columbus*. But she was covered up and out for the count on the back seat of Worm's big black Delage.

She woke up in a bed. Blood on the pillows. Blood coming out her ear. Pain in her hand. More blood on the duvet. The end of her little finger had been hacked off — a clean cut, wrapped in a bandage. She sat up, swung her legs over the side of the mattress, but the fright knocked her onto her back. She was thirty feet off the floor. The bed was more like a tower block. Hundreds of mattresses piled on top of one another. A jump like that woulda broke her neck.

A couple of goons came to check on her. They brought ladders, climbed up, gave her food and something to drink. One of them redressed the finger wound. Then they left.

Worm returned with them later. Had Beatrice brought down to him. He led her to a dining room. Sat her at one end of a mile-long table sagging with food, and took a seat for himself at the other end.

Fat fuck was a big eater. That was his weakness, the way to his heart even after Beatrice stole the fucking thing. To him, every day was like one long Roman feast. Motherfucker was a real Caligula. Swallowed anything from doughnuts to dolphin brains, ortolan to orphan. Only time he ever left his mansion on the hill was to go sample some outlandish dish in the city.

Word was he got through about a chef a month. These guys, lured by the promise of riches beyond their wildest, would come from all over the world to cook for him. If they lasted three months at nine meals a day, never making the same spread twice, he let them go free with all the gold they could carry. But any less and he had them crucified. Tested the mettle of the next sucker by having him carve up the previous chef and serve him as a Sunday roast.

Dining room was a king joint. A gold-encrusted hole with hangings and fountains. Big windows faced on to dreamy scenes lifted straight outta da Vinci or Perugino: hills, forest, lakes, castles, wild white horses, gold skies and deep blue valleys smouldering in the distance.

When Beatrice asked where they were, Worm told her this was his house. But she remembered him saying, during the faro game, that he lived in London.

This is London, he said. It's what you might call a hidden corner of Highgate.

He gave her a grand speech about how, now she was his, he'd make sure she wanted for nothing. So long as she didn't try to escape she'd live out the rest of her days like a queen. If she managed to give him the slip somehow, he'd find her, bring her back and nail her to the battlements. No joke.

Turned out the missing fingertip was a badge. Worm's way of laying claim. Keeping track of property. Also his way of letting a motherfucker know he meant business.

At the end of the meal, he had his monkeys hold Beatrice down while he force-fed her a clutch of black seeds that looked and tasted like peppercorn, but were, in fact, real heavyweight barbiturates. He called them cannonballs, and man they packed a punch.

Took a few weeks to work her up to a super-dependence on the dope. After that Worm let his henchmen take her out on the town from time to time. But even though she was fucked up, Beatrice managed to bribe one of these blockheads into passing a message on to Roosevelt. Only she and God know what she had to do to get round that motherfucker, but then, I guess true love knows no bounds.

So Worm's man, he left this note at one of the bars me and Roosevelt hung out at. A bar Roosevelt'd told Beatrice about in his letters. Of course the grunt read the note. Made sure it didn't say anything it shouldn't, and delivered it to the landlord. Thing was Beatrice and Roosevelt had their own code. They'd been outlawed lovers in one of the most racist states in the Union for years. Had their own way of doing and saying stuff. Cryptic shit no ordinary motherfucker could understand. To Worm's stable boy, the letter must've read like some kinda lame holiday postcard, but to Roosevelt, man, to him it was a call to arms.

He played it cool. Didn't tell me what was going down. Thought I'd panic if I knew. Try to talk him into a safer later plan. Fuck the whole thing up. A surprise after the battle with Legion. But who knows, what with Blossom and everything, maybe he thought I messed that up too.

The night we prised Beatrice out the grip of that spic motherfucker, she had it all planned – situ, time, place, getaway, everything, candied up in the soft-core words of that letter. She spent all that day on the spic's case. All day playing on the motherfucker's weakness – a real man would do this; a real man would do that – until he was just aching for somewhere to happen. She set him up. Lured him to no-man's-land. Served him up on a plate and watched Roosevelt eat him alive.

Once we got hold of Beatrice we fled London for a safe house on the rim of the Weald. Place was owned by Livingstone, our generous cigar-smoking city gent, and we hung out there for a month or two, waiting for the dust to settle and for Bea to get over going cold turkey.

The withdrawals were real bad. Took us weeks to get a handle on the puking and cramps, the seizures and hallucinations. Even after all that crap, the craving could come on awful powerful. I didn't say a thing to Roosevelt but every other day I was around Beatrice I never felt she was one hundred per cent. Always something about her that wasn't quite there. Like Worm kept a little piece of her clamped in his hand.

Once the fits and shit were finished with, she and Roosevelt caught up on the stuff they hadn't been able to do. First off they got married. Had a priest come over from a nearby village and perform the ceremony out on the lawn. Just him and the three of us. I was best man. It was autumn. Leaves on the trees, red and gold. Leaves carpeting the lawn. Everything else a mist-laden shade of blue. When I handed Roosevelt the ring he'd had made out the spic pimp's gold teeth, he said, This is all down to you.

Honeymoon seemed to last for ever.

Wasn't easy staying out of the way.

I walked in on them one time, but they were so engrossed they didn't see me. Roosevelt on his back and that white-chocolate blonde riding him real slow all the way home. Starstruck Negro couldn't keep from coming for long; big religious glaze seeping into his eyes, motherfucker looking like a Renaissance portrait of holy ecstasy, and I knew he was seeing things I never would. I got more out of watching them that one time than I did out a year of screwing Blossom.

Wasn't long before the two of them were driving to nights out in the city. They'd come back in the early hours, smashed, laughing, after the opera or a boxing match and share a bottle of wine in the gazebo over-looking the grounds. I didn't like it. Not one bit. Too much noise too soon. Roosevelt was a face and there were sick sons of bitches out looking for Beatrice. On top of which, she wasn't in any fit state to be out on the streets. Not with what was at stake. She was a loose fucking cannon. No matter how well she meant or how much she loved Roosevelt, she couldn't be trusted. No knowing what shit she'd get that lovestruck nigger into. No knowing what Worm got planted in her head.

I put these things as kindly as I could, but they wouldn't listen to me. Couldn't hear a word I was saying. They were too full of each other, and they were sick and tired of living under some other mother-fucker's boot. Of making like they were ashamed of their love. This was as close to being a free couple as they'd ever gotten and no way were they gonna give that up for anybody.

Come new year, all that shit, all of it, hit the fan.

Come new year we were good as dead.

I got woken by a noise in the downstairs hall one night. At first I thought it was the lovebirds come home to roost, but I didn't hear any voices – no fooling, no laughter. I got out of bed and put on my dressing gown. Pulled the bowie knife out the pocket of my pants. More noise. This time quieter. Strange kinda rhythm. Something jangling. I crept on to the stairs, peeked over the railing and saw Beatrice in furs shovelling spilled gold and trinkets back into a suit-case. It was the last of the money Roosevelt and me had stolen from Legion in New York.

What the fuck are you doing?

She looked up, gave me something between a gasp and a smile and got right back to raking the brass into the case.

I dashed down to the bottom of the stairs, shouting, Where's Roosevelt?

She was shaking, her eyes shadowed with tear-smeared liner, hair hanging loose.

Roosevelt's in trouble, she said.

I wasn't in the mood for any shit. Maybe I shoulda been cooler. But I yelled, *What the fuck have you done with him, you bitch?*

She didn't look, scrambling around on her hands and knees.

Where the fuck is Roosevelt! I pushed her back. She pulled a gun on me.

Now you listen to me, she said. Roosevelt's in trouble. I'm going to bail him out. Worm's got him.

Worm what? Oh man, lies. *Lies!*

He's done it to get to me.

Bullshit. Worm's after *you*, Beatrice. If he was close enough to get Roosevelt, he sure as Hell was close enough to get you. But you're standing here. How come?

We were at the opera, she said. I guess one of his guys spotted us soon as we hit town, and brought reinforcements. Roosevelt went to the men's room and didn't come back. Worm lifted him. He's no fool. He wasn't going to come into the box and drag me out my seat in front of hundreds of people. He took what he could and split knowing I'd go after him.

I don't know what kind of dope you're on now, I said, but it must be awful potent before you try to spin me a story like that. The shit you're telling me just doesn't add up. Why the fuck didn't Worm wait until you and Roosevelt were driving back here to make a move, instead of busting into a toilet in the fucking Royal Opera? Why didn't he have his guys tail you and grab you when you came out on your own? How do I know he's not waiting for you outside right now?

281

She brought her other hand up to support the gun. Didn't say a thing.

Oh boy, I said. You're going to Hell. You mother-fucking, double-crossing Delilah. Roosevelt's lying in some ditch with his brains blown out. Worm's still your pimp. All that time you say he was keeping you prisoner, you and him got snug and drugged-up, hatched plans to fuck Roosevelt over. You kill Roosevelt, the man who loved you more than anyone, then you come here in the middle of the night thinking to steal his treasure right from under my fucking nose and go live happy ever after on Worm's Highgate estate. Maybe you got plans to snuff him too. Plunder his African bounty.

That's crap and you know it! I don't want any fucking money. All I want is Roosevelt.

You lying bitch! You fucked up somehow, or you made some deal, and now Roosevelt's paying for it.

She cocked the gun, trying to smother the jitters. You bitch me one more time, she said, and I'm gonna bitch you back. Bitch! Now, be a good little dog, and get the fuck out of my way.

If you want me out the way you're gonna have to shoot me. Either that or you tell me the fucking truth.

Every word a real effort, she said, I told you . . . we were at the opera . . . Roosevelt went to the bathroom during the break and didn't come back . . . I went looking for him . . . found the men's room swarming with cops, all of them holding handkerchiefs over their noses because of the god-awful smell in there . . . It was like *dead* people. Real hot too. The window was smashed. A big hole in the brickwork below it. The walls, the pissing ditch and the shit-coops were all scorched like someone had torched them. Big pool of blood on the floor. Footprints coming out of it, climbing up the walls. Footprints on the *ceiling*. And Worm's signature in the corner: a handful of nails and a gold hammer. I saw him do it hundreds of other times. It means someone's gonna get crucified. You keep me here any longer and you'll have good as killed Roosevelt.

She was shaking. Almost hysterical.

The story set my heart clattering round its cage. Do you know what you're saying? Man, you got some *fucking* nerve bringing that shit up in front of me. You trying to spook me? Huh? You mixed-up junkie bitch. Has all that dope messed you up so bad you can't tell the difference between fact and fairy tale, between truth and downright fucking lies?

I stepped forward. She stepped back.

You know what happened to us over in New York, right? How Roosevelt lost his fingers and shit, got his guts all twisted?

He told me he got that in a fight in the Bowery. She came on real uneven. Wouldn't look me in the eye.

Oh Beatrice you sick, mixed-up little bitch. You trying to tell me Legion's *here*, in *England*? That he's in cahoots with *Worm?*

Who's Legion?

Like you don't know.

I'm just telling you what I saw. It's the truth.

Bull *shit!* I kept creeping forwards, forcing her back.

We're wasting time.

So let me come with you. If Legion's here you'll need all the help you can get.

No way. All Worm wants is me. If he suspects anything, he'll crucify Roosevelt before I can get to him.

I'm coming with you.

Oh, Faulkner, just let me go. Please. I don't want to

hurt you. Just trust me. Let me go. I'm in enough shit already.

I lunged for the gun but she was ready. She skipped back and fired. The bullet hit me just below the collarbone on the right-hand side, went straight through. Blast knocked me on my ass. I couldn't get up. All my strength slipped out through the slughole. Beatrice flung herself down beside me, muttering like a madwoman, *Shit shit shit shit, look what you made me do. Oh Christ, I can't leave you here to bleed to death, but then I guess they'll come find you anyway.*

She made for the suitcase, stopped and came back, stood over me wringing her hands, then hauled the case outside. Once she got the stash in the car, she grabbed me by the ankles and dragged me the same way. Managed to get me strapped up in the front seat, and drove off with the hood down. The whole world was spinning like a top. Pain pushed me under after a few minutes.

I'd come round from time to time, see Beatrice in furs, her hair blazing like a comet's tail, framed by shifting sapphire skies, hazy constellations and blood-red rocket spoors. Every time I woke, she looked a little more beautiful, and even though she'd shot me, even though she'd fucked everything up for ever, I could see why Roosevelt called her his angel.

We cruised over the moor, engine buzz changing gauge the deeper the dell the thicker the wood, and me, shot-up in the passenger seat, kinda lulled by the tilt of the hills and bass vibrations. The wind made my eyes water. Tears rolling cold, pooling in my ear. I'll never forget the smell of lavender as long as I live.

Maybe she'd been telling the truth. Maybe Worm *had* lifted Roosevelt from the opera. Maybe she really was on her way to bail him out. As for Legion, I for one was ready to believe he was in London. Ready to believe he'd come looking for me and Roosevelt, and had got hooked up with Worm. Ask enough of the right sorts of questions in the right kinds of places, before long you'll strike gold or, in this case, shit. Wasn't such a crazy idea that those two monster motherfuckers had cooked up some kind of a deal. It's like I said already, love and hate: all kinds of shit's possible if you're gunning on either of those. All kinds.

We crossed over Westminster Bridge, past Big Ben and rode up Whitehall. Next time I woke we weren't moving. Everything was real quiet. Car was parked outside a country mansion. Chimneys puffing out grey smoke.

The pain in my chest had bit its way up and down the rest of my body. My head was on fire, but my feet were ice-cold. Every breath I took, my lungs ached. No knowing how dead I was or how long Beatrice had been gone.

Driveway was a steep one. The house on some kind of ridge overlooking a valley lifted straight outta Perugino. I saw white horses galloping along a river-bank. Rocky bluffs and woodland. Mountains miles away. No doubt that this was Worm's place.

Someone bust out the front door. Fur coat and suit-case. It was Beatrice. She staggered on to the grass and loped off down the hill. I tried to call out but my voice broke up into a cough that flecked my chest with specks of blood. She kept running, all lopsided with the case. Two goons came sprinting out from under an archway and charged down the slopes after her.

Footsteps crunched round the back of the car. My door swung open. I crashed out onto the ground, face-down, just about kissing two sets of feet. Didn't have the strength to turn over. Spread-eagled, snuffing stone chip.

One of the guys spoke with a Slavic accent, It looks like Beatrice came up trumps again, he said.

The other one stood on my hand. His boot was red-hot. The smell of sulphur unmistakable. Voice like a fucking landslide: Yeah.

I spotted Beatrice as I lay there. She was way down the valley. Worm's goons had almost caught up with her and I remember thinking, before I blacked out for the last time, that if she could just jump on one of those white horses, or make it to the trees, she'd be OK.

Standing ovation. Faulkner bowed to the house and stepped off the stage.

beurre noir

In which fairy tales are made flesh.

As Faulkner stepped down, Bohemond barged forwards. Deaf to the cries of dismay, the sound of shattering glass, he skidded around the side of the stage, stumbling over wires when he saw the side door swinging open. All he wanted was to find out whether Beatrice was real.

He crashed through the backstage and emerged wheezing in the darkened foyer. Thom had knocked off hours ago, but Faulkner had his own key. He came this way to avoid the bar crowd: sycophants angling to kiss his hands; worthies too ready to tell how profoundly his tales had touched them.

Bohemond rumbled towards the porch, afraid that Faulkner might escape, too late to see the man himself standing in the open doorway holding court with the rest of the band. Too late, because Bohemond in full flow with only half a foot to go knew it would take an act of God to stop or deflect his momentum. And so it was that, just before he sent Faulkner flying from the top step into the heads and bellies of his henchmen, a prayer leaped to his lips: —Jesus! Please! No! But what Bohemond required right then wasn't merely divine intervention, it was a truly biblical miracle.

The band landed heavily, awkwardly. Hard enough for trouble. In later life some of them would complain of cramps and pains and attribute them to this instant; the time – they'd tell others – they'd had a run-in with some fat black cross-dressing schizo cunt in the East End.

Bohemond scratched his head and wished for wings.

Francis the pianist was first to his feet, his trouser legs soaked in snow. Like the others he was unshaven, black-eyed, tie loosed, cuffs unbuttoned, as though he'd been rampaging, sleeping in his suit.

His hat lying in the road twenty yards nearer the Thames, Faulkner sat up and laid a hand on the back of his head. The palm, when he examined it, to Bohemond's horror, was red with blood. Amazement glazed the old man's eyes; the blue loop of his lips and stunned silence quite childlike.

Bohemond thought it better to fake bravery than to fly away. He came down into the midst of the massacre, mumbling, —Sorry, sorry, sorry. But as he stooped to help Faulkner to his feet, Lili stepped in and lashed out, his fist like a firework exploding in Bohemond's nose. He stuttered back, dazed by the pain and double vision. Blood bubbled in his gullet, spilling on the snow as he crumpled and rolled across the road. He came to rest against a lamppost. Almost immediately the far-flung reaches of his innards ignited, pumping and ferrying sedative humours to vital organs with such life-saving ferocity, he felt himself flooded as with quality drugs. Maybe his girth was good for something after all.

As he sat there, slush seeping through the seat of

his pants, the world whirled before his eyes. Words uttered by Faulkner and his so-called sons sounded songlike. Their movements became balletic, as though this street scene were part of a musical, and that at any moment they might each unfurl an umbrella and waltz away into the clouds.

Lili took off his jacket, swung it around Faulkner's shoulders. —*We were just coming to get you*, he crooned, the rest of the band backing him with a chanting a cappella: —*Coming to get you/Coming to get you*.

—*It's time to leave town*, Lili went on. —*We're in deep shit/Or rather you're in deep shit/I don't know how you talked us into this fucking mess/Worm's on the warpath. If we hang about he's gonna getcha/He'll get us all!*

Faulkner hummed something *sotto voce* and Lili let fly in full song: —*Forget the fucking girl!/She's dropped us right in it!/Look what's happened to Petra already!*

And for the first time Bohemond noticed that Petra might be headed for his deathbed. Propped up by Jugs and Mr Lewis, the front of his shirt was steeped in more blood, his complexion as dull as dumpling. Looked as though holes had been hacked in the backs of his hands.

Faulkner nodded and bloodied his other palm on the back of his head.

And what about ladyboy? Jugs nodded at Bohemond without looking at him.

—*I'll fucking fix him!* Lili came storming on, a flick-knife springing open in his hand, but Francis pirouetted ahead and pulled him away. —*Maybe later, Lili. Maybe later.*

They filed after Faulkner and the others. Every one of them – including Petra who hopped as best he could

– seemed to dance and sing all the way down to Shad Thames.

Bohemond tried not to black out, but he couldn't keep up the struggle. What sent him to sleep in the end were not the soporific ichors coursing through his system, but the intolerable horror that, for the first time in his life, he'd been hit.

Snow woke him: bite-size praline-flavoured flakes. The glorious euphoria was gone, in its place what felt like poison pounding round his frame. A stalactite of curdled blood hung between his nose and lips. Frost fixed his fingers to the ground.

It was still dark, but the sky was lightening. Bohemond unfastened his hands, losing the bandages wrapped round his right, and, ignoring the rawness, the almost mortal wounds, crawled across the road, back through the still-open foyer door, deeper and deeper into Delphi. His pants clung to his backside, freezing-wet with snow or piss or both, he wasn't sure.

By the time he reached the restaurant he'd made it to his feet. Wading through tables using chair backs as crutches, he careered into the corridor and curved into the dry store almost smashing his cache of curaçao. He grappled for the bottles, snapped cap after cap, gulped down gallons. The rum warmed him up, but didn't still his shivering – rivulets dripped over his chin.

Finished, he wiped his nose and mouth, smudged his sleeves and front with bloody fingerprints. A triple shot of Ventolin turned his shivers into shakes, but he felt fortified, just able to carry on.

He limped into the kitchen, sniffed back a hunk of blood, stopped and sniffed again. The familiar smells of supper had mingled with other scents: wet fur and a sweetness like skin – Seeta on a night off but softer –

soap dashes and vodka breath masking the merest hint of lavender.

Bohemond swayed around the bain-marie and shuddered to a halt in the laundry. Slow to sink through the sea of rum he'd swallowed, shock rocked him back against the wall, and there he stayed, dazed, for ages, nibbling at a thumb knuckle. An undone suitcase lay braced against the mess-room door. Gold coins and glittering trinkets poured from its open wings.

When he found the strength to edge closer, the first thing he saw was the hem of a fur coat, followed by the full slip of the weightless woman sprawled on the floor. She was unconscious. One hand stretched out above her head, gesturing towards the upset stash. The other was clawed over a cobalt box. A trail of soil skittered from the mess-room garden to the soles of her feet. No trace of snow in her trainer treads, only clods of earth and blades of grass as though she'd come running through the mess-room grove, just as Hanswurst claimed he had more than a year before.

Bohemond sank to his knees, scooped the loose riches into the suitcase and stuffed it under the linen cupboard along with the cobalt box. Another six quick fixes of Ventolin, he gathered the woman in his arms and carried her upstairs to his room.

thighs and biceps

peaches

In which Bohemond's daydreams gain weight and he
learns the truth about beauty.

The woman was as light as a bouquet. Once Bohemond
reached his room, he laid her down on the bed,
watching for a while as she drifted on the rippling
mattress, her hair fanned out like sunrays, the nine
blue nails almost starlike.

He crept back down to the mess-room, grabbed the
suitcase and metal box – which felt hot against the
palm of his hand – and lugged them upstairs, swearing
out loud as he swung into his room to find the woman
awake and waiting. She sat stacked up against the
headboard. Fur coat bundled around her trunk.

Bohemond stumbled, dropped the box.

—Was I that heavy? She spoke slowly, her voice
weighed down by drowsiness.

—Sorry?

—You're sweating.

He flushed again, every pore suddenly steaming.
—*You?* No. You weren't heavy at all . . . it was the
suitcase.

—You're bleeding too. She pointed at her nose.
—And your hand.

Bohemond drew a sleeve across his face. Glanced at his ruptured knuckles. —Hectic New Year, he said.

—It's Boomer, isn't it?

He sniffed, twitched, dabbed his nose with a hanky, raging against a faint, pain, utter amazement.

—Sounds French.

—It is. You're . . . Beatrice, aren't you?

She shrugged. —Bea, Beatrice, whatever.

—*It's you*.

—You look like you've seen a ghost.

—I'm . . . sorry. Beatrice, sorry . . . but . . . *Jesus Christ*.

—What?

—*You!* . . . You . . . Faulkner. And Petra: ah . . . so much *blood*. It looked as though . . . He shook his head. Picked at the damp seat of his pants.

—As though?

—He had *holes* in his hands.

She frowned.

—As though . . . someone had tried to crucify him.

—I know a few people who'd like to've done that.

—*What?*

—What yourself.

Bohemond licked his lips. Beatrice in his bed. Red-hot threads of lavender. Goldilocks with luminous blue nails. —What about these? He nudged the case with a foot and nodded at the box on the desk.

—The box is mine.

—What's in it?

—Nothing.

—It's warm.

—So?

He nodded. —And the suitcase?

296

—Belongs to a friend.

—Roosevelt?

Neck arched, she squeezed her eyes tight shut. —My head hurts. I must've bashed it when I fell over.

Bohemond stepped towards her. Withdrew as she looked up. —Are you OK?

—Don't know.

—Can I get you some aspirin or something?

—Wouldn't help.

—You fell over?

—Last thing I remember was running through trees out Highgate way. I tripped up, lost it . . . next thing I know, you're carrying me upstairs.

—Doesn't that *alarm* you?

—Aye it fucking alarms me. Do I look unalarmed?

Bohemond swallowed another bloody nugget. —Did the band bring you here?

—I just said: I don't *know*.

—Were you with them in Highgate?

— Look . . . can I have a smoke?

—How can you be *so cool*?

—I just told you, I'm *not* cool. That's how I want a fag.

He paused. —I've got . . . asthma . . . There's a balcony around the roof of the dry store. You can smoke out there. But I think it's snowing.

She slid down from the bed. Bohemond stepped away from her again. —What d'you think I'm going to do? she muttered. —Bite you?

—What about Faulkner and the band? They might be looking for you.

—They are *so* the least of my worries.

—This is bad, isn't it? All this . . . it's really bad.

Frustration softened by a smile, she tutted. —Come on, will you, I want a smoke.

—. . . If we go out, I'll have to lock the door.

—Big deal.

He switched the key and turned around, stunned into silence – Roosevelt's beautiful back-stabbing beloved, glowing, arms folded, eyes angled towards the ceiling.

Bohemond bounced into the bathroom, led her up the brass staircase and around the banks of the bath, her voice a volley of sighs behind him: —Jesus, this place is *amazing*. It's like a tropical forest.

At the faraway end, he unlatched the swinging window, allowing her to step on to the balcony before he crouched out after her.

The snow had stopped and hadn't stuck. Thunderously white columns of cloud rolled off towards Shoreditch, revealing clear stretches of sky. Stars winking. Beatrice hunkered down with her back to the glass dome. Bohemond remained standing, shuffling away from the train of smoke as she lit up.

—Cool, she said. —I thought we'd be freezing our bollocks off. Does the balcony go all the way around?

—Almost, yes.

She stood up and sidled past him, stopping halfway to look out across London. Street-level lights illumined the underside of her face – the fur coat and cigarette smoke, everything smouldering gold. —You must be up here all the time, she said. —You can see everything: the Tower . . . and St Paul's.

He glanced back into the bathroom. Drew up alongside her. Couldn't hold back a smile.

—Yeah, yeah, I know, she said. —Tourist. London's not my favourite place in the world.

—Where is?

—Ullapool, easy.

—Another from the West Highlands?

—You know someone else?

—Hermione, the owner of this place . . .—He ran a finger under his collar . . .—Her parents live up near Torridon . . . She was going to be getting married up there.

—Was?

—Might still . . . It's a long story.

—You OK? She glanced at his mangled hand.

—Hm. Why?

—You're mumbling.

—I've . . . seen better days.

—I'll go in a minute.

—*No, no.* He bit his tongue, backed up, blew out. —It's not you.

She looked him up and down. Took another draw on her cigarette. —I know Torridon. It's not so far from Ullapool.

—Is that where you're from?

—Kind of.

—I thought you'd be American.

—*Christ.* Spittle and surprise. —That's a wee bit exotic. You disappointed?

He closed his eyes. Muttered a couple of nothings.

—What's that supposed to mean anyway: you thought I'd be American?

—I've just heard a lot about you, I suppose.

—Who from?

—Faulkner.

—Ha. *Him?* What was he saying?

Bohemond whistled a single note and thrust his hands in his pockets. —Every now and again he gets up onstage in the bar downstairs and tells these stories. The latest one's set in the Twenties and it's all about his adventures with a man called Roosevelt, whose wife, Beatrice, fits your description exactly.

—He said that? Onstage? *In front of folk?*

—He finished off the last instalment by suggesting that you'd . . . I mean *Beatrice* had double-crossed everyone and run off with a suitcase full of money and a heart in a box.

—*A heart in a box?* A box like the one I've got? Is that why you were asking?

—It was a *rumour* . . . in the story. We were never told what it actually held. *Oh* . . . and she shot him too.

Her face lit up with something like delight. —*I shot Faulkner?*

—So he said.

—Talk about tempting fate . . . And this all happened in the Twenties?

—Yes.

Beatrice snickered. —Do I look that old?

—Not sure.

—Piss off.

—How old are you?

—Old enough.

—You look about eighteen.

—Don't be creepy. What about you?

—Older than I look.

—Thirty? Thirty-one?

They exchanged glances. A sparkle in the split-second of silence. And then Bohemond said: —So what about the money and the box?

—What about them?

—Where did they come from?

—Did Faulkner not say?

—According to him . . . Bohemond rocked under the weight of the rum . . . —the money in the suitcase was stolen from a demon policeman's hoard in New York. And as I said, the rumour was that the box had a heart in it.

—Whose heart?

—Worm's.

—And who the fuck's he?

—A big gay Slovenian gangster.

—Oh yeah, right. Worm.

—*You know him?*

—Get real.

—Look, Beatrice . . . he was gasping again, losing his place, shaking his head, —. . . shouldn't we call the police?

—Fuck the police. She drew sharply on her cigarette, smoke scattering as she spoke. —If I don't get the stuff I've got to where it's got to go sometime soon, my friend's had it. Call the police and you'll drop me and him right in it. And then I'll have to drop *you* in it. Carrying me upstairs, hiding me in your room – all that's aiding and abetting.

—I was trying to help . . .

—God's truth, Boomer, shop me, and I promise, you're coming too. Faulkner's not so far off with some of the things he says about me. She ran a hand through her hair. Her voice, after three more draws, much softer. —You know Lili and that lot's had it coming for a long time. And anyway, I'll be gone soon. Just keep your head down till it blows over.

—But I'm thinking of you. This is serious. There are people looking for you.

—Aye, and if you get the police involved that's more folk looking for me. I've done all the running I'm going to do tonight.

—But our lives might be in danger! Someone tried to murder Petra!

—*Calm down*, she stood straight. —Calm down, OK . . . *OK?*

—OK . . . OK.

301

—You saw Petra. He's alive and you don't owe him anything. God knows, him and the rest of them think little enough of you.

—What?

—They were *always* on about you: Lili bragging about the time he got you a silk bra and suspenders for your birthday; and the time they forced you to do a striptease . . . The fat white bird they call you, seeing as how your eyes are blue and everything.

—You know all that?

—Aye. But it was bullshit. You're nothing like I expected.

—. . . What did you expect?

—Not this anyway. She sniffed. —Only thing they came close to was your eyes.

—I dread to think.

—Like a puppy about to be put down.

—Ah.

—Their words, not mine. But you've got to admit, your eyes, they are really sad-looking. Beautiful though . . . really beautiful . . . but, yeah . . . sad.

—Beautiful.

—That's what I remember about the night you hauled me through the window . . . I'll never forget it. Your hands were like shovels, but really gorgeous with all that varnish on, and dead gentle, lifting me up. And as I was coming down, all I remember is these big sad blue eyes. Wee oceans. Couldn't get them out my head all night. That's kind of why I sent you the card.

—Uh . . .

—You just looked so sad. I sent it to say thanks, but it was meant to cheer you up too.

He shook his head, words winding down. —That's one of the kindest things anyone's ever done for me.

—Huh . . . You've had a wee bit to drink, eh?

—Why?

—No reason . . . You're slurring a wee bit. That's all.

—It's not the drink talking . . . I meant what I said: that card was like a bolt of lightning.

—Steady.

—So thoughtful.

—I am thoughtful.

—Are you very familiar with Chagall's work?

—Chagall? Why?

—Don't you remember? On the front of the card?

—I know a couple of the more famous ones, like that one where he's in the kitchen with his wife and he's kissing her, but he's flying off the ground and his neck's bent right round and he's got no arms. That's the one I really wanted to send you.

Bohemond blushed. —*The Birthday?*

—That's the one.

—They say it's one of the most sublime and abiding evocations of love ever committed to canvas.

—Do they?

—It's probably my all-time favourite painting. Why that one in particular?

—They're both floating off the ground in it – he is anyway – and his wife's got this sad far-off look in her eye. She kind of reminded me of you, the other night.

—But in the picture they're kissing.

—So?

Butterflies fluttered in his gut.

—But like I say, she said. —I couldn't find that card, so I made do with the one of the folk on the flying horse. It's still a nice picture.

—Do you know the story behind it?

—It's part of a love poem: the 'Song of Songs'.

—I thought you said you didn't know much about Chagall.

—Couple of famous paintings is hardly much, is it? A ribbon of smoke streamed between her nose and mouth.

—Did you mean it?

—What?

—That next time you'll fly me home.

—Course.

—You think you could carry me?

—Easy.

—You did mean it, then?

—Every word.

—I suppose you must have . . . you gave me six kisses.

—Aye well . . . she tailed off, —. . . you got me out of a lot of trouble.

—Ditto.

—Cryptic.

—If I tell you any more, Beatrice, you'll think I'm mad . . . Perhaps I am.

—Try me.

—Suffice to say . . . I was in dire need of a miracle . . . and there you were.

—*Me?*

—You. Your letter.

She edged closer. —What were you needing a miracle for?

He inhaled. Held his breath. Fireworks sparkled over the Wapping wharves.

—That bad?

—It's nothing.

—You're bleeding again. She went through her pockets, found a crumpled paper handkerchief which she handed to him.

Bohemond nursed his nose and knuckles, nodding thanks.

—Is all this part of it?

—The knuckles, yes, the nose, not really . . . but in a way . . . I suppose . . . yes.

—What happened to your nose?

—Lili hit me.

—That lot . . . She leaned forward, looking for him. —. . . they give you a hard time, eh?

—This is one I deserved.

—I doubt it. What about your knuckles?

—. . . *sss*.

—Boomer.

He forced a grin, but it snapped to a gasp, felt like water welling around his heart. Beatrice straightened away from the railing and dropped her cigarette over the side.

—Sorry, sorry, this is shit. I wasn't thinking. I should go?

—*No please don't.* It's not you.

Already on her way to the swinging window, she turned around.

—It's not you, said Bohemond.

—You've got problems . . . haven't you?

—You will have too, if you leave here now.

She sighed, rolled her eyes, mulling for a moment.

Bohemond looked away again, blood back up in his throat. —Really, I'm fine.

—But you're *not*.

—I will be. Just give me a moment.

Beatrice saw all the sorrow and returned to his side. Made a play of not meeting his gaze.

—I just want something I can't have, he said.

—Join the club.

Neither of them spoke for a long while. Beatrice

305

lit up another cigarette, smoked it through. As she
flung the butt over the balcony, she looked at him,
narrowing her eyes against the wind. —What's that
smell?

—Huh?

—It's like peach? Is it you?

—Eh . . . sorry . . . it's sweat.

—Sweat? No way. It's nice.

—Oh.

—Don't look so surprised.

—I saw you a few times . . . before I pulled you
through the window at New Year . . . Every time . . .
the air was full of a wonderful scent of lavender. Is it a
perfume?

—I don't wear perfume, she said. —And I haven't
had a decent wash in ages.

—Sweat.

—Away.

He watched her smoke a third cigarette – speedy
puffs working up to something. She flicked it half-
finished into the air, its tip shedding orange shrapnel
as it spiralled down to the street. —Listen, she said. —I
don't like to ask . . . but can I stay here . . . *just for
tonight* . . . I'll go first thing.

Bohemond blinked.

—No? OK.

—No, *wait, wait*. Stay. You can have my bed. I'll
sleep on the floor.

She smiled. —No you won't. I will.

—But I insist.

He led her back through the bathroom into the
bedroom and sacked the cupboards hunting for extra
bedding. There was none. Seeta was the only overnight
guest he'd ever had, and she hadn't even been a real
guest.

Beatrice dumped her fur coat on the floor, un-covering a silver shirt and matching silver trousers. —There's room for us both in the bed, she said.

—What?

—It's *massive*.

—Maybe I'll just . . . sleep in my armchair.

—Don't be daft. She undressed. Darted under the duvet in nothing but silver knickers and a bra.

Bohemond swung away eyes closed, the gold wings he'd glimpsed tattooed on her shoulderblades glimmer-ing on the backs of his lids. —My prayers answered, he whispered, so quietly he more felt than heard the words coming out of his mouth. —*Heaven has sent me an angel.*

—I promise I won't watch you getting changed, said Beatrice.

He peeped, saw her head above the covers; a shaft of neck and shoulders buried in blonde.

She rolled onto her side, away from him. —I won't.

He slipped off his shoes, slithered into bed and lay on the edge of the mattress.

—Aren't you going to get undressed?

—This is how I sleep . . . sometimes.

—But your trousers are all soiled.

—No matter.

—. . . Can we set an alarm?

—What time?

—Before the staff start coming.

—Seven?

—Great. Goodnight.

—Shall I turn out the light?

—Aye, whatever.

He flicked the switch. Lay frozen with his eyes open.

Many minutes later she rocked towards him. Breath

307

on the side of his face, the sound of moisture popping in her mouth. —Can't you sleep?

He couldn't, *wouldn't* look.

—I'm sorry, she said. —I feel really shit about this.

—*I* carried you up here.

—I was wondering about that.

—You were in trouble.

—Aye, but bringing me up here to your bedroom? Why not just call the police?

—I was dazed, not thinking straight.

—Is that it?

—Why else?

—You mentioned a miracle.

Bohemond pinched his own thigh. —I'm afraid if I question it or tell you, it'll prove to be something much less.

—Aye, well, after what Faulkner said about me in those fucking stories, it'd have to be a miracle for you to bring me up here.

—I just wish I knew more. Given the last few weeks of my life, especially the last few days, the situation we're in right now is unbelievable. For all I know, this is a concussion-induced dream . . . I mean, the way you say you got here . . . Faulkner and his stories. You fit the description of his Beatrice right down to the smell of lavender and the missing tip of your little finger, but . . . Bohemond pursed his lips as Beatrice ruffled the bedclothes and he saw the silhouette of her lifted hand.

—How did he say I got this?

—I'm sorry?

—What did he say about my finger?

—He said that Worm chopped it off to show that he owned you.

—That's *sick*.

308

—I know.

—I got it jammed in a car door when I was six.

—*Sorry*.

—Anything else?

—No. Chance-taking, drugged-up murderess just about sums you up.

—Not so bad a handle given the scum that's after me.

—But why risk your life?

—I told you: my friend.

—*Is it* Roosevelt?

—Shut up with these names, will you?

—Is he black or white?

—What kind of a question's *that*?

Bohemond swallowed spit.

—It's got *nothing* to do with you.

—But it does. I'm aiding and abetting a criminal, *remember*?

—I'm not a criminal and you're not dreaming.

—Well then, tell me what's going on.

—I don't want you to get hurt.

—All the more reason why you should tell me. *Christ's sake*, someone tried to crucify Petra.

—Look, you're getting all panicky again. There's no *way* I'm telling you. And I can't believe that Faulkner would be so arrogant, or just plain insane, as to get up onstage in front of a room full of people and make a story out of it.

—But if I'm in danger, I have a right to know. You've come barging into my life. Already it sounds like it might never be the same again . . .

—I didn't barge into your life! It was you brought me upstairs.

—But I had no choice.

—Course you had a choice! I told you . . . ah for

fuck's sake! She shunted away from him and sat up.
—I knew this was a mistake.
  —*Sorry. Sorry. Sorry. Sorry. Stay. Please. Stay.*
· He could see she was looking down at him. Strands
of hair glowing like filaments, gold tattoo smattered
across the moon-blue arc of her shoulderblade.
—Please.
—Are you going to shut up then? Cos I'd rather go
out there and take my chances than lie in here with
you whingeing all night.
—I just don't know what any of this means.
—Why's it got to mean anything?
—You *are* real . . .
—You're drunk.
—Curaçao.
—Rum.
—Yes.
—Good choice. Tangerine goes with your peaches.
He smiled, quite light-headed.
—You calm?
—Calm.
—Right, goodnight.
—Goodnight.
During the night she was restless, drifting back and
forth. Bohemond spent each sleepless hour stroking
the mattress, feeling the warmth of where she'd
been.

When the alarm trilled Beatrice sprang out of bed and
almost cartwheeled into her clothes. Bohemond lay
low, watched her come and go, his gut and groin
rumbling at the show of thighs and biceps. —It's as
though you're famous or something, he said.
  She grabbed the suitcase and the metal box. —What
is?

—You being here after all that's happened. It's like a film or a fairy tale.

—What a thrill.

Ambushed by a hangover, he almost tumbled out of bed. —I'll have to let you out.

—Fine.

—Let me take the case.

—I can manage.

—Some breakfast?

—No.

It was cold on the way down to the foyer. The bones in Bohemond's ankles crackled. Gold coin chimed behind him as Beatrice battled with the case. Snow swept in when he unlocked the front door. Day was on its way, the street blue-white. —This is it, he said.

—Thanks a lot. I owe you two now.

—I feel like I should come with you. Keep an eye out.

—Don't be daft. Stay here and get better.

—Just be careful.

—Always.

He watched her shuffle up the street towards Shad Thames. Stayed where he was long after she'd slipped out of sight.

love birds

Strange visitations.

For the first hour of the morning shift Bohemond blundered and bungled and botched. Dazed by day-dreams of the previous evening, he careered around the kitchen torching everything he touched. The second hour he sat out, genuinely fearful of doing himself, or someone else, real damage.

Dinner was disrupted by a din in the dining room. The kitchen staff scuttled in to find a pack of dogs dashing after a canary. Diners sprawled on the floor amid overturned spreads, their suits and slips spattered with soups and sauces, while the bird fluttered on just beyond reach of the dogs' snapping jaws. It flew into the corridor, through the kitchen, the laundry, dis-appeared into the mess-room grove. One of the dogs galloped after it and didn't reappear. The waiters railed against the rest with raised chairs, forcing them out the door, on to the back lot. Hanswurst pranced in pursuit, a cleaver swinging in either hand.

When the cooks returned to the kitchen they found a

man and a woman standing by the deep fryers. He was obese, bearded, blue shirt and jeans, while she was altogether smaller, younger, thinner – cropped blonde in a thigh-length sleeveless dress, a tiny nose stud winking silver and gold. When Bohemond saw them together, breathless as he was, he couldn't keep from smiling.

—Are you the chef? asked the man.

—We all are.

—Well, we've been here a few times before and we'd just like to say we think the food's absolutely fantastic. Really incredible.

—Thank you.

—Oh, and the band you sometimes have playing in the bar is pretty good too.

—You're very kind.

—I used to play in a jazz band myself and those guys are pretty good.

—What was your band called? asked Morrissey.

The man teetered up onto the balls of his feet. —Oh, you wouldn't have heard of us. We only played in Scotland. Nearest we got to the big time was a tour we did around the Highlands.

—You're a long way from home, said Bohemond.

—Well . . . The man looked at the woman. She gazed back at him swallowing a smile. —. . . I, eh . . . I've been here a wee while now, he said. —Anyway, we just came in to say thank you and we'll definitely be back. He shook Bohemond's hand, glanced past his shoulder, and cried out: —*Gee whiz! Look! Gee whiz!*

Bohemond turned to see an egg rolling around on Seeta's worktop.

—Maybe there's a chick in it, said one of the waiters. —Y'know, trying to get out.

They all crept to the edge of the table, quite mute as the egg spun like a compass needle.

Bohemond glanced at Seeta, sadness in her eyes despite the marvel. —You and I should have a chat, he whispered.

She nodded but didn't look at him.

Everyone squealed as the dancing egg dropped onto the floor and rolled, still whole, out the door.

wish bones

In which Bohemond opens his heart and Hermione
bares her soul.

The egg danced on and on, Bohemond waving everyone back to work as he chased it out into the corridor.
It whisked through the restaurant, and the foyer,
across the deserted bar floor and broke open against
the leg of a table. The two halves were empty; no yolk,
or white.

—What the Hell was that?

He whirled around, saw Hermione behind the bar
sipping from a tumbler, and, struggling against a stutter,
muttered: —Egg.

—An *egg*?

—It rolled out of the kitchen. I came after it. He
glanced around the empty room, off-balance, off-key.
—Stocktake?

—All day. She hooked a bottle of lemon Looza up
onto the bar. Grabbed a glass from the draining board.
Bohemond approached and sat down, his backside
spread across three bar stools. Hermione poured his
drink. —Cheers, she said, waiting for him to take a sip.

315

—What've you got?

—Mother's ruin.

—Cheers. He drank and looked round again. —Any word from Faulkner or the band recently?

—I got a call last night. They're taking a break.

—Any reason?

—No, why?

—Just something I overheard.

—What?

—Nothing. Gossip.

She eyed him over another sip of gin. —I haven't seen you since you ran out of my room, Bo.

—No . . .

—I would've come after you.

—But?

—Didn't know if you wanted me to.

People passed by outside, their laughter drifting in through an open window. Bohemond set down his drink. —I *wish* you'd told me, Hermione.

—I thought you knew.

—I only realized that night, after I had made an utter fool of myself.

—But New Year . . . all the stuff about the letter and Seeta . . . *I thought you knew*.

—Seeta didn't say anything.

—So what were you talking about?

—Something else . . . Does Paris know?

—You were the last person I wanted to hurt.

—*Does he know?*

—Yes, he knows. He's always known. She patted her chest, swallowed the last of her gin and poured another. —Paris tries, he really tries to be a good guy, but he's a little boy . . . Me being bi was a turn-on, believe it or not. Yeah, he was into the thought of me getting off with other women, but it was more about him wanting to play open-minded man of the world. And it wasn't like a challenge to his manhood either, cos it's different with girls, sort of thing. It was like, so long as I didn't get off with other guys, no problem. Just so he could be the one to cure me with his big black cock.

Bohemond jolted.

—His exact words; meant as a joke, but no joke.

—Paris . . . *as a misguided but sensitive man*?

—Yeah, but once he finally got that he wasn't going to *cure* me, he started to feel like he was missing out and doing stuff to try and make me jealous.

—Your games . . .

—Since Seeta he's gone up gears.

—So . . . *all the time I've known you*, Hermione . . . you've taken female lovers?

—Before then too.

—Other women?

—And girls.

—*Girls*, he grunted. —Good God.

—*Eighteen and over*, Bohemond. I'm not a cradle snatcher.

—Even when you lived in the flat above my bedsit?

—That's what me and Matt were always arguing about.

—I had no idea. *No idea*.

—But they were all just flings.

—Seeta too?

—Christ. *Seeta?* No. No way . . . She turned my whole world upside-down. Was the real thing. I got the fright of my life. Paris did too. That's why he proposed.

—Ah, Bohemond nodded. —*You* got the fright of your life. *Your* world was turned upside-down.

—What's that look for?

317

—What look?

—*God.* You, of all people.

—*What?*

—I've got nothing to feel guilty about, Bohemond.

—Don't think I'm judging you on your sexual peccadilloes.

—*Peccadilloes?*

—It's the people caught in the crossfire.

—Seeta's going to be fine.

—I wasn't thinking of Seeta.

Hermione lowered her eyes.

—You used me to get back at Paris.

—Bohemond, please. I was confused. Well and truly fucked. *Fucked.*

He felt for the gold feather in his pocket, found it between the leaves of Beatrice's card. —You were ready to run away with me, Hermione . . . Told me there's no-one you'd rather run away *with*; how my love had been staring you in the face all these years; could I imagine what life would be like with you . . . You sounded so sincere. And the way you looked at me . . . *my God* . . .

—But I meant everything I said. It's just . . . when it came to the crunch, I wimped out. Not because of you, but because of me.

—You got cold feet?

—In a way.

—You broke it off with Seeta, you ran away from me . . . what now?

—Not sure.

—Back where you started? With Paris?

—I think.

—So then explain it to me, Hermione, because I don't understand, I just don't *understand*, after all the things you said and did, why you'd want to stay here

318

and *make do* with a man who falls so entirely short of you.

She shrugged. —He's always been there for me. He's a good friend . . . maybe the best. And if I'm totally honest, we've been together such a long time . . . the thought of *not* being with him scares the shit out of me.

—Seeta was right . . .

—Seeta said what?

—You're settling for second best.

—*Always*, she's trying to tell me what I am and what I'm not. She's fucking twenty-one years old.

—A child, said Bohemond. —But she was right. You just admitted as much.

—*Crap*. I'm marrying Paris because I love him.

—Is it true love?

—True enough.

Bohemond closed his mouth and clenched his teeth, summoning strength. —And what about Seeta?

—It's really knocked you for six, hasn't it?

—Is that so *surprising*? You're my oldest friend and suddenly it's as if I've only half-known you all this time.

—Nothing's changed.

—*Everything's* changed . . . There I was waiting for you at Liverpool Street station, my head full of all the things you'd said to me over the preceding weeks, ready and waiting to spend the rest of my life with you, when all the time . . . you were dreaming of Seeta.

—A woman?

—Don't put words in my mouth.

—That's it though, isn't it?

—I told you, I'm not here to criticize your shifting sexual preferences.

319

—*Stop saying that*. You make it sound like I can't make up my mind or something, like I'm confused.

—'Confused' is the one word I've heard you use more than any other over the last few weeks.

—Yeah, but not about my sexual orientation.

His voice hardened but his shoulders and hands were all apology. —But if it was something you in no way felt guilty or confused about, surely at some point over the last fourteen years that we've been friends, you would have told me.

—Oh stop.

—I'm not suggesting for one minute that you *should* feel guilty. All I'm saying is maybe you do.

—Could you be any more patronizing?

—I just wish you'd said *something*!

—*Keep your voice down!* She glanced at the door. —Look, you know about me and Paris because you work here. You knew about Matt, but only because I fell through your roof trying to get away from him. Apart from them I never said much about anyone I've been out with. I don't see why this thing with Seeta is such a problem, unless you're lying when you say you're not bothered by me liking boys and girls.

—. . . You know, you and Matt fought just about every night . . . I remember the ceiling rumbling, all the screaming. It was horrible. The police came that night because I phoned them. I thought he was going to kill you.

—Wasn't far off.

—When I heard you and Paris fighting just before Christmas . . .

—The time you knocked on the door?

—Has he ever hit you?

—No.

—Have any of your *other* boyfriends?

—I can see where you're going, Bohemond, and I think you better stop before you say something you regret.

He scratched his nose, dug knuckles into his knee, inhaled the scent of lavender wafting from his pocket. —No.

Hermione finished her gin, poured another. —D'you want to know why Seeta?

—She listens . . . ?

—It's cos she's mad about me.

—I was too.

—Not like her you weren't . . . When we were together, the way she'd look at me, it was so . . . *fierce.* I knew she didn't need anyone else.

—I'm sure I've looked at you in the same way.

—When you look at me, Bo . . . there's something missing. Same with Paris. It's like you're holding back. Seeta gives me everything.

—But she's *so young.* No wonder she's in awe of you.

—Age has nothing to do with it. She's more mature than most people I know.

—She's a *child*, Hermione. She doesn't know what she wants . . .

—Don't be so naïve. Her gaze was calm, but quite final.

—. . . And if I *had* looked at you the way Seeta did, obese and freakish as I am, would you have come to meet me at Liverpool Street station?

—*Hey . . . hey . . .* after all this time, you think the way you look would have *anything* to do with how much I could or do love you.

—Noble words, but would you?

—I wouldn't have had any choice. But it's like I said, the way you look at me now isn't enough. It's like there is, or could be, someone you'd love more. So you see, me not coming to Liverpool Street's got nothing to do with you being *obese and freakish*. I told you – it's not you. It's not even *me*. It's just a question of who we're *meant* to be with.

—. . . You probably don't remember, but that night, in the shower, all those years ago, you gave me a look I'll never forget. Just for a moment, I thought I'd found my way . . . After you left, your phone calls kept me going. Believe it or not, my life *literally* revolved around hearing your voice. But my time . . . working for you here has been *torture*. Watching you with Paris . . . how he *treats* you . . . The wedding announcement broke me. I was ready to kill myself. I wrote you a letter . . . had enough sleeping pills to fell a herd of elephants. One sign, I wrote, that my love for you wouldn't remain unrequited and I'd relent. At that moment Paris and his lady-friend came in through my window . . .

—These things, Bohemond . . . *I'm amazed* . . . but, Christ. *Suicide?*

—I feel so *fucking* . . .

—Well I feel like shit too . . . but since we're being bold, I've got to tell you . . . I still don't think you love me like Seeta does.

—*How can you say that?*

—Because it's true. And because maybe it's what you need to hear.

—Do you think *any* man could love you as much?
She toyed with her glass, made no reply.

—Then why not go and be with Seeta?

—I told you.

—Fear of life without Paris? Well then the love

322

you talk about can't be true, because true love conquers all.

—I'd like to believe that, said Hermione. —More than anything. But it's another of your fairy-stories.

—If you loved Seeta as much as you claim, you'd do anything to be with her. Even call off a wedding.

—But I *can't* call off the wedding.

—Why not?

—Because people are so fucking awful. She turned away from him, glazing over. —And because I'm a coward.

—Ah.

—At the end of the day, how I feel about Seeta comes second to how other people would feel about *me* and Seeta: it'd kill my dad. He'd have a heart attack. It'd kill my mum eventually too. Look at Seeta's dad, he beat her up and threw her out the house when he found out about her.

—Of course, *the house of shame* . . . But he certainly didn't hit her on purpose.

—So you say. But there's all that shit. And then there's everyone making out like everything's cool while they're whispering behind my back. It's just fucking pressure . . . All I want, Bo, more than anything, is to start a family.

Fingers pressed to his temples Bohemond attempted to stem a headache. —You could do that with Seeta.

—*What are you playing at?*

—I just want you to be happy.

—Seeta doesn't want children, she's way too young. And I don't want to be injected with jism. I just want a regular family, with regular kids, kids who know who their real parents are. But I . . . I also . . . think maybe it's not *right* for children to have two parents of the same sex. Not just for the kids getting hassle at school.

But sometimes . . . I wonder whether a mother and a father can naturally give a child something that two mothers or two fathers can't.

—*Ha . . . amazing*, given the life you've led, that you'd make such a remark. Surely to be loved by *someone*, be they gay, straight, black, white or *blue*, is better than not being loved at all.

—But just a moment ago you were making out I was some kind of *deviant*.

—*Christ* . . . He wiped his brow, swept sweat back into his hair. —This whole thing depends on which is most important to you: a family or happiness. For myself I can't understand why you'd commit to spending the rest of your life with someone you *don't really love*.

—How many times? I *do* love Paris.

—Maybe, but you say you're *in* love with Seeta.

—I don't think I'll ever feel like that about anyone ever again . . . She was smiling, miles away. Unhappier than he'd ever seen her. He glanced at the stage, the place where Faulkner, full of fairy tales, had aided his renaissance. —. . . Maybe, in the gap between the heavenly but impractical love you bear Seeta and the more, shall we say, *earthly* love you bear Paris, there's room for someone else to steal through. Someone who can give you the best of both worlds.

—Not now.

—It's your *life* we're talking about. Don't settle for second best. If it's Seeta you want to be with, be with Seeta, whatever your reservations, *love will find a way*. If the thought of that is too much, wait, rather than coasting into a marriage of convenience. The right person will come along.

—Bohemond, wake up. That's TV talk.

—Your letter to Seeta was *full* of such talk. You

324

know as well as I do, sometimes there just aren't the words.

She smiled, breath cleft between her teeth.

—Don't you ever wonder . . . he said, slowing down, —. . . what might've been if you'd stayed in Brixton? If you'd lived alone in that flat above my bedsit and we'd become friends?

—Don't, Bohemond.

—When I think of you and Seeta together, I feel so . . . He shook his head and hands searching for words: —*helpless*.

—Please don't.

—It's bad enough picturing you in Paris's arms, but when I think of you with Seeta and suppose there's nowhere you'd rather be, it fills me with despair.

—Why despair?

—Because I'm a *man*, of sorts . . . the wind went out of him; —. . . and you'll never feel the same way about me.

—I honestly think, said Hermione, —that the person you find most attractive in all the world will be the person who finds *you* most attractive. You just haven't found her yet.

—That's almost what I just told you: *the right person will come along*. But if you really believed these things, you wouldn't be marrying Paris.

—Come on, Bo, in your heart of hearts you know it's not me you want.

He stuttered to a stop, snorting as he started again. —But maybe . . . I could give you the things Paris, and now Seeta, have been unable to give you.

—Bohemond . . . Hermione's voice was tiny, —don't get upset. If you get upset I'll get upset. She swerved out from behind the bar and wrapped an arm around his shoulders. —You're beautiful, she said, pulling him

325

closer, words warming his neck. —The most beautiful person I've ever met . . . but I'm not in love with you . . . and I never was.

He flinched, bit the back of his hand. —*But I don't understand!* All those omens . . . so many signs. Heaven sent me an angel. She saved me . . . for you I thought. It was a *miracle*, Hermione. I nearly died . . . *I nearly died, I nearly died, I nearly died* . . .

—*Miracles?* Bohemond, what are you talking about?

As he reached for the letter in his pocket Hermione pulled away, one hand left resting on his shoulder. —Can I help you?

Bohemond turned around, nearly keeled: wrestling with the suitcase and cobalt box, Beatrice was on her way across the floor. —I just wanted a word with the chef, she said.

Hermione let go. —How did you get in?

—The door was open.

—*Shit.* She glanced at Bohemond.

—It's OK, he said, still astonished. —I know her. This is Beatrice. Beatrice, meet Hermione.

They nodded at one another, Hermione on her way out.

Beatrice watched her go. —She looked a wee bit spooked. What've you been saying to her?

The seat of his pants soaked through with sweat, Bohemond slouched off the stool.

—Jesus Christ, she said, —has someone died?

He pressed the heels of his hands against his forehead. —Are you all right?

—Me? I fucked up, didn't I?

—More trouble?

—No-one knows I'm here. I was careful. She levelled her eyes at his chest. —Can I stay again? I was going to stay with Faulkner or one of the guys in the band, but they've done a runner.

Hermione leaned around the doorpost, face flushed. —Quick, it's Hanswurst.

Bohemond bolted, Beatrice beside him like a day-dream. —To tell you the truth, he sniffed, —nothing would make me happier.

chargrill

How Bohemond is almost beheaded.

They found the kitchen crowded: Vic shielding himself
with a raised chair, Morrissey poised to strike with a
brass enamelled pan, the waiting staff wielding an
assortment of cutlery, all working to corner Hanswurst
as he swung about the floor, the cleavers still gripped
in either fist, both wrists scorched raw.

Innocent backed towards Bohemond, a fish slice in
his hand. —He comes in from chasing the wild dogs,
he said, —and he has these burns, and then he tries to
attack Loretta. She is in the mess-room with Seeta
now. I think that she is hurt.

—Hanswurst, for God's sake. Bohemond came
around behind Vic. —Put the cleavers down before
you hurt anyone else.

Hanswurst's eyes widened and rolled. He cocked
to the side, saw Beatrice, thundered, —CUNT! and
lunged, breaking through the human ring. Beatrice
ducked, chicaned about-face and, holding onto the
hems of Bohemond's overalls, thrashed out, catching
Hanswurst with a foot below the knee. He pitched,

cleavers like wings, one of which clipped Bohemond's collarbone – a blue hot nip singing round the rim of his frame – and Vic charged with the chair, grinning vengeance as he pinned the kitchen porter to the ground. Morrissey and the waiters fell on top of him, pressureholds and headlocks, the cleavers finally unfastened from his hands.

Bohemond slumped against the sideboard, a million fingers trying to stem the flow of blood from his neck. It was Hermione, in the end, who sat him down, washed and wiped the wound. —You've got a tiny notch, she said. —Nothing serious.

—Thanks, he said, leaning back, looking for Beatrice. No sign. The suitcase and box gone too. He stood up. —Where's Beatrice?

Hermione stumbled away from him. —Who?

—The girl in the fur coat? asked Vic, still sitting on the chair caging a now-subdued Hanswurst against the ground. —She just left.

—Fats!

—Hanswurst?

—I'm sorry . . .

Bohemond howled and spun around. Hermione moved to stop him, but he blundered past, into the hall, chasing the trail of lavender, convinced that the burns on Hanswurst's arms were Legion's red-hot handprints.

horseback, chicken breast and bubbly

In which Bohemond opens his eyes and succumbs to the wonders of the world.

Lavender drew him through the restaurant, into the foyer and out the front door. He stumbled towards Shad Thames, swung back up the stairwell on to Tower Bridge. Beatrice was well ahead, struggling with the suitcase, over the Thames by the time Bohemond caught up with her. Breathless, bent as double as his belly would allow, he begged, —Beatrice, please come back.

She glanced at him but kept on. —And get you lot up to your necks in shit?

—Running along Tower Bridge like this is asking for trouble. It's safer back at Delphi.

—It's better for you if I'm not there.

—Not for me it isn't . . . Not for me.

—Cab! Flag it.

—Let me come with you.

—Oh for fuck's sake! She dropped the suitcase and hailed the taxi.

330

—Beatrice.

—No.

—Please.

—Go home.

—Please!

The cab pulled up beside them. Beatrice hauled herself inside. Gave him a stiff wave goodbye.

Bohemond squatted, one hand pressed against the ground, the cleaver notch throbbing hot. He watched the taxi drift off and stop for the traffic lights. Blonde hair blew through the open window. A tiny voice mingled with wind. —Come on then.

Joy brought a wiggle to his walk as he made his way along the pavement.

Beatrice opened the door, arms spread wide. The unbuttoned coat showed off softness. Glitter in her grin and too-blue eyes. Bohemond set his foot on the step, testing the suspension, wheezed with dread as the lights changed and engines revved.

—What the fuck's wrong with you? she smiled. —Get in.

He pulled himself up, sat down beside her, astonished that the cab hadn't capsized. Hadn't even *creaked*.

—I thought you were gone, he gasped.

—Well . . .

—Thank you so much.

Half an hour later the taxi pulled over on a street bordered by a canal. Yachts and barges cluttered the quaysides. Bridges arched off further up. Once she'd paid the driver, Beatrice slid down the verge to the waterside. Bohemond rolled after her, grabbed hold of the suitcase. She let go and led on along the canal path. Literally walked on board a barge.

Bohemond followed, rocked the boat and almost

toppled. Sat at the stern as quickly as he could.

—Don't worry, said Beatrice. —You're not going to sink it.

—Is it yours?

—Sort of.

She took off her coat and grabbed the tiller. Bohemond gripped the lip of his cushioned bench, as the bow swung silently away from the quay. —Has this thing no *engine*?

—It just works.

—Where are we?

—Little Venice.

—And where are we going?

—Who knows?

Houses on either bank seemed to grow and lean, at one point became so stooped, their roofs so close, that Bohemond felt himself indoors, drifting down a huge hall. Diners, drinkers and dancers thronged on balconies. Skin and brickwork bathed in candlelight. Voices amplified by the plunge. Flamenco guitar stuttered down from miles up, slicing through air fat with the scents of mint and venison. A hidden Latin soprano flew into the finale of an aria, its dying notes lost in a deluge of applause, and the barge was obliterated by a blizzard of confetti. A man leaned out of a riverfront window and handed Bohemond a magnum of champagne, the head chef at long last actually laughing. Beatrice popped the cork with a penknife and they boozed straight from the bottle, waving at women and wild white horses swimming in the water before them. —Mermaids, said Bohemond.

Beatrice beamed and sat down beside him, one hand still on the tiller. —In London?

He shook his head, grasping at the shower of tinsel. —This isn't London.

—We were just in your kitchen.

—That's what I mean. I'm . . . not there any more.

The confetti fluttered to nothing, more applause roaring up the inlet. Beatrice took another swig of champagne and handed him the magnum. —Is it that bad, Boomer?

—Bohemond.

—OK, *Boo*. Will Boo do?

—Boo will do.

—Is it? Is it that bad?

—Just promise me that you're real . . . he took a sip of champagne, pointed up ahead, —. . . and that I'm not dreaming.

Half-naked acrobats had formed a human bridge, tumblers in turbans riding full-grown elephants across.

—You've been too long in that kitchen, said Beatrice.

—If this is what it's like outside, I could just keep going . . . sail away.

—So do it.

He swung his feet, scattering heaps of confetti. —I might just.

Something bumped against the underside of the barge, the water around them suddenly white, slashed by the dorsals of six speeding dolphins.

—It's thingy, isn't it? said Beatrice. —The woman in the bar. Harmony or whatever.

—Hermione.

—When we were out on the balcony that night, it was her you were talking about: wanting something you can't have.

Lips puckered, he nodded.

—Have you not said anything to her?

—I tried.

—And?

—Failed. Miserably.

—That's her loss.

—Ha.

—She work in the bar?

He told her about his arrival at and flight from the goth squat in Hackney. About how Hermione had fallen through the roof of his bedsit. Her eventual offer of a job. As he finished, Beatrice smiled and said: —So that's how you met the woman of your dreams: she fell out of the sky.

—She *was* the woman of my dreams.

—What's changed?

—So much.

—Like.

—I just found out she's bisexual.

—Is that a problem?

—Best friends for over fourteen years and I only found out two days ago.

—Fourteen years, *and you didn't know*?

—We weren't together every day. She moved away soon after we met. Phoned occasionally but I didn't see her again for quite some time.

—So how much time did you spend with her?

—Not much, but that wasn't what was important. It was the connection between us.

—Some connection if you didn't even know she was bisexual.

—She didn't tell me.

—But it doesn't sound like you were that close.

—How would you know?

—*One shower and a few phone calls?*

—And then she asked me to come here and work for her.

—Is that when you got it together?

—She was involved with Paris by then.

—You hardly saw her, Boo. How come you fell in love?

—I fell in love with her as soon as I saw her.

Beatrice watched the dolphins disappear a while, before she faced him again. —You don't really know her, do you?

Bohemond took another swig of champagne. —. . . I had nothing else.

—Don't say that.

—Ah . . . perhaps you're right. Maybe there was something missing. She said herself that the way I looked at her wasn't enough. And now I'm out here, with you, really seeing things for the first time, I'm beginning to understand what she meant.

—Wow.

—Stupid to've thought, even for one second, that she might have feelings for me.

—*Jesus Christ*. And you were doing so well.

— But seriously, what beautiful intelligent woman, any woman for that matter, what woman in her right mind would be attracted to me?

Beatrice sagged against the stern, exasperation in a voice and eyes aimed at the sky. —Do you have to act so pathetic all the time? Last night, I thought, OK, guy's had a hard time. But you just play up to it. It's so *boring. Oh God, I'm a fat ugly repressed bag of shit.* Fuck off.

—It was . . .

—I mean, what kind of a question's that? Could I imagine a woman being attracted to you. *Of course I could*. Christ.

He looked around him – white horses swimming in the barge's wake, boys diving into the water from the top floors of bankside houses, a brass band massed on an imminent bridge blasting out Strauss's *Chitchat*

Polka, rockets passing overhead. Beatrice reached out and swept a hank of hair away from the side of his face. Her skin glittered. Glitter in her eyes and lips. Her expression so benevolent, so bewitching Bohemond only just managed to muster a whisper. —What's your story?

—None to tell.

—All I've got to go on is Faulkner's colourful account.

—*Christ, yeah*. Can you remember any of it?

—Almost every word.

—Do you mind?

—Not at all.

—Wait a minute, she said, and stood up. —Will we stay sitting out?

—It's January, but it feels like mid-summer.

She opened the cabin doors, clattered down the stairs, and when Bohemond saw that, on her way back, she was dragging a mattress, his heart flipped. He helped haul it through the narrow gap up onto the deck, nowhere left to stand but on top of it.

Beatrice buzzed to and fro, swarms of oversized fireflies exploding from the folds of the blankets and cushions she flung up from down below. Last thing was a handful of candles that she placed all over the boat. Bohemond made the bed, the two of them before long under the covers, leaning back against a hillside of pillows propped against the stern.

The barge drifting on, steering its own course, Bohemond slipped into an abridged rendition of Faulkner's fairy tale: the shooting in South Carolina, the cross-country chase and near-lynching, the enchanted tree and golden birds, Blossom and the Fleece, stealing from Legion, sailing to England and the tussles with Worm, all because of one wry smile.

—It's a bit spooky, said Beatrice, her voice creaking after an hour of silence. —The truth's in there but it's been blown up. Makes people I know sound super-human.

—So Legion and Worm *do* exist?

—Aye, but they're nothing as supernatural as Faulkner made out.

—Is your relationship with him as it is in the story?

—We don't see eye to eye . . . and we're in the same pile of shit. But like I said, he's done a runner. Left me to pick up the pieces.

—And Roosevelt?

Her voice tailed away. —I know someone who could be Roosevelt.

—The friend you were talking about.

—Aye.

—And?

She grabbed the magnum of champagne propped between them. Took a swig. —We're not married or going out.

—But you're in love with him.

—Ages ago.

—And what happened?

Her glances darted across the water. Houses had given way to trees and grass banks, all illuminated by the halo of onboard candlelight. —Just stuff, she said. —Things change.

—But you still intend to hand over the gold to secure his release.

—Course.

—If I was as powerful as Worm, I'd just abduct you. Pluck you from this canal right now.

—No you wouldn't. Cos you'd know if anything happened to me or my friends, you'd be going straight to Hell.

337

—You really do have his heart in that box, don't you?

—Close.

—May I have a look?

She reached around and handed it to him.

The box's walls were warm. Its gold padlock almost too hot to touch. Unsteady in Bohemond's hand, it rocked and tilted, swayed by the weight sliding inside it. He held it to his ear, straining for any trace of Worm's beating heart; even smelled it. —What is it?

—Leverage, she said, and took it from him.

The canal grew narrower. Strange vegetation soared from the waterbed. Bohemond's stomach burbled as Beatrice shimmied down the mattress and rolled towards him.

—Can't get over it, she said, inhaling, eyes closed. —That's the other thing that got me about you the first time, apart from your eyes: the smell of food on you . . . I was hanging there in that window, and I smelled you before I heard you. I can't describe it, kind of meaty but sweet at the same time. And then the peaches . . . You just smell so . . . *delicious.*

He looked at her, lying on her side, hair bunched back from her face, the gentle whirl of her ear. —Let me cook something for you.

—You have already.

—*I have?*

The barge passed through a water-filled courtyard. Palaces on four sides glowing silver and gold.

—Before Christmas, I was at a dinner party on another boat in Little Venice, with some of the people you mentioned earlier. Just before everything went wrong.

Bohemond wiped his lips and hurriedly huddled

338

down beside her. —It was snowing right? Lili and the band were playing.

—They tèll you about it?

—Paris, Hermione's fiancé was there . . . *Good God*, do you know him?

—Never met him. There were a good few of us out that night. If we go along with your fairy tale, Worm and the gold-toothed Cuban were there with a few other folk you don't know about. Lili and them did all the music. It was them that brought the food too. From your kitchen. All we had to do was heat it up and I tell you, Boo, I've never tasted anything like it. Even second-hand, it was better than anything. I had chicken breast. I think Worm had calf liver. And, Christ, everyone shut up. Just the band playing in the background. And you could see folk sitting there, stunned by how good the food tasted. I swear, at the end, Worm's got tears in his eyes. He stands up and says, A toast to the chef, and everyone got up and toasted you. That really got Lili's back up. He started a fire down below. Sank the ship. We all had to swim for it.

Bohemond glanced back at the sparkling palaces. Palm trees looming over lucent blue straits. Beatrice moved even closer to him. Her hair bunched under his chin, fingers resting on the back of his scarred hand.

—I could cook for you again, he said. —Properly this time.

—I'd love you to but I'm going to have to make a move.

—But would . . .

—Yeah?

—OK . . . OK . . .

—What's wrong?

He grimaced, winded, waited for courage to come.

339

—What is it?

—Will I see you again?

She slid her fingers over his wrist and raised her head, the faintest outline of her features caught in the glare of golden palaces. —I'm not sure you will.

He shrugged. —. . . I thought not.

—I'm going to do a deal with the man, give him what he wants, get what I want, and retire. I've had enough.

—What stopped you so far?

—He's insisting that the only way he'll bargain with me is over dinner at his place and there's no way I'm going to do that. I'd wind up on the menu.

Bohemond glanced up at the sky and mouthed a silent thank you. —Maybe we can get him to come to us.

—We?

He turned onto his side, facing her head to head. —If he thinks I'm such a great cook, and he's as great a glutton as I've been led to believe, it shouldn't be too much of a problem.

—Stay out of it, Boo.

—I don't feel like I've got any choice.

—It's not a game. They'll come looking for you.

—So where are they now?

—I told you – I've got the box.

—Then it'll be my protection too.

—This isn't the Hobbit.

—So he'll come after me and do me harm?

—Maybe, maybe not. But he'll definitely try to scare you out of helping me.

—Let him.

—This is for real, Boo.

—And so is right now.

Beatrice paused, sighed. —Look, I've asked him to go

to other restaurants, places out in the open, but he always refuses.

—Ah but he's already under my spell.

—*Boo*.

—So you're going to go into the lion's den even though you may never come out again?

—I don't know what else to do.

—Then hear me out. All of the staff are going to Hermione's wedding. Delphi will be empty. You invite Worm to dinner, tell him I'll be cooking and that there'll only be the two of us in the restaurant. That way, if he's been watching you as closely as you say he has, he won't feel threatened. You dine, make your arrangements and then it's over.

She sat up, hands pressed against his chest.

—Delphi's going to be empty?

—For a week.

—Right . . . He'll take some persuading.

—Well then your luck's in: the wedding's not until the end of spring.

—Uh . . .

—Well?

—It's going to be *empty*?

—Yes.

—And you'd do that for me?

—I'm afraid to say more in case I jinx things, but . . . I think this is it. What I've been waiting for . . . maybe all my life. All I'm worried about is not being in Scotland in time to prepare the wedding meal. I need a whole day. If I'm here cooking for you on Friday evening, the first full day that Delphi will be empty, it doesn't leave me much time before the Sunday ceremony.

—You're definitely going to go, then?

—Beatrice, I don't feel like the same person I did

this morning. I want to be at that wedding. I *have* to be.

—I'll drive you.

—You have a car? You can *drive*?

—I'll sort something. We can leave on the night we do the deal and be in the Highlands by the middle of the morning. I'll drop you off and go spend some time in Ullapool.

Bohemond petted his neck wound with quivering fingers. —If I cook for you . . . will you do something for me?

—Just about anything . . .

—Instead of dropping me off, could you see your way to staying for the wedding.

So dark now she was all outline, her hands slid from his chest to his shoulders. He heard her lips click, swallowing, the boards shifting beneath her knees. —I'd love to.

—Honestly?

Whispering, —Yeah.

—Oh.

She lay down again. —Would you do *me* a favour?

—Anything.

—Take the suitcase back to the restaurant and look after it until I can come and pick it up.

—Of course.

—Is the champagne finished?

He groped around the deck to his left, giggling as his fingers found the bottleneck. —There's a little left.

—Cheers, she said, and took a long sip, rockets passing overhead.

Bohemond woke in the night. Beatrice was lying next to him, her body moulded around his, one arm draped high over his hip. He quavered with concentration, afraid he'd lose control; that he'd submit to the weight of his body, the bob of the barge, roll over and crush her; or that he'd tumble forwards, across the deck, dragging her in his wake – lips and tongues and teeth, his head between her breasts, cock popping out.

Breath held, he kept perfectly still for the two minutes it took her to drift away from him.

She wasn't there in the morning; warm sheets and lavender mist all that remained. Bohemond rose to find the sun hazy gold over Canary Wharf and the barge idling in silt at the corner of Tower Bridge and Shad Thames. He grabbed the suitcase – maybe the only guarantee he had that Beatrice would come back to him. One chance to make himself matter.

Dinner.

A magical meal like the wedding feast, moving along ancestral lines: France, Africa, possibly Scotland, the America of Faulkner's fairy tales . . . Tenuous links, but tough enough for Bohemond's belief that the key to Beatrice's heart lay in the cosmopolitan Creole cuisine of New Orleans.

He hoisted the suitcase high above his head, stepped over the gunwales and waded ashore.

roast goose with smoked ham stuffing and spicy fig sauce

In which Seeta fuels Bohemond's blues with a true story.

A bird to symbolize the bond between Heaven and Earth – Bohemond was nothing if not a creature of the Earth; Beatrice, weightless as she was, looking like she did, something rather more divine.

Spices, as with the Turkish wedding soup, to mark the meeting of east and west, north and south.

Best of all, the fig sauce: ancient wisdom from African kingdoms, hexed by centuries of voodoo in the bayou, and thickened with great dollops of butter.

Any direct derivative of milk – which, as he well knew, was the stuff of life – shared the sanctity of the original element. So for some, just as milk was the original elixir, butter, which rose from its richness, was first amongst fats. If Bohemond were made of butter, people would bow down and greet him like

344

a sex god, because butter myths abounded with abandon. Best was the great Deluge of Hindu myth, during which amrita, the balm of immortality, was swept away by a raging tide of milk. The gods and demons joined forces in churning this strange sea until it yielded, amongst others, the Healer of the Gods, who advanced bearing an ivory chalice brimming with brand new amrita. When Bohemond pondered that image, his mouth watered: the host of Heaven and the hordes of Hell, north and south, east and west, joined in an orgy of fucking, more or less, desperate to hold on to immortality.

Seeta began leaving the kitchen early. At first she'd wait until all the wiping down was done, and slip away without saying goodbye. But soon she was bolting at the back of the last sweet, leaving her work-top littered with crusts and bits of biscuit. So immersed was Bohemond in meditation of the meal that would bind him and Beatrice closer together, it wasn't until Innocent took him aside that he noticed anything amiss.

The following evening he tailed Seeta out on to the street, stopped her on the corner of Shad Thames.
—What next? he said.

She turned around, fright dissolving to melancholy.
—What do you mean?

—*You're* miserable, *Innocent's* miserable, Hermione, *me.*

—What've you got to be miserable about? You've got yourself a girlfriend.

Bohemond scratched his neck.
—So it's true.

—She's just a friend. I've only seen her twice.
—That's a start.

He took her by the arm. —Shall we go for a seat by the river?

Seeta resisted, but he made off, nothing she could do but go with the flow of his bulk. He smiled, she smirked, falling into step as they emerged from Maggie Blake's Cause. —So who is this mystery blonde, Chef?

—Her name's Beatrice.

—Fancy.

—No more fancy than Seeta.

—Give me the gory then.

—I met her out here one night.

—*And?* What's she like?

—A marvel. A miracle even.

—Déjà vu.

—I just feel so different.

—And you've seen her how many times? *Twice?*

—But, Seeta, for the first time I think I can truly comprehend how you feel about Hermione.

—*Hermione?*

—It's all right, he spoke softly. —I know.

—How?

—Worked it out.

They came to rest on a quayside bench.

—I owe you an apology, Seeta. You were right at New Year to tell me that I was in love with Hermione. I was obsessed. Ready to believe the worst of the ones I love most. To believe the worst of you. I just hope you can forgive me.

—Everyone's in love with Hermione; the words bobbed and wove melodiously.

—No more.

—I can't believe you sent those letters to me and Paris. And those *photos*. *Morrissey* . . . what a *wanker!* Still makes me angry. It was so *fucking* poor.

—Clutching at straws, Seeta.

346

—. . . You used me.

—I asked him not to spy on you.

—But you *still* came to that party armed.

—Desperate.

—Fucking right.

—Can I ask you though . . .

—What?

—When you met Paris that night, didn't you suspect anything?

—Hermione had been trying to get us to bury the hatchet for ages. And Paris is fucking winking at me in the kitchen the day before, cos he thinks I've sent him the note and it's like we're on the same side or something . . . *ugh* it was horrible. But we met, and soon as we got over the *But I didn't send you any letter* bit we immediately thought it was one of Hermione's ploys. Nice try, we thought, and we both love her, so we called a truce for the night. It was a laugh. I did it for Hermione. I still think he's a wanker though.

—It was as I thought. He wiped his hands on his trouser legs.

—You can breathe out now.

—I just can't believe I didn't know about you.

—Obsessed and self-obsessed.

—Say whatever you like, I deserve every word.

—*Oh*, wait. Seeta reached out, fingers flicking through his fringe. He backed away and, as he did, felt and then saw the long blonde thread she was pulling from his hair. She held it up to the quayside lights. —And you've seen her *twice*.

Bohemond blushed.

Seeta wrapped the hair around her fingers and presented it to him as a tiny gold wreath. He slipped it into his pocket alongside the feather and the letter.

—There goes Innocent.

—That was quick. Bohemond glanced up at the snow-white head bobbing across Tower Bridge.

—He's been grilling me, said Seeta, —for information about you and Beatrice.

—But I told him all about it.

—Maybe he thinks you're keeping something from him. Ha. Maybe he's jealous.

—*Please*.

—I swear you two are like a married couple.

Perhaps, but he was holding himself back for Beatrice. When she came to dine with Worm in Delphi, one mouthful of Bohemond's roast goose would be enough to charm her away from the table and lure her through to the kitchen where she'd ravish him. While he waited for her to return, Worm would eat the rest of his meal, so moved by the tang, the texture, so appreciative of the effort, that he'd simply let Roosevelt go. Weeks later, Beatrice pregnant, Bohemond somehow slimmer, they'd be wed on a sun-kissed peninsula, all those instrumental in bringing them together present as guests of honour: Innocent, Seeta, Worm, Hermione, Legion, Roosevelt, Vic, Paris, Morrissey, Faulkner and the band, Hanswurst, Blossom, Blanche, Beauregard, Vegas, maybe Eli the dressmaker, the gold-toothed Cuban, even Sol, Clarence, Onlie, Jacob, Walter, Petrova and the North Carolina lynch mob. Disco-dancing under a downpour of confetti, skies alive with fireworks, they'd applaud as the bride and groom flew away to their honeymoon on the back of a ruby-winged horse. And as they soared out of sight, the train of Beatrice's wedding gown blazing like a comet's tail, Hermione would make a celebratory speech tinged with regret that she hadn't been brave enough to bag Bohemond for herself.

—. . . U told anyone?

—Sorry, Seeta, told anyone what? About Beatrice?

—No, about Hermione and me.

—Oh . . . no . . . and I'm not going to.

She nodded.

—Have you made up with your father?

—No chance. That one's fucked for ever. My sister keeps coming and staying over. Drives him mad . . . Not bad for a few months' work, though . . . I've lost him, lost Hermione. Lost you too, I think . . . in a way.

—*What?*

—You know things can never be the same between us. Not after this.

—Oh, *Seeta*, please . . . don't say that. I was just trying to do the right thing.

—Bohemond, you *used* me.

—That's not true.

—. . . I try not to think about it. Makes me depressed . . . If I leave Delphi, which is what I want to do, you all win. But why should I go? I wasn't the one with the camera and the forged letters. All I did was fall in love.

Bohemond looked down at his shoes: brass-buttoned clogs, big as dinghies. —You're still in love with her, aren't you?

—What do you think?

—How did it happen?

—You sure you want to hear it?

—It's something I should have heard months ago.

—Last Easter. The night the fox jumped out the mess-room garden. I chased it upstairs. Hermione was coming out of her flat and it got in through the door. We chased it round the living room, but it just kept going, running round and round, so fast it was virtually running round the walls, y'know, like those bikers on the wall of death, and it was knocking

349

everything over. Everything getting trashed: all the stuff on the shelves and that. It was like a cartoon. This copper-coloured streak flying round the room, and nothing we could do about it. Hermione sat down on the settee in stitches, and whenever the fox got anywhere near her it sent her hair flying over her face. And then it was gone. Straight out the door. Both of us pissing ourselves. I sat down beside her and went to brush the hair out of her face . . . and she grabbed my hand, just like that . . . she grabbed my hand and kissed my wrist. I can still feel her teeth, scratching along my thumb as she let me go. That *little scratch* . . . Christ, I don't know, but *God* . . . the way she was looking at me, Chef, and just . . . fuck . . . I'm laughing, but her hair that the fox had messed up, I couldn't help myself. I couldn't help it.

Bohemond dug fingernails into his knuckles. —So *you* seduced her?

—She made the first move.

—I wonder how she knew? About you I mean.

—Sometimes you can tell.

—If . . . *a woman is lesbian or not*?

—Yeah.

—Can you do it?

—Nine times out of ten.

—But how?

—I don't know. I just can.

—Did you know Hermione is bisexual?

—Hermione's not bisexual, she's just scared.

—What makes you so sure?

—Because I know.

—So she's a bona fide lesbian?

—In spirit.

—I don't believe it. I don't think she could've carried on with Paris this long if she was. It would be like me being in a relationship with Innocent. Though I love him dearly, the thought of making love to him turns my stomach.

—Nasty.

—I just don't think you're right about her.

—That's up to you.

—How often did you meet?

—Lots. Any time Paris went off on some escapade, which was most of the time. Sometimes while he was around. I remember one night, after a late shift, I was walking to the bus stop and she came round the corner in her car. We drove to the coast. Talking all the way. She's got this knack. That's the only way I can think of to put it. Not anything she says really, just . . . I don't know, kind of like you sometimes, but not quite so airy-fairy. And all the way I was thinking, Don't stop, just keep driving. We went for a moonlight stroll along one of the piers in this little town we stopped at. The sea was really calm, like glass, and there were dolphins or seals or whatever it is they've got out there, making ripples in the water. I got off with her. Right by this boarded-up hut at the end of the pier. I just gave in. And the thing I remember best was the smell of cherry on her. You think it's perfume or something, but it's her, she tastes of the stuff. Everything. All over.

Bohemond stood up, mumbled an apology as he stumbled away. He reeled on to Shad Thames, groaning at the way the heavens whirled around him, and crumbled under the awning of the cornerstone bookshop.

trotters and conserve

In which Bohemond weathers two storms and
slays a dragon.

When finally he staggered back into the foyer, overalls
smirched with grit, Bohemond found another envelope
bearing his name on the front desk. This one was
golden, the writing reminiscent of Beatrice's, but all
the ellipses were a little loose. No sign of Thom or
anyone else, he picked it up and fanned himself with it
as he lumbered up the stairs.

Once he reached his room, he slumped into the desk
chair and ripped the envelope open, but the picture
inside blasted him back onto his feet. It was a collage
– magazine cuttings spliced with what looked like
bits of photo – showing a white woman fellating a
black man. They were both naked, she on all fours,
trotters pasted in place of hands and feet, a pigtail
wriggling at the base of her spine, while he was sitting
on the ground, legs spread, his prick more like a
forearm forcing her jaws apart. There was a noose
around his neck, the eyes popping out of their sockets,

trailing tails of blood over a mouth full of monkey teeth. At the bottom, in small black type the words:

Eat at Delphi's

The phone rang. Bohemond picked up without thinking. —Hello?

—Hi. An American voice – snappy velvet like a gameshow host's.

—Hello?

—Is that the fat black French head chef?

—Who is this?

—Come out on the balcony. I've got something I want to show you.

Bohemond hung up, hands shaking, shining with sweat. He grabbed a corkscrew from the drawer and edged out on to the balcony. The air was mild, but still he shivered, creeping round the dry store roof, corkscrew raised like a sword. Roland ready to rebuke the hordes of Hell.

But there was no-one there. He straightened up and gazed towards the north bank, drawing down deep breaths that almost choked him when he spotted a white balloon hovering above the river. It swayed in the wind and began to swell. Soon the size of a beachball, it changed shape – seven blunt appendages sprouting like the barbs of a star. As the inflation accelerated, these extremities morphed into hands and feet, breasts, and a blonde-haired head. The beachball became a hot air balloon, the balloon became a blimp, the blimp became a zeppelin: a pneumatic nude goddess of mythical proportions floating above the waters of the Thames – face blacked-up, eyes white-ringed, full fat strawberry lips, and finally, as the breeze rolled round, massive black capitals stamped on the backside:

LOVE SEE NO COLOUR

Bohemond collapsed as the leviathan floated close overhead. He threw the corkscrew into the air, cowering as it spangled up and up and found its mark between the eyes. The blast knocked him head over heels through a shower of shattering glass, shockwaves snapping at his clothes, dragging him to the very edge of the shelf. Feet and legs prised away from the ground, he grappled for the railing as his chest took off — the big fat black head chef flapping like a flag.

The storm ceased in an instant. Bohemond dropped to the floor, three metres of rubber mouth hanging above his head. The doll's body was draped over the skeleton of the dry store dome. Gallons of strawberry conserve oozed from its wounds.

garlic and hawthorn

In which Bohemond shields himself against evil.

Bohemond didn't sleep. He fetched a corm of garlic from the kitchen, pruned a bough of hawthorn from the mess-room grove and hung them around his bedroom door. Soothed by the scents of herb and sap, he nursed a skinned nose with sassafras solution and paced his room until dawn. Morning brought him to his knees. He found the doll skin gone, but the glass dome smashed, jam spattered over the dry store floors.

The glaziers came before breakfast. Bohemond told Hermione he'd heard nothing suspicious during the night, and she replied that nor had she. But then she'd been out on a bender with her friends.

As he watched her walk away, Bohemond instinctively braced himself, but his blood didn't boil, nor did his guts rumble, a measure of how much his love had changed.

earful

Another close call.

Weeks passed. Sleepless weeks. Almost broken, dozing at his desk early one morning, Bohemond was woken by the phone ringing.

—Hello?

—Bohemond.

—Beatrice! *Good God!* Where are you? Are you OK?

—Fine. You?

—Yes.

—You don't sound it.

He glanced at the wreaths hung around his door. —I haven't been sleeping.

—Why not?

—Things haven't been too good around here.

—Nasty?

—In places.

—Nobody hurt.

—Not yet.

—I told you they'd try to spook you.

—They've certainly done that.

—Mr Big's agreed to come to dinner.

Bohemond smiled and stretched out. —I told you he wouldn't be able to resist my cooking.

—Are you still up for it?

—I was beginning to think you'd forgotten about me.

—Really?

Distant drums. A wave of static.

—I've missed you, she said. It was a laugh on the boat and that.

—I haven't been able to stop thinking about you . . . he pinched his thigh, clenched his teeth, pressed his head against the edge of the desk, aching as he waited.

—I'll be in soon to pick up my suitcase. See you then, eh.

—If you . . .

—Yeah?

—Nothing.

—What?

The moment folded. —Nothing.

—OK, bye then.

—Bye. He sat back in a sweat and readied himself for another disastrous day.

hands and feet

pumpkin and ricotta ravioli with basil and parmesan

Hell comes to Delphi.

—Chef, Chef, *Jesus*, what's this? José the waiter spun a starter onto the hot plate.

Innocent coughed. Kept a hand over his mouth as he stepped back. —Good God, he said.

Bohemond put down his knife. Vic and Seeta came swishing around the bain-marie.

—What is it? asked Vic.

—It *was* pumpkin and ricotta ravioli with basil and parmesan, said Innocent, scratching the back of his neck.

Charred, fused together, the pasta shells were speckled with ricotta mush and globs of chewed-up pumpkin.

Hanswurst had crept up from the other end of the kitchen. —It looks like an abortion to me. Are you changing trades, Polski?

Innocent didn't reply, but Seeta did: —Fuck you, Hanswurst, she said, glancing around as more staff gathered. —Who took it out front?

—Not me, said José. —I just picked it up when the guy complained.

—If he complained, said Bohemond, —that means the dish reached him in this state. But it didn't go out like this, right, Innocent?

Innocent shook his head.

—So what happened? Because I've never seen anything like it in my life. Did you say anything, José?

—Have you *seen* the guy? He's fucking huge.

—What table?

—Fifteen. He's with this blonde ˙Spanish-looking girl.

Paris swaggered in clapping his hands. —Come on, you lot, we've got a full house. People waiting.

Bohemond slipped the dish from the hot plate onto his work bench.

—What's happening? asked Paris.

—Someone sent a starter back, said José.

—Why?

—It was burned.

Paris sputtered, almost laughed. —*What the fuck?* Where is it? Chef. Chef! Where is it?

—Don't worry, said Bohemond, —it's all under control.

—To France with control, you get me? Show me the plate. He snapped his fingers, —Come on, come on. What's that on the side behind you?

—Paris, forget it, we'll get another starter out right away.

—You give me that fucking plate, *right* now.

José loitered at his back, smiling at the scent of a set-to.

Bohemond put the dish on the hot plate. Paris gaped. A few seconds and he was shaking. Very quietly he said: —What the fuck is this?

—It *was* pumpkin and ricotta ravioli with basil and parmesan, said Innocent.

—Say again, old man.

—I said—

—Did you make it?

—Yes I made it.

—You learn your skills in a concentration camp?

Innocent cocked his chin. —I learned my skills in Poland.

—Well maybe you should fuck off back there.

—What?

—Jesus *H* . . . Paris turned away, slapped a hand on his hip, bowed his head and looked up again, pointing. —This is the last fucking time, boy.

—What?

—You *what* me one more fucking time and I'll . . . *Jesusfuck*!

—Please calm down.

—Don't you tell me to calm down, you fucking . . . *fuck*! You've turned this joint into a *zoo*.

Innocent raised his hands and rolled his eyes.

—Is this a fucking zoo?

—I don't understand.

—It's a simple cunting question! Is this a fucking zoo?

—Zoo? What do you mean?

—I mean is Delphi a place where we feed animals fucking slop like the fucking slop you put on this plate? That's what I mean. *Is Delphi a fucking zoo!*

Innocent gasped.

Paris played to the kitchen crowd, tapping his fingers on the hot plate. —I'm waiting.

—I can't . . .

—I should've fucking known. I been saying to Hermione for ages we should sack that daft old cunt, but, *oh no*, she's got a soft spot. This is it though. You are fucking *finished*!

—Paris.

—Don't Paris me you Polish pissflap.

Vic set his cleaver down on the chopping board.

—Don't you Polish pissflap him, you black bastard.

Everyone puffed except Bohemond who nodded.

Paris screamed, —You fucking racist! And you a Chinaman!

—Vietnamese actually, said Vic. —And I'm not a racist.

Bohemond stepped between them. —Relax, both of you. I think we get the point, Vic. Now, why don't we just make another starter and forget about the whole thing.

—No way, said Paris. —This is the straw that broke the camel's fucking neck.

Innocent drifted against the sinks rubbing his wrists together.

—You think Innocent *let* the plate go out front like that? Vic pointed at the out-door.

Paris banged into Bohemond as he backed up. —No way am I talking to no fucking racist.

—Paris, said Seeta. —Grow up for fuck's sake. Why would any of us make a meal like that? And who would take it out front?

—You're saying whoever ordered the dish deliberately fucked it up and sent it back here?

—There's *no way* it would've got out of the kitchen in that state.

—Not unless pissflap cooked it, it wouldn't.

—His name's Innocent.

364

By now the entire waiting staff was gathered round.
—OK, said Paris, holding up the ruined platter, —who took this out front?

Heads down, no-one spoke.

—I see. As the man said, your silence speaks volumes. Well, at least we know who made it.

—*I* made it, said Innocent, scratching his head with both hands. —But not like *that*. I am not *mad*.

—Yeah, but you're past your sell-by date. Something like this could fuck us *right* in.

—But Paris.

—Paris me one more time and I swear I'll knock you out, *I will knock you out*. Fuck off back to the salt mines, or wherever it is you crawled out of. *Go on!*
—Fuck off!

—That's enough, said Bohemond, but Innocent had already undone his apron. —Innocent? No. Wait. Wait a minute.

—This is ridiculous, Seeta hissed. —Innocent, for God's sake don't go.

Innocent shook his head. —I will not be spoken to like that. I quit.

—That's right, said Paris. —If you can't hack it, you should pack it in. Go home and swallow some fucking sleeping pills, you silly Polish sod.

Vic lashed out but Paris was too swift, a smile flashing as the flailing fists missed him and hit Seeta. She and Vic toppled over the sweet tray, Innocent dragged down as Vic's heel hooked his back, all three of them dashed against the floor.

Bohemond helped them to their feet. Innocent limped towards the door. Vic made to follow him but Bohemond snatched his wrist and pulled him aside, whispering, —Don't go. If you go he wins and tonight's a write-off.

Vic's chest heaved. He glanced at the roof and nodded. —What about Innocent?

—I'll go and get him. Hold the fort and do another
pumpkin ravioli. I'll be right back.

Innocent was limping along Horselydown Lane
when Bohemond caught up with him. He was still
dressed for the kitchen, no coat or shoes, just nylon
whites and clogs. —Innocent, wait!

He stopped, turned, upset glinting in his eyes.

Bohemond staggered to a standstill.

They stared at one another, breath clouding in the
quiet.

—Oh no, said Bohemond.

Innocent reached out, kissed him on either cheek.

—What about your clothes and coat? You can't go
home dressed like that. It's freezing.

—I'll be fine, said Innocent. —Goodbye. And thank
you.

Bohemond watched him walk away and then stormed
back up the street. Outside Delphi, he swerved around
a parked stretch-limousine that seemed to recede and
keep receding. The number plate shone with gold
letters and numerals:

NIL
000

A bruise already budding on her cheek, Seeta
stopped Bohemond as he strode back into the kitchen.
—What's going on, Chef?

—Oh, Seeta, are you OK?

—Where's Innocent?

—He's gone home.

—Is he all right?

—No.

Vic came round behind them. —What?

—I don't think he's coming back. Where's Paris?

—He's in the mess-room, said Seeta.

Bohemond pushed past wiping his hands on his trousers. —Why the *Hell* is he in the mess-room when we've got a full house and we're minus one of the best chefs in all London?

Paris was sitting on the table, puffing on a roll of dope.

—*You shit!*

—Not now, Chef, eh.

—*Yes now!*

—The guy from New Year is here. He looked up, his face wrought with worry. —Cunt that melted my fucking shoes.

—I don't want to hear it!

—I'm not going back out on the floor until he's gone. Serious. *Winked at me.* Fucker.

Fists, teeth, toes, everything clenched, Bohemond blasted: —*Get back out front and do your job!* Stop skulking in here like a frightened little girl!

—It was his plate. The burned stuff. *It was his.*

—Well if the Devil was responsible, you should apologize to Innocent.

—Go and look for yourself. Table fifteen, biggest guy you've ever seen, black suit, grey quiff, sitting with this blonde bird. *Go on.* Then tell me I'm bull-shitting.

—*Get back out there!*

—*Fuck* you! Go see the guy.

Bohemond stomped through the kitchen, into the corridor, and held one of the restaurant doors slightly ajar. The couple at table fifteen were nothing like the ogre and Latino queen he'd been led to believe. Fairy tales.

—Excuse me!

He started as Loretta barged past.

—Wait a minute.

—Chef?

—Are the couple at table fifteen the ones who sent back the burned plate?

—No. They left already.

—Did you see them?

—Yeah.

—What did they look like?

—Normal. He stank though.

Bohemond frowned. —He what?

—Smelled like a slaughterhouse.

—*No*.

—Yeah.

With Innocent gone, the balance listed, everyone shouldering their share of misfortune: Morrissey slashed his forearm on a broken bottle; Seeta knocked the only remaining chocolate cake onto the floor; José sprayed himself with boiling oil, and Vic twisted his ankle. Toasters exploded, the bain-marie leaked, the waste disposal choked and the dishwasher flooded the floor. At the end of the night, all hands helped Hanswurst wash and dry the avalanche of crockery and cutlery.

Everyone but Paris retired to the mess-room well after midnight. Bohemond and Seeta dished up shots of rum and vodka, slabs of marzipan and Belgian chocolate. The sugar and spirits loosened some tongues, José and the waiters hooting about what a prick Paris was, poor Innocent, all jabber stammering to a stop when Hermione appeared, half an hour in, signalling to Bohemond from the door. —Chef, she said, —I think you better come and see this.

He followed her, fearing the worst, Seeta right behind him.

Hermione led them to the restaurant and table fifteen. —First there's this.

One of the chairs was scorched – varnish and veneer flaked and blistered, the seat cushion burned through to foam and springs – while the immediate wall was blemished by a man-sized heat stain.

—That's just the tip of the iceberg, she said, and waved them downstairs to the toilets.

The stench of sulphur had Bohemond gagging before he saw anything. Seeta led the way, into the women's room, one hand held over her nose. —*Fuck . . . me*, she said. —See this.

All the damage was contained in one cubicle. The walls, toilet seat and cistern were charred black, the matting on the floor melted. A great mound of blood-streaked shit rose up out of the bowl, and on the ceiling directly above, written in shit, the words:

EAT SHIT!!!!!!

Seeta turned around scowling. —That's just sick.
Hermione nodded.
—Oh Christ! Have you seen that?
Bohemond followed Seeta's pointing finger to lipstick letters smeared on one of the mirrors:

WE FOUND THE PUMPKIN AND RICOTTA RAVIOLI A LITTLE OVERDONE. BUT WE BELIEVE THE CHEF TO BE INNOCENT. HOWEVER, THE CHARGRILLED VEGETABLE SALAD WITH GOATS' CHEESE AND TOMATO VINAIGRETTE WAS UNEQUIVOCALLY EXCELLENT.

X

Bohemond thundered out of the room. Seeta took one more look and came after. Hermione let go of the door, blowing out, sucking in. —It is bad, she said, as they climbed the stairs, —but I've seen worse. It's just shit that it happened here. Bastards. We had the dry store roof a few weeks ago, and now this.

Seeta scowled. —Did anyone see anything?

—I was hoping you or one of the waiters might've.

—There was that guy that sent back the starter. Do you think he *knew* Innocent?

—What guy?

—We had a bit of trouble tonight, she said, and glanced at Bohemond. —A punter sent some food back to the kitchen. Paris blamed Innocent for it. Shouted him down in front of everyone and Innocent walked out.

—He quit, said Bohemond. —Didn't Paris tell you?

Hermione's shoulders sagged. —*Oh no*.

—It was disgusting. The result of another one of your games, no doubt.

—I'll see what I can do.

—Utterly disgusting.

—Yeah, *all right*, Bohemond, I'll see what I can do.

He glanced down towards the toilets as Seeta told Hermione about the couple at table fifteen – the giant in the green suit and his Latino-looking girlfriend – could be they had caused all the damage, although they seemed too mature, so maybe someone had come in off the street, but that didn't explain the mess in the restaurant, someone would've seen something, shouldn't they just call the police? And Bohemond replied, Why call the police, what could they do? And another thing, her description of the man didn't fit with Paris's or Loretta's; had either of them heard

Faulkner's stories about Legion and Blossom and Beatrice and Worm, Seeta's sceptical tut and smile cutting him short, a flat glance from Hermione that left him pondering what good quick wit and culinary creativity would be against the Devil himself.

strawberries

How true love finished Innocent.

Sunday afternoon, Bohemond was on the doorstep of Innocent's house in Whitechapel rapping at the letterbox. No word in three days, all his phone calls ignored, he'd come with wine and ready reassurances.

When the door creaked open Innocent was already back inside, out of sight.

Bohemond pushed his way into the porch, turned left into the living room where he found his friend sitting by a bay window, hands on his knees. Whitish light bleached the wealth of his wrinkles, the well-pressed downs of his tank top, shirt and corduroy trousers.

—Innocent?

—Come in.

Bohemond closed the door.

Swathed in poppy-patterned wallpaper, the room smelled musty but sweet. There was a settee along the back wall, an armchair to the right, a carriage clock on the mantelpiece alongside a sepia wedding photograph. Bohemond gazed at the newlyweds: Innocent was handsome enough, but Sara was truly beautiful.

—Innocent, are you all right?

—So-so.

—I've been trying to call.

—I thought it might be you.

—I brought you some claret.

He glanced to the side but didn't look up. —Have a seat.

Bohemond sank to the floor at Innocent's feet. Propped himself against the wall beneath the window. —I was hoping you'd come back to work. Paris has apologized. Hermione wants you back. We all do.

—Where is Paris now?

—At Delphi, I suppose.

—And Hermione?

—She's there too.

—They could not come here and speak to me in the flesh, rather than sending you to do their talking for them?

—I came because I was worried about you. They've been trying to phone you, just as I have.

—I'm sorry, Bohemond – but I can't come back. I am finished with Delphi.

—Rough patches, Innocent, it's nothing new.

—You don't understand. Paris is right, all I'm fit for is the waste disposal.

—Oh no, *no*. I can't believe you're talking like this.

—It's true.

—*Innocent.*

—You remember asking me if I believed in ghosts?

—Yes, a ghost that turned out to be Beatrice. No ghost at all.

—But when you first saw her, it was like a miracle. The beginning of a new time in your life.

—Perhaps I see that now, but at first . . .

—Well, I do not believe in ghosts either . . . but in the last day or so I have come to understand that a new time is beginning for me also.

—*My God*. Bohemond smiled —You've met someone else.

—I think that coming to Delphi after Sara died was what I was *supposed* to do. As though I was here to watch over you. To give you hope. To make sure you didn't get too sad about how you look. Don't think I don't know that you meant to kill yourself.

—*How* . . .

—Because I know you, Bohemond. But now you are beginning to find your way, now you have seen things are possible that before seemed impossible, you don't need me any more.

—I don't quite understand. Have you met someone?

Innocent lifted his eyes higher. —The first time Sara collapsed she was only sixty-two. It was a Sunday afternoon, at the end of winter. We were walking in the park, she complained of feeling a little dizzy and then suddenly she fell to the ground. Someone passing ran and called for an ambulance while I stayed with her. She was in hospital for two weeks where she got worse and worse. Not one doctor knew what was wrong. They had no name for the illness that was killing her. So many treatments, so much medicine and nothing working. It was clear very early on that nothing would save her. I was with her all day, every day, able to do nothing but watch her die. In the end she said that she would rather pass away at home than in a hospital and so the doctors allowed me to take her there since there was nothing more they could do.

I tried to make her last days as comfortable as possible, and after a while she seemed to respond to being with me in her own house. Soon she was sitting up, smiling, by no means well, but much better. A week later she was walking again. One of these happier days she told me she lay awake the night before thinking about how we used to pick strawberries in the mountains around Piwniczna, which is the place we were reunited after our childhood exile in England. She said in the morning she had thought about the strawberries so much that she still had the taste in her mouth, could I perhaps go to the fruit market across town and get her some? At first I was not happy to be leaving her alone. Her cousin did the shopping for us every week and she was due to go again in a couple of days, but Sara wouldn't wait. Go, go, she said, you could do with some exercise, some fresh air, I'll be fine, look at me I'm walking. And she was smiling then, in the sunlight, like the old Sara. So I kissed her goodbye and took the bus to the market. I fell asleep on board. I was so tired after weeks of being a nurse and hardly any sleep. When I woke up the bus was almost there, but I was still a little dizzy from sleeping. I found the strawberries I was looking for after a long search, then I checked my watch. It said twelve nineteen. The buses back to my house went once every half hour, so that meant I had five minutes to walk around. That's what I did, quite glad to be out of the house for a while. Eventually I made my way to the bus stop. I checked my watch again and that is when my life changed for ever. *It said the same time*: twelve nineteen. It had stopped. I asked someone for the time, and I remember very clearly, they replied, Twelve twenty-six, which meant I had missed the bus and would have to wait almost half an hour for the next one. I ran and ran, through the streets, hoping to catch up with the bus, dropping the strawberries along the way. But I

375

kept going, on and on, a foolish thing to do because the next bus passed me between stops.

Innocent held his breath. Let it go slowly. He was rubbing his wrists. —When I did finally get home, I found Sara lying on the kitchen floor. Her eyes were open but she was gone. The watch I carry with me everywhere. The hands have not moved in six years. For six years they have said twelve nineteen and forty-seven seconds. Like prison gates that never open. There to remind me how I failed my wife when she needed me most.

Daylight ebbed and flowed over Innocent's face.

—When I left you the other night, he said, —I walked across the bridge to get the Tube train at Tower Hill. As I was about to go down the steps and past the Tower I saw a woman in a hooded fur coat, walking up Minories. I wouldn't have stopped but there was something so warm and familiar about her I couldn't help myself. I couldn't see her face and so the familiar thing was all in the way she walked, in the way she carried herself. And then the wind blew her hood down and I almost fell over. She had red hair. I could tell even in the streetlight. And I don't mean red the way people mean it nowadays when the colour they are thinking of is really copper or ginger. I mean red like a good Pomerol. Like blood or embers of a fire. I don't know what is happening to me, Bohemond, but I swear to you, it was Sara. I called out her name and she turned towards me. I told you I don't believe in ghosts, *but it was her*, just as she was the time I found her in the mountains all those years ago. I waved but she didn't seem to recognize me. She just walked away. By the time I reached Minories she was very far ahead. My clogs made running slow. The road got narrower and narrower. Up through the houses, getting higher and higher. I saw her turn right up ahead, but when I took the same turning a few moments later I found a dead-end with no sign of her. There were no windows or doors that she could have run or climbed through, just bricks and pipes. I cried out. A voice that came up out of me and took all of my strength with it, causing me to fall down. My lungs were in agony from running and I noticed for the first time that it was raining. My clothes were heavy and wet. I sat up against a wall and saw my watch on the ground. It must have dropped out when I fell over.

Innocent plucked the silver wristwatch from his pocket. Stared out the window as he handed it to Bohemond.

The face was misted over. Bohemond held it up to his ear. Closed his eyes when he heard it working.

last supper

In which Bohemond prepares to descend into the Inferno.

Bohemond visited Innocent once a week. Bearing flowers or chocolates, sometimes a chess set, he'd arrive mid-morning and sit, often in silence, until midnight. Innocent preferred to lounge by the living-room window. After some initial awkwardness Bohemond fell in love with the hush, full of nothing but Beatrice.

Work was a different story: lengthening shifts made worse by a new sous who didn't fit, Bohemond's hands constantly balled into fists, as he muttered and stuttered round the kitchen trying to beat the teething problems.

The day before everyone left for Scotland he begged Innocent to accompany them. The old Pole's eyes glimmered, but his lips whitened and his fingers drew in. Bohemond left him with a kiss and two bottles of claret.

At the end of the evening shift Bohemond sat with Seeta in the mess-room.

—Are you looking forward, Chef?

—Perhaps I should be asking you that.

She shrugged.

—The next few days may be very hard for you, Seeta.

—Could be for you too.

—Maybe once, but not now.

—Ah yeah, she nodded, —I forgot, your new muse.

Her smiles made him bashful but he said, —You'll find someone too.

—I keep thinking about them at the altar, Paris and Hermione, and the bit where the priest goes if anyone has any objection speak now, and I can see myself standing up and saying my piece, and it makes me feel sick, like I'm actually there doing it, like I might even do it, just not be able to help it.

—Perhaps you should. Stand up, declare your love.

—Maybe I will.

—Have you spoken to each other since I found out?

—Yeah, we decided . . . she looked away, voice tailing off, — . . . don't want to talk about it, Chef.

Bohemond wrapped his arm around her shoulders. She laid her head on his breast and closed her eyes.

Hermione's office door was ajar, gold light glimmering in the gap. As Bohemond reached the top of the stairs she called him in.

—I thought it was you, she said, reclining in her swing chair, a half-bottle and glassful of gin on the desktop.

—You're working late again.

—A few things to tie up before tomorrow. Sit down.

—I'm just off to bed. Is Paris around?

—Stag night.

Bohemond blenched. —Aren't you supposed to do something similar: girls' night out?

—Didn't feel like it.

—. . . Don't get angry with me, Hermione.

—What?

—Are you sure you want to go ahead with this?

—Bohemond . . .

—All right.

—All right?

—All right. One other thing if I may.

—What now?

—Since your life is about to be changed for ever, I'd like you to clear something up for me.

—Yeah?

—I was talking with Morrissey some months ago now and he intimated that you and he had had a liaison in the bar after hours.

Softened by the gin, her eyes and mouth sagged wide with surprise.

—He even went as far as telling me that you have a star-shaped scar on your bottom.

—You didn't believe him.

—The intrigue within these walls, I'm not sure.

—You're too good to that little shitbag.

Bohemond smiled. He felt light as a feather. —Well?

—I wouldn't spread my fingers for that scrawny twat, never mind my legs. And in the bar!

—I thought not.

—I hope so.

Papers stacked on the desk slid to the floor, some wafting through a series of loops to the other side of the room. Silent, smirking, stoned, Hermione watched them go.

—Listen, Bo, about New Year and everything . . .

—It doesn't matter.

—I've been such a bitch.

—Maybe that's just what I needed. You helped open my eyes to what's important.

—. . . You look so different these days.

—Really?

—Yeah. Inner thing. Sort of a glow.

—I certainly feel different.

—You're in love, aren't you?

Bohemond made for the door. —By the way, he said, stopping with a hand on the snib, —Seeta's downstairs.

—Hmm.

—I think she's alone.

Hermione stumbled up and out from behind her desk, lunged and hugged him.

fat

On the difference between gourmandism and gluttony.

—Have you decided what you're going to cook for us then?

Bohemond gazed at Beatrice, stunned anew by her furious beauty. —It's a secret.

She'd woken him that morning with a phone call. Five minutes later she was in his room rummaging through the booty-filled suitcase, looking for money to pay for a getaway car. Utterly unwilling to let her leave without him, Bohemond backed out of a full-blown row saying he'd simply follow her wherever she went. Now they were walking across Tower Bridge, the day sunny blue and baking: Beatrice in fake fur carrying a handbag full of cash, Bohemond in a leather coat and corduroys, the cobalt box in his pocket.

—Why the secrecy?

—Cooking is magic. If I give the secrets away the power of the discipline dissipates.

—I only wanted to know what you were making.

—According to you, the man you mean to sup with

is a glutton. He'd find any kind of slop seductive, so it's not that important.

—He's a greedy bastard, yeah, but he's also a connoisseur. You won't win him over with pie and chips.

—If he is, as you put it, a greedy bastard, he can't be a connoisseur. Therein lies the difference between gluttony and gourmandism. My illustrious predecessor Jean Anthelme Brillat-Savarin put it best. Gourmandism, he says, is a passionate, rational and ritual preference for everything which delights the organ of taste; it is the enemy of excess. Indigestion and drunkenness are offences of the worst kind. So, from what I can gather, though Worm and I share what one might call a generous constitution, he is most definitely a *glutton*, whereas I am a *gourmand*.

—God, you sound like him.

—Like Worm?

—No joke.

Bohemond fingered his throat. —What time is he coming?

—Ten o'clock. He's bringing one of his guys. That's the plan. I get you, he gets to bring one of his. We dine, do the deal, and if it works out, he'll make a phone call. Then we all drive to somewhere with lots of people – I'm thinking Trafalgar Square – I give them what they want, and they give me my friend, you and me drop him off at Heathrow airport, and then we drive to Scotland.

Bohemond's blood glutted at a vision of a moonlight drive, but thinned at the premonition of his bulk jammed in a chassis: *Head Chef Hacked Out Of A Four-Door Saloon By Five Hundred Firemen*; ranks of ambulances, news teams, police, helicopters with spotlights. —This car, Beatrice. Will it be big enough?

—Oh God, wait till you see it.

—It's big then?

—I just said.

—And how long have you been driving?

—Relax, will you.

—Try to, he said, mumbling a prayer as she hurried him down into the Tube station.

They changed trains at Moorgate, then again at Highbury and Islington. From there they rode an overground to Hampstead Heath. Beatrice led the way once they were outside the station. A few steps behind, Bohemond hummed about beautiful houses, what a day for sitting out on the balcony with a cup of tea and a touch of Verdi.

The heath was crowded, swarming with sunbathers, millions of children. Beatrice shrugged off her coat, and swung it over her shoulder, waiting until Bohemond drew level. Sunlight and sweat killed his clothes. His shirt clung like a damp dishtowel. Shrunk around the crotch and higher thigh, jumbo-corduroys shortened his step. His good new shoes were already ruined. But it hardly mattered.

They drifted uphill, both grinning at how the hubbub dwindled to a hum. Trees loomed, shading the pavements. Heat broiling above flagstones condensed the scents of heavy-headed flowers. Plumed birds sailed overhead. Vast butterflies fluttered past. Arms entwined, Beatrice drew Bohemond off on to a smaller leafier road.

—Where are we? he asked.

—Don't know the name of the street.

—If my memory serves me, it should be Well Road, but I don't remember it being *anything* like this.

As the road rose out of a dip, she pulled him over at

384

a black door hung deep in a dry stone wall. —Listen, Boo, you can wait here if you like, or go back to the restaurant, I'll come for you when I'm finished.

—I'm not leaving you alone.

—That's nice. She whipped a set of keys from her coat pocket, fitted one into the lock and swiftly forced a way in.

—Besides, muttered Bohemond as he squeezed through after her, —I'm not sure I could, even if I wanted to.

Beatrice closed and locked the door behind them. Nodded at a short stone ramp on the right. —Up there.

The slope opened on to an overgrown garden, the only way through via a dried-out swimming pool. Hand in hand, they descended a flight of crumbling marble steps, trawled across the tiled floor and climbed out the other side. Beatrice forced another door at the corner of the plot, Bohemond holding his breath as she curled around the post. —OK. Go. Go.

Another garden; trimmed, landscaped, full of sunlight. Chairs scattered on a patio surrounded a table topped with a bottle of wine and glasses. A shotgun was propped against the wall. Music from one of the front rooms crackled through an open bay window, Bohemond in some cod show of cool purring along to Cab Calloway's 'A Ghost of a Chance' as he staggered down the banking into a maze.

Beatrice didn't hesitate. The hedgerows grew to well above head height, but she seemed confident of every turn. Even when he felt as if they were re-treading their own tracks Bohemond kept quiet.

They emerged on the edge of a field of weeds. Stone walls towered above them on three sides, the one opposite formed by what looked like the gable ends of two houses.

Bohemond wheezed, breathing pollen. —Are we there?

—Almost.

—Thank goodness. Whose land did we trespass?

—A couple of cricketers. They're mad old colonial bastards. They saw me walking across the lawn one time, and asked me up for a drink. So I went, and we were talking, y'know, about this and that and I said something, I don't remember, some wee off-the-cuff remark about England or something and next thing I know one of them's going for the shotgun. I had to run for it, this old prick shooting at me for real. Next time I saw them they were all sweetness and light. Senile as fuck. You've just got to be a wee bit careful.

—So you've been this way a few times before?

—A few.

—You say you're a stranger and yet your London is like another world to me.

At the gable ends, they found a narrow alley looming between the buildings. —Down this gap, said Beatrice, —and that's it.

The gap looked more like a *crack* to Bohemond. —I'm not sure I can get down there.

—This is the last of it, she said. —It's easy after this.

He sucked his teeth.

—Really, Boo, it's been a nice walk, but maybe you should just go back to the restaurant. I won't be long.

—I'd never get through the maze. And if I did, your cricketers'd shoot at me. I'm coming with you.

Beatrice crept into the cleft and he sidled along behind her, turning side-on as the alley narrowed and forced him flat. A knot of brick pinned one of his knees. Another outcrop fettered his chest. He heard a key turning in a lock, a door opening. A gust of wind mingled lavender with honeysuckle. —Beatrice! he gasped, his lips pasting the brickwork. —*I'm stuck!* Head wedged upwards, he felt her fingers slide between his, savoured the coolness in her voice: —It's OK, she said. —I've got you. A good grip for such a small hand, she pulled and the walls seemed to give, only to clamp shut on his crotch. Bohemond squealed and squirmed, testicles punched up into the undercarriage of his gut, the same white-hot shock Faulkner had described all those months ago when Beatrice belonged to Roosevelt, whereas now she was with Bohemond, trying to prise him from between two fucking houses. The struggle wrenched his head down and up again, enough time for a clip of landscape beyond the gable ends: tracts of forestland, a lake under a waterfall, blue mountains, and wild white horses cantering past so close he could hear the thunder of their hooves. Beatrice set her hands against the walls, swung her legs and booted Bohemond back along the alley. He shot out the other end, dazed, but amazed to find her kneeling beside him.

—Jesus. Are you OK?

He began to reply but the pain in his groin was just too excruciating.

—I couldn't see how else to get you out.

—*Ffftthh!*

—Sorry. *Sorry.* Look, I've got to go. I'll meet you back at Delphi, all right. She stood up, glancing left and right. Walked off. Came back. —*I told you*, you shouldn't have come.

Tears stung the backs of his eyes. Spit trickled down his chin.

She grabbed the cobalt box and kissed his forehead, licking peach-flavour sweat from her lips as she skipped off into the gap.

Bohemond rolled onto his back, as always, gasping.

hands and feet

In which Bohemond makes a mad dash from the Devil.

Legs spread, Bohemond did his best to keep still, since any exertion killed him a little. Heat made him sleepy but the pain kept him awake. Near dusk he heard a knocking at the door down the alley. —Beatrice?

Almost an octave higher, the reply mimicked his voice. —*Beatrice?*

He stood up, his lungs and heart and limbs tugging on his testicles, everything commingled and outrageously agonizing. —Beatrice?

—*Beatrice?*

—Beatrice is that you?

The voice lowered. —*I'll huff and I'll puff.*

—Who is it?

No answer.

Bohemond limped away from the wall, tripping into a trot as whoever was on the other side of the door snapped into attack. Weeds and gorse snatched at his ankles, snagging him back, but the scent of sulphur snaking in his wake drove him on. Weak, depleted, all but obsolete, he only just made it to the maze when he heard the door give way. The door smashed off its hinges, roaring up the gap between the gable ends. Legion. *Unleashed!* The very Devil himself flying in pursuit of the fat black French head chef, who huffed and puffed, making a meal of making a break for it, outsize thighs buffeting his swollen gonads. He veered left and left again, came about right, jostled down a long corridor. If he ran too deep he'd get lost and die of hunger before he found a way out. But the next left brought him close to the brink of the maze, to heavy footsteps crunching the overgrowth. He winced, dashed back towards the interior, threw himself to the ground in a rough-cut dead-end. Huddled under over-hanging gorse, he breathed through his nose in an effort to smother the sound of wheezing.

Black boots blurred past hedge stalks only one partition away – a weight much greater than Bohemond's making the earth shake. One hand clamped over his mouth, ready to push back a scream or stream of vomit, he listened as the rumble circled, its rhythm slowing down a few feet behind him. Slowing to a stop. Bohemond closed his eyes. Gripped the gold feather in his pocket. Heat clawed at his back, growing in intensity as the ogre behind the hedge lowered himself to the ground. And when he heard a guttural chuckle, knew he'd been found and was being fucked with, Bohemond began to roll. He wriggled away from the stench and heat, from the first twists of smoke and baby flames, on his feet screaming by the time his hideout ignited. The maze forced him left and left again, bang into another body on the next right – a blur of blonde and fur almost trampled underfoot. It was Beatrice. She leaped up, laughing, grabbed Bohemond by the hand and dragged him after her. They ran through avenues of fire, the heat searing, flames rising high above their heads, the ground still thundering under Legion's stampede. Smoke filled Bohemond's nose. It stuck to the back of his throat sparking a coughing fit that ripped through his lungs. He pitched forwards, whirled back, and eyes tight shut sucked in a mouthful of soothing ice cool. Beatrice whooped, and Bohemond looked up to see the sky wiped out by snowflakes; snowflakes and flame. The whole maze hissed like a pressure cooker.

They cleared the last hedgerow, clattered past the colonial mansion, through the marble swimming pool, and sprawled into the street. Bohemond covered his head, more a guard against Legion's fists and feet than a brace against the ground. But Legion wasn't there, and the snow had stopped. He came to rest on his knees, no time to recoup as Beatrice hauled him to his feet and led him on, down towards the station, one backward glance at great peaks of flame consuming the summit of the hill. Hampstead going to Hell.

nut roast

How Bohemond glows while London burns.

She had him by the hand again – her thin white fingers slipped between his fat black ones – sprinting on and on, Bohemond's legs not made for mad dashes, flailing crazily, all the momentum sunk in an unwieldy waddle, just a question of whether he could keep himself upright long enough to make an escape. Part-way down the hill, Beatrice swung him hard into a parked car. He bashed a shin on the bumper, tumbled headlong into some kind of somersault, the whole world slowing down as he looped over the boot and open roof and landed arse-first in the gap between the back and front seats. Deafened by the dredge of his own hysterical breath, he grappled with his shirt collar trying to clear an airway, somehow widen the width of his windpipe, but his fingers wouldn't work. Beatrice vaulted overhead, shooting through the stars, her blonde hair wiring towards Heaven as she plumped down into the driving seat. She gunned the engine, sped towards the city, physics finally forcing Bohemond into the back seat where every ounce of his puff petered out.

*　　　*　　　*

Her whispers woke him.

When he opened his eyes she drew away shimmering in silver shirt and shorts. —Are you OK?

Bohemond eased himself up, freezing as he realized that not only had he been undressed and bedded, but that this was not Delphi. He glanced round the room – television, wardrobe, dresser, bedside light – and sighed with relief to feel briefs still clinging to his crotch and bottom. —Where are we?

—The Tower Hotel, said Beatrice. —Just in case.

—*The Tower?*

—We've got a balcony, she said, nodding at a billowing curtain. —Delphi's right across the river so we can keep an eye out. You can even see the fire way over in Hampstead.

—*Oh Jesus.*

—You sure you're OK?

—*Yes!* No. He gnashed his teeth, wincing at the storm in his scrotum. —We were in a big convertible, driving away from the maze.

—Don't you remember? We were going to spend the night in the car, but you were too hysterical.

—I passed out.

—Not the whole time.

He tried to recollect, but nothing would come. —How did you get me up here?

—The lift. Then I pretty much carried you.

—*You carried me?*

—Yeah.

Faulkner's fairy tale shimmered behind Bohemond's closed eyes: Beatrice fleeing from the strip-poker party with Roosevelt draped over her shoulder. —What if he comes here?

—Who?

393

—Legion.

—How many times, Boo? Beatrice swung her arms. —Legion's a figment of your imagination.

—So who chased us through the maze and set fire to it?

—You saw him then: your ten-foot-tall demon policeman?

—I saw something . . . legs . . . *the ground was shaking*.

—What did I *say* to you?

—Beatrice . . .

—I fucking *said* not to get involved, didn't I?

—I could've been *killed*. Burned alive. Just running like that could've finished me.

She sat down beside him, limbs loosening. —We'll be fine, Boo. Just hold on.

—I saw horses. When you unstuck me from the alley. Wild horses galloping behind you. There were mountains and trees too. And a lake.

—I took a shortcut to Hampstead, not Narnia.

—Promise me, Legion and Worm and Roosevelt don't exist.

—*Fuck's sake*, you know they exist, but they're not freaks from a fucking fairy tale!

—Does that mean no?

—You're losing it, Boo, she said and almost smiled.

—But you said . . .

—You should come and have a look out here. She sprang up from the bed, keening towards the window. —It's quite a view.

When he wavered, she parodied the look on his face with a clownish scowl.

—It's not funny, Beatrice.

—*Come on.*

He slouched forwards. Bit his lip at the jab in his

balls. But still he came on, forgetful of his semi-nakedness, spitting oaths as soon as he hit the floor.
—God! My feet!

Beatrice dipped into the bathroom, while Bohemond curled up on his side. A slice of city twinkled past a chink in the curtains. Flames on the faraway horizon.
—What are you doing?

—Your feet, she said, and re-emerged carrying an ice-bucket full of hot water, a bar of soap and a towel.
—They're fucked. I'll give them a wash.

Bohemond drew back.

—Looks like you've been walking over hot coals . . . Oh hey . . . what's that stuff on your toenails?

—Polish. It's nothing.

—The same that's on your fingers?

—It's old goth stuff called Arabian Nights.

—Cool.

—It won't come off.

—What?

—Nor will any of this gunk on my face.

—What gunk? Beatrice peered at him.

—You haven't noticed?

She set the bowl on the floor, crawled up onto the bed, slowing down as she edged her face into his.

—See? he said, turning his head towards the light.

—No. Fucking. Way. Her breath smelled of blueberry. —How come it won't come off?

The words a blur, filtering after the drift of Bohemond's roving eye, he sang more than spoke of his adolescent depression. The six-week long-lie that changed his life for ever. —It's like a tattoo, he purred. —Pretty much inked into the skin.

—Christ. She looked down at his skinned soles and bucked back onto the floor. —You ready?

—I . . . was thinking that I might have a bath.

—It'll take me two seconds. And she was kneeling down, coaxing one of Bohemond's feet onto her lap, smiling as he draped the duvet over his crotch and lower belly. The fit between the arch of his foot and the curve of her thigh made his blood rush. Beatrice seemed to feel the change in heat. She plunged the soap into the water and spun it between her palms. Bohemond began to say something else, but his tongue turned tail once she slid fingers between his toes. His soles glowed, a miniature inferno shifting to his instep and ankles, raging up the insides of his thighs. He bubbled and gurgled, Beatrice watching him all the while, thumbs running deep between his tendons.

—Your face, she whispered, —*fuck's sake*, it's a picture.

He crashed back onto his elbows, moaning.

Beatrice rested the flat of his foot between her breasts and massaged the muscle all the way to his calf. Bohemond rolled onto his side, flapped back over, the fire in his thighs shooting up to the root of his prick, roasting his already battered balls.

—Ticklish? she asked.

—Foo! he said.

Footprints stamped on her shirt, she rinsed him off.

—Is that better?

He lay still, looking up at the ceiling.

—Well?

—. . . I can't believe you did that for me.

—What? She climbed onto the bed, stretched out face-down, head tucked into the crook of her arm.

—No-one's ever done *anything* like that for me before.

—Washed your feet?

—I've had massages . . . from Morrissey, but . . . I paid him for them and . . .

She reared up, the frown knotting her brow suddenly undone. —*Boo* . . . what's wrong . . . hey, hey . . . calm down.

—I'm in a mess. *I'm in such a mess.*

—Don't cry.

—*I'm not*, he gasped. —I'm not . . . I'm happier than I've ever been.

—*You're crying*.

He wiped his eyes and stared at her. —See? Dry as a bone.

—It's been a shit day, eh?

—Best day of my life, apart from being with you . . . *on that barge*!

—Boo, hey . . . *hey* . . . calm down.

—*OK. OK.*

—Is it your asthma?

Speech snapped over every short sharp breath, —*No. No. OK. OK. All* right. *All* right. *I'm* fine. *Just* fine.

—You're not hyperventilating then?

—*No. No. No.*

—I can't believe I let you come with me today.

—*I'm. Like* this. *Because. I* am. *With* you. *I'm happy.*

—Christ, she said. —I'd hate to see you sad.

He laughed. Barked like an ass.

Beatrice slid to the floor and darted on to the balcony. Bohemond's seizure ceased almost simultaneously. Quiet curses slipping between his lips, he pulled his hair, slapped his face, pinched his nipples, abusing himself even as he began to get up and follow on. Hobbling on the edges of his feet, the duvet clutched to his waist, he found Beatrice sitting on a chair, legs hooked over railings, silver polish twinkling on her toenails, gold wings glinting through the sheen of her shirt.

—Sorry, she sighed and lit up a cigarette. —I wasn't abandoning you, I just needed some fresh air.

—I'm really sorry.

—Aye . . . well . . . so am I. Today's been a fucking shambles.

—Panic or anxiety or something. *So* embarrassing.

—Just forget it, eh?

—I bet you wish you'd never . . .

—D'you see the flames?

Hardly winking at the blaze rising up the sky, Bohemond sat down on the doorstep, obsessed by the form of Beatrice's legs, by the fresh recollection of how her hands had felt digging into his feet.

—It's just . . . I've never been touched like that . . . *ever*.

—*Boo* . . . all I did was wash your feet.

—*All?*

—You've made your point, OK?

—You must think me a pathetic idiot.

—Fuck me, she mumbled, —here we go. What did I just say? Can we change the subject? Can we? Please? It's *you you you* so far.

—*Your wings*, he stammered, toes curled so far in the concrete powdered his nails. —I keep meaning to ask you about the tattoos on your back.

She took a long slow draw on the cigarette, held down the smoke while her eyes searched his. —You're not well, are you?

Bohemond sneered and slobbered, sucked in hard to keep the spit from dribbling. —Don't *pity me*. I'm just tired.

—You're fucked.

—Not now.

—I wish I could just say let's just forget the whole thing, but we're so close now. Tomorrow, and that's it.

398

—We were changing the subject, remember? He pinched the corners of his mouth. —I was asking about your wings.

Beatrice smiled. —So you were. She turned away from him, lowered the shirt and bra straps over her shoulders to reveal prints of intricately detailed butterfly wings glimmering like gold leaf. Bohemond blinked against the glare and bared skin, nothing more than a mutter coming to his lips. —*That's why you can fly*.

—I got them done ages ago now.

—Why wings?

—I'm not saying. It's daft.

—But they're beautiful.

—Thanks; she shrugged the shirt and straps back over her shoulders, —but it's still daft.

The fire on the horizon seemed to be spreading west. Sirens winding up Haverstock Hill.

—I'm better now, OK.

—OK, Boo. Just try to relax.

—But I've got to ask . . .

—Christ, what now?

—. . . only because so much has happened between now and then . . . and maybe you think of me . . . differently, especially after today, whereas before, we were on the boat, and I was so much more in control . . . and probably seemed like a different person . . .

—Get to the point.

—Do you still want to come to the wedding with me?

She glanced at him, blowing smoke into the sky. —Course.

Giddied by the ease and speed of her answer, he laughed a little. —Why come?

—Why not?

—For a moment I thought it might be because you enjoy my company.

—Oh *please*, stop doing that fucking fishing for reassurances thing.

—No really? Why?

She didn't answer.

He hugged his knees, rocking gently, words and eyes directed at the ground. —When we were on the boat that night, and I invited you to the wedding . . . you paused before you answered, and the way I imagined it, there in the dark, was that in that pause you were smiling, just as I would have smiled had it been you who was doing the asking . . . smiling because I couldn't think of anything I'd want more. And then when you said you'd love to come with me, the very words that were flying around inside my head immediately before you said them, I thought, again just for a moment . . . that perhaps you feel about me the way I do about you.

—And how's that? Beatrice unhooked her legs from the railing and faced him.

—Isn't it obvious?

—Boo, where the Hell's this come from?

—But we just drift and drift always making excuses not to seize the moment, don't we?

She bent even closer to him, darker and warmer. —You're on the rebound.

—I'm what?

—From Harmony.

—Hermione and I were never in a relationship.

—Can I be honest?

—You think I'd want you to lie?

—I think you've got real problems – lots of heavy stuff to deal with – and somehow you're projecting it all on to me. If I knew you better, I might even say maybe you should go and see someone.

400

—A *psychiatrist*?

—Believe me, Boo, the *last* fucking thing you want to do is make me a Hermione replacement.

—And believe me, the last thing I need is a shrink. Beatrice, the way I feel about you has nothing to do with Hermione.

—It's got *everything* to do with her. I've been up to my neck in shit. I'm constantly having a go at you. What happened today? I broke your balls, *and* your feet, by the looks of it. You've no reason to feel anything.

—I have every reason.

—*But you don't know me.*

—I feel as though I've known you all my life.

—But you *don't* . . . and I hate to say it, but you're doing the same thing with me you did with Hermione.

—No. At first I thought you were a ghost. When Faulkner began his story of how you and Roosevelt kept your forbidden love alive despite all the obstacles fate threw in your path, I took sightings of you as signs that I shouldn't give up my pursuit of Hermione. And sure enough, you'd always appear immediately before or after some portentous event. The first time was just after I told Hermione that Paris, her fiancé, climbed into my room with a strange lady-friend; the second, just before she suggested that she and I should run away together; then at New Year, before she kissed me and told me to wait for her at Liverpool Street station. And finally, the night after I find out that she's bisexual, I find you, out cold, on the mess-room floor; then you're with me in my room, on my balcony, in my bed.

—*Boo* . . .

—Remember that night, I mentioned a miracle?

—. . . oh shit.

—Seven hours I waited for Hermione at Liverpool Street station, dreaming about the places we'd go. I almost killed myself running back to Delphi. After that, her bisexual revelation was just too much . . . I remember lying on my bathroom floor . . . the sky catching fire. I started floating up towards the flames, thinking, *My time has come.* But the scent of your letter, the scent *of you*, kept me anchored to the ground. That's when I began to think you were an angel. And when I saw your wing tattoos for the first time, remembered how you'd almost flown away at New Year, I was convinced.

—Oh *Boo* . . .

—There were times, during that first night we spent together, I thought I was hallucinating. But when you appeared in the bar, as soon as Hermione had finished telling me that she and I were never to be, I knew you were real, and that you were the one.

Beatrice murmured something, her voice carried off by the breeze.

—You look as though you've seen a ghost.

—That was the miracle you mentioned . . . out on the balcony that night? You being brought back from the dead? *By me?*

—I certainly would've died if it hadn't been for you.

—*God*, Boo . . . I'm just . . . *fuck* . . . this is what I'm saying: you've got a lot to get over. This thing with Hermione . . . I don't know . . . you flipped or something. There's nothing remotely miraculous about any of this.

—I call it a miracle, you call it something else. But the result is the same: we're here, together.

—Just hang on till tomorrow, yeah?

Police boats buzzed upriver. The sky behind Butler's Wharf grew blue.

—I told you already that Hermione said she knew I wasn't truly in love with her by the way I looked at her. It was as though I was holding something in reserve. Remember? As though there could be someone I'd love more.

—Yeah, you said.

—Well, that first night on the balcony you seemed captivated by my eyes. Wee oceans, you said.

—Boo, do we have to do this now?

—Yes, or I'll never forgive myself. Yet another chance of happiness allowed to go to waste.

Pursed lips.

—After my chat with Hermione, I remembered thinking on the night you floated out of the ruins on Curlew Street that you were the most beautiful creature I'd ever seen. Why? Well now I understand why. It wasn't so much the way you looked, although you were and are stunning. It was how you were *looking* at me. First time, most people see a cartoon. A fat black blue-eyed hermaphrodite. But you saw everything. And for those few seconds, as, I'm certain now, I had never done with anyone before, I gave you *everything. All* of me. That's why you sent me the card. It's why you kept coming back. *It's why I'm still alive.*

—How can you *know* that?

—Because everything fits.

Beatrice sat up. She raised her heels so only the balls of her bare feet met the ground, and lit a new cigarette with the butt of the old. —I'm just trying to remember that night.

—Think about it, said Bohemond. —Worm's coming to dinner *because of me.* I'm going to bewitch him with a dish to help you get what you want. *Think about it.* It's a *bizarre* scenario. A chef, for God's sake, helping to save the day, and yet, here we are. I knew after my near-death experience I was being kept here for some reason, and this is it. My whole life meant for this moment in time. *Meant for you*.

Beatrice backed away, but she was smiling. —D'you have any idea how melodramatic that sounds?

—Do you have any idea what my life has been like up until this point? It's as though I've been blundering along in black and white all this time and now suddenly, because of you, I can see things in colour.

She smiled lazily and shook her head. —It's really nice of you to say so, but it sounds a bit like bollocks to me. Worm, or whatever you want to call him, is coming to dinner because that's the way he works. He's mad. Pretentious. Thinks he's a sophisticated player. But he's too into TV and ketamine. That's why he'll only talk to me over dinner: he probably saw it in *The Sopranos* or something. It's got nothing to do with fate. He's tasted your food already and yeah he loves it, but he also knows the restaurant's going to be empty. So he's got room to make a move. And the other thing is, I *know* Faulkner, *he* knows you, *you* met me, *I* know Worm. There's no mystery.

—Maybe you can't see it yet. There's a lot to take in.

—I hate to spoil your party, Boo, but I think Faulkner's stories came along at a time when you were really vulnerable. But you've *got* to remember, they're based on people and things he knows, *including you*.

—Beatrice, I know there's a chance I might never see you again after tomorrow night. And I suppose if I was as mad as you seem to think I am, I wouldn't entertain the possibility. But whatever happens, nothing will change the fact that the days I've spent with you have been the happiest of my life.

She stood up. Flicked her lit cigarette towards the Thames. —I'm knackered.

Bohemond ducked. —My revelations have scared you away. You think I'm a madman.

—We've got a long day ahead of us tomorrow. There'll be time for all the revelations in the world when we're on our way to Scotland.

—You're still coming, then?

—That's the deal.

—Please don't think I'm mad, Beatrice.

—I don't think you're mad. Maybe just a wee bit sensitive. And anyway, now isn't the best time to try and get off with me.

—Is that what you think this is? *A pass?*

—Well, isn't it?

As she squeezed past him, he leaned over and said, —You take the bed, I'm going to sit up and watch the sunrise.

—What you're doing for me, Boo . . . you know I'll probably never be able to thank you.

He felt her crouch behind him, the hair pulled back from his face on the right-hand side, the warmth of her mouth next to his ear. —You. Are. The. Bees. Knees, she whispered, and kissed him at the very corner of his jaw, her lips shifting, nothing but breath on the ramp of his neck, lingering, lifting.

She bounced into bed, left him stifling giggles.

A few minutes later, her voice uncoiled sleepily. —By the way, she said, —all that cast-iron furniture you've got back at your bit . . . the bed and everything . . . you should get rid of it. This bed held you no problem and I pretty much carried you up the steps to get in here.

Bohemond bent forwards, eyes on the flaming horizon. He was still grinning.

nectar

In which a single kiss breaks an ancient spell.

Eight hours later, making for the mess-room, they crept across Delphi's back lot. Bohemond expected to find his home utterly trounced, but it was untouched. Within seconds of stepping over the threshold, he knew, by scents, echoes, the weight of the air, that he and Beatrice were alone. The staff had bailed out the day before. No trace of any unwelcome guests. Leading on through the kitchen to the foyer, he wondered whether he imagined a sharpness in the silences between them. The thrill of the chase killed by his early-morning epiphany.

They pushed upstairs. Crept along the landings. Ready to rush just in case. As Bohemond unlocked the door to his room, the clank and rattle of keys and latches gave way to a pitter-patter skittering across the lower floor. He turned around, saw Beatrice peering over the stairwell, a machete dangling in her right hand. She glanced back at him, mouthing, *What was that?*

—Probably a fox.

—A fox? She rolled her eyes, strode towards him, tucking the machete inside the lining of her fur coat as she breezed through the open door towards the bathroom.

—Is that yours?

—What? Her voice dulled down behind the wall.

—The broadsword.

—It's my friend's.

Roosevelt; the name not spoken, just rolling round his mouth.

—I've never had to use it.

—I suppose even a guardian angel has to be armed.

—Don't start on the angel stuff.

—Apologies, I . . . Silenced by the sound of trickling piss, Bohemond's grip on the handle slipped, his heart jittering as the door slammed shut.

—*And stop apologizing*. Flushed water babbled down the pipes. Beatrice popped back into the room tugging at her zipper, stepping out of her shoes. —You got the time?

Bohemond gazed at her. Couldn't answer.

—What're you standing way over there for? She slung her coat onto the bed, glanced at the clock. —Nearly twelve. *Boo*. What's wrong?

How to say, without ruining everything for ever, that he'd die without her.

—*Boo*.

—I should make a start on dinner.

—Already? She ambled towards him, hands in pockets, head cocked. —You still haven't told me what you're making.

—Roast goose . . . with smoked ham stuffing . . . and spiced fig gravy. The key is in the cooking: five and a half hours at two hundred and fifty degrees for that sumptuous . . . Cajun cum Creole character.

407

—Sounds good, but Cajun?

He tapped his nose, finger frozen over his lips as the glitter in Beatrice's eyes and skin spread to the very air.

—You mind if I stay up here and go back to bed? she asked.

—Not at all. By the way; he fumbled the cobalt box out of his pocket, —what will I do with this?

—Here. She took it from him, groaning as he limped towards the door. —Boo, your feet. Have a lie-down first.

—If I lie down I'll fall asleep, and if I fall asleep now, I may never wake.

—*Five minutes*.

One foot in the hallway, he stopped. Eyed the box in her hand. —Will you ever let me see what's in there?

—If I did that, she said, her face half-hidden under a curtain of hair, halo hotter than a spot lamp, —you'd take back everything you said about me last night.

ROAST GOOSE WITH SMOKED HAM STUFFING AND SPICED FIG GRAVY

Goose

Smoked Ham Stuffing

First Seasoning Mix

Second Seasoning Mix

Goose Stock

Cornbread Dressing

Clogs on, Bohemond brought two geese from the dry store to his chopping board. He plucked, cut and eviscerated both, held one back for the focus of the feast, while he set about making stock of the other: its rudely carved backbone and neck, slung onto a tray – with onion, garlic, celery – and shoved into the oven to roast. Once the veg and bones were browned, he tossed them into a stock pan and brought them to a boil.

Time to kill. Beatrice best left alone. He swept and mopped the kitchen and corridor floors, watered plants in the mess-room, tidied all the linen in the laundry, drained, scrubbed and re-filled the bain-marie, polished all the cutlery in the restaurant, played piano on the bar-room stage, finally climbing to the top floor of the dry store, where, looking out across London, he vowed he'd visit all the places he should've, and every one of these with Beatrice.

Three hours and a thousand daydreams later he came down to tackle the main course.

The first seasoning mix whistled through his fingers: whole bay and dried thyme leaves, black, white and cayenne pepper, sea salt, and onion powder. Preparation of the stuffing, quicker still: smoked ham ground down; onions, celery and green bell peppers suddenly fine-chopped. Cornbread dressing in seconds: salt, pepper, sugar, butter, milk, eggs, margarine, garlic, flour, cornflour, cornmeal, oregano and goose giblets, mixed and melted, packed in a pan to be baked until blonde. Dressing in the oven, he prepared the second seasoning mix; same ingredients as the first, with the addition of ground sage, paprika, and, in true Creole style, gumbo filé.

He slapped fat, flayed from the good goose, into a saucepan, bronzed it over a low heat, poured a portion of the sweet yield into a skillet and melted it over a high heat. To this he added ham, followed two minutes later by the first seasoning mix, then onions, celery and bell peppers seven minutes after that. Meat and veg tossed and turned until burnished, tender to taste, he doused the lot with exactly half the stock.

The mixture grew thick, and, with the addition of fine-flaked cornbread dressing, quite sticky; suffused with the second half of stock, there was enough for five cups' worth of stuffing. Satisfied, Bohemond set the pan aside, smeared every crevice of the goose with the second seasoning mix, stuffed it, and thrust it in the oven.

He followed the scent of lavender up the stairs, just as he'd followed it down all those months ago. But far from thin air at the end of the trail, there was Beatrice asleep in his bed, lying diagonally, her arm spread out to keep his share of the sheets warm.

Hunched up, painting her toenails, she was there beside him when he woke.

—This is just too perfect, he said, his tongue thick as beefsteak, both eyes honeyed up.

—What's that? she asked, tautened towards a middle toe.

—Waking up with you here as though you'd always been here. It's the second time in two days. The kind of thing you want to go on and on.

—Sounds nice.

He rolled onto his side, watching her hands, the skin baked gold by sunshine, snow-white at the crest of her severed finger. —Varnish, he said. —I forgot about the smell. It's great. Like bubblegum.

—Hmm.

—Back when I was a goth, I always wondered if it would taste as good. Do you ever get that?

—Nope. Her lips popped on the last flick of paint.

Bohemond gazed at the row of shimmering toenails.
—They're beautiful, he said.—Regal even.

Brush and bottle held up in either hand, Beatrice mused upon the finished effect. —D'you want some?

—Haven't used it in years.

—Come on. I'll go over the stuff you've got on already.

—OK.

She crawled around to his feet, her silver shirt two-thirds buttoned. Bra cups arced over the parted hems. Bohemond was quick to shed his clogs and socks, his toes curling as she hovered above him.
—You ready?

He nodded.

—You're not going to go cracking up on me like you did last night?

—About last night . . . I wanted to . . . *sayyyyy!*
Beatrice wrapped herself around his foot, laughing as he came close to blacking out. Hair cascading to his ankles, her chin brushing the tips of his toes, she stared at him and said, —The swelling's gone down. Blisters are dead already. Is it still sore?

—*Bit!*

—You've got sensitive feet anyway though, eh?

—*Dunno!*

—A friend of mine's always on about how she made a guy come just by sucking his toes.

—*No.*

—Aye, she replied, and began to paint. —He was a younger guy, about sixteen or so, that she got off with one night, and all he wanted was to get his cock sucked. But she didn't really fancy it, y'know. She just wanted a shag, pure and simple. So she says to the guy, Y'know in China they've taken oral sex to new heights. They've got this thing called a toejob.

411

It's like blowjob but on your toe and it's supposed to be incredible. And this young guy, apparently he just swallowed it all up. He's like, Fuck yeah, give us a toejob. So she starts sucking his toe, thinking, Great, lesser of two evils, he'll get bored and I'll get my shag. But she's not at it five seconds and he comes.

—*Comes!*

—Yeah . . . I reckon there's two things you can take from that: one is, there's hundreds of ways to turn someone on, really turn them on, that most folk just don't know about; and two: it's proof of the power of packaging, the might of a wee bit of myth. I don't think I'd have sucked his toe though. Maybe his finger or something. But not his toe.

Bohemond closed his eyes, opened them and said, —What if his feet smelled of peaches?

—If his feet smelled of peaches, I would've sucked his cock and swallowed every drop.

—*Beatrice!*

She smiled, —I tell a lie, if his feet smelled of peaches I would've made him give *me* a blowjob.

—*Good God!*

—Listen to you – *God this, God that* – *you* started it.

—Yes, but . . .

—Keep still. Unless you want your toes all silver glitter too.

Job done, she stretched out next to him, her feet alongside his – twenty toenails, all sparkling.

—It's armour, she said. —For later. Shows we're on the same side.

—So long as I wear it, even when I'm not with you, I'll feel like I am.

—We've still got five days in the Highlands to go.

—And then what?

—Who knows?

—Do you think you'll come back to London?

—I've had enough of this place to last a lifetime. She moved further up the bed, her head coming to rest against his, the two of them gazing at the ceiling.

—I understand.

She glanced at him, the twinge momentarily flattening his ear. —I'm surprised you haven't. Might be just what you need: to get out of the city for a while. Get your head together.

—I wouldn't know where to go.

—I'll show you if you like.

—What?

—After the wedding.

—*You're serious?*

—We could go out to the Hebrides. Up to Orkney. Shetland even.

—But Beatrice, last night . . . Bohemond turned on his side, snuffling back a noseful of blonde hair. —You were so . . . *angry*. You said I was mad.

—Yesterday was a shit day. I said things . . . it's not that I didn't mean them . . . it's just . . . fff! . . . they came out wrong.

—Me too . . . All that talk of fate . . . I feel like a fool now . . .

—No need . . .

—All I know for sure is how you make me feel and after everything I've been through over the past six months, I wasn't about to bottle it all up. Last time I did that, I wasted fifteen years. So if what I said last night seemed a little melodramatic, it wasn't due to madness, just lack of practice.

—I don't think you're mad, said Beatrice, shielding her eyes against the evening sunlight. —I just think you need to get away from here for a while. I've made things worse . . . I know. But every time I see you,

413

you're so . . . I don't know . . . *sad*. I think I've seen you laugh once. And yesterday . . . *fuck* . . . that was me . . . leaving you like that after I kicked you . . . but Christ, the *state* you were in before we got to the hotel. I really thought you'd lost it.

—*That* frightens me . . . I remember blacking out, waking up in the hotel room, but nothing at all in between. Would you believe I'd never so much as broken a fingernail before I met you?

—You've got a heart of gold, Boo. I owe you . . . bigtime.

—Orkney though? What will they make of me up there?

She reached down, grabbed his thumb, her fingertips not quite meeting the palm of her hand. —Fuck them. We'll go to the tropics.

He blushed, steaming peachy sweat, thumb throbbing.

—Your skin, she whispered, —I meant to say. It's like baby skin.

—Childish, right?

She tightened her grip, turning to face him, toes touching. He waited for her reply, vaguely alarmed that she was looking at him as though she expected something else; Bohemond, with his scant knowledge of coquetry, foxed by her silence, his hush pure proof of frigidity, especially now she was so close, lips inches from his, eyes unswerving, could it be he'd misread *everything* – her fingers still wrapped around his thumb, the way she'd fondled his feet, last night's parting kiss in the wake of his revelation, the talk of baby-skin and blowjobs, holidays in the tropics and hearts of gold – all of that just sham and chat, so that as he leaned over to kiss her, she'd resist, spitting rape, but as usual his weight would take him, Beatrice writhing, fighting for her life, gradually flattened by avalanching fat, Bohemond rolling on, his eye cut, lip split, skin heaped under her fingernails. He jerked back. —I must have a bath.

Beatrice let go of him. —You OK?

He nodded and stumbled into the bathroom, only half-closing the door. The sky over the dome was almost dark. Cirrus cloud cooling to blue. Criss-crossed lanes of plane exhaust. Plug in, taps on, he waltzed around the blind side of his pot plants and sat down, legs dangling over the bowl. When the rising water tickled his glittering toes, he stripped off and slipped in.

Relief from the evening heat. From any further *faux pas*. Time to think. He plunged all the way under and stood on the bottom. Tiny fish flitted past. Reeds he'd never seen swayed at the deep end. Back on the surface, he sidestroked towards another glimpse of Beatrice.

—I'm here, she said.

He thrashed to a stop, swallowed water needling the core of his nose.

Just a head above water, hair hitched up in a bun, Beatrice emerged from the shadow of fully flowering boughs. —Do you mind? I was stinking. If my sweat smelled like yours I wouldn't have bothered.

Bohemond backed into a corner, his tiny knot of a cock rock-hard. —*You could've waited until I'd finished!*

—It's nearly nine.

—*Oh God!* He covered his crotch with one hand, the other clawed over his mouth. —*Once we leave here tonight, we won't be coming back will we?*

—Wasn't planning on it.

—*I haven't even packed.*

—We've got time for that.

—*I haven't wrapped Hermione's wedding present either!*

—Stop shouting.

—I'm shouting?

—Aye. What is it you've got for Hermione?

—A stone from the banks of the Lac d'Hourtin Carcans. It's white, *like ivory. Looks just like a pair of wings* . . .

—You're shouting again.

—*Yeah.* The night she fell into my room, she fell in love with it.

Beatrice straightened up, arms tracing arcs below the surface, the dimmer suggestion of breasts and belly lower down, legs treading slow-mo like a cyclist's.

—Your eyes, she said. —I can't get over it. They're fucking *luminous.*

—God knows why they're blue.

—Maybe you're descended from Roland. He was French, wasn't he?

Bohemond gaped, amazed.

—I was watching you asleep, she said. —When you've got your eyes closed you just look like someone sleeping. Big deal. But see when you open them . . . I always get a wee bit of a flutter. It's like the sun coming out or something.

Eyes angling down the closer she came, he glimpsed her glittering toenails.

—You sure you're OK?

—Think so.

—I keep going over that kick I gave you yesterday.

—Don't.

—I hurt you.

—A bit.

—Is that why you've been walking funny?

—It . . . was a tender spot.

—You're still in pain, eh?

—Better.

—Still bad though.

—Not great.

—You hear women go on about that, don't you? Wondering what it'd be like to have a cock. What it'd be like to get hit in the balls.

—*Uh* . . .

—I can't imagine. She drew level, Bohemond cowed by her closeness. —The look on your face when you hit the ground.

He blinked back a UV flash, breathing spittle in the pit of his throat as her hip or thigh, or stomach, *something* brushed against the nub of his prick. She laid a hand over his left breast, fingers drawing in to pinch the nipple, softly at first, tightening to a red-hot hold, the whole tip and aureole screwed up between her knuckles. He muttered, Fucking Christ, cut short by a kiss, and as her tongue drew back, sliding around the top row of his teeth, he came.

cooked

How Bohemond lost his way and found himself.

The kitchen wouldn't sit. Floors rose and sank, walls revolved and arched, Bohemond throwing surf shapes trying to stay on his feet, dizzied by the bliss of lost virginity. The glow in his groin blossomed all the way up to his belly button, and beyond there, where the glare died out, nothing but a luscious lethargy; limbs swinging without his say so. He swooned through preparation of the spiced fig gravy. Stabbed his other thumb with the stem of the gold feather and dripped blood into the mix. Top lip curled under his nose, he inhaled the musk of Beatrice's kiss, its scent still embedded in his skin. —You and me, he muttered, —for *ever*! the last syllable more of a scream as he caught sight of a man hovering in the corridor.

—You some kind of witch doctor?

Bohemond wiped his bloody thumb on the hem of his trousers. —I didn't see you.

The man smiled, teeth glimmering gold in the shadow. Slowly, leisurely, he brushed fluff from the collar of the Crombie draped over his shoulders.

—You trying to give my boss some of your African AIDS?

—It's part of the recipe . . . Old Creole . . . Where's Beatrice?

—In the restaurant.

—With your boss? *With Worm?*

—Who?

—Worm.

—*What?*

Motionless for a moment, they stared and glared at one another, both stepping back at the sound of swing doors flapping, and there was Beatrice blazing in the hallway. —OK Boo?

Bohemond nodded, speechless.

—I'm fine, all right. Just bring the food in whenever you're ready, yeah? She glanced at the gold-toothed man. —Yeah?

—Yes. OK.

—And don't let this idiot mess with you.

The man watched her go. —What a waste, he said, and rivets singing in his heels, clopped into the kitchen, his Latino features muddled with bemusement, dismay and outright ill-will. —What the fuck *are* you anyway?

—I might ask you the same thing, said Bohemond puffing himself up.

—I expected a whole lot more than you. After what I heard? A whole lot more.

—Oh really, and what did you hear?

—What I know now to be a crock of bullshit.

—Well, rest assured, you're everything I've been led to believe.

—Oh yeah?

—Yes actually. Bohemond turned to the stove. —No starter. Right?

419

—Straight to the main.

He fetched a pair of plates, prepared relative portions, quashing a quick pang that the meal was in no way geared towards parley. That it had everything to do with desire – love-lotus to boil the brain and inflame the heart – absolutely everything to do with how much he wanted Beatrice to be his.

The stranger reached over Bohemond's shoulder, the aroma of his cologne overpowering. —I'll serve em.

—No, it's all right.

—No. It's not all right. If the boss sees you, he'll have a heart attack. Fat black faggoty-looking thing like you making it with his prize girl? Uh, uh. You better off stay in here.

Both dishes balanced on one hand, he swayed out. Bohemond peered after him, almost gasping with relief when he buffeted back into the kitchen. —Is everything OK?

A frown, the flash of gold teeth. —What the fuck?

—Is it?

—Whatever you do, don't go in there. I mean it. It'll kill my boss stone-dead.

—Beatrice, she's . . .

—*Relax*. He leaned against Seeta's sweet bench and folded his arms.

—I'm relaxed. Bohemond shrugged. —Totally. Relaxed.

—So tell me . . . said the man, shaking his head; —. . . what's the ah . . . attraction. How'd she fall in with a fat black faggoty thing like you anyway? Was it while she was on the job?

—I don't know what you mean.

The man chuckled and hung his head. As he looked up he said: —You know she's a pro, right?

—A what?

—A pro. A prostitute. *A hooker.*

—I know what you're trying to do, said Bohemond, —and believe me, it won't work.

—*No way*; neck craned, eyes alight; —she didn't tell you.

—I know what you're doing.

—What *did* she tell you?

—Everything.

—Oh yeah? Like . . . ah . . . what happened to that little finger of hers?

—Amongst other things.

—She told you she got it clipped in a car door, right? *I got it shut in a car door when I was six . . .* Yeah?

—That is . . . what happened . . .

—You clueless fuck. You wanna know the truth? How far in over that freaky fat black head are you? She's a *pro*, OK?

—No.

—Yes. My boss owns her. He's in big business and when Bea ain't out on his arm, playing play-thing, he's passing her round his associates to keep em sweet.

—*Lies.*

—There's a Japanese gentleman, high up in some multinational. There *was* a hotshot French lawyer, an Arabian sultan, got an Austrian aristocrat, and a senator, flies over from the US, special.

—She . . .

—Oh *come on*. Even you gotta know how guys get when it comes to beautiful women. Especially women with the gift. And believe me, Bea's got it. Just a *whiff* of that lavender thing she's got going on is enough to get most men in a sweat.

Bohemond bore up with a brave face, but his heart was on its way to breaking.

—Don't look so hurt, said the man. —She duped me too. I was the one who took her round these guys' palaces, not knowing she was in cahoots with the nigger who pimped her before my boss saved her ass.

—*Roosevelt was her pimp?*

—She's wild. A few doses of Beatrice and these high-rollers are ready to surrender everything. She's got bank details, knows where the secret stashes of cash are, plus she's sitting on the mountains of dough they paid her for services rendered.

—You're wasting your breath, said Bohemond. —I'm not listening.

—But wait, this is good. One night she set us all up, see. She got the boss drugged somehow. Took a heap of stuff she shouldn't have. I got ambushed. Nothing I could do. I'm left for dead in an alley while she and the pimp go collect from the big cheeses. They got notes and gold enough to last a lifetime. Motherfuckers. But she was so doped up, she fucked up.

—Drugs?

The man sunk a hand in his pocket. Pulled out a palmful of black seeds.

—Cannonballs.

—Fucking A. One of these and she'll do anything. She'd even fuck *you*. He looked around the kitchen, nodded at the stack of unwashed pans and the half-carved goose. —Looks like she has already.

—The cannonballs . . . they're real?

—Oh *please*. In your pants one minute, cold as ice the next. She was so fucked up on these, she left herself wide open. We found her, no problem. And

422

sure she got away, but as I *guess* you know, we got the pimp. He's locked up right now.

—Your story, said Bohemond, his voice half-hearted and hoarse, —it's make-believe. You're talking like a walking cliché. It's ridiculous.

—No more ridiculous than you look, sweetheart. But wait a minute, *wait*. I'm off-track. That *finger* . . . ? Big-shot French lawyer bit it off when she choked him to death. I found the fucking thing in his *mouth*.

—But . . . that's impossible. A man couldn't bite through bone.

—The fuck do you know? Struggling for your life. Weird death throes and shit.

—No.

—Why not? She's throttling the life out the guy and somehow gets her finger caught in his mouth. He gets the rigor mortis or whatever and *Bang*! Bites her finger clean off.

—Couldn't be done.

—Or maybe she cut it off herself. Maybe . . . she couldn't get it out his mouth once he'd snuffed it – a deadlock or a deathgrip kinda thing – and she had to *hack it off* . . . *to get free*! You saw the machete, right?

—These things . . .

—You see her use it yet? *Man*, it's like something out a kung fu movie. Livid-eyed, hands slashing through the air, the man danced forward, backing Bohemond into a corner. —*Crouching Tiger, Hidden Dragon* kinda stuff. *Fuck knows* where she learned those moves. *Fuck knows!*

Bohemond ducked around the other side of the bain-marie. Grabbed a cleaver from the magnetic rack behind the deep-fat fryers. —*Keep away from me!*

423

The man bent down and plucked a dagger from a sheath strapped to his ankle, his face when he straightened full of joy. —Put down the chopper, Jungle Jane, else I'm gonna serve you as dessert.

—You wouldn't . . . dare, I mean . . . we've . . . got what you want.

—Oh yeah?

—The box.

He smiled, turned his head to the side as he edged forwards. —She told you what's in it?

Bohemond stumbled backwards. —. . . yes.

—*Oh man* . . . he cried . . . —*she didn't tell you?* Jesus. She didn't tell you that, either?

—I *do* know . . . and if you come any closer . . . you'll be sorry.

—No. *You'll* be sorry, you . . . fat . . . man-woman . . . nigger . . . faggot thing.

A suffocated shriek snatched the man off-step. He dashed into the corridor, only just beat Bohemond to the swing doors, both of them bursting into the dining room to see Beatrice scrambling up from the floor, Worm down there on his back, out cold, maybe dead, bald head, red lips, bigger than Bohemond, it was true, and much uglier. The gold-toothed man crashed after Beatrice, but she doubled back and, without warning, Bohemond's body lunged, him more of a passenger, thrown into a flawlessly judged punch, every ounce of his great weight distilled into a single fist: – POW! His wrist clicked, elbow bones popped, the hit ricocheting down to his knees, and the gold-toothed hoodlum soared over the tables like a *motherfucking rainbow*.

True love.

The man landed tangled in tables and chairs and lay quite still. Dazed, elated, Bohemond watched as

Beatrice frisked the bodies, her hands soon full of a mobile phone, the dagger and all kinds of keys. —We've got to go, she said. He made the call. Said to meet at Trafalgar Square in two hours. I say we go straight to Highgate. I've got the keys so it'll be fine.

Bohemond yanked out of his trance, knuckles numbed. —What about these two? We should call the police.

—Christ you're bleeding.

His sleeve had been sliced from shoulder to wrist, blood showering from the ends of his fingers. —He must've caught me when I hit him. Doesn't feel like much.

—Are you sure?

—Sure.

—And what's this? She nodded at the cleaver in his other hand.

—Protection, he said and dropped it on the floor.

—We've got to go. There's sheds out the back, eh?

—Oh, no.

—Can they be locked?

—Beatrice.

—We lock these two up in there.

—*Beatrice!*

—*So you make a fucking suggestion!* We're wasting time. I'll phone for someone, maybe even the police, to come and let them go once we're out of reach, if that makes you feel better.

They dragged the two men out on to the back lot, crammed them into the tool shed, Bohemond half-hysterical, retching at the doughy yield of Worm's skin. No sooner was the door locked than Beatrice pushed him into the street. —Wait! Wait! Beatrice! My clogs! I can't run.

—*What you doing in your clogs anyway?*

—Cooking . . . I always wear them in the kitchen . . . for luck . . .

—Fuck it! We've not got time. *Come on!* She hauled him around the block to the blood-red convertible. Bohemond tumbled inside. Beatrice beside him but miles away. Far too cool. She flicked the ignition, thumbed a black button on the dash, the car beginning to coast as the roof rolled back, up to speed on the bridge approach.

—What did you do to Worm? Did you kill him?

Beatrice scowled. —*No.*

—He was very still.

—I chinned him with the wine bottle.

—It sounded like you were throttling him.

The car swerved as she glared at him. —What are you *on* about? He made a grab for me, so I whacked him with a bottle. Fuck's sake. *What about your guy?* Did you kill him?

—All I did was punch him.

—Some punch. He left the *ground.*

—I didn't see any marks on Worm's face, Beatrice. No sign he'd been hit.

—That's cos I smacked him on the back of the head.

—Beatrice.

—*I'm telling you the truth.*

—*The truth?* You told me you didn't know any fat Balkan gangsters.

—I didn't.

—*You did.*

—No, I told you these guys were real, just not the film villains Faulkner made them out to be.

—We're driving to a mansion in Highgate, next thing I'm going to lose you to Roosevelt.

426

—*Fuck Roosevelt*. I'm coming with you, to Scotland.

—But you don't need me any more.

—Boo, I could've run off and left you any time.

—No you couldn't. Not until you and Worm sat down to eat . . . and the drugs. The cannonballs.

—*Ah shit!* What did that fucking idiot say to you in the kitchen? Come on. *What did he say?*

—Did what happened in the bath mean nothing to you?

She fell silent, her hair fluttering in the wind, Bohemond – his hub swilling with honeydew, nipple still tingling, upper lip thick with the kiss that'd made him come, sky-fucking-high on one killer punch – failing awfully fast. —Did you try any of the food?

—*No.*

—Not even a taste?

—*Boo*, you let Gold-mouth bring the fucking meal to us. Christ knows what he put in it.

—*Oh shit . . . shit . . .* I didn't think. *Shit!* He stamped his feet, shook the chassis. —*Shit!*

—What's the big deal?

—I . . . made it for you and me.

—But you were never going to eat any of it.

—I sample my dishes as I make them.

—What are you on about?

—I thought . . . if you tasted something I'd prepared especially for you, you'd feel for me the way I feel for you.

—And I thought you were feeling better.

—And I've never met anyone like you either.

—Bewitching people with food? Boo, the sooner we get you out of this shitty city the better. Believe me, food's just the tip of the iceberg with you.

427

They stopped at traffic lights, silence ruptured as a team of men packed into a minuscule Citroën pulled up alongside. Wheezing, hollering, leering out the windows, they bared their chests, unbuttoned their trousers.

—Let's just go, said Bohemond.

Beatrice turned to him, framed by a furious play of semi-nakedness.

—To Scotland. Let's keep driving.

She became still, sadness dragging at the corners of her eyes.

—Right now. He leaned towards her, laid a hand on her arm. —Just us.

Car horns shrieking, Beatrice blinked back surrender, cranked the convertible through the green light. Bohemond left her alone, his heart sinking once he recognized the outskirts of Highgate. A left at the top of Muswell Hill brought them dipping down smaller, leafier roads. Streetlamps and houses gave way to moonlit moorland. —I can't leave him, said Beatrice.

—We take him to the airport, then we go.

—I'll die without you.

—*For fuck's sake stop talking like that!*

—It's true.

—One more time, and I swear, I'll stop the car and you're on your own. She turned out the lights, swung the car off the road, bounced it down a dirt track – scrub scratching the windscreen, scraping along the doors, rocks rifling against the undercarriage – ground to a halt in a grit plot. Bohemond's ears rang in the sudden calm. He bowed down as the roof crackled overhead, a moment to reflect on mad love, before Beatrice climbed out.

She led him back up the track, on to the road, skirting bushes that circled a palatial white-brick mansion.

A few feet short of the driveway, she crouched down and pointed to a light glowing in the window of an ivy-covered turret. —He's locked up in there.

—Now, take these. She handed him a set of three keys.

—What's this?

—If we get split up for any reason I want you to meet me on Primrose Hill.

—What?

—Just go to Primrose Hill, along the main street and about a hundred yards down on the left as you go towards Camden you'll find a flower seller's between a café and a clothes shop. Go in through the big iron gate, straight across the courtyard till you come to a wooden door and open it with the bronze key. Go along the wee path and open the glass door at the end with the silver key. Then you go up the stairs, across a catwalk and open the brass door at the other side with the gold key. There's an orchard at the top of the hill. If I'm not there, wait for me. If I get there before you I'll wait until you come. Don't worry, it's totally safe.

Bohemond put the keys in his pocket. His slashed arm had become numb, fingers slick with blood. —Promise me you'll come.

She drew a finger across her breast. —Swear on my mother's life.

—Do you have a mother?

—Fuck you.

—Promise me, Beatrice.

—Cross my heart and hope to die.

—Remember your letter: *next time I'll fly you home.*

—And I will.

—I mean it. I think . . . I'll . . . I'm not sure how long I'll last without you.

She cupped his face in her hands. —Don't try to blackmail me, Boo, OK. I'll meet you, by the orchard, like I said. *I promise.*

—I'll be waiting.

—And if I get there before you, *I'll* be waiting. But hopefully it won't come to that.

—Hopefully.

—OK. Now there's usually two guys stay here and look after Mr Big; you just flattened one of them so there's only one left. He'll be in there somewhere, getting ready to take my friend to Trafalgar Square.

—You're still calling him, *my friend.*

—OK, Roosevelt.

—How are you going to get him out?

—I've got Worm's keys too, remember.

Bohemond smiled.

She let go of him. —You like that better: Worm?

—Much better.

—There's no way I'm going to sneak in there and run around trying to find my way up to the room. I'll climb up the ivy and give Roosevelt the key so he can let himself out. Just keep watch, OK.

She kissed him on the cheek, pranced towards the wall and leaped into the creepers. Bohemond scrambled out of the scrub, astonished by how quickly she was climbing. Once she reached the window, she drew the machete and hacked at the glass, almost falling when it smashed. She passed the knife and keys between the bars, Bohemond as he watched lost in pondering how Roosevelt must've longed for this moment.

A voice at his back said, —Howdy, and suddenly he was flying – lifted off the ground by monstrous hands, screaming at their heat, a molten pain that speared his sides, frying his liver and kidneys, cooking the blood in his veins, boiling the urine in his bladder, liquidizing shit in his bowels, tears, sweat and spit dried up in their ducts, *his whole soul driven out by an inferno. By Legion.*

As he shot up he saw Beatrice jump down, her fur coat spread like wings. Distant city lights blazed into and out of sight. Close to the moon, he saw stars twinkling, comets and rockets trawling across the sky, city lights smouldering again, before he realized his great weight was too much even for Legion. And as he began to arc towards Earth he remembered his new-found strength. Pure kung fu, his knees swung up, like cannonballs, fifteen years of everything from anchovy crostini to hot chocolate fondant packed into a smash that launched Legion into the air. Jaw snapped, nose broken, teeth shattered, the Devil's sheriff bested by God's own gourmet.

Bohemond hit the ground, bouncing on his bottom, glimpsed Legion squeezing his ruined head between red-hot hands, bare shoulders and back like a mountain range. —Come on, time to go! Beatrice again, out of nowhere, pulling him to his feet. They ran hand in hand around the side of the house, crunching through a patch of biscuity grit, down a flight of stairs and headlong over a parapet, the drop knocking them into somersaults that lasted the length of a Moorish arcade, a hanging garden, smothered under buds and blossom. Clouds of moths and butterflies burst out of flowerbeds, exploding in size, shade and abundance every time Bohemond's head bashed the brick, and still Beatrice held onto his hand, even as they broke through the gates at the bottom of the slope. White horses scattered before them, some dashing for cover under the boughs of a nearby wood. Others galloped down the moor towards a waterfall.

Crazy with concussion, clogs lost, Bohemond was up and running, surprised, despite his desperate plight, that his feet felt fine. Grass tingling between his toes, he glanced at Beatrice, began to thank her, but stopped when he saw she was hand in hand with another man. A man no bigger than she was – skinny, shirt and shorts, barefoot too – Bohemond knew, by the missing fingers, it was Roosevelt. But so *slight*. So *frail*.

The earth rumbled. Legion's screams bubbling with blood. Beatrice tightened her grip. —River, she said, and the ground was gone, all three of them sailing way beyond the bank, screaming at the wintry blast of water. The blow made a bellows of Bohemond's chest. Bigger, fatter, blacker he sank, while Beatrice swam on, her legs smudged above him, kicking with the current. Swift to the surface, he splashed after her, swept back by a whale-sized wave as Legion plunged in.

He hurtled through clouds of sulphurous steam, crashed onto the bank, Beatrice suddenly leagues away, blonde hair blazing along with her voice. —Wait for me at the orchard! Legion shot past, wallowing, out of sorts in the water. No sign of Roosevelt.

Bohemond tottered to his feet. Watched as the rip-tide whipped Beatrice out of sight. Didn't doubt for a second that she'd be all right. Maybe Roosevelt was further upstream. Legion on the other hand was lost. Overcome by the undertow. All that fire and brimstone extinguished.

One step away from the river, Bohemond threw up. He'd left his suitcase full of clothes, and, far more importantly, Hermione's wedding present, at Delphi. But then he couldn't have foreseen the chain of events that'd led to him standing on this riverbank with a bellyful of stewed viscera. Then again, he should've prepared for all eventualities – put his belongings in the car after the bath . . . although after the bath he hadn't been in any fit state for anything much. Weak and delirious, he'd just been fucked by his first real kiss. Blown away by how Beatrice, even when she knew he was coming, continued to pinch his nipple and chew on his lips, right up until the orgasm undid his limbs and lulled him under.

If he went straight to Primrose Hill and found her waiting, she'd insist on leaving the city immediately, sure that Legion and Worm and Gold-mouth would be out looking for them, or waiting at the restaurant, whereas Bohemond reckoned Delphi was the last place they'd be. And anyway, besides Hermione's present, he *really* did need to get some clothes. No way would they find anything to fit him on the road to Scotland.

Some ancient tributary of the Thames, the river wove towards London's corona. Bohemond followed the flow, every step upsetting his entrails, but still his feet held out. The ground beneath them seemed softer than a bed of petals.

He climbed higher, found a path and, following it away from the gorge, cried out at the sight that met him at its crest. There, hanging in the branches of a roadside tree, shining twice as brightly as the moon, was Beatrice's fur coat. She must've discarded it to aid her escape. Left it here for him to find as a sign that she'd survived. He plucked it down, its weight tripled by water, and slung it over his shoulder.

The track sank through a copse. Bohemond emerged amongst the back gardens of terraced houses. Cars thrummed along an obscured road that he eventually recognized as Muswell Hill. He juddered down to Highgate station – concrete more like mallow against the soles of his feet – and hailed a cab on the corner of Archway Road. —Tower Bridge and then Primrose Hill, he said, steadying himself against the door. —I'm afraid I'm a bit wet.

The driver, whose hair shone snow-white, glanced at him, and nodded lazily towards the back seat. —It's waterproof.

Fifteen minutes to Delphi. He left the fur coat in the cab and limped around to the back-lot door. It was wide open. The tool shed in splinters as he expected. Worm and Gold-mouth gone. They'd be looking for him in Highgate now.

He dipped into the mess-room and crawled through the kitchen. Pans and utensils lay as he'd left them, air still warm with the scent of roast goose. The dining room bore signs of the earlier struggle: one broken table and two broken chairs, scuff marks on the floor, blood. He reared up on his knees to inspect the laid table – Worm's roast goose was stripped to the bone but Beatrice's was untouched. Bohemond's blood in Worm's belly.

Only when he reached Hermione's flat did he finally stand. Delphi was sleeping. No-one home – good guys or bad.

The lights in his room were out. No need for them really since the suitcase was on his bed already half-packed. He gathered his belongings in the gloom, succumbing every moment to increasing waves of pain.

Clothes, the cobalt box and Hermione's wedding present stuffed into the case, Bohemond stripped. Blood and bile churned in his gorge as he ran fingers over the vast handprints branded on his flanks. They were for ever, but he could learn to love them, their symmetry and span suggestive of Beatrice's wings.

434

Legion, however, could never love his wounds: a crushed skull meant sucking soup through a straw for eternity.

No time to salve or bandage, he jiggled into a blue suit, stepped into his last pair of moccasins, and grabbed the suitcase, on his way to the door when the phone rang. Worm wouldn't call and expect anyone to answer. Not unless he knew Bohemond was here and was trying to spook him. But why bother when he could just bust in and behead him. It was Beatrice, trying to reach him from Primrose Hill. Ringing to say, I'm waiting, where the fuck are you, or, Stay where you are, I'm coming to get you. He picked up the receiver, but whoever was on the other end rang off as he pressed it to his ear. Another blunder. 1 . . . 4 . . . 7 . . . 1 . . . No response. —Bastard! He replaced the handset and made for the door. The phone rang again. He dived back, slipping to the floor as he answered.

—Bohemond?

—Good Christ, *Hermione.* Is that you?

—Who else?

—Your voice sounds strange. Are you on your mobile?

—No.

—Did you phone a moment ago?

—No.

He grabbed a handful of his hair.

—Why are you whispering?

—Sorry, Hermione, but I've got to go, I . . .

—There's someone here wants to say hello.

Tap and clatter as the phone changed hands.
—Chef?

—Seeta?

—Oh, you sound knackered.

435

—It's been a long day. Is everything all right?

—Yeah, great.

—Everyone ready for the wedding?

—Eh . . . I suppose.

—Don't take it too hard, Seeta.

Another phone rang in the background: one long bell, a short pause and so on, not the two jingles Bohemond was accustomed to. —Seeta, where are you?

Her voice blunted as she covered up the mouthpiece and relayed the question. And then he heard Hermione, calm and clear amid the ramble of sounds, say: —Just tell him.

Bohemond stood up, stepped back, sat on the bed. His wounds were beginning to prickle, premonition of the agony morning would bring. —You're not in Scotland, are you?

—Bohemond.

—*Hermione*. Where are you?

—It's called Big Sur.

He closed his eyes. Visions of the sea. —Big Sur.

—Yeah.

—California?

—Yeah.

—You're there with Seeta?

—Got in about an hour ago.

—Just the two of you?

—Yeah.

—What about Paris and your parents, and everyone up in Scotland? Do they know where you are?

—I left them a note and I'm going to phone them next. I can't imagine, though. Me and Seeta saying we're going to drive up the coast for the day, and we go to Glasgow and get on a plane. I bet Paris is having a heart attack.

Bohemond licked his lips. —You've eloped.

—You could say that, but then we were thinking you might like it out here too.

—Me?

—You.

—What would I do out there with you and Seeta?

—I might try to set up another restaurant. I'll need a chef. You talked about us running a place in Spain, remember.

—And what about Delphi?

—Paris can look after Delphi.

—You don't sound as though you plan on coming back.

—I'm out here with Seeta and the sun's shining. The only thing that's missing is you. How about it?

He shook his head, massaged his eyelids, holding down a fountain.

—Bohemond.

Time to go.

—Bohemond . . . are you still there?

—That's your problem, Hermione: you think you can have your cake and eat it. You string people along until you're sure you don't want to be with them, hedging your bets so you can jump ship whenever it suits you. Well, I'm sorry, but I'm not going to come out there and be the consolation prize when things don't work out with Seeta.

—It's not like that.

—I can't believe how selfish you are.

—I want you to come out here because you and Seeta are the two people I love most. If it's selfish, fine, I'm selfish.

—You don't love me, Hermione.

—Maybe I don't love you like you want me to, but that's your hang-up, not mine. Come out here

437

and sit in the sun for a while. Chill out. You might like it.

—Can I speak with Seeta again please?

—Chef?

—Seeta.

—Yeah.

—Are you happy?

—Very.

—Hermione's not suddenly going to change her mind and fly back to Paris.

—I got in the car with her yesterday evening thinking we were going for a drive, but she had our suitcases in the trunk and she'd somehow got a hold of my passport. She said did I want to go to California with her and I thought she was joking until we got to the airport in Glasgow. It was all her idea.

—You'll be OK?

—Chef, I don't feel anything like I did . . . I feel . . . bigger or something . . . just . . . *more*.

—All right.

—Are you going to come out here then?

—Do you really want me to?

—I'd love you to.

—I may just. Might bring someone with me too.

—Beatrice?

Something bashed against the building, so hard and heavy the bed shifted. Bohemond stood up, wincing at his fried sides. —Seeta, I have to go. Say goodbye to Hermione for me.

—Bohemond?

—Goodbye.

—Let me just give you the number.

Another explosive blow, wood splintering.

—Quick, Seeta, *quickly*.

She reeled the number off, he wrote it down, hung

up and shoved his desk against the door. He opened
the window, threw his suitcase out, stripped all the
sheets from his bed and knotted the corners together,
butterfingers slipping on every pull tight, dread
doubling as the sulphur stench seeped into his room.
The west wing quivered as Legion overturned the
kitchen, heat creeping through the soles of Bohemond's shoes, working him up to a dance as the
floor became too hot to stand on. He tied one end of
the makeshift rope around the bedstead and hurled
the remaining bundle out the window. Pandemonium
crashed from the kitchen, into the corridor, through
the restaurant. He slugged up on to the window ledge
and, holding onto the bedspreads, slowly lowered
his legs over the edge. Balance tipped, his grip on
the sill withered and he was falling, screaming, teeth
chattering as he jolted to a halt. A corner of his bed
had smashed through the window and wedged in the
gap. Safe enough for the moment. Hand over hand,
ankles tangled in blanket, he shuddered down, slow
but sure until he passed the first-floor window and
saw Legion's legs striding up the stairs. Panic spun
him around. His collar hooked on a metal crook jutting
out the wall. Rope yanked out of his hand, he dangled
like a hung duck. The descent had sapped the last of
his strength. Nothing left to stop his own garrotting.
Saliva slicked over his chin. His eyes bulged and
rolled. Tongue filled his throat. Blood ballooned his
limbs. Piss trickled into his pants. Tears of agony and
embarrassment blurred his final view of the world.
Typical.

A knot in his neck popped, torture so new and
exquisite that even as he yielded he lashed out. The
spasm snapped the catch. He hit the ground head-first.
Twisted a wrist. Still choking, he grappled for the

suitcase, and raced for the gate, overtaken by a dog, a fox and a hundred different species of brightly coloured birds. A python kept pace with him all the way to the alley where the cab was ready waiting. The snow-white driver reached an arm out of his window and unlatched the back door. Bohemond toppled inside, one last look at Delphi as the taxi pulled away – the mess-room garden in flames, more animals escaping from its sub-tropical habitat, Legion leaping out of his bedroom window.

Streetlamps were dead on Primrose Hill. Guided by moonlight, Bohemond finally found the flower shop. Its ornate iron gates were wide open. He crept across the courtyard to a wooden door, and, just as Beatrice had told him, opened it with the bronze key. Hemmed in by hedge, a flagstone path led him to a glass door set back in the wall of a white-brick tower. He unlocked it with the silver key, shuffled down a short hallway and mounted the spiral staircase on the right. The suitcase and fur coat weighed heavily on his aching arms and legs. His phlegm and blood speckled the steps and shaft. And for the first time he felt welts on the back of his unbloodied fingers. During their flight, Beatrice had held him so tightly she'd bruised his hand.

The stairs rose to a metal catwalk, which he crossed on hands and knees. Rusted shut, the brass door at its end only gave under the full brunt of his weight. He waded up through a rampart of weeds, swooned once he saw the orchard. It seemed to hang on the hill top. Trees leaned towards the clouds, the boughs beneath their vividly green leaves home to a thousand golden birds; their dizzy heights decked with apples that flickered like rubies and emeralds. Bohemond sighed with delight. Tears in his chuckling as the first traces of day drew him on.

Exhausted by the orchard gates, he leaned back against the wall and slid to the ground, his fall broken by Beatrice's fur coat. The suitcase spilled open by his feet, scattering gold, while the cobalt box rolled off down the slope.

He was high up. London looked different: a glittering city balanced on the rim of the world. Spanned by an outsize Tower Bridge, the Thames arced and sparkled like an ocean. Spume sloshed against the shores. He spotted the white stretch-limo meandering between east end tenements. Smoke belching from Delphi's back lot. Hands clasped, he hoped that Beatrice would find him before Legion, prayed that she hadn't given up waiting for him while he'd been babbling on the phone to Hermione. Just one mouthful of roast goose, and he could be certain she'd come. But she hadn't even unwrapped her napkin.

Sunrise spilled across a soon-blue sky. Helicopters and aeroplanes zipped above the city, their windows, wings and blades glinting intermittently. And far above them, where the sky darkened and stars still shone, comets and rockets drew glittering tracers. Bohemond curled his top lip, smiled at the still-fresh smell of Beatrice, grinned at the dying glimmer in his groin, and, just as he fell asleep, muttered with relief that the wedding was off, because he hadn't had time to decide upon a sweet.

He opened his eyes in daylight; same day or not, he couldn't tell, but his wounds were so inflamed he thought not. Breathing was as much movement as he could bear and even then a swollen throat jammed the flow to his lungs. The city looked the same only closer. He saw Innocent's house in Whitechapel. Could just make out the old Pole sitting by his living room window. He was in for a surprise. The look on his face when Bohemond and Beatrice appeared at his door. They'd take him for a spin in the red convertible. Catch a plane from Heathrow to Big Sur, where they'd hook up with Hermione and Seeta on the beach, the five of them in surf gear and bikinis, drinking exotic cocktails.

When next he woke, it was dusk. Birds had come to roost in the branches above his head. Sunset on their feathers dappled the ground around him. Reflections played across his face as they had when Beatrice uncovered her wings on the balcony of the Tower Hotel; an omen that she was coming to fly him home, just as she'd promised; her bond hallowed by Chagall's Song of Songs and six marker-penned kisses.

Lavender roused him a third time, his excitement wrung out by a slow realization that the fragrance was in the fur coat. It was night, but he was hot, his legs blanketed with gold feathers that the birds had shed. He kicked off his moccasins, blinded momentarily by star-bright toenails. Not long now before he was able to walk. To stride the summit of the hill; a point so high he could see the Cheviots. He'd circle the orchard until Beatrice beheld his beacon feet, an astronomical phenomenon seen the length and breadth of England, but that only she would recognize. All he had to do was walk and she'd come running (or falling), gold hair sparkling like a meteor storm. She'd feed him with a kiss to restore his strength, and guide him down to the red convertible parked at the bottom of Primrose Hill. He wriggled his toes. Cooed at the coolness and ease of movement. City clocks struck quarter to the hour. Fairy-lit paddle steamers wove up a ruby-red Thames. Rockets passed overhead. Both hands full of fur coat, he waited for the bells to ring out, and began to heave his great weight heavenwards.

THE END

LONDON IRISH

Zane Radcliffe

'VERY FRESH, VERY FUNNY. I LAUGHED UNTIL I
STOPPED'
Colin Bateman

There are 750,000 Irish living in London. One of them
has to get out. For good.

Summer 1999. Only 157 shopping days until the new
millennium and for Bic (half-Irish, half-Scots, and
half-cut), who ekes out a living selling crêpes to the
hordes descending on Greenwich market, the year 2000
can't come quick enough. One severed ear, two bizarre
deaths, and the arrest of his dog for civil disobedience –
so far Bic's *annus* has been pretty *horribilis*.

But a silver, or rather, a raven-haired lining appears in
the guise of Roisin. She's from Home, she's
heart-stoppingly beautiful, and she's taken the stall
opposite Bic's. Despite her over-protective brothers,
things are definitely looking up.

At least they were until Bic wakes up
the-morning-after-the-night-before, in his clothes, in
Edinburgh, to find he's the UK's Most Wanted Man. On
the run with fourteen murders to his name . . .

A glorious comic thriller bursting with outrageous
shenanigans, shot-to-pieces with black humour, while
retaining a heart of gold, *London Irish* introduces a
singular and entertaining new literary voice.

0 552 77095 7

BLACK SWAN

STICKLEBACK

John McCabe

It's Wednesday morning. You hate your job so much you haven't done any work for two weeks and nobody's noticed. You share an office with a sad and obsessed Trekkie whose computer manuals are encroaching on your workspace. Your breakfast routine has gone wrong. It's your 29th birthday.

So you have the worst hangover in the world and you're on the Number 11 bus circumnavigating the dreariest suburbs Birmingham has to offer. The bottle of red you've been necking is nearly gone and the passengers on the bus are freaking you out. You slip into the Jug of Ale for a pint.

And now you're trapped in the gents by a man-mountain with only one eyebrow and if you thought things could only get better, YOU WERE WRONG . . .

Stickleback is a novel about men's need for routine and what happens when life intervenes. A funny, poignant and fast-moving tale of office life, drinking, drugs, love, friendship, clubs, football, computer programming and the perfect financial heist.

'WITTY AND INCISIVE ABOUT THE PREOCCUPATIONS OF MODERN LIFE'
Observer

'NOT ONLY DO YOU HAVE A COMPULSIVE READ ON YOUR HANDS, YOU ALSO HAVE A FASCINATING PROFILE OF THE RITUALIZED MEDIOCRITY OF CONTEMPORARY LIVING'
Big Issue

'THIS FINE FIRST NOVEL . . . MAKES A VERY WELCOME BREAK FROM THE NORM'
The Times

0 552 99984 9

BLACK SWAN

THE WISDOM OF CROCODILES

Paul Hoffman

'INSPIRES SENSATIONS OF TERROR, NAUSEA,
BEMUSEMENT AND EXHILARATION . . . THIS IS
FICTION ON A GRAND AND AMBITIOUS SCALE'
Daily Telegraph

When Steven Grlscz saves a young woman from throwing
herself in front of a train, he finds himself consumed by
a love affair which transforms her from a suicidal, angry
anorexic into a happy and beautiful young woman. Then
she vanishes without trace.

Across the Thames on the morning George Winnicott, former
head of the Anti-Terrorist Squad, is to begin his new job in
charge of the City of London's most powerful anti-fraud body,
he wakes from a nightmare screaming that he knows the
meaning of life. Later that day, a huge bomb explodes in the
centre of London.

How are these events linked? What connects modern
economics, a new take on the vampire concept, parachuting,
pornography, the Leaning Tower of Pisa, financial fraud,
terrorism, aliens, artificial intelligence, the meaning of life
and the hardest crossword clue in the world?

13 years in the writing, this is a novel that engages with the
way the modern world works – and in admitting that
contemporary life is complex, impenetrable and often
terrifying, it also asserts that there are ways to see the
patterns emerging from the chaos.

'THE ONLY WRITER, ENGLISH OR AMERICAN, WITH THE
GUTS TO TAKE ON THE MODERN WORLD IN ALL ITS
TERRIFYING COMPLEXITY'
The Week

0 552 77082 5

BLACK SWAN

A SCIENTIFIC ROMANCE

Ronald Wright

Winner of the David Higham Prize for Fiction

'AMBITIOUS AND ENTERTAINING . . . A HEADY MIX OF LOVE
STORY, PESSIMISTIC PREDICTION, SATIRE AND LYRICAL
ADVENTURE'
Sunday Times

'PURE PLEASURE . . . A DEEPLY SEDUCTIVE AND BRILLIANTLY
SUSTAINED PIECE OF ADVENTURE WRITING, ENTHRALLINGLY
DESCRIPTIVE, FRAGILE, SCARY'
Julie Myerson, *Observer*

It is 1999, and David Lambert, jilted lover and relectant museum
curator, discovers that H. G. Wells's time machine really existed –
exists, in fact, because now it has returned to London. Motivated by
unanswered questions and inescapable curiosity, he propels himself
deep into the next millennium. Exploring the utterly changed,
luxuriant and menacing new landscape of the future, he also explores
the ruins of his life, in particular the web of erotic obsession and
remorse which ensnared him and his old friend Bird, and Anita, the
beautiful, eccentric Egyptologist they both loved and lost.

A *Scientific Romance* is a rich, imaginative novel of contemporary
culture and conscience refracted through the lens of the distant future
– and a darkly comic work of outstanding narrative power.

'THE MOST APOCALYPTIC DYSTOPIA SINCE RUSSELL HOBAN'S
RIDDLEY WALKER . . . IN 100 YEARS TIME THIS BOOK SHOULD
BE A CLASSIC'
Guardian

'THIS NOVEL WORKS ON ALL LEVELS . . . ITS FLAIR FOR
DESCRIPTION CAN BE POSITIVELY DICKENSIAN. THE RESULT
IS A FRESH TAKE ON AN OLD FORMULA – THE DYSTOPIAN
POSTAPOCALYPSE NOVEL – AND A PROFOUND MEDITATION
ON THE NATURE OF TIME'
John Vernon, *New York Times Book Review*

'INTELLIGENT, MOVING AND ABOVE ALL WONDERFULLY
ENTERTAINING . . . BRINGS RONALD WRIGHT INTO THE
FELLOWSHIP OF ORWELL AND H. G. WELLS'
Alberto Manguel

0552 77000 0

BLACK SWAN

A SELECTED LIST OF FINE NOVELS
AVAILABLE FROM BLACK SWAN

THE PRICES SHOWN BELOW WERE CORRECT AT THE TIME OF GOING TO PRESS. HOWEVER
TRANSWORLD PUBLISHERS RESERVE THE RIGHT TO SHOW NEW RETAIL PRICES ON COVERS
WHICH MAY DIFFER FROM THOSE PREVIOUSLY ADVERTISED IN THE TEXT OR ELSEWHERE.

99588	6	**THE HOUSE OF THE SPIRITS**	*Isabel Allende*	£7.99
99313	1	**OF LOVE AND SHADOWS**	*Isabel Allende*	£7.99
99946	6	**THE ANATOMIST**	*Federico Andahazi*	£6.99
99921	0	**THE MERCIFUL WOMEN**	*Federico Andahazi*	£6.99
99860	5	**IDIOGLOSSIA**	*Eleanor Bailey*	£6.99
99925	3	**THE BOOK OF THE HEATHEN**	*Robert Edric*	£6.99
99910	5	**TELLING LIDDY**	*Anne Fine*	£6.99
99898	2	**ALL BONES AND LIES**	*Anne Fine*	£6.99
77082	5	**THE WISDOM OF CROCODILES**	*Paul Hoffman*	£7.99
99796	X	**A WIDOW FOR ONE YEAR**	*John Irving*	£7.99
77109	0	**THE FOURTH HAND**	*John Irving*	£6.99
99859	1	**EDDIE'S BASTARD**	*William Kowalski*	£6.99
99936	9	**SOMEWHERE SOUTH OF HERE**	*William Kowalski*	£6.99
99984	9	**STICKLEBACK**	*John McCabe*	£6.99
99874	5	**PAPER**	*John McCabe*	£6.99
99873	7	**SNAKESKIN**	*John McCabe*	£6.99
99907	5	**DUBLIN**	*Seán Moncrieff*	£6.99
99901	6	**WHITE MALE HEART**	*Ruaridh Nicoll*	£6.99
99861	3	**IN A LAND OF PLENTY**	*Tim Pears*	£7.99
99862	1	**A REVOLUTION OF THE SUN**	*Tim Pears*	£6.99
99667	X	**GHOSTING**	*John Preston*	£6.99
99817	6	**INK**	*John Preston*	£6.99
77095	7	**LONDON IRISH**	*Zane Radcliffe*	£6.99
99865	6	**THE FIG EATER**	*Jody Shields*	£6.99
99948	2	**HENDERSON'S SPEAR**	*Ronald Wright*	£6.99
77000	0	**A SCIENTIFIC ROMANCE**	*Ronald Wright*	£6.99

All Transworld titles are available by post from:
Bookpost, PO Box 29, Douglas, Isle of Man IM99 1BQ
Credit cards accepted. Please telephone 01624 836000,
fax 01624 837033, Internet http://www.bookpost.co.uk or
e-mail: bookshop@enterprise.net for details.
Free postage and packing in the UK.
Overseas customers allow £1 per book.